# What is Secret

12/07

Emily,

Words to add to your Chilean experience/adventure.

Merry Christmas!

Love,

Dad

# What is Secret

## Stories by Chilean Women

Marjorie Agosín
Editor

White Pine Press · Fredonia, New York

ACKNOWLEDGEMENTS: "Scents of Wood and Silence" by Pía Barros is
reprinted by permission of the publisher, from *Scents of Wood and Silence,*
1991, Latin American Literary Review Press, Pittsburgh, PA.

"The Boy Who Took Off in a Tree" originally published in English by the
Latin American Literary Review Press under the title "The Boy Swept Away in
a Tree" in Jacqueline Balcells' collection *The Enchanted Raisin,* 1988.

An exhaustive effort has been made to locate all rights holders and to clear
reprint permissions. If any required acknowledgementshave been overlooked,
it is unintentional and forgiveness is requested. If notified, the publishers
will be pleased to rectify any omission in future editions.

Publication of this book was made possible, in part, by grants from
the National Endowment for the Humanities
and the New York State Council on the Arts.

Book design: Elaine LaMattina

Cover painting: "Quiet Resistance,"
©1983, Emma Alvarez Piñero, oil, 48" x 70"

ISBN 1-877727-41-5

Printed on acid-free paper.

Manufactured in the United States of America

First printing 1995

10  9  8  7  6  5  4  3  2  1

Published by
White Pine Press, 10 Village Square, Fredonia, New York

# What is Secret

# Contents

*To the valiant women writers of Chile*
*whose defiance and courage continue to be our hope*
*and to my mother, Frida Agosín.*

# Introduction

Pablo Neruda once defined Chile as an expanse of fruitless geography. Historian Benjamin Subercaseaux characterized the country as having an unruly geography. This narrow strip of land is mysterious, suggestive, and unforgettable. To traverse the Chilean territory is to enter a land of cities and green valleys, a land where the heat of enormous deserts rises toward Andean snowstorms. The great ocean and the great mountains guide the voyager through a territory generous in its variety of landscape and attitude. To travel through Chile is to lose oneself in a labyrinth of landscapes and lives.

The majority of voices that have left their mark on the Chilean imagination have been masculine, especially within the poetic realm. Pablo Neruda, Pablo de Rocka, Nicanor Parra, Augusteo D'Halmar, Oscar Castro, José Donoso, and Antonio Skármeta are well-known and widely read by a public unaccustomed to hearing the voices of Chile's women writers. In my country, writing and disseminating the written text was, and continues to be, a largely masculine endeavor. Newspapers at the turn of the century show only the existence of male writers praised in masculine critiques. Among the sacred male voices, the only female voice heard is that of Gabriela Mistral, the first and only Latin American woman to win the Nobel Prize.

Yet within the mysterious strip of land that is Chile, there is an invisible and lost geography, a constellation of women with a hidden, but omnipresent, tradition. The landscape of feminine voices in the Chilean narrative is powerful. These voices of unusual and varied richness are the voices of the earth, the city, the children. They are the voices of women who have always acknowledged the power of words. These women have always written, and they have done so with elegance and wit. Yet I peruse the literature of these women, approach their legacies, and I find them invisible, separated from the artistic endeavors of their male counterparts. It is difficult to find texts of the pioneers, those born around 1800, but they are there, filled with the ideals of the vanguard and that which is modern, creating a powerful body of work that is yet to be fully read and analyzed. This marginality has its origins at the turn of the century when women saw writing as an activity that could be performed in the confining spaces of the home. They never aspired to contribute to the society they were part of because they were denied the right to interpret and be part of history. Even in the 1990s, it is difficult for women to garner reviews in prestigious journals and newspapers. I am amazed that the large number of women who wrote in Chile, silently and covertly, did not cease their creative endeavors but survived by living in a dislocated state between their writing persona and their feminine persona, between the domestic spaces and the public ones.

Set apart, relegated to the backrooms, forced to follow rules of silence and censure in a society which instilled in women the belief that *En boca cerrada no entran moscas,* women created and recreated their own geography, forging a new landscape for the written word. We can analyze the writing of women at the turn of the century only by perusing personal diaries, the novels written in episodes, the poems created in a hurry on busy afternoons. Regardless of how they chose to express themselves, these women wrote, and the act of writing inscribed their names in history.

This is the only anthology of its kind in either English or Spanish. It gathers the voices of the women of Chile, both those who wrote at the turn of the century and those who continue to write as the end of the century nears. I researched and compiled this anthology as if it were a precious object, a familiar and dear gem. Through this collection, I feel that I am discovering a vast, lost history, a history as varied as the Chilean landscape. I dedicated myself to searching the great books of literary history for the presence of Chilean women. With the exception of Mistral and María Luisa Bombal, the panorama was desolate, so I perused marginal journals and old fashion magazines. It was there, bringing to the realm of power and knowledge a verbal originality that inscribed them in our literary history, that I heard the voices of these long-lost women. My search was fruitful and I found an unforgettable legacy: stories of untold beauty and power. And among the writing of the younger generations, I found a vital and touching literature that continues to map the territories women have claimed as their own. This book vindicates and actualizes an invisible territory filled with voices that write from a feminine perspective. By gathering them in one book, we can appreciate certain themes, some unexpected and subversive, that weave through the women's daily lives. There is in these narratives a concern with the preservation of memory and the negation of oblivion, especially in stories with political content.

Each story in this anthology is a deep reflection of the woman who wrote it and of her historical situation. The backdrops can be startling: the women's voices appear with incomparable beauty in contrast to the violence surrounding them. In light of the fact that the so-called *criollista* literature, or the literature of the earth, has been dominated by male authors in Chile, the names of many of these women are unknown. I have attempted to gather a multi-faceted ensemble of voices and visions that despite chronological and social gaps, maintain great similarities.

The authors and texts that were selected cover a vast period of Chilean history. The texts attempt to map the voices of the different women and to find for them their rightful place in history. The reader will discover the language of various periods, and the simple relationships that have always existed between women and nature. But most of all, these texts are imbued with, and have their origin in, a feminine imagery that creates within a traditional culture of silence the language of a new territory: women's words.

The first section of this anthology, "Of Angels and Voyages," begins with "Memories of Clay," a myth of creation and identity. This fine story by Cristina da Fonseca gives tribute to the indigenous past of the Americas. Clay is the emblematic symbol of an Indian woman sharing the secrets of the birds, and the flora of the American continent. It is a powerful and poetic meditation on the nature of identity and heritage in the Americas. "The Pilgrim's Angel," by Violeta Quevedo is a story of travel, which has always been for women both an act of courage and an act of defiance. The woman traveler has been an explorer through the intricate complexities of language and identity, but her language has been very much her own. A long piece, Quevedo's writing is unique within the framework of Chilean narrative by either men or women. Her writing is difficult to catalog. She does not write within the traditional canons and is considered the first *naive* writer of the country. Violeta Quevedo was the pseudonym of Rita Salas Subercaseaux, whose family belonged to the Chilean elite. From an early age, and disobeying paternal authority, she wrote letters, stories, and diaries. There is a sense of astonishment in her work and she has, according to Eduardo Anguita in his prologue to the book *Six Stories by Violeta Quevedo,* a "primitive innocence." Her writing is luminous and passionate because she speaks without the self-censure imposed by a sense of what literature should be. It is a pleasure to read her texts, to observe her manipulation of languge and subtle nuances. In her narratives, writing is truly a way of defying the established order, and they seduce the reader with their ingenuity and by the author's innate ability to mingle everyday occurences with the supernatural. Her work, like that of many others, was published in small, self-financed editions. These were collected and edited in the 1950s and a new edition, soon out of print, was issued in the 1980s.

The second part of this anthology approaches that which is supposedly feminine — accessories and clothes — and the language of intimacy. Marta Jara is one of Chile's most extraordinary writers due to the uncommon strength of her language, yet she has been undervalued and little-known. Despite having published one novel and two short-story collections, it wasn't until recently that Jara began to achieve recognition within the landscape of Chilean narative. "The Dress" is from her best-known collection, *Surazo.* In this story Jara's daring language unleashes through the images it creates all the violence and pain experienced by a woman in the countryside who is relegated by her gender to marginality. However, it isn't patriarchal power that keeps the protagonist in a state of pain and misery, but the mother figure, a woman who perpetuates and imposes the schemes of male dominance on her family. "The Dress" is a story of undisputable power about feminine solidarity.

I first met María Asunción De Fokes almost three years ago. She intrigued me because of her determination to write at the age of seventy. "Vanessa and Victor" is Ms. De Fokes' first story, written with an extraordinary sense of passion for the landscape and the people who inhabit the dunes of northern Chile. "Vanessa and Victor" represents a history of passion and sexuality often sublimated in Latin American culture, a culture interested in the denial of female sexual experience. De Fokes creates a most unusual story where the protagonist represents almost a double marginality, one caused by the isolation of living in the dunes and one caused by living in ill-fated poverty. "Vanessa and Victor" also represents a most unique style in Chilean literature, a mixture of elaborate lyricism as well as images of desolation and destitution.

If "The Dress" presents the eternal dichotomy of the country woman faced with industrialization and the city, "Elegance" by Ana Vásquez insinuates the conflict between woman and her social class. In this subtle story, Vásquez, through imagery associated with clothing, manages to unveil a series of conflicts surrounding what women wear and the garments that sometimes validate or invalidate their presence. These conflicts can be seen as different ways of entering dimensions of power and acceptance beyond one's own class. Oddly enough, these two stories from different time periods both reveal the ways in which women are conditioned to perceive their own bodies and of how the opinions and descriptions of outsiders effects them.

The brief story by Flor María Aninant, "The Department Store," evidences woman's mysterious condition in relationship to garments, to the display window, and, most of all, to the passers-by that give life to those dubious and immobile mannequins. "Cleaning the Closet" by Margarita Aguirre leads us closer to this feminine imagery, to those spaces where everyday domestic tasks exert an enchanting power. Aguirre leads us to the magically surreal, to that which one cannot confess, to the limited and closed territory of the closet where a woman can enter the often-desired private space. Aguirre also belongs to the world of the invisible. She began to write in the 1950s, a time when Chilean literature thrived, yet her name does not appear in the lists of writers from that period. This is true as well for her colleague, Marta Blanco, whose story is surprising for the period in which it appeared, the 1960s. In "Maternity," Blanco defies the predominant perception that happiness is obtained with motherhood. Like other stories in this section, "Maternity" defies the established norms that condition the actions and rites of women.

Next we have a recent text by a young writer, Luz Orfanoz. The brevity and pace of "Insignificance" reflect the high tension in the narrative and the violence of its ending. Sonia Guralnik, author of "Sailing Down the Rhine" is a very interesting writer. Like De Fokes, she began weaving her texts in her seventies. She is one of the few Jewish immigrants who write in Chile today based on their condition as immigrants exiled between two worlds. "Sailing Down the Rhine" has a haunting and extrordinary power that reminisces the World War II years. It is a story the encompasses both a sense of remembrance and a sense of forgiveness. The Jewish women on their vacation recognize their sailor and finally dare to speak. Guralnik speaks openly of the relationship between two women of alternate identities as well as of the secret jealousy that exists between them. The elements of emptiness, of being and not being, the sense of feeling like a "worm woman" make this story similar to the texts of Marta Jara and Ana Vásquez.

The second story by Marta Jara to appear in this anthology, "The Englishwoman" clearly shows the various roles that women of yesteryear played as servants and governesses. In this story we observe that condition of exile and distance imposed upon women who arrived in a new and strange country and the pain they felt when faced with the indifference of both their employers and the children in their charge.

Elena Castedo, who has resided in Washington, D.C. since the 1970s, writes about this topic in "The White Bedspread" as well. This time, though, the story does not take place in the Southern Cone but in Washington. The conflict of classes and the ways of approaching power are similar in both stories as the writers explore how these same situations can take place in very different physical locations.

The last story in this section is by Marta Brunet, who, like the others, describes the country folk, their world and its zones of pain. In her story, "Down River," the theme of incest acquires an unsuspected violence, and once again we are visited by beings who seem lost in an alienating geography.

To speak of love, of sensuality, of eroticism, the themes of the third section, has been the main focus of women's narrative, although many times desire had to be presented in a hidden and subtle way since to write about and from love has been the patrimony of the masculine language. María Luisa Bombal, back in 1933, created in her novel *The Final Mist* an imaginary lover to manifest her own eroticism. Fortunately, eroticism and women's writing in Latin America have acquired strength, although their development has been slow. Only the youngest generation of writers can write about sex without false modesty.

This section, "Encounters with the Skin," begins with a story by María Flora Yáñez, a noteworthy writer of the 1930s who was relegated to obscurity by the few publications of her work. In her story "The Pond," desire appears hidden by the lyricism of words and by scenes filled with magic and dreams. The story takes place in an abandoned house at dusk. It was in this dimension of the invisible that women could speak of sensuality. Here they could speak of their own bodies in a darkened universe where the lover will never be embodied by a man. Through this powerful story, Yáñez approaches the portal of feminine sensuality with a deluge of words and images that conjure touch on skin more than words on paper. It is a place where it is difficult to separate love from eroticism.

The next story was written almost thirty years later by a young and vibrant writer, Pía Barros. "Scents of Wood and Silence" has the same enchanted atmosphere as the text by Yáñez and speaks of love from the bewitching zones where it is not clear whether the words are part of a dream or part of reality. It is interesting to note that to speak of eroticism and pleasure, both writers make use of the ambiguous realm of nightmare, dream, and fantasy. Both authors invent the objects of their desire, both speak of eroticism in the languge of poetry, and both see themselves with imaginary lovers.

The story "Subway" by Ana María del Río is surpsising in its constant agility and its perception of human relationships. The author's vision of a long-term marriage is set against the circuitous world of a subway.

Alejandra Farias represents the voice of the newest generation of Chilean women writers. In "The Fish Tank" she presents eroticism and sexual tension without euphemisms. Her narrative can be seen as an open stage where sex functions apart from love and modesty.

The raw eroticism of Carmen Basáñez's writing, represented her by "Not Without Her Glasses," is similar to that of Farias'. This time, though, sexuality and psychology transcend and subvert the established order. Here, women's discourse penetrates the forbidden zones, those dominated by male sexuality. This section ends with "A Requiem for Hands," a suggestive tale by Alejandra Basualto where images of love and of the body give the story unsuspected strength.

Lucía Guerra, like Elena Castedo and Barbara Mujica, is a Chilean expatriate and professor of literature. For these writers, discovering the themes of marginalized women writers have been an essential component of their studies. In "Encounter in the Margins," Guerra explores with passionate lucidity the struggle for woman writers today to form alliances with those women whose voices have been long neglected. What seems at first a futile attempt to give value and meaning to a trivialized writer's work ultimately reveals the way women writers had to hide the true themes of their work in "tears from a broken heart, women who faint in the throes of love."

Imagination, magical flight, and intuition have been essential characteristics of the literature written by women in the southern tip of South America. The astonishing universe of children is the appropriate territory to penetrate the open spaces of freedom. Therefore, many of the women in this anthology also write children's literature. The book's fourth section includes texts from the boundless realm of children's literature, where these women's contributions are viewed as fundamental and innovative. Heading this section is a story by Jacqueline Balcells, "The Boy Who Took Off in a Tree." Balcells is probably the most renowned writer of children's books in all of Chile. In this story, drought and the barreness of the land merge with the prodigious arrival of a child, creating that magical union of earth, women, and fertility as well as conjuring ancestral knowledge in the psyche of the child.

Amalia Rendic in "A Dog, A Boy and the Night" has been able to masterfully recreate the divided world of the rich and the poor in a dilapidated mining town in northern Chile. Rendic is able to depict the subtleties of class as well as ethnic divisions while showing the generosity of the human spirit transcending social and economic boundaries.

"Butterfly Man," "Up to the Clouds," and "Endless Flight" have in common the elements of flight, freedom, and learning that can only be obtained when the imagination is unleashed and subverted. Elena Aldunate, in "Butterfly Man" builds the image of a precocious girl tired of the regime imposed by established order and of ritualistic birthday parties. Her greatest desire is to venture outside this existence, and she gravitates toward the countryside where she finds danger but also the possiblity of a new identity. In "Up to the Clouds," Ana María Guiraldes takes a similar approach by placing at the center of her story a girl who, in the solitude of her house, plays the dangerous game of running away by donning adult clothes and ascending to the sky. In "Endless Flight," María Cristina da Fonseca created a story which approaches the myths of magical transformation. A little bird becomes a clay vessel, and, after endless days of navigation and small deaths, becomes the true sustenance for the lives of others.

In "The Secret," Maria Luisa Bombal, in a highly lyrical prose, approaches intuition, the secrets of the universe, and the mystery of water and its supernatural secrets. Finally, taking up the thread of da Fonseca's story, we have "Hualpín" by anthropologist Sonia Montecinos which once again builds on the model of legend and the supernatural universe of the Mapuche culture. These stories are revealing and lyrical in the usage of highly metaphorical language, as well as in their subversion of order.

In the southernmost tip of America, the decade of the 1970s signaled a period of cruelty, terror, and fear. Sinister military dicatorships dominated what was spoken and written. However, in a paradoxical manner, this was the period in which women began their incursion into public spaces and in which they began to participate in areas previously forbidden to them, such as politics, street life, and men's language. The years of the military dictatorship in Chile forged a new space for women and gave them the possibility of creating a literature about their condition as political subjects and of developing strategies that would expose the military government's censure.

Aside from the chaos and terror created by the government, the 70s and 80s were a period of intense internal struggle where a great number of women writers emerged. These women did not fear using and "un-using" words. They published marginal books, many of them hand-bound, and they carried forth the ancient image of the written text as a form of weaving. The interesting phenomenon of women's workshops also emerged in the 80s. Here groups of different ages gathered to discuss literature and their situation as women. These workshops were a bridge to unite them in their activities as women and allowed them to introduce themselves as writers. These women attempted to re-integrate themselves into a history that had ousted them and made them women without names, without words. Many of the authors in this anthology, including Sonia Guralnik, Pía Barros and Alejandra Farias were great organizers and participants in various workshops.

The final section of this anthology addresses the political and social context of repression, but it also accentuates the fact that women continue to create, to denounce, and to speak. The condition of the woman exiled from herself, her nation, and her identity acquires unprecedented power. The topics of absence and search, as well as the image of woman as the receptacle for memory, are the central motifs as these authors attempt to defy death and oblivion.

The first story, "Description of an Image," is by a young writer, Claudia Escobar. The language of her story is wounded: it reflects the pain of being part of a generation of invisible and disenchanted youths whose memory encompasses the years of endless political violence. "The Bicycles" in the story by Agata Gligo are obviously a parody of the aburdity and obsessivenes of fascist regimes. The theft of the bicycle accentuates, in a paradoxial and parallel way, the thefts of the country and the uselessness of daily ritual against a military attempting to maintain order. The "bicycle thefts" cannnot be controlled, but this is the only story in the anthology that has a suggestive sense of humor.

In "Because We're Poor," journalist Elizabeth Subercaseaux speaks about the lives of the peasants, the existence of desolate beings whose marginality, especially in rural areas, is exacerbated by the disappearances taking place in their country. This story juxtaposes the language of the peasants with the urban and more precise language of the characters in Escobar's story. However, the terrifying political background invites the reader to a profound reflection on the social climate of that period.

"The Bone Spoon" by Luz Larraín manifests the results of violence within a country that functioned through the gestures and rituals of its inhabitants. The main theme of this text is the alienation of the main characters. The home space is, par excellence, women's territory, their place for daydreaming. The surprising tale by Margarita Niemeyer, "The House," portrays a house that acquires an ominous presence when the memory of a disappeared child invades every corner and permeates even the sweet summer fragrances. This story subtly conjures the deep and endless grief caused by a sinister dictatorship.

Journalist Ana Pizarro presents in her story, "The Journey," the return after a long exile to a city in which no one lives in the familiar places anymore. This story is complemented by "Journey of the Watermelon" by Virginia Vidal. Here a mother's ecstasy in visiting her son in prison and the dilemma of what she can bring to him draw the reader into the issues presented in the piece. This story speaks of rendezvous, but it also addresses the pain caused by disappearance and the destruction of a whole life, a whole existence. The Chilean *arpilleras*, those colorful weavings created by the female relatives of the detained and the disappeared, appear in this story in all their splendor, following the traces of memory.

"Mitrani" by Bárbara Mujica, which speaks of the different exiles and holocausts, is also included in this section dedicated to women and their political endeavors. Mujica narrates, in a magnificent text, the exile of her main character from Nazi Germany to a place almost at the end of the world, Chepén, Peru, and of subsequent relocation during the years of civil war to Santiago, Chile, where he discovers the same terror he'd known in Germany.

This section ends with the ambiguous and lyrical story by Sonia Gonzalez, "Matters of Distance," where the narrative is located in a imprecise time frame. We hear a daughter remembering her mother through letters received from a distance, from an unnamable exile in a small guest house in Santiago where it is still possible to create dreams of a sunny and free country.

These are the stories of my country's women. Beautiful, intense, gripping, violent, and lyrical, they are like the language of the earth. Some speak of islands, of absences, of shipwrecks; others place themselves within the boundaries of cities, of spoken words. These are all powerful stories, possessing the luminosity of a clear summer's day. They are creations where memory and words do not vanish but establish themselves forever. Spoken from a woman's threshold, these are women's words.

— Marjorie Agosín

# Of Angels & Voyages

# Memories of Clay

## María Cristina da Fonseca

*To the indigenous nations of Latin America
who still know what we have forgotten.*

She, my mother, was the best potter in this entire vast land. Her earthenware vessels were famous for the strange power that they possessed to keep water fresh and cool. Seated on the ground, with her black hair draped over her back, she spent her mornings bending over the clay. A part of her own life's breath went into this labor because she touched the clay, she pounded it, she kneaded and caressed it until it gave way to the whims sketched by her mind.

That is the way my mother was.

Tall Mountain was her name. Her hands were as rough as the earth that she shaped, and her skin bore the scent of smoke and the color of clay.

I loved her with the river's depth and the height that the waterfall sometimes reaches. And I kept very still by her side, never tiring of watching her work, attentive to her every word and movement, because I always carried within myself the ambition to possess the secrets of the moist clay. Like a shadow I would follow behind her when she went to gather the pieces of clay and left them to soak in turtle shells and open gourds. Afterwards, she would set about joining the female sand to the masculine lumps of earth: to put in motion the world of earthen jars and dishes she had to mix them together!

Then, with a probing eye, she set about examining the alligators who lay in wait at the edge of the water channels, the iguanas suspended high in the trees, or some snake sleeping among the rocks, and making their shapes her own she molded them in the raw clay, opening their eyes with a twig and marking out their scales with her fingernails.

As if by secret magic endless flocks of lizards, alligators and serpents burst forth from the earth. It does not seem at all odd to me, for those animals with their harsh and stony hides are brothers of the rocks and lava.

My eyes still feel that they can see her stacking up her pieces of earthenware to dry, in the shadow of some large tree. Once the water was out of them, in accordance with the size of the moon and the wind that might be blowing, she made a big pyre on which to fire them with a lot of wood and straw. Repeating prayers such as "Ignite little fire. Burn brightly. Don't spoil my works of clay," she stayed right beside them, keeping watch over the flames' slow work. "One must feed the fire well, because the spirit that dwells within it teaches the pots to cook the corn," she explained. And in case they did not learn anything from their first experiences with the coals, on the outside face she drew two bright eyes so that they might discern the exact moment when the food was tender.

Because of the rare ease with which her little pots cooked the kernels without burning them, it was said that my mother had secret dealings with the elements, and they called her Great Lady of Earth, Fire and Water.

I wanted to live to be just like her. Because I loved her so much I thought it had been she who, hill by hill of moistened sand, had made the world all in one morning. So immeasurable the power of her rough kneader's hands seemed to me as she kneaded.

And while I knew that she could not have molded the universe, the heavenly canopy and the ocean floor with her fingers, I had the feeling that the one who made valleys, coasts and mountain ranges necessarily had to be a kneader of sand, minerals and elements just as she was, her mother, her mother's mother and every woman of the earth.

It still seems that I am listening to the long litany of deeds and words with which Tall Mountain tried to teach me, the first of her daughters, everything that her head contained about what it meant to be a people who had risen from the dust. "We are people of the muddy clay," she would tell me, "and from afar in their long canoes come those who seek our decorated ceramic pieces."

And thus it was, because at regular intervals during the year the boats would appear riding the backs of the rivers and carry away our earthen water vessels, leaving us in exchange palm wine, beautifully woven baskets and chewing resin.

Of the many treasures that the water travellers hid in the bellies of their dugout canoes, what we most appreciated were the shells that they brought from gleaming sands. We made use of them to polish the clay or to leave them next to our dead as a sign that life is eternal and always returns, even though, like the snail, at times, it may hide.

"Some clans arose from the water. Others came from the world beyond the clouds or they were brought forth by the moon. There are people of corn or of wood. There are some others who were born of the sun. We are made of clay and are children of the earth," said our first grandparents who lived on this the most ancient soil of all.

And because it was that way, because our blood and its substance were made of clay, the shaman healed cuts, bites and bruises by applying a layer of mud over our afflictions.

"If one of our people dreams about a full pitcher it is a sign of happiness. But if the person sees while asleep a pitcher breaking open, she or he will soon die," they pronounced. From hearing so much that our true mother was the earth, sometimes I wanted to cease to be just so the women of my kin might make pottery with my body.

"When the suns were first created, people ate only earth," Tall Mountain remembered. "Some day we will all be earthen vessels," she repeated. And I believed it, because often her belly would become more swollen than an earthen jar for collecting rain water. It was as if some silent potter, with knowing fingers, were working her from within.

Only when her womb was about to split open did my mother put down her clay and go off to the woods with the woman who knows how to help others give birth. There, after preparing a hollow in the ground, she squatted down to wait for the water of life, in one of its surges, to bring forth the little one who was navigating the inland sea of her body.

One morning when red flames of dust were enveloping our huts, my mother, before setting off into the forest, let slip from her hands the jar that she was creating and tumbled over into the dust. The earthen vessel and she seemed to shatter at the same time, and I had to go in search of the Master of Suffering.

With his necklace of blue feathers and wild boar teeth, the shaman appeared in the place where our hammocks were strung up. He brought with him his most powerful maracas, but in spite of the chants, the secret charms, the ground tobacco and the bright red clay poultices with which he covered Tall Mountain, he did not succeed in sucking out the illness nor in making a living creature come forth from her. Crestfallen, then, he went deep into the jungle in search of a place to bury his powerless rattles.

When, at last, that tiny blood-smeared shape – that could have been my brother – appeared between my mother's legs, I felt that the hills were crashing down around me. Never before had I seen a newborn face emerging, with its nostrils still closed to the air's breath, with lips that knew nothing of words. That time Tall Mountain spent many moons lying in her string hammock, listening to the wind go by, her eyelids closed, while in our corn field, the plants – refusing to grow – dried up.

And although, after many attacks of fever and outbursts of grief, she got up from the hammock, some part of her remained behind there, sleeping forever. She did not go back to being the person she was before. She kept quiet for long periods of time. Or she talked about strange things – about the river that her son never played in, about the tree that he didn't climb, about the many things that he could have seen but did not, about his own name that his own mouth did not pronounce.

Then one dawn, when the sun was already clearly visible in the sky, she sat down again before a mound of clay and after kneading it and caressing it lovingly, she set about making a figure still uninhabited by movement, with pupils whose gaze was turned inward, with lips that were unopened, with nostrils that still did not breathe. Then she took that idol devoid of sight, movement and sound, and after hollowing it out, she put into its interior a handful of little singing stones. As soon as that small clay man was fired, with coloring from the achiote fruit and some red earth, she dyed it the color of blood. Then, with milk from her breasts and a burned chip of wood, she set about marking it with white talismanic signs and black formulas.

Tall Mountain was transformed in that way into the first of many potters who have walked upon these lands—the first among her mother, her grandmother, and the grandmothers of her grandmother in giving form to a person's body and head. "But how did you do it? How did you conceive of it?" they would ask her, and she responded, "The clay kept telling my hands where it wanted to go." If I questioned her about why she had made it hollow, she would explain to me, "The blood of our kin is made from mud, of mud is our flesh, of mud are our bones. At birth we are only an empty vessel which, throughout suns and moons, must go about filling itself with echos and songs. Your brother did not have moons in which to fill himself with the world, and I had to fill him with little stones." From that time on, the women of the earth continued to model the ecstatic face of my dead brother. But one morning at dawn, when suddenly the heavens began to be tinted with pink (a sign that somewhere on the plain a tiger was giving birth), they felt the impulse to fashion their own bodies; and they made a standing figure, with a long thin opening between the legs to mark the place where the moisture of life makes its nest. And many moons later, one of them depicted herself at the moment of giving birth to a daughter.

My mother was also owner of the hidden secrets of color. She knew how to pull it out of each plant. She knew with certainty which herb, bark, root or leaf needed to be heated. toasted, soaked or ground up in order to dye the white foam from the wool bush and weave loincloths or hammocks. By extracting the juice from the buds of the tall trees that grew next to the river, she got the color yellow. With the moss from the stones, green. The little roots of some slender plants gave violet. And the plants that the men of the long canoes brought from distant beaches gave indigo.

Likewise, she sensed with accuracy just when the moon was in its precise phase so she could add to the resulting hues a drop of her own urine to add brilliance to each tone. It was not only for the sake of imitating the beautiful fur of the ocelots that Tall Mountain taught us how to paint our bodies with oil and achiote extract, but also to protect us from the insects' assault. During the season of heavy rain showers, in spite of the incantations that we sang around our huts, they attacked us inexorably. If we were not poking at the clay's heart or yanking the muffled color from the plants, we were stringing snails, armadillo claws and feathers so that the men might show them off in neck pieces and banners.

While gathering up the radiant tufts that the birds dropped as they passed by, my breast filled with anxiety, as if they contained messages from the world beyond the sun. "We belong to the ground, the birds to the sky," I said to myself then, to my own self to drive away the thoughts that were tormenting my imagination. But since there was something of the egret in me, when no one was watching, I picked up a little clay and modeled a bird with a woman seated upon its back. It was our custom to observe the flight of the birds. The hunters learned, in that way, to put feathers from the curassow and the turkey hen on their arrows to make them push forward through the air. We had heard of towns that learned to count by watching the macaws. And of sorcerers who foretold the future by the flight of flocks of birds. But we were most impressed by the music with which they swam through the sky, and we tried to repeat it in our dances.

When I, in my insatiable curiosity, pursued Tall Mountain with relentless questions about who had revealed to her the mysteries locked up in things, she invariably responded, "My mother, who for long moons carried me in her womb and for many more on her back, taught me to stir in the clay. But the language of the grass was imparted to me by the place of the many trees."

Yes, the jungle and the corn field, because after our work with the clay, when the moment in which the sun falls like an enemy arrow over our shoulders had passed, we went off to gather the fruits of the jungle and tend the plants. "The women are to devote themselves to the earth which is sacred because they bring forth children, and the earth gives birth to plants," the ancients said. Our garden was not always located in the same place. No sooner than we noticed that the garden plots were tired—they tire out just like animals and people— we began the search for another spot in which to sow the yuca for the cassava cakes, the plantains that we had to chew for the newborn children, the cacao that we used for trade, and the tobacco that we offered to visitors .

The choice of the exact spot to prepare the corn field was a delicate matter. To determine the site where the men would slash and burn, Tall Mountain looked at what trees were growing nearby, examining closely the color and the density of the earth, squeezing it between her fingers and sniffing it for a long time. When the moment to plant the corn arrived, we had to try to find snake meat to eat so that the ears would give a good yield. As regards the other plants, we only concerned ourselves with carefully painting our bodies and our faces and with adorning ourselves in our most beautiful finery. The more beautiful we were the better the harvest would be! So many moons, so many instants of so many afternoons lived among shrubs and wild climbing plants impregnated my mother with the hidden mysteries of the barks and herbs. Secrets that she tapped with brilliance when the evil spirits penetrated one of our bodies. With the juice of the sorrel plant she cured blurred vision. With the resin of the guacayán's bluish-purple flowers she soothed toothaches, and with the milk from certain bushes she caused the sterile—who had not been able to bear descendants to give proof of their existence and to remember what they looked like—to flourish.

It was not, nevertheless, from my grandmother or from the garden where she learned the art of joining threads together. The spiders taught her how to weave. Tall Mountain told me that before, long before, I saw the radiant source of our light and warmth, the women of my community did not know how to transform cotton into thread or to make hammocks. One afternoon spent staring long hours at the beautiful nets that the spiders extend into the air made them want to imitate them. To learn how these creatures made their webs, one of my grandmothers decided to pretend that she was sleeping in order to spy on them. Night after night she did the same thing until she succeeded in learning all the details of the task. Finally, early one morning, she placed a tiny ball of cotton in her mouth, she filled it with saliva, she twisted it until it formed a thread, and imitating—with her feet and hands—the movements of those insects, she wove a deli-cate web.

My father's name was Catatumbo. Hunting, fishing and keeping enemies and dangers at a distance was his job. He, like all our men, was a great lord of the jungle and the lagoon. Catatumbo knew the things of the forest and the savannah. There was no mystery in them that he could not explain. It was sufficient for him to sample a little bit of water to know from which river's shore it came. For him all the streams and mountains had a name. And he knew why each one of them was called what it was called.

The stones were glistening from the rain the afternoon my father scaled the glowing walls of the mesa—from where blood-red waters leap—and discovered that on those magic-charged summits dwelled animals and plants forgotten to all because the same sun that shone the day life began was still giving them its warmth. My father was also a visitor to the mysterious streams whose fish, leaping up, would get into the dugout canoes. And he visited others where the fish went away laughing bubbles because they knew how to use magic charms to free themselves from the traps.

Catatumbo asserted that he had seen wondrous fishhooks that caught an abundance of fish because they were made of human bones. And also that he had seen, thanks to the luminous eels that burned in water like submerged suns, the towns that rise beneath the river bed.

When there was no war going on or they weren't in the forest, my father and the other men of the earth were busy fashioning arrows and blowguns, preparing nets and fishhooks or weaving baskets for the gathering of the fruits of the jungle and fields. They had the custom of getting together early in the morning or towards twilight to talk about the dams to be constructed and the wild beasts and birds that they wanted to hunt (they named them and they drew them over and over again to begin to take control over them). Similarly, they practiced the song of the male birds in order to trap the females. Or they prepared curare and the powders that aid in the hunting of wild turkeys and toucans. Our men would often allow themselves to be caught by the evening shadows, chewing on a sliver of wood. They conversed tirelessly about when there was no world. About when everything was in suspension and the firmament's expanse was empty. About the birth of the oceans and the mountains which rose up from their waters.

And at the moment when they felt the necessity of communicating with the jungle spirits, they chewed tobacco wrapped in palm bark, or they inhaled *coba* so that the spirits would enter their open eyes and fill them with dreams. On occasions the medicine man would rack their brains with riddles and guessing games. On other occasions he would recite poems and songs that narrated the history of our people from the age before the time when the animals talked. If people from other regions came to us along the pathways of land or water, Catatumbo and the men would engross themselves in new deliberations, and they would sit around commenting on what each traveller reported having seen on other soils and shores.

That was how we found out about a race of wise people who told their story by making drawings on the rocks, who kept a record of the passing ages, and—in order to keep watch over the things of the night—had raised up buildings that touched the sky. Foot travellers also arrived saying that they had heard of the infinite pathways marked out over the face of the earth by a distant nation that harnessed the god of the waters, forcing him to work for their crops.

When the men got up from their string hammocks, it was to hunt or make war. And they seemed to enjoy both things. We women, on the other hand, were afraid of fighting. Our sons perished. Our daughters were stolen. The pottery, although polished with great care, would break, and the morning of calm to model those pieces that we had imagined making some day—and which were going to be the best of all that we had made until then—did not exist. The cries of war brought nothing good. Of the lances and arrows that had been so carefully crafted, nothing remained but shoulders and bellies ripped open, hearts and intestines exposed to the air, bones being bleached by the sun. In times of peace, on the other hand, the fruits of our wombs would burgeon, and the land—transformed into flower, nutriment and earthen vessel—would issue forth from our hands.

On certain occasions I would wander away from my mother's side to go over to where the boys were, to learn shaman word games and to let the wonders of the planet enter my ears. I felt that I would have enjoyed being a man in order to traverse strange jungles, defy rapids, scale the impenetrable mountains until I reached their powerful summits, recognize the track of the tiger and the capybara, or simply to remain in the hammock spitting out oceans of words. Nevertheless, I have not thought about straying from my own path since one morning when—as I was watching envious how the men were getting ready for a hunt—an old woman potter (my great-grandmother, who had been dead for many moons) appeared. She came from her distant dwelling to walk among us and converse with me.

That day she wanted to talk to me (from the depths of the earth where she resided, from the bosom of the ground where she lay waiting, she felt that my hands were the hands of a fine potter just as she herself had once been, that between my fingers she could be changed into an earthen vessel and return to life). And she did it through the song that the women were singing to bring about a bountiful hunt. She spoke to me of her existence together with the clay. About the four-faced figures that she modeled to show that the clay was moving, about the effects that she obtained by applying different fabrics and elements to it, about how she obtained the colors, about the ways of polishing it. Finally, she said, "The challenge for some is in the jungle, yours is in the muddy clay." Then singing softly a poem that went, "Earth hides life in its breast. Woman with her hands awakens life and sets into motion the world that the mud conceals," she went back to her tomb.

Since then, I have not doubted any more. I knew that my calling was to bring into flower the universe, the birds, the fish, the men and women that the muddy clay hides in its womb. And satisfied with carrying a damp nest between my legs, just as my mother had done, her own mother and all women who have arisen from the dust, I prepared myself to spend my mornings and my afternoons making pots, caring for the corn field and for my children. And although many of my earthen vessels would break with use and time, I knew that others were destined to survive as a record of the epoch when our kin sang, planted and suffered under the sun. For my grain storage jars would be, some day, guideposts for those who would come afterwards, cries of old clay that other hands would surely awaken, between whose fingers the earth would come to life over and over again.

Thus, when my womanhood first flowered in me and I had abstained from eating during the three days that the blood lasted, the other potters left me to choose my own place where I could create my clay pieces. And I, in turn, was to learn to negotiate with the flames, to carry always little sticks of cacao to light them, to look for oil to feed them, to engage in battle with them so as to tame the spirit that possesses them. I had to know how to spy on the rain's footsteps so I would not be surprised by its tears and to keep myself alert to its gestures and silences, for when its murmuring drops arrive, the pottery work falls behind, and the clay—just like curare—loses its strength. And in time I too was a mother and filled with the power of earth, fire and water.

That the clay speaks I knew after sharing my hammock and giving birth to my eldest child. It happened, one of the many times when without knowing what jar or pot to make, I was caressing, pensively, the lump of clay. I noticed, then, some murmurings coming from its grainy surface. I thought it was, perhaps, the mockingbird that had its nest nearby, which entertained itself imitating the sounds of daily life. But when I put my ear right on it, I could sense that it was the clay that was whispering. Then the feeling came to me that it was my kin speaking in that soft sound. And besieged by the desire to trap the voices hidden in the mud, I began to fashion whistles in the form of corn ears, pottery pieces that sing when they are filled with water, and large earthen jars for storing the sounds of anguish.

With the sun's movement I discovered these things: clay retains memories that sometimes overtake it and they oblige it to assume a determined appearance; the memory of the earth continues to flower with the dampness of water, and when that occurs it is the earth that adopts a design, old although apparently new, not the hands; and it can be the countenance of someone long dead or the round surface of a water pitcher which—pulverized by time and longing for what it once was—obliges our fingers to travel back over the road of its ancient body.

One dawn when I was feeling somewhat drowsy from the aroma of the golden tobacco leaves that were drying above the string hammocks, I was able to test the veracity of something that Tall Mountain had confided to me at an early age. On taking a ball of clay that was already prepared, it seemed to me that it remembered something because, without intending to, I drew a man with a harpoon and a blow gun, carrying an alligator on his back. According to one of our wise old women, it turned out to be the silhouette of Lanza Rapida who, in life, was the great lord of the streams (none of the hunters of his time succeeded in hanging from the roof of his hut as many alligators jaws as he, who had for so many moons resided in the world of the dead). Since that time, on beginning my labors every morning, I never fail to ask myself about the memories that can cause the clay to tremble. And if it does not obey my fingers and persists in taking paths that are to me unknown, I allow it to speak through me.

When they arrived, it was already many moons since my mother's eyes had become filled with earth. Her body and hands had turned to clay and were already earthenware when they arrived. We did not see them coming. The moriche palms suddenly stopped their gentle waving; the breeze became saturated with the stench of vultures and the rubber plants wept their dewy drops before their time. (The corn seeds foretold the end of our shamans' power. Again and again the corn announced with its kernels that a time would be upon us in which we would despair. Beings not naked like ourselves would destroy us.) We listened to them descend from the mountain's most hidden opening. The cicadas suddenly fell silent. Suddenly a great silence fell upon us.

They came from above, like the gods of the rain and the wind. They arrived from the most distant clouds, and they proclaimed their ability to extinguish the moon's fire. We believed that they, like the first fathers of the river walkers, were inhabitants of the world of the beyond and were bringing signs of the dawn in their hearts. Or perhaps they were children of the stars who, during the night, appear and disappear. Nevertheless, the people of the lake dwellings said they had seen them arrive from the sea, in dugout canoes larger than an island, for one evil day they appeared on the line of interwoven feathers that marks the place where the waves intermingle with the arching sky. The roads that led to their dwellings were not known by anyone, nor was it known where they had left their women. They did not reveal a single part of their bodies. They covered themselves completely with a strange bark that glowed like the water's skin. Some had four legs and they expelled smoke through their lowermost head. But all displayed long shags of hair on their faces and cheeks, which were pale like the light of the moon.

# María Cristina da Fonseca

On catching scent of them, we determined that they smelled of death. They were seeking the sun's yellow sweat, which we at times hung from our noses and necks. Gold, they called it. Gold, it was the only thing that they wanted. To find it they burned our houses made of palm. They broke the bows and the arrows belonging to our men. They killed our sons and they took our daughters to be slaves. When they arrived the fire in which I was baking my earthen vessels suddenly recoiled, injured by invisible enemies, and crackling and sobbing it put itself out, breaking all my clay jars at once.I took refuge in my hut, but my hut was falling down around me.I climbed up among the pink flowering apamate trees, and the trees threw me to the ground.

I wanted to return to the bosom of my mother earth, and I ran to the most secluded of all the caverns. And the caverns closed their open lips before me. I invoked the seeds, their power to turn themselves into trees and that of the caterpillars who transform themselves into cocoons, but I did not succeed in taking the form of a nocturnal butterfly and escaping among the shadows.

Our huts erected on plots of land where the jaguar had not set foot and the owl had not made its nest; our huts built according to old and wise laws (the houses have to be round like our world, round like the sorcerer's maracas); our huts that had not been brought down either by the ground with its tremors or by the whirlwind with its pounding blows gave way before the thunder and the flames vomited by their harpoons. The voices fell silent and our bows and arrows spoke. Death followed upon death. "Christ is the true life," they said while they went about bringing our end. "Only we are human," shouted the chieftans as we were turned into slaves. And nothing was as it had been before. The hilltop roared our misfortune like a wounded ocelot. And I felt as if all my pottery pieces, those already made and those still to be created, were about to break.

I tried to run far away. I tried to find the people of the long canoes and flee in their floating tree trunks. But the universe that I believed to be big, abruptly shrunk. Suddenly the mountains fell down on top of me and the swamps covered the roads. The paths to the jungle, the cornfields and the savannah opened out like a fan, but there was no route that would lead me back to what had been before. The shaman

39

with his word could not retrieve yesterday's sun, nor did the talismans still have the power to force our enemies to depart. Where could we flee and not find them there? Where could we turn so we would not have to look at them? What could we cover our ears with in order not to listen to their incomprehensible language? What place could I go to if I was their prisoner? From seeing what I was seeing. from looking at so much hatred and violence, I wanted to go blind so I would not find myself in the new world that they had brought under the hooves of their beasts.

Between bursts of rage and tears, a thousand and one times, I asked myself how my mother might have behaved had she suffered the curse of seeing our people conquered. And with the certainty that she would have kept on modeling earthen jars, as if she did not hear the screams of our kinspeople nor listen to the sounds of the whips with which we were forced to sow the strangers' gardens, I did as she would have done. Then turning my gaze inward, even if my hands felt heavy with a new fatigue, I began to knead my clay. Dreaming that I was already dead, erecting underneath the ground another world of free earthen jars. And I kneaded clays, animosities and laments as if in doing it I might bring back the life of each one of our people. The rest of the women soon began imitating me, although the pain of their hearts was great and their mouths and eyes were sad. And we worked as if we did not see nor hear all that was happening. But our earthen containers were no longer the same. Even full of water or food, they gave the appearance of being empty. The faces that we put on them looked more and more like ourselves, and we looked more and more like that first form of people—inert and hollow, made one day by my mother, who in life had the name of Tall Mountain.

Seeing my white hair and my spent breasts, the newcomers left me alone to work. From time to time they sent someone in search of my ceramic pieces. I learned that they valued all that my hands made by the gleam in their eyes and the torrent of words that burst from their mouths when they looked at it.

One day, three of their sorcerers came up to me under the palm leaves of my roof. They were not wearing face paint as is customary for medicine men but they were carrying two crossed sticks to scare away the evil spirits. They were the ones who conversed with the

Great Heart of the Sky, whom the conquerors petitioned for rain. They had with them a piece of wood that spun around. According to the explanation of the man from my town who understood what they were saying, I was supposed to place a lump of clay on top of this thing and push it along with my fingers. But we, the daughters of the earth, worked so rapidly and perfectly that we had no need of such an instrument. The foreign shamans made a habit of coming to look for me. They sat down near where I was working and asked questions about my craft. They talked to me about how ceramic ware was made over there in their distant land. And about some potters—nuns, they called them—who perfumed the clay as they kneaded it, a secret that they promised to trust me with if I came up to the fire that they were preparing to model the stones of the god that they worshipped.

They envisioned erecting a dwelling, out of boulders and packed earth and as big as a mountain, to be the home of the spirit who had brought forth the entire universe and then each one of us from a handful of clay moistened with its own saliva. They wanted it to have a tower from which would hang a maraca made out of seven metals, and at the sides they wanted two enormous pieces of carved bark so that the Indian men could enter through one, and through the other, the Indian women (that is what they called us). They asked me to make the one who created all things—his hands and feet nailed to two crossed branches, as he was at the moment of his sacrifice. I remained silent. But even so, I was tormented by the desire to know how those distant women managed to fashion vessels that smelled like the resin of certain trees and the flower of certain plants.

In the afternoons, I walked among the cacao fields to spy from afar on the giant kiln that they had set up to fire the walls and the idols of the temple. Guando, Totumo, Petaquero and Colina—who like myself had fallen prisoner—were in charge of preparing the packed earth to build the walls that were reinforced from the outside with additional stair-stepped walls. and they carved their names into them as they worked. This was an extremely dangerous thing to do, because to reveal one's name is to give possession of one s life to another, it is to hand over to another the power to enslave our breath and to make us victims of their evil chants. (I never wanted to pronounce mine or to write it on any of the objects that I created.)

Again and again they returned to invite me to fashion the ceramic pieces for their altar. And I explained to them that this was a matter for discussion between my fingers and me. Something in me refused to please them, but when I saw how the mist that for moons and moons had woven its grey tresses among the reeds of my hut was now becoming entangled in the roof of the foreign sanctuary, it seemed to me that I might as well go where it went. Sun after sun they continued coming to enjoy the protection of the shade under the thatch of my hut. By observing them closely, I could see how the power of little things conspired against them. I saw them succumb under the mosquitoes' and gnats' assault. I saw them turn deathly black from the merciless spike of the red sting ray and other creeping things, their sorcerers not once turning to the power of the juices locked within the fragile herbs. Their weakness lay in not knowing the secret powers that insignificant things possess. Our chieftains, who fought them from the forest, were right not to believe them invincible as they unleashed a guerrilla war against them, surprising and insistent as the mosquitoes' attack. Such thoughts helped me not to fear them, and finally, overcome by the desire to know what I did not know, I walked up to the kiln and agreed to depict their idol in fired clay. That was how I came to understand that the deity whom the foreigners called upon in time of drought was the same one who inhabited our rivers, although their shamans might be adorned in a different way and they might not know the incantations that the Guardian of Rain pronounced to make the clouds come near.

They had explained to me how the Great Spirit had created the universe; how the Great Spirit separated the elements and set them in order making oceans, lakes, land masses and mountain ranges and extracting male and female from the clay's open bosom. I concluded, then, that the one who had given shape to everything of necessity had to be the potter and great lord of earth, fire and water, as was the one who gave me life. And therefore, as the Heart of the Heavens I made a woman whose breasts were wounded yet so abundant with milk that they could nourish the stars of the firmament, the fishes of the ocean and all the creatures of the universe. And I fashioned for her a spacious womb capable of giving birth to skies, lakes and volcanoes. I gave her hands that were raw from so many long hours of kneading, the same clay-colored skin that Tall Mountain had, the warm eyes that she had, the nose and the mouth that accompanied her in life, and her long tresses crowned with thorns.

I transformed my dead mother into Christ because it always seemed to me that there was an infinite power in her wondrous hands. And that just as she wrested humans, birds and animals from the clay's generous womb—by kneading with those potter's fingers—the one who created the world had to be, of necessity, a kneader of broths, minerals and elemental substances. As had been all the women potters descended from these, the first and most ancient soils of all.

But, in spite of the fact that I took the trouble to conceal with a red-tinted loincloth what they called "the shameful parts" of my woman-heart-of-the-heavens, the foreign shamans ordered me flogged. Having no respect for the snow of my temples, they beat me again and again. Mercilessly they beat me to the point of exhaustion. They dragged me, then, to a hole that was so dark, so small and bearing such a resemblance to a tomb that I thought I had died. I do not know for how many moons I was abandoned there, eating larvae, worms and insects and drinking the rain that filtered down through invisible crevices. At the beginning, I did not care that I could not see either the light or the fog, (the pain in my back, great as the black immensity of the rocks, did not allow me to feel anything). Nevertheless, as suns came and went, their light never touching me, a great nostalgia began to spring to life within me. It made me grieve to evoke the jungle, the smell of the plants, the deafening call of the howler monkeys at dawn and dusk, the slow, aimless wandering of the sloths under the silvery shadow of the *vagrumo* trees. The absent songs caused me pain, and into my eyes there flowed a green so intense that the memory of it hurt

The hills still caressed my gaze, my feet still listened to the babbling of the deepest streams, and in my innermost ear I still retained hidden within me the rumble of the waterfalls dropping in transparent reflections over the old harshness of the stones. And in spite of the fact that from where I was, I was able to listen to the movement of she who appears and disappears in the sky at night, to savor the perfumed song of the rain embracing the jungle, my legs longed for the freedom of the roads. Then I was seized by the strong desire to feel once again—just like when as a little girl I walked at my mother's side—that I was part of the cloud-filled forest, at one with the mist that plays in the light and the branches that sing in the darkness, sister of lianas, beasts and birds, and of the children of the grass. And so that they would never abandon me, so that they would never run away from me, I called out their names.

One by one I began calling *Picures,* tapirs, ocelots, capybaras and rabbits. I invoked ceiba trees, shady *bucares, araguaneves,* bushes and climbing vines. Then I summoned together the nocturnal light of the glowworms, the humming of the insects that buzz in one's ears, the incessant clamor of the cicadas announcing rainshowers, and the snakes bearing their silence. I called the violet flower of the *bora bora* floating in the rivers, the white water lilies submerged in the lagoon, the waters of the great sea, arid rocks and stones shining from the rain. Into the dark shadows that surrounded me I invited the colors red, green, yellow and indigo. I summoned the aroma of the damp earth and the white orchids. The taste of cassava cakes crunching between my teeth and the flavors of the avocado also came to me. In that way I began to fill up my cell. It happened that during seven consecutive nights I had the same dream: I was sitting very still on the floor when a thousand golden dragonflies came to rest on my body and then, picking me up, they carried me far away through the air.

I learned in this way that my freedom existed somewhere (I had seen it while I was asleep), and remembering how our ancestors drew the animal that they wanted to trap. I said to myself: "If I make my sisters the butterflies in clay, if I draw their flight. they will come to this place and I will escape between their wings." My jailers refused to bring me any clay, but since the images that I was longing to make were breathing within me (their breath was as strong as the wind that cannot be held captive), I soaked my fingers in the blood of my still open wounds and I traced on the walls of my tomb a dragonfly more red than the fire's red flower. And I do not know what secret incantations I unleashed on drawing it, because the flutter of its wings brought warmth to my heart.

I was assailed by a great desire to keep sketching the birds, the flowers, the fish and animals that inhabited my memories, and taking a little bit of the moss that covered the stones, after dampening it in saliva with a clump of my own hair, I drew a macaw in splendid shades of blue. Using my urine to alter the earth's color and procure new tones, next I made a troupial becoming one with the clouds. Then I felt that I was flying! I traced a little tuna leaping playfully in the radiance of the river. And I was a fish in the water! But when I painted the purple flower of the sweet potato, I was transformed into a plant, burgeoning with roots, moist with sap. And I kept on working, never resting for a moment, until I turned my jail into one great jungle. Finally, I fell asleep and slept as I had not for many moons.

And how did they find out about what I had done in silence? I never knew, but one morning they opened the night that surrounded me, and before my blind eyes the strangers presented themselves. I thought that they were coming with new punishments and torments, but—in a friendly manner—they lifted me up from the floor and after looking at my designs they withdrew, begging me to agree to paint the main altar of their temple with the motifs that covered the fortress walls that imprisoned me.

This had already happened many moons ago. I remember, nevertheless, that when I finished creating the great altarpiece, I felt that my breath was being cut off. With the few gasps of air that I held stored in my chest, I walked toward the place where—seated on the ground—the youngest of my daughters was working with the clay (on her back, my granddaughter, whose hair had the color of corn, was playing with her mother's dark braids). When I came up to her, she raised her eyes in my direction and began to express her grief even before listening to what I was going to tell her. "My children and your children are grown. My pottery has been fired," I began to tell her as if I did not see her tears. "My days have already been accounted for. My moons no longer shine. My suns have gone out. The bats with their wings are announcing a more important flight. I, the one who came from the earth, am going back to the earth. I am leaving and I shall not return. Look after our hut, our corn fields, our water jars. If you think about me, you will be able to hear me through the song of the musicians, during an afternoon's dancing. If you do not forget me, my voice will reach you through the whispers of the clay…"

"How have our enemies been able to cast a spell against you if they do not possess your name?" she interrupted me sobbing. "What powerful evil have they done to you—twice a mother, you who gives movement to the muddy clay, you who with it creates music and poetry—to extinguish your light?"

Without responding or turning to see her, I started down the road to the string hammock that was to ferry me toward life's horizon. (While she was beginning to burn pine resin in my memory.) Such was the last time that I, still living, looked at my daughter and at her own daughter. But because—when the same wind that gave me my first breath gathered up my final sigh—they buried me facing the heavens, from here, from the warm insides of the earth where I find myself, even with my hollow eyes, I never stopped looking at them. Before their ashes and my ashes were mingled together, I came one morning to talk with them. I had much to entrust to them, but I saw that there no longer remained any signs of our existence (neither they nor the other women devoted themselves to the clay), and I sealed myself in silence.

It was then, only then, that I understood that I—who have for so many dawns been inhabiting the dust—was really dead. For centuries I remained silent. For centuries I tossed about in sadness in my tomb without undertanding how our people could become estranged from the earth. But today taking sustenance from the infinite patience with which the dead are nourished, illuminated by the memory of the dawns when I would knead my earthen jars, I wait for the oblivion accorded me to be forgotten...

Like the snail that sleeps in its shell, I wait to be reborn! The chattering river sometimes brings to me here where I lie hidden the hum of life in its daily passing, the echo of events that are transpiring in the world of those who have still not died. I know therefore that the women of my kin, in spite of not working the clay, learned to embroider clothes with threads of intense hues which repeat, a thousand and one times, the pictures that I, the daughter of Tall Mountain, drew on an alien altar. But, even though a little bit of me still travels on the shoulders and backs of my people, the muddy clay of my old body still sorrows because there are no longer any hands to knead it. My eyes, my mouth, my ears. my arms, my womb and each part of my body which has now become sand burn with desire to be transformed into an earthen vessel. The ashes of my blood, seasoned by time, still tremble with the memory of the earthen jars that I dreamed of making but never made! Sometimes I feel that the dawn is not far away when new hands, hands unknown to me, hands ignorant of mine, working together like sisters with those that were once my hands may take up, caress and knead the mud of my ancient body and bring forth the world that throbs in the earth of my breast.

*Testimony gathered in the lands included between the basin of the lake that was later called Lake Maracaibo and the settlement. today known as San Miguel de Bocono, sometime during the year of 1499.*

Translated by Elaine Dorough Johnson

# The Pilgrim's Angel

## Violeta Quevedo

### On the Way to Buenos Aires

There were about twenty of us in our group. We were taking the Transandean Express as far as Mendoza. From there we would go on to Buenos Aires to embark for Europe. Only one cousin, a really close friend of ours, came to the station to see us off.

As we crossed the border, my heart felt heavy; I was about to leave my country for the first time by myself, without my parents, who had always gone places with me when I was younger.

Once we got to Buenos Aires, we checked into the Majestic Hotel, where we had reservations. Here I began to feel the hand of Providence, which I attribute in large part to the sacred blessing bestowed upon us as we left Santiago by an ancient priest, a good friend of ours, whose advice to me had always been sound, and who approved of my pilgrimage. When we said our farewells, the good old man was moved to tears. His name was Hernán Domeyko. His recent death was truly admirable, the death of a real saint. I remember him affectionately and gratefully, since he was always a true guide for us, with his prayers and his advice.

Buenos Aires is all life and activity! It is a great city. I will make note of a little incident which happened there.

At tea time, around five in the afternoon, we were sitting beside an Argentine lady, who was also preparing for a pilgrimage to Luján. Little by little we got to talking and we found each other most congenial. She invited me to visit the church of the Holy Sacrament, which

48

was the one my sister and I most wanted to see, and she took us on a tour of the principle avenues in her magnificent car, with stops along the way at a few shops.

I marveled at the beauty of the church's interior. We attended a religious service and I was very impressed by the elegance of the ceremonies. People are quite right to say that this is one of the best things that Buenos Aires offers.

On the morning we were leaving, our new Argentine friend came to see us off. Our companions were surprised by such kindness and courtesy. We said farewell, perhaps forever.

THE SHIP

We arrived on the La Plata pier with the rest of our group, ready to embark. I could hardly believe that my journey was becoming a reality. Along with everything else, I felt very nostalgic about the country where I was leaving behind the beloved remains of my parents and so many relatives, and of course I never dreamed that during my absence I would lose one of my favorite aunts. When my uncle hugged me goodbye at his splendid country home, he said, "Pray on the tomb of St. Francis that I'll be chosen as Minister to Rome, because there's more for us there..." And that's how it turned out, but at what a terrible price. Soon after they got to Barcelona, his wife, my aunt, got sick. They tried everything, but to no avail. God took her away.

The crossing was really tedious. The food served on board was terrible. My appetite, which had been poor since we left Chile, was completely destroyed. It was positively providential that I arrived at our destination still alive.

Our stateroom was very close to the steamship's engine. The heat was stifling. When I saw my pale sister with her eyes closed, gesticulating wildly in her sleep, I was so panicked that I threw myself on top of her, shaking her violently to wake her up. She was furious at me, but when I explained to her what had possessed me, she told me she had reacted the same way when she saw me sleeping so restlessly.

One of our companions made this prediction to me which, thank Heaven, did not come to pass: "Your sister will not reach Paris."

We were lucky that a Mr. Besa, now deceased, demanded that the captain switch us to another stateroom.

## GENOA

We began our sightseeing very haphazardly. We lunched and immediately afterward went to visit the city's main attraction: the cemetery. What a flood of memories crowded us there! It had been so many years since we had passed through with our parents and the rest of the family that we didn't expect to remember anything. But our young minds had been so impressed, we found that we could still remember everything clearly and very precisely: the beautiful marble lacework, the little children draped in porcelain embroidery cradled in their mothers' arms, and oh, so many other things.

It was a real struggle to find our companions again since we had gotten separated from them when we stopped to say the rosary. We also visited the corpse of Saint Catherine of Genoa which is on display. It is intact just as it was when she died. It has turned completely black, just like the body of Saint Clara.

## ROME

We arrived at last at our journey's real destination. Our major purpose was to visit the Holy Father, and next we wanted to see the great churches, monuments, museums, etc.

We had lots of problems while we were preparing for the visit to the Vatican. At the door there were women who inspected the "toilettes" of those who entered. My sister's dress was too short, so since I'm older I had to lend her one of mine, and we fixed up the one I wore as best we could. Each pilgrim had to cover up her neck and shoulders so as to enter into the presence of the Holy Father with proper decorum and respect.

Our companions had not waited for us, and we had to take a hired car in order to be there on time for the audience. Even so, we waited an hour.

At one o'clock the Holy Father entered the hall, under a canopy, and he was cheered and applauded by all the pilgrims gathered there. One of the Chileans presented him with Chile's flag. The Holy Father received it graciously and made a short speech.

The Bishop who was with us undertook to translate it, and these were the words, more or less: "I greet you all and am pleased that you have made such a great effort and traveled so far to be here and gain the jubilee."

Next, he said a few friendly words to several of us, and gave us his holy blessing. As he said farewell, he gave us each a medallion that I still have.

The Pope is of normal height and has a very intelligent face.

In Rome, we visited several churches: St. Peter's, San Giovanni in Laterano, and the chapel which houses the Holy Stairs, the Scala Santa, which we went up on our knees, as you're supposed to. I was really impressed by one of the Chileans who had very bad legs, which meant that his climbing the stairs was of greater merit. Even though I was quite frail, I climbed up on my knees, too.

We also visited the Catacombs. The bishop officiated at a mass there, and my sister took communion. We also saw the church of Santa Maria Maggiore where, with great solemnity, they showed us the authentic portrait of the Holy Virgin, painted by St. Luke. I could distinguish her features quite easily and I thought she looked remarkably similar to a relative of mine in Chile, especially in the oval shape of the face. We went through several museums and through the Roman Colosseum, with all its rows of spectator boxes from which those barbarian emperors watched the Christians being tortured and killed by wild animals. We also visited the galleries of the art museum.

I am really sorry to have to repeat it, but "This city makes no sense to me," I said to my sister, crying. "I don't like it. I think that if I could come back alone, I would enjoy it. Right now I just feel tired...and bored."

These words must been premonitory, because after we had left the rest of the pilgrims behind, I managed with great effort to arrange another little tour of Rome for us, and despite my ailments, I enjoyed it much more and could better appreciate the beauty and the ancient art and the historical and religious memorabilia that the city contains.

My aunt had suggested that we go visit a Chilean she knew who lived in a small castle, where there were also various other Chileans and some of our relatives. It was a great pleasure for us to greet and embrace them. They received us with a splendid meal, really a feast, and they invited us to visit the most interesting attraction there: the church of Santa Croce.

We were able to gaze at the sacred goblets, relics of the First Supper, the thorns of Our Lord, and the Finger of St. Thomas. The monk who showed us all of these treasures was extremely surprised and told us that they were only shown to the public on very rare occasions. Even the friend who accompanied us said that even though she had lived in Rome for a long time, she had never been able to see them before.

Some of our cousins came by to collect us in their splendid automobile, and took us on a sightseeing tour of the outskirts of Rome. It turned into a very long day. My sister got really tired, but she enjoyed seeing the little town of Frascati.

NAPLES

In Naples, we were welcomed with a supper given for us by the consul, the son-in-law of Mrs. Valdés who had referred us to him. We can attest that he fulfills his diplomatic post admirably.

Once we had seen the city, we went on to Pompeii. I invited my sister to go visit the sanctuary of the Virgin of the Rosary, Our Lady of Pompeii, to whom I have always been greatly devoted. My sister accepted enthusiastically.

The beautiful Virgin, elegantly attired, the Queen of the Holy Rosary, was in the center of the church. I think that the rosary held by the Divine Infant in her arms was made of real pearls or diamonds. What a wondrous chapel! We went with the pilgrims to visit the famous ruins of Pompeii. Even skeletons are still preserved the way they were when the volcano erupted.

It is very moving to see so many bones frozen into position: men, children and animals. The tour was a long one. There we bought mementos of the basilica to take back with us to Chile.

# Violeta Quevedo

## MONTE CASSINO

It was founded on the mountain peak by Saint Benedict in the 6th century. At its foot lies the city of Cassino, about halfway between Rome and Naples. The road to the abbey climbs up through rocks and olive groves. From up above there is a wonderful view out over the valleys and neighboring peaks. The beautiful abbey is a jewel of an example of the baroque style of the 17th century. Saint Benedict constructed a church right on the site where there had been a temple dedicated to Apollo, which he had ordered destroyed. There he established monastic life and wrote his Rule, which governs the Benedictines. He was buried in the crypt of the abbey church. Nearby one can visit the rooms where the Saint lived, in the oldest part of the immense monastery.

The monastery of Monte Cassino is governed today by an abbot who is also the Bishop of the entire region. Some forty monks live in the Abbey. The Abbey includes apartments where pilgrims can be lodged and also an astronomical observatory. The library possesses manuscripts which are very old and valuable. For me it was a real joy to have visited this Abbey. A relative of mine who is a member of that order kindly told me all these details and described to us what we were seeing while we were there with the other Chilean pilgrims.

We returned to Rome to continue to visit churches and monuments.

## MILAN

Here we visited the tomb of St. Charles Boromeo, the Duomo of Milan, which is in the Cathedral. It contains 3600 statues.

## COMO

Our group of pilgrims arrived at this lake on a little launch, since the bishop who led this pilgrimage brought a greeting from Chile from the convent of the Visitation to this house. The Mother Superior was called, a pleasant elderly woman who had been the teacher of the young saint, Benigna Consolata, a nun in that convent. I can remember every word of the conversation she carried on with the Bishop. Since I knew French quite well, although she spoke it with great difficulty, I could understand her easily. She recounted, "Benigna Consolata often said that a lack of confidence in Our Lord was what most grieved her. She said that for Him, the greatest shortcoming of mankind was the inability to just fall into His arms and trust in His infinite mercy, regardless of any sins committed."

VENICE

Its originality is its location right on the water. Wherever you want to go, you have to travel by small launch or gondola.

We went to see the great church of St. Mark. My sister and I saw the great bronze clock with a man on it who strikes the hours, and a lovely dovecoat where pilgrims usually want to have their pictures taken surrounded by a circle of little doves. We also visited the great factory where glass and fine porcelain are made. Almost all our companions bought lovely statues and expensive sets of dinner china; but we did not do that, since such purchases were beyond our means. We contented ourselves with seeing the queens' apartments, and pretending to ourselves that we were exploring fairy palaces, right out of children's tales.

SAINT FRANCIS OF ASSISI

Although this summary does not follow the exact order in which our activities took place, since I am just putting things down as I remember them, I don't want to skip over an interesting story, so I'll tell about it here.

We were staying at the Hotel Subasso very close to Assisi. The proprietor welcomed us warmly when he learned that we were nieces of the Chilean ambassador to Rome, whom he esteemed.

We took communion right on the Saint's tomb. I asked him to grant that my aunt's trip with her husband should take place, since before I left, she had requested me to ask this. How badly it all turned out! It was beyond belief how much I suffered when my aunt died when she got to Barcelona, since I was expecting that she would accompany us on our return home. She was a truly exceptional person for her strength of character, her kindness and her intelligence. She was always very practical in her deeds of charity. She wasn't one of those people who think they can accomplish a lot with theories and good excuses. When I found out about her death, I nearly lost consciousness. May God's Will be done!

We visited the little room where the Saint's mother gave birth to the great St. Francis, and all the buildings which were interesting because they are so old.

We were really racing along on this trip. Once we had gotten our suitcases packed, I gazed out of our window at the marvelous landscape, never dreaming that my travel companions were all the while waiting impatiently for me in the car. I blamed them for being in such a hurry to leave, without allowing even a moment to contemplate those glorious panoramas of the fields of Assisi.

How I yearned to escape from my group and spend a week there, but it wasn't possible. I had to climb into the car and bid farewell to that charming and picturesque city of Assisi. While we we were there, we had also visited the Portiuncula, enclosed within the basilica of Santa Maria degli Anglia, where the Portiuncula Indulgence may be gained for the dead. We visited the convent of Saint Clara, and saw her famous chair and the tomb where they have her actual body, unembalmed and kept right where visitors can see it. Even though it has turned a little bit black, it's really well preserved.

This sanctuary was an Eden of peace and tranquility. I thought I was really justified in my quarrel with the others, since that way I demonstrated that I had known how to appreciate how beautiful it was there. I was sorry to leave that sanctuary since I might never see it again.

## LOURDES

That same night we split apart from the group of pilgrims, since we had decided to travel on our own. Our parting of ways was accompanied by a rude shock. We were charged a very steep price for our last night's stay there. You could just see the indignation on the face of our companion, a Chilean gentleman, but he didn't say anything, although he made every effort to make our journey more pleasant.

While I was at the post office, I received a welcome surprise. I bumped unexpectedly into a cousin of ours. He invited us both to a splendid supper at the Grotto Hotel.

He was there in hopes of clearing the way for a marriage to take place. Unfortunately, he did not receive what he asked for. We were so glad to run across him in a foreign land, especially since he turned out to be so pleasant and affectionate toward us. That same night he took us over to the convent run by the little sisters of Bleaux. He took communion there with us.

We had come from Chile with a letter from Father Victor, who is dead now, asking that we be able to stay at the convent of the Soeurs Bleu, the Blue Nuns of the Immaculate. They have a beautiful convent where I spent very happy days with my sister, who yearned to move right in and stay there, until because of my health and the terrible cold, which was impossible for me to tolerate, we had to hurry up our departure.

IN THE BASILICA OF LOURDES

Each morning Sofía and I went to the Grotto of Lourdes to hear Holy Mass. Along the way we gazed at the beautiful and picturesque countryside that only Divine Wisdom could have created in such perfection.

One is left ecstatic gazing in amazement at all that, and it is beyond one's capacity for description. I will simply say that we were both enchanted with those beautiful landscapes that surpass what the most skilled painter could copy; even with all imaginable talent and ability, no human painter could come close to imitating those scenes, for those colors and that range of shades could only be achieved by a celestial hand.

We went out into bright sunlight even though the sky looked glacial. Since we were so unaccustomed to the sudden treacherous rains of European countries, it never occurred to us to take our umbrellas along.

One day when we were already in the Grotto and while we were hearing Mass, it began to rain so hard that we were soaked through.

When he saw us in that state, the sexton, a kind and compassionate man, realizing that we were foreigners, allowed us to pass through a shortcut as a special privilege. It was a passageway that went right through to the Basilica, and this way we did not get so wet.

The next day we forgot again and once more went out without our umbrellas. Suddenly we were caught in a torrential downpour. I was entirely soaked; but I said to myself, "I know what I'll do, I'll go through that same passageway the sexton showed me." Then something totally unexpected happened which I ascribe to the protection of the Most Holy Virgin and which could be considered as a favor granted to me by this Holy Mother.

I opened the door and went down into the subterranean vaults through which the sexton had guided us the day before. I walked down one passageway, then another...and nothing; I couldn't figure out where it came out nor did I remember how to get back.

I found all the doors locked. I was so tired that it didn't even occur to me to call for help, and I sat down on some marble steps.

Just then the sexton appeared, like an angel sent by the heavens. When he saw me, he exclaimed: "Que faites vous ici Madame?" He was extremely surprised and said, "Believe me, Miss, it is amazingly lucky for you that I've come through here, because I came just by chance to look for some keys I had left here. You've run the risk of being shut up here by yourself for three or four days."

"Since you brought me through here yesterday," I said, "I thought I could come through here again, since I was so soaked..."

"I brought you along this route yesterday as a great favor," he replied. "This area is always locked up." It began to dawn on me what a great favor he had done us the day before.

My sister, who had no idea why I was delayed, also marveled when I told her what had happened. It seemed to her to have been a celestial favor.

We visited Bernadette's house. We swam in the pool, which was frozen over with ice. My sister did it for the sake of her weak limbs and I did it for my stomach. This probably kept me from getting any worse than I had been.

I found the Grotto very similar to the copy of it in Santiago, which is an excellent imitation. It's really too bad that we weren't here for any of the main festivals of pilgrims. They say they are really impressive.

We met the family of Saint Bernadette, including her brother Bernard. Among other gifts, we gave him a cape which had been a gift to my sister from my dear aunt, who died just after that. Bernard was sweet as an angel, with blue eyes. He gave me his picture with his autograph, and I brought home several pictures of his saintly sister. He had been born fourteen years after the famous apparitions. She was his godmother. We said goodbye to him. My sister said to him, "We'll see you in Heaven!" And quite rightly, as it turned out, since only a few days after we'd gotten home to our country, we read in the paper that Saint Bernadette's brother had died.

SAN SEBASTIAN

One of the items on my travel itinerary was to go visit my cousin who was a novice in the order of the Catechists of Aspeitía. From Lourdes itself I wrote her asking if we could come stay with her. Her answer was delayed in coming. We went directly to San Sebastián. There my sister wanted to find lodging in a convent. Our stay there wasn't very enjoyable. The young nun showed us the beaches, but I didn't see anything else of much interest. We found out how we could get to Aspeitía. We took the right buses and arrived at the Catechist Noviciate, a really pretty house. The nuns there were the most pleasant people we met while we were abroad. They served us a wonderful meal in their splendid house. I told my cousin Marta that she was the luckiest of us, since she seemed to be living in a real castle. But this was not Our Lord's Plan for her. For reasons of health, she returned to Chile. After many tribulations and difficulties and setbacks, her health is more or less all right again now, and she is wearing the Catechist habit in La Cisterna. She was delighted to see us. My sister felt really emotional and had a kind of premonition: When we got back to Chile, she wrote to Marta inviting her to come see us. Marta came back to Chile later with her religious sisters.

The convent was lovely, and so was the chapel.

In the city of San Sebastián, I went alone to visit a Sanctuary I'd been told had a miraculous Christ, similar to the Lord of May of Saint

Augustine, called the "Christ of Lezo."

Something very odd happened to me. Since I didn't know the way, I went along asking people and everyone answered me "Right where the road ends, there's where it is." I couldn't understand what they meant by "road" and I walked on and on...but I didn't see any road...until I finally found out that in Spain, "road" means a path and I'd been on it all along and there I was. I said a prayer to that very ancient Christ and also brought back a picture of it.

## SAN IGNACIO

Right next door to the Catechists' Noviciate was the beautiful house of St. Ignatius Loyola, transformed into a true religious museum. The church is magnificent, rich in relics, antique decorations, etc. I touched the holy medallion I always wear to each of the relics. They showed us the place where the Holy Virgin appeared to him when the saint was converted. The little chapel, decked with the finest jewels, had its own history. High up on one wall, you can still see the sootmarks from the smoke from the kitchen hearth of the Saint's house. In the room where they used to pray, there is a golden altar. In another room they have the relics of the saints of the Jesuit Order displayed in special reliquaries.

When I got there, I requested that a mass be said for my mother in that very house, since she had been so devoted to Saint Ignatius. A little after I had returned to Chile that order of saintly priests suffered persecutions and they were ousted from many of the places they lived, but I don't know whether this house that I remember so well was also destroyed.

While I was in the hotel buying some mementos, the proprietress took an interest in our last names and told us a story about the leave-taking of some ancestors of ours, who had bid each other farewell right in that very place, saying goodbye to their lives as a married couple and henceforth dedicating themselves to God and going off to live forever after in separate religious orders.

It was a very unusual case and it has been much discussed, since such sublime and singular acts are truly incomprehensible to the world.

# Violeta Quevedo

## LIMPIAS

My sister and the nun we were staying with suggested to me that we go see the Christ of Limpias. We took the train after a certain amount of discussion. We were going to see the New Year in while we were there, and we got there on the rainy afternoon of New Year's Eve. They were getting ready for the midnight Mass. We were lodged just across from the church. That day of torrential rains, I made my confession and took communion at that midnight mass. Just me, since my sister preferred to wait until the morning mass. At the communion rail they gave each of us a slip of paper telling us who our Saintly Protector for the year would be. I got the Sacred Heart with Saint Margaret Mary Alacoque.

When I entered the chapel and first looked at the Holy Christ, I'll have to admit that I felt afraid, since I had often heard that he stared angrily at people. Nothing happened to me, thank God, and when I talked to the priest there, he said that he hadn't seen anything in all his years there.

I brought home mementos and holy pictures which had been touched to the Holy Christ of Limpias, since they move Him down from His pedestal so that objects can be touched to Him.

## TOWARD FRANCE

We traveled through several French cities. In France, I can truthfully say, I learned how to look out for myself, since the French don't think well of Chileans. I often wept, and sometimes people assumed that I was French. Despite my afflictions, my sister made me laugh, since her squabbles with the French were so comical. I'll tell one anecdote.

My sister went to get a pair of shoes mended. She wasn't satisfied with the repair, and she started to argue about it. The Frenchman called me over, saying that my sister didn't understand him. They went back and forth about it. The Frenchman got furious, picked up a knife and made as if to slice into the leather. My sister calmed down and told him in French, "C'est bien vous dever aller vous confesser." The cobbler calmed down, too, and answered, "Elle ne pas mechante cette dame lá." I almost died laughing.

We had several other encounters like that.

## PARIS

We strolled along some of the beautiful avenues, the Champs Elysees, etc.

In the shabby little hotel where we were staying, in the Rue Hamelin, we met an Englishman who invited me and another person to go see the Eiffel Tower. We went and climbed right up to the top. From that height, people looked like ants and flies. I was reminded of stories of the Tower of Babel because down below, the city and people looked all tumbled together in confusion. Sofía didn't want to go up.

The shops in Paris are huge and have so many different sections and choices that it is exhausting. I left without being able to buy anything since I felt faint and dizzy surrounded by all those buildings and enormous spaces. Chilean shops seem tiny compared to the huge French Magasins.

## THE FRENCH CLERGY

I don't want to neglect to mention something that was so important on our trip.

I think I can say that my sister agrees with me, despite our very different personalities.

It's hard to say which of all the French priests was most kind, most gracious and most paternal.

When they saw that someone was sad, their word of consolation was always: "Courage mon enfant."

Words fail me to describe the chaplain of the hospital, and I can never thank him enough for his kindness. I still feel guilty that I didn't say goodbye to him. I feel very sorry about that.

Once in Belgium when I was pestered by a child when I was really tired, a priest came to my rescue so forcefully that the youngster didn't even dare look at me let alone beg from me. The same priest told me that that child didn't have permission to beg for alms.

I have the most agreeable memories of my confessions in France. Often my sister and I think how wonderful it would be to be there to go to confession with those priests who have such clear, sharp minds!

I went to confession in many different languages, including some I didn't know well, like Italian. The Father calmed my anxiety, assuring me that he had understood me.

## A DREAM

Just after my mother died, I was living with my sister in a shabby boarding house on Santo Domingo Street, and one night I dreamed something that later came true.

"Last night," I told my sister, "I dreamed that someone asked me, 'When your financial affairs are all sorted out, what are you going to do?' I heard this answer: 'You will live for two months in Lisieux, and your siser will be with you. You'll go window shopping and buy gifts for people.'"

## LISIEUX

Since we had so many problems—poor housing, bad health and really high rent—in Paris, I decided to write to Lisieux to the Santa Teresita sister, Mother Paulina, who is the Mother Superior. She answered on behalf of her order, recommending that we stay at "The Hermitage."

We moved. My sister was in her element. So was I, but less than she, since I was still suffering from poor health.

We began to visit every place that was connected to the Saint. We went to Buissoniers, the little house where she had lived with her father and sisters. It was a real gem. They have kept her childhood toys and put them on display there: a small bronze doll's bed and other little things. In the garden, there is a bronze statue of her with her father, showing them in the scene where she asked his consent to become a Carmelite. And he gave it, right there. You can also visit the room which contains the copy of the true Image of the Virgin "Notre Dame des Victoires," that is, the "Vierge de Sourire," an image of which I brought home with me from Lisieux. We also got to see the convent where the young saint was educated and we talked to the teacher, Mother Gertrudis. She was now very old but quite well preserved. She talked to us a bit about the young Saint. She said she was very sensitive in temperament and cried a lot about everything. I went to see the confessional where she received communion for the first time. What happiness that day must have brought to the heavenly angels, as that little girl with her celestial soul received Our Lord King of Kings in her heart!

My sister and I went every day to the chapel. The chasse where her bones are preserved is there, under a beautiful wax image. It's not like the way they've displayed Saint Clara of Assisi, out in the open, which doesn't give a good impression unless you know that it is the relic of a Saint. There was such a crowd of pilgrims that the little Chapel seemed very small.

My sister and I heard many masses going on at the same time, said by priests of various nationalities, who came from as far away as Africa and Greece.

I saw different kinds of bread and wine being used in holy communions offered by these various priests. Anyone could take communion. At one, wine was being administered with a spoon: this took place after the communicant had received the Holy Host. I wanted to take communion this way, too, but since I hadn't spoken up in time, they couldn't include me since it is all very organized. They had the wafers all counted out ahead of time and couldn't divide them. Despite the rules, several times I was shoved aside by Frenchwomen when I went to take communion at one of the special altars.

One day something curious happened to me that I attribute to being favored by Saint Teresita, given the circumstances in which the event took place. I was with my sister as usual, hearing the masses that were so numerous they were like a "shower of roses." She was hearing hers at the Altar of Saint Joseph, with a Frenchwoman, and they had requested Holy Communion for the two of them. I went by chance to hear that same mass but I wasn't planning to take communion since I wanted to do so later, which is why I hadn't requested to be included at this earlier time.

The moment of communion arrived and my sister went up to the rail; just then, the other person with whom she had requested communion disappeared, I looked over at the priest, and much to my amazement, the priest himself, with the Holy Host in his hands, beckoned to me. I hesitated a moment, because I was not yet prepared. My sister said "Come on!" I thought, "I have to accept this Divine Invitation." It would have been worse to turn it down.

But how could the priest have known that I was fasting and that I was intending to take communion? This incident left me profoundly moved, for in it I saw a divine kindness that thus recognized my ardent faith and yearning.

I visited the cemetery where the young Saint and the whole Martin family had been buried. I also went to visit the Saint's church, still in the early stages of construction but the grandeur of which could be seen in its details, its steel beams, its framework...I think that it must be finished by now.

The contractor of the temple project happened to be there and he walked around with me and with a Frenchwoman who also wanted to see the construction. He said he never took people around, so I considered myself privileged and was very grateful for this favor. He showed us all over, telling us about the areas designated for the church, for the convent, and for many other buildings; I don't remember now exactly what.

When I descended, two people assured me that I would return in another six years. I don't know but such odd things have happened to me that I wouldn't be surprised if after six years, I were to go back there again. Only the Lord knows what will happen in the present and the future.

From there I wrote to a Chilean friend, the Duchess of Descars, whose name is Teresa, who received me in her palace, and showed me her lovely castle. She invited me to lunch at her house and sent me to see Doctor Carnot, who was the one who later opposed the plan to operate on me at the Hotel Dieu Hospital. I was deeply grateful to my Chilean compatriot.

On one of my trips to Paris from Lisieux or Paray-le-Monial, I don't remember which, something so astonishing happened to me that I can only be deeply grateful to my Guardian Angel.

It was more or less midnight when I reached the Rue Hamelin in Paris, and I was all alone, weighed down with a suitcase which was just incredibly heavy, especially for my feeble strength...and here I was in Paris where they aren't like the English, but can be summed up generally as egotists.

Imagine my stupefaction when a young Frenchman, as handsome as he was kind, introduced himself as a concierge and said, "I'll carry that suitcase for you, Miss, right to your door."

"Je n'ai fait avec personne Ça." I had to tell him that I had almost no money in my purse (since I was afraid that he only wanted to do me this favor in exchange for *francs* or *sous*). He told me he wasn't the least bit interested in money...but that he himself wasn't sure why he'd felt inspired to carry my bag for me and that I shouldn't worry about it, since he'd take it right to where I was staying. Thanks be to God who watches over His creatures, even though the young man himself was unaware that Divine Providence had moved him and made him notice my expression of exhaustion that revealed that I was in great need of help.

I thanked him a million times and parted from him gratefully. Since he wasn't expecting more, he seemed pleased with just the single franc I gave him as a tip, a really tiny sum in those days.

## DAUVILLE

We had stayed about two months in Lisieux, but because of the problems caused by my poor health and the wretched food, my sister and I decided to leave there.

We were very friendly with a nice Frenchwoman, Marguerite Vacher. She wanted to repay me for making her a dress by taking me in her car to Dauville. She came by to get us herself, with her husband, a very kind gentleman. I was very grateful to them, and still remember them with affection.

They themselves assisted us and left us happily installed in a sweet little cottage that reminded us of Saint Teresita's little house in Lisieux. We stayed there about ten days.

Thinking that it would strengthen me, I committed the folly of bathing in the sea. It gave me a chill and I was very ill. We went to the shops and to a pretty little chapel that had a lovely park through which they carried the Holy Image in processions. This reminded me of the processions of Parisian nuns at Les Oiseaux. When we were little girls, my mother had enrolled all three of us in that school.

The church was called Saint Augustine's. I took a photo of my sister standing in front of its doors.

We went on trips to the nearby beaches of Trouville, so filled with memories of my relatives, who went there often. Here I bathed and before we left those Baths, a photographer took my picture there, despite my protests. I still have it, since it is a good likeness. French photographers do good work, not like the Chilean ones who roam around the squares and main avenues.

What most surprised the French was that after I lost my scissors in the sand, even though they laughed skeptically, I later found those scissors right on the beach where I had gone with my sister to sew.

## BELGIUM

Something truly strange happened here. One of the Cenacle nuns became really crazily obsessed that I should become a nun in her convent. Day and night she followed us around, even telling me that she would make me go on "retraites" by her own authority alone. She kept after me so tenaciously that I couldn't go anywhere without her tagging along, and I got really fed up.

"Sofía," I said to my sister, "here comes that nun to hound me again." Since by now it was Holy Week and she had bothered me so, I went to talk to a priest about it. He thought the nun's idea was a good one. So we moved up the date of our departure for Paris.

## PARAY LE MONIEL

In Belgium, I perfected my sewing skills, since I made friends with two Frenchwomen, despite always having to dodge that insistent nun. She got so angry when we left that she wouldn't even look at us. She wanted my sister to come back to Chile to arrange a dowry for me. She had her plans all made and she didn't care whether or not I had a vocation. Her idea was amusing, but it got so it really irritated me.

We also went several times to the *Criste Roi*. We signed ourselves up for the Friday masses in Paray.

From Rome, a Chilean friend sent money so that I could sign her up, too.

The priest who was there told us that we would come back. And in fact we did go back twice; but he wasn't certain about a third return. That priest was really kind and good to us.

We were in the little chapel dedicated to Father Colombiere, a Jesuit who was Saint Margaret's confessor. His skull is there to be venerated, and is on public display for that purpose. The little chapel is a modest one, but alongside it they are building a bigger one. I brought home a sketch of the plans. It must be finished by now, since it was well along in construction.

I signed up lots of Chileans, friends and relatives, for the masses which are said on Fridays at the altar of the apparitions.

It's not a bit like the Paray le Monial in Santiago, not like the Sanctuary of Lourdes which is a perfect copy.

## NEVERS

Since we were going right by there, I couldn't resist making an overnight stop to visit the city where Bernadette took her vows as a nun.

Since my sister wasn't interested in this trip, we traveled halfway together and then she went on to Vichy.

I arrived half dead with fatigue right on the doorstep of the nuns' house in Nevers.

A very nice young sister named Victoria received me, and when I told her I was Chilean and had come to stay there, she laughed and said, "You're not the first to want that, but we don't accept guests here," and she added: "Vous avez l'air trop fatiguée."

She sent me on to the Hotel Blanc, where, since she had recommended me to them, they graciously gave me an inexpensive room.

"Demain viens a la chapelle," she had told me, and this is what I did the next day. I made my confession and took communion in the sanctuary of Bernadette.

They have her there exactly like Saint Teresita of Lisieux, as a statue which looks as though it is made of wax.

Later they got a little girl to accompany me, who took me to see the Saint's tomb, and the convent with its big gardens. They showed me their relics. I bought lots of illustrated cards and pictures there, and their book; I still have all of these.

Just recently, one of my newborn relatives has been given this nice name. This has made me recall that I had the pleasure of seeing all the places where she saw apparitions, and that I met her brother and saw the convent where she died.

The only thing worth seeing in Nevers is that nuns' house.

LAUSANNE

We toured the city, but since my sister was feeling tired, she didn't go to the castle of Chillón. It was interesting there to see the place where ten political figures of that time were tortured most cruelly.

They showed us where the guillotines had been, where they hurled the bodies down into pits, and where they tortured them.

We also saw the place where the poet Byron declaimed his poems.

I felt very pleased to have completely understood the whole lecture given by a young Frenchwoman who spoke with a clear accent in impeccable French. My companions were frustrated because they could not understand her well, but I'm really convinced that you shouldn't go to France without having a firm grasp of languages. I am very grateful to my parents, who taught us these languages without ever suspecting that we would turn into such travelers.

Translated by Mary G. Berg

# The Dress

# Vanessa and Victor

## María Asuncion De Fokes

The old woman recognized him from far away without realizing it. His stride, his stooped shoulders, his stubby arms echoed something engraved years ago in her memory.

Again she looked toward the dusty track that came up from Las Dunas, following the figure which grew as it advanced, becoming more and more clearly delineated. Impatiently, she snapped her prayer book shut. Go on, it can't be, she thought, not after all these years. Why would he come? He's up to no good, her gloomy side said. He's come to stir up trouble, to ask for money, to tell me all about his disappointments—for the silhouette, even at a distance, threw off an air of repeated and definitive failure.

How old is he, she wondered. He must be fifty-two: she calculated exactly. She was barren now, but she'd had him at twenty-five, the first of her four children—one daughter and three sons. Headstrong and insolent from an early age, possessing a certain quirky ability with numbers, he alone had rebelled against the destiny that would have made him a fisherman. As if rebellion were possible; as if he could avoid that curse—the curse an old crime had already cast like a shadow across three generations of his family!

Doña Amanda's husband's clan had come to Las Dunas more than seventy years ago, driven out of their country town toward the coast by shame and by nasty fingers of blame. The sea's expanse swallowed their sin, their shame, and they settled int othe primitive community that was Las Dunas. Doña Amanda's husband became a fisherman. She had met him as such and loved him as such, and her two younger sons still eked out their living from the waves. Her daughter had also married a fisherman in Las Dunas. The ocean and the sand dunes which ruled their lives had brought them dignity and poverty, and most of all resignation.

"Resignation is the important thing," repeated the evangelical pastor, Doña Amanda's spiritual advisor, who assumed in the old woman's life almost the status of a private deity. And she had needed a full measure of resignation, upon the arrival of her children, to accept a hard, poor life, a life permeated by dirty diapers in old pails on the patio where one miserable grape arbor failed to shield them from the sun; she had needed it to gut and scale innumerable jurels and sardines; she had needed it, during tourist season, to kowtow to capricious strangers, to flatter them and to mop up their grime; she had needed it more recently, after Asian fishing fleets decimated the local fishery, to sit by while her sons took their families off to foreign countries from which they mailed Easter greetings in incomprehensible languages.

Doña Amanda had been abandoned with a tiny income and a stretched and battered acceptance of her lot. Only when the young gringo arrived with his handsome face and his clear, hypnotising eyes, exhorting her to a surprising new fervor, had she gotten another lease on life. After that her granddaughter Vanessa had come. And now Juancho.... An insight flashed in her mind like lightning: He's looking for the girl. How could he know? He's chasing her down; he'll hurt her. Thank goodness she's gone today. If we're lucky, he'll clear out before he can find her.

She got up, pushing the wicker chair into its place against the wall with hypocritical calm. Shaking sand from her slippers she went inside her small house, clean now without children running underfoot. Black and white photos of forgotten relatives hung on the walls and stood out against the dingy screen. Among them here and there hung verses from the scriptures printed in North America: "And ye shall know the truth, and the truth shall make you free." In a corner a Sacred Heart and a picture of the Virgin of Lourdes shared a niche. It was a heterogenous salad of symbols, philosophies, and truths.

Señora Amanda was no illiterate. Though her schooling stopped at reading, addition, and subtraction, her vivid old mind had arrived at a synthesis of divergent heresies and theologies. Catholic in girlhood, she had converted to evangelism in her age. In Las Dunas she was a pillar of the new faith, a helper and protector to the archangel (as she called him) with bronze skin and blue eyes who, with his trembling testimonials, his visions from God, with pamphlets and songs, had come to save souls in a style reminiscent of television comercials.

But Juancho was getting closer.

He'll be hungry, she thought, and thirsty. So, falling into her ineradicable habit of doing whatever a man needed, she went to fix him something to eat.

He came in through the kitchen door. They stared, sizing one another up without speaking, each studying how age had ravaged the other's face. "Hi, Mother; it's me," the man said.

"Hello Juancho. You must want some lunch. Sit down, I'll get you something."

He dropped the bag he had carried slung from his shoulders on a bench, and without washing up fell into a straw chair. His eyes roved around the dining nook, over its clean furniture, its china cupboard full of cheap ceramicware, to the frame from which his parents stared in their wedding clothes. The dining room appeared unused.

"How are Marietta and your kids?" the old woman asked.

Juancho burst out in a voice taut with anger: "Don't talk about that bitch and those good-for-nothing ingrates! Don't mention them to me, Mother."

And with that he launched into his story, into their story, the story of his troubles, without letting the woman get a word in edgewise. "Who else would have done what I did for that whore and those children? After I joined the Navy—remember, Mother?—I took every blasted workshop and training session they offered me. I was no sailor like my brothers. I hated the sea. I hated it even when I was a kid. I had no desire to exist in the stink of fish guts and rotten oysters my whole life, so I got into management. If a 'buddy' of mine hadn't cheated me out of a promotion, I'd be a comptroller right now. But never mind. I did okay by myself: I became a deputy accountant."

He brooded for a minute, silent. The woman waited without taking a breath, her hands folded in her lap. Juancho was irascible, danger-ous, and trying to stop his temper was as useless as putting brakes on the south wind. He kept quiet now, but not because he'd recovered his good humor. Rather, she sensed him raking through his memories, stirring up his poisonous anger, getting ready to fly off into another fit of recriminations.

"I did everything for them—I gave them everything they could want, everything! I got out of the Navy because the pay was lousy. I became the personnel manager in a large construction firm. I built a house. I played basketball at night and on the weekends to meet a better class of people, because with sports social differences aren't so important. And when Vanessa was seven, I put her in school. It was a beautiful private kindergarten. I took her there myself while she held my hand."

He sighed deep in his chest. "My little girl, my beautiful blond-haired, long-legged little girl. Kids around the neighborhood always called her 'the gringa.' I used to wonder if Marietta's father wasn't some German guy from down south, not that old mapuche she calls dad."

Or maybe Marietta pulled the wool over your eyes, the old woman thought. I wouldn't be surprised. She simply got tired of your demands, your unbearable boorishness. She cheated on you.

The man exploded: "They're gone! I gave them everything I had. They left me when I couldn't give them anything more. I hope they burn in hell!"

"So you lost your job?"

"Of course I lost my job. Like everyone else—thousands, hundreds. This was during the troubles. And I was one of the good guys; I knew some powerful people."

"So that's when they abandoned you?"

Juancho hesitated. "No, not then exactly. The truth is they stood by me for awhile, good as little saints. Bunch of hypocrites! But I said I didn't want to talk about them—didn't I say that, mother?"

Instead of answering, the old woman put some fish soup and a couple of rolls on the table in front of Juancho. He wolfed them down without speaking. As he ate the woman speculated about the reasons for his visit. Had he come to get away, to rest? Or had he suspected Vanessa's presence here, had he sniffed her out, guided by some uncanny olfactory instinct like a bloodhound?

"I must warn the girl," she thought. As Juancho went to the basin and began cleaning himself up, she left the house, saying she needed some vegetables, and disappeared down into the village.

It was Monday. The market fair had started early. In its stalls, thrown together that morning out of wood and cardboard, the towns-people could find things that would have been prohibitively expensive in Doña Carmen's store, Doña Irene's little shop, or Don Juan's grocery. Salsa music seething with dance rhythms blared from cassette vendors' stalls. Rock-and roll and the protest songs, which were banned in the capital, injected a modern hum into the hubbub. Next to the tape racks one might see, jumbled together in no particular order, shoes, socks, maize leaves, long, prudish nightgowns, or old women's bloomers, thick and warm, out of use in the city but ideal for winter wind. Right next door were see-through blouses and bikinis for young girls with developing breasts. A little further on came the stacks and stacks of produce. Fruits and vegetables straight from the field—farm-fresh, juicy, treacherous with pesticides, fresh as morning sun, without expiration dates or refrigeration. Pumpkins and squashes, like ladies' fat asses, lolled on their sides. Mounds of lettuce and cabbage; tomatoes lined up red, red; dark chilies; little green or mottled beans; huge baskets of corn so tender that milk welled up when an ear was squeezed.

The market stretched across a block and a half. Through it, like ants carrying their loads to a secret and collective destination, the women of the town crawled, pushing between stalls. Perched on the little porch in front of the post office, Doña Amanda took it all in with a glance. If Vanessa had been there she would have spotted her. Her hair, a deep and unfeigned gold, distinguished her from the dark or dyed heads of the townspeople. No, she wasn't there, but maybe someone could tell Doña Amanda where she was. Ah, Erika. What names, Erika and Vanessa! In Las Dunas, whose people came from Indian or mestizo stock, Germanic names were all the rage. Doña Amanda often chuckled to herself over these gringoisms, and over the daydreams they betrayed. "Maybe in their dreams," she mused sometimes, smiling, "the gringos imagine themselves with dark eyes and dark bodies like ours."

She picked her way toward the girl. "Have you seen my grand-daughter, child?"

Erika looked around, surprised. "Doña Amanda, you know she works in Los Pelícanos today. She'll be back the day after tomorrow."

"Yes child, where is she staying exactly?"

Her arms loaded with lemons, oranges, and prickly pear fruit, Erika answered hurriedly. "There are only two places she can stay: with La Maruja, the woman who has black hair, or at Mañungo's house."

"How can I get a message to her?"

Erika, more and more surprised, put down her load of fruit. "Hmmm, let's see. I suppose in an emergency you could send a note with Martin, the bus driver. He could take it to the clinic."

"Okay. But I don't write so well, child: can you do it? Just say this: 'Don't come back until I send word. Your father's here.'"

Erika's eyes flew open. "No. Is it true?" She grew silent, amazed. Distractedly, then, she assured Doña Amanda that she'd take care of it. She could rest easy that night. "I'll tell her to stay in Los Pelícanos. I can cover for her here; I'd be glad to."

Erika and Vanessa worked in the surrounding countryside as nurses. With one paramedic and, sporadically, a doctor, they cared for twelve thousand patients between Las Dunas and Puerto Profundo, a district which included Los Burros, Los Pelicanos, and Agua Clara. Neither of the two had a license to practice nursing, but they could administer injections, tie a tourniquet, perform mouth-to-mouth resuscitation, and dress wounds. In grave cases they took people to the police station for transportation to the regional hospital. In addition, in an ongoing truce with the medicine women of the community, a truce ruptured only intermittently, the two diagnosed people's day-to-day pains, comforted them, and prescribed aspirin or bicarbonate of soda as needed. In these wind-scoured coastal villages, where everything was scarce, Vanessa and Erica provided a bit of everything. And though they lacked official diplomas, they possessed something that science and technology could never have given them: they loved their patients. They spent three days in Las Dunas, two in Los Pelícanos, and the odd day they alternated among the several outposts scattered between the coast range and the sea. From place to place they took the rattletrap bus, or accepted a ride in a donkey cart or in some businessman's car if one was offered.

After Doña Amanda had bought what she needed she began her slow trip back with the woven sack of market goods dangling heavy at her side. She mused as she walked the twelve blocks, turning the situation over and over in her mind, trying to puzzle out what could have separated her son so irrevocably from his family. Why was her granddaughter so repulsed when she had brought up the subject of her father? What kind of mystery, what secret caused the girl to stiffen as soon as her grandmother alluded to Juancho, either directly or by insinuation?

These allusions had ended abruptly one day when, very serious, with anguish in her blue eyes, Vanessa had said to her, "Please, grandma, don't mention my father to me again. He died—do you understand? For me he's dead, though he's still alive. He died without dying. It's a very sad thing. If you want me to stay here with you while I'm on duty in Las Dunas, don't talk to me about him any more."

She had promised, and she had kept her word. She never spoke of Juancho again. Gradually she began to understand, also, that with this exquisite granddaughter of hers it was impossible to bring up matters of love, or to crack jokes about the young men in town.

When Vanessa had first come to Las Dunas the young fishermen and artisans had gaped in amazement. By blood, by birth she belonged to the town, but her movements, graceful as a gazelle walking, her lank blond hair, her oval eyes seemed those of an exotic tourist woman. The more forward among them courted her favors immediately, but in flirting with her they ran up against something they had never encountered and didn't understand. No rough rejection, nor disdain such as a beautiful or snobbish woman might show for her admirers, they found, rather, sorrow and a benevolent, almost saintly isolation, a camaraderie devoid of coquettishness.

Home from the sea, from the mines, or from a construction site, after a stiff drink or two by themselves, without women, they discussed the phenomenon. "She's touched..." "Half crazy..." "She's sick..." "Perhaps she's secretly married..."

Until one night in winter, red with wine and enlightened by alcohol, Guillermo, the deflowerer of several questionable local virgins,

proclaimed slowly but without faltering, "She's going to be a nun...
That's why she looks at you so strange... She sees things, visions..."

And because it salved their vanities, and mollified their desires, the
explanation stuck.

"Shit, man, that's it. You put your finger on it! I had that same
hunch..."

And the hunch swept through the male population of town like a
tinkling, subterranean bell, placing Vanessa exactly where she
belonged: among the townsfolk but apart, set on her own cloud, a
cloud that never faded. During her hiatus out of the convent she
would occupy the post of their empathetic virgin nurse, who awakened neither envy among the women nor jealousy among the men of
Las Dunas. All alike viewed her as a lovely but slightly touched and
sexless saint.

As soon as Señora Amanda closed her front door, Juancho's tired-
ness evaporated. He peered onto the patio, where four rude rooms
and a primitive bathroom, improvised by some poorly trained mason,
permitted his mother to rent out the little wood house facing the
street in summer. She, meantime, or perhaps an itinerant worker,
occupied these quarters built like lean-tos against the walls. A sneer
settled on Juancho's lips. His mother could barely read and she wrote
even worse, yet her profit instinct and her constructive drive never let
her alone. All day long she made cakes and sweets, selling them in
the neighborhood; she rented out the patio rooms in winter and the
house in summer, filling out, by these makeshift measures, a retire-
ment income that would have left her hungry.

At the back of the patio a rickety arbor cast shade on the table
where the old woman took her meals. But Juancho hadn't come all
this way to view her remodeling projects, nor for that matter to find
out how she fared with her meager subsistence. He sought a clue, the
clue which would clarify what, in the capital, had become a muddled
mess in his brain. He had been searching, as always, for Vanessa,
when, one night, an idea took hold of him. Fed up with vague explanations from the detective on duty, with friends' well-meant but inept
analyses, Juancho felt the idea hit him square on the head like a blow:
"Mother knows where she is." A current of sympathy had always run

between granddaughter and grandmother; Vanessa used to write to Doña Amanda every once in awhile.

But if he wanted to search the house he should get moving before she returned. He crossed the dining room and tried the bedroom doors. To his surprise he found them padlocked. "The old biddy doesn't trust a soul," he thought. Anyway, she must live outside in one of those asphyxiating little hovels. So he went back to the patio, tripping over the basin where she washed herself, straight to the first door. He kicked it open. The room was empty. Just an old bed without sheets, and a crippled table. His mother slept in the second room in an iron bed from the colonial period. On the walls surrounding it, keeping her company he supposed, hung a jumble of evangelical images and posters. A color TV and a misshapen armchair, slightly broken down, bespoke the moments when the old woman entertained herself with news from the outside world.

A high night table with a chamber pot underneath and a small drawer, belonging, he supposed, to some ancestor, was the only thing worth searching in that room rank with old age and fish. He opened the drawer. Pictures, lots of them—all ancient, washed out. Photographs of his brothers, of himself as a child, dressed up for first communion, of his father...suddenly he glimpsed a picture of Vanessa when she was fifteen. His heart pounded. How beautiful she was!— his great love, a love so personal and involving, so possessive, that his other affections had paled to nothing!

He gazed at it a long time. With renewed urgency he rifled the drawer, and pried into every nook of the room, without finding anything that could help him. Afterwards, feeling worn out and dirty from his trip, he thought he might shave and freshen up. He decided to shower, went back to the main house, into the modern bathroom, collecting his bag from the kitchen. There was no way he was sleeping on the patio. He'd tell his mother he was going to stay in the house. He was no beggar fisherman but a man of importance, though just now in reduced circumstances. He was somebody. He started the water and water heater, stepped in, and even whistled as he showered. When he got out, drying his body with the white towel, a curious sensation took hold of him. This house, everything so clean, its padlocked rooms next to a fully functioning bathroom, the brand new towel, the mirror—there was something that didn't fit. No spider webs, no dust, clean windows... Someone lived in this house, and his mother had clammed up just a bit too much. As he approached the washstand he saw something that sent a shiver down his spine: on a shelf, arranged in a neat row, lay a woman's comb, a toothbrush that had hardly been used, and some toilet water. He opened a little white cabinet and discovered tweezers, rubbing alcohol, cotton, gauze: a first aid kit. Vanessa was studying to be a nurse's aide before the family abandoned him wholesale, before the atrocious last scene where she confronted him. He squeezed his eyes shut to get rid of that vision, and joyous at the discovery, screamed aloud, like a man possessed: "Vanessa's in Las Dunas! I've finally found her!"

Rage flooded his arms and legs like a drug. His mother was an old fox with her innocent questions: "And how are Mariett and your children?" Goddamned bitch—just like the others. Fine, let's play cat and mouse and we'll see who's better at it. She was probably scurrying through the town right now to warn the girl he'd come. Okay old woman, I'm going to have some fun... He clamped his eyes shut in a shivering paroxysm of delight. His face acquired a yellowish cast as if a malignant wave, entering his veins, had surged through his circulatory system to the skin's surface.

It was already three o'clock. Going into town in this heat would be pointless. Pitilessly the sun beat down, falling directly onto the wood and adobe houses, glittering off the distant water and off the island where tourists summered, withering the pines and eucalyptus trees. The southeast wind lifted dust devils among the dunes and enveloped the roads in orange clouds. The town was taking its siesta. There would be no one around to tell him anything. He'd wait for his mother and ask her to open the bedrooms. That's when the fun would begin. What was taking her so long?

She rattled through the kitchen door just as he was posing the question. He came out clean and perfumed, concealing his ire as best he could, and went over to the old woman. "I'll take that sack, mother. Wow! what's in there? It's heavy."

"Fruit and vegetables, son, fruit and vegetables. It's market day. Things are cheaper than in the stores. Every month it gets harder to make ends meet."

"Don't you rent one of those rooms out back? You must get something for that."

"A little, but they're poor people, like me."

"Oh, by the way, mother, how about opening the bedrooms for me. You can put me in one of them. I'm from the city and I'm not sleeping on the patio."

The old woman dropped the package of chard she had been about to place on the counter, and stooping after it, hid the hot blush that rose to her head. Red, she straightened to answer him. "Yes of course, Juancho. Absolutely. I'll fix up one of the bedrooms for you. The other's rented out."

"Rented? Who to?"

Dear God, forgive me these lies, she said to herself. "Who?"

"Yes, that's what I said. Who to?"

"What do you mean, who to?" she stalled for time.

"Oh come on, mother, don't make an idiot of yourself. If the room's rented and padlocked, I figure someone must live there. Unless it's a ghost."

Juancho sat relishing his mother's confused reactions. But she had learned something from her life as a petty businesswoman. She could handle his interrogation. She was ready for whatever query or demand he threw at her. "It's reserved for the pastor."

"For the pastor? The pastor? Oh that's excellent. Now this podunk fishing village has a pastor. And where is his flock, may I ask?" he sat back, jovial.

"Yes, he's an evangelical pastor. He comes twice a year. I put him up here." She uttered a half-truth. The young preacher had in fact visited Las Dunas twice, staying with Doña Amanda, and investing her, in the town's eyes, with a certain reverend prestige.

When she locked Vanessa's door, she had snapped a rusty padlock on the other as well, without thinking, to keep up appearances. She could put Juancho in there, while Vanessa's room would be officially reserved for the pastor, a figure endowed with a sort of mysterious halo. Superstitious as unbelievers generally are, Juancho would not profane that sanctuary.

Even so, Doña Amanda didn't feel completely comfortable. The walls were of thin wood, and she couldn't help imagining that the perfume, the smell of youth that permeated the room from Vanessa, could seep through the boards.

Gathering his resolve, Juancho renewed the attack: "I noticed that you have a first aid kit in the bathroom. Does it belong to this pastor too, then?"

"Why yes, it does. He's a wonderful, caring person." And, swept up in the game, soaring on the wings of her imagination, the old woman pressed on. "He studied medicine. He heals people, takes away their pains—and with nothing, nothing: a few herbs, tweezers, a bit of cotton. He fixes anything. And the way he looks at you, son, his eyes—like Jesus, like Jesus," she chanted, entranced.

Juancho assessed her scornfully: That's all I needed, he thought: she's gone off. "All right, mother, tell me about it some other time. Why don't you make the bed. I'm going to lie down for a bit before I go into town."

Fifteen minutes later his snores put Doña Amanda at ease. She'd won the first round: at that moment, in a rattletrap bus, her message travelled toward Vanessa, and thanks to Erika everyone in town knew Juancho had come.

For an entire week Juancho played the prodigal son in the bars and shops, on the beaches and the wharf of Las Dunas. He got re-acquainted with his school chums, called on former teachers, flattered old sweethearts, and made himself a hearty fellow all around. Not a man, woman or child escaped some sort of declaration of his affection. He struck deals, set up small businesses to tempt the greedy hearts of the poor and disadvantaged. All for nothing. He changed his wardrobe, appearing one day in a three-piece suit, speaking authoritatively as if hidden strings linked him to the government. Another day, dressed in white shorts and carrying a racquet, he talked about the necessity of putting in tennis courts.

Of course he tried the police station. A ray of hope shone out suddenly when he described his daughter to the young private on duty. The man's face lit up and he said, "Ah, I think I know the girl you're looking for. She's blond, isn't she?"

The words were barely out of his mouth when the landlady of the inn, an enormous woman who happened to be waiting for the lieutenant, jumped in belligerently: "What foolishness are you talking now, Cabo? The girl you mention stayed at my hotel. This gentleman (she spat out the word with distaste) is seeking Vanessa Rojas, his daughter, who came to Las Dunas three years ago, and hasn't been back since."

She glowered at the youth who immediately fled to the back offices, babbling excuses, for he knew what all-powerful influence the hotel owner wielded.

Another time, on the beach, some brats shouted something which sounded like:

> Vanessa went off to the war
> And she ain't coming home no more.

His daughter's image seemed to peep like a phantom from every corner, only to vanish when he was on the point of perceiving it.

On Sunday he went to Mass. He would question the Padre. The Padre couldn't lie, so if Vanessa was somewhere in Las Dunas he'd have to tell him. Juancho didn't know this priest they had now. When he was a child and his mother used to take him to Mass, his ears washed and his hair combed, the priest was a fat, bucolic man whose prestige consisted in the mysterious phrases he used, which his parishioners mimicked like magic formulae:

> Kyrie eleison,
> Kyrie eleison.

In a daydream once, Juancho had answered 'open sesame,' and his mother had poked him so hard in the ribs it still hurt. He looked around at the pews. Men came to church these days, a rare occurrence forty years ago. And the priest was a well-built chap whose virile good looks could have won a woman's heart. He began to speculate on the unsavory possibilities.... But the sermon, too, was different. He didn't recognize the scripture. The curate spoke of fair salaries, of solidarity with the weak and oppressed. A fury built up inside Juancho. When would this damnable comedy end? Words, words, words, all those words! He wanted hard facts.... He positioned himself at the sacristy door, waiting for the priest to emerge. He can't lie. Eighth commandment: "Thou shalt not bear false witness." He'd recite it if that became necessary. He'd make the priest sing like a canary. Plenty of times he'd watched how the police made people sing, people of all stripes....

The curate had noticed Juancho also as he said the Mass. From the day Juancho arrived Padre Fernando had known the reasons, for Las Dunas, with its 2,000 souls, formed an ideal agar for gossip. Vanessa belonged to his congregation; as her confessor he possessed a much clearer picture than Doña Amanda of the girl's tragedy, her odd desperation. Like the fisherman Guillermo, but for other reasons, he suspected that one day she would devote herself entirely to God. "All roads lead to God,"—he recalled Saint Augustine. He left off musing at the sight of the solid figure waiting for him on the sacristy's threshold, and sent up an urgent prayer: "Lord, help me wrestle this lost soul without having to lie. Help me protect Vanessa." In the seminary they had taught him diplomacy, how to skirt hidden rocks and reefs, harming no-one. His mother, his holy Mother the Church, whom he served and loved, had existed for two thousand years, praying, teaching, dominating in the world, getting kicked down, picking itself up out of the dirt after persecutions and internecine wars—all with words alone. "Give me charisma, Lord, guide my tongue, show me how to get inside this stony heart...."

With a friendly nod Juancho hailed him. "Good morning, Father. I wanted to tell you how much I enjoyed your sermon." (He wasn't going to make the mistake of mentioning Vanessa right off).

"Good morning my child. I don't believe I know you: are you from Las Dunas?"

"Yes, sir, I am, but I moved away years ago, which is why you don't recognize me. But my mother still lives here. May I talk to you about her for a moment?"

"Of course. What's her name?"

"Amanda Lopez de Rojas. She lives on the north side of town."

"I think you've made a mistake, child. Your mother doesn't belong to my parish. She's evangelical these days, I believe. Of course I'd be glad to help her if you want me to, don't mistake me. What's the problem?"

"She's going crazy, father."

"Crazy? What do you mean?"

(Now was the time to shock this newfangled priest.)

"She claims she has visions. She chants. She trembles. She rambles on about some 'pastor'. She also swears up and down that Vanessa, my daughter, is here in Las Dunas."

"And you believe that not a word of it is true, is that it, my son?"

"Well, I really don't know. My daughter left home more than a year ago after an argument with her mother and me. We've searched everywhere, but can't find her. Actually, that's why I came to Las Dunas, to ask you about her. Nobody around here seems to know anything."

"You know, I've always thought it curious," Padre Fernando pondered aloud, "how easily people disappear in a country as small and thinly populated as this. Everybody knows everybody, everyone talks about everyone else, everyone asks questions, but all at once, poof, half the population are ghosts."

This conversation had taken a turn that didn't suit Juancho one bit, former toad of the police that he was—and so, falling back on the habits of his delinquent youth, he bid the priest a hasty goodbye, and left.

Father Fernando sighed through his teeth in relief. He had told no lies, but he hadn't furnished Juancho with any clues either. Instead, touching on a subject that rankled his conscience, he'd scared him off. "He won't be back," thought Father Fernando. "Soon he'll go away for good, and the girl can return."

Juancho was furious. Not only had his sleuthing instincts failed him absolutely, but more and more his mother appeared to be not the old liar he'd suspected, but a dotard whose mental faculties weakened before his eyes. He decided to get out of Las Dunas immediately. What good was it doing him to listen to her sing psalms of David every morning when she got up and every night before bed? What good had it done to spend all that money on the town drunks, talking about his daughter in provocative terms, even, hoping to make the old lechers break a quiet that grew more eerie with each passing day? At the simple mention of her name, indifferent silence spread, as if she'd never been seen in Las Dunas.

Though he knew he was wasting his time, he decided to give it one last shot. It that failed he'd pack his duffel and catch the local bus which would take him by way of Los Pelicanos to the regional capital.

From there he'd catch another bus to the big city. At that point Vanessa would become the true needle in a haystack.

When he got to Don Vitelio's watering hole it was already seven o'clock, and almost all of the tables were jammed. The men raised a shout of welcome, mixed with what might have been mocking laughter—he couldn't tell. (What harm could it do to get another round or two out of this jerk, this cockroach, this hypocrite, this informer, if it didn't hurt the girl's position any?) Vanessa had fallen under a sort of collective male guardianship which had developed this last week among the men in town. It ran contrary to reason, contrary to the age-old decree which stated that unmarried daughters belonged to their fathers. They did away with Juancho's patriarchal authority at a blow, without any spoken agreement, without commentary, without a whisper among them. Perhaps Juancho's contemporaries recalled the scorn he had scattered right and left as a young man, before he went away. Perhaps the airs he put on, always acting like a city slicker when in fact, at heart, he was as provincial as everyone else, rubbed the young men wrong.

After two drinks Juancho could hold back no more. He launched into his theme. "I tell you, if my daughter ever comes to Las Dunas you're going to see something beautiful like you've never seen before. She'll sweep you off your feet. No beauty queen's got anything on her, no sir—and here's my address if you care to place a wager."

"You're leaving then, Juancho?" they asked, surprised.

"You bet. I'm going back to work." (To look for a job, rather.) "I can't waste any more time in this two-bit town. I came because I thought Vanessa was living with my mother. I was wrong." The words seemed wrenched from him. "I was wrong," he repeated haltingly, already drunk.

And like the somber chorus in a Verdi opera, his drinking buddies echoed in unison: "You were wrong, you were wrong!"

At that moment, the moment of Juancho's capitulation, that traitor Fate who has plagued the human race under a thousand disguises from the beginning, intervened to seal Vanessa's doom. No-one had noticed a second earlier when, by the door that gave on to the beach, Martín had entered in the first giddy stages of drunkenness—Martín the low-life, part time conductor for the bus line. Stepping on stage with his ego bloated on its own importance, he declaimed solemnly and poetically. "I saw her... I saw her.... She was beautiful like a princess out of a fairy tale, and holy like the virgin. Her body was gold and her hair was blond. The sun shined like a halo on her hair..."

And though his buddies leapt on him, squelching him immediately, it was too late. Inside Juancho's skull the words 'I saw her, I saw her' resounded like the thunder-clap at the beginning of the world.

With a power disproportionate to his physique he lifted Martín by the collar and screamed at him. "Where, punk, where have you seen her? Don't lie or I'll kill you right here!"

Wheezing through his constricted wind pipe, Martín could not manage to lie. "Los Pelícanos. North side of the beach. She goes swimming there every afternoon."

"That's bullshit, Juancho, he's drunk," the others yelled.

Juancho went limp, calm. "Of course he is. of course. That's a load of crap. I've been to Los Pelícanos and my daughter isn't there. He's drunk."

"I saw her on a cloud," Martín murmured, " 'cause they say she's a saint. She was in a shrine, I think, floating on a cloud..."

"A cloud of alcohol," said Don Vitelio. "Get out of here, you imbecile, and don't bother coming back."

They pitched him out onto the cold sand, muttering among themselves. Talk turned to other matters. The gathering broke up and the men went to their beds sure Juancho had forgotten the incident.

Each afternoon she bathed at the northern tip of Pelícanos Bay, where the beach ran together with the estuary in a pronounced seashell curve. Black rocks, which bore the brunt of the weather during a storm, hid the spot from the village.

Almost an extension of Las Dunas, but ignored by the bigger town, abandoned to the waves' ceaseless rocking, the fishing hamlet of Los Pelícanos seemed to let the years slide away without caring. None of the technological or commercial developments that changed life elsewhere penetrated to this sleepy corner of the coast. For its most basic services—health care, governance—it still depended on Las Dunas. Only in summer, when a few nature-loving tourists pitched their tents and ran their launches up onto the beach, blaring radios and buying the entire day's catch, did unruly life invade for a couple of months. All the enterprising young men got out, escaping either to the mines or to construction jobs. The most audacious of the girls boarded the bus which stopped at the side of the highway and carried them to the happy metropolis of their dreams, where they ended up as maids or prostitutes according to luck and looks.

Vanessa loved Los Pelícanos. Only its immense beach witnessed her reveries. Sitting there in the sand soft and yellow as fresh bread, she traced the pelicans' flight. Those pelicans who nested in the estuary's scrub had given the place its name hundreds of years ago, time out of mind. She watched them glide above the regular blue swells that arrived from the interior of Asia, or from Australia; she listened for the snap as their wings collapsed, and they plummeted sure and speedy toward the particular sardine their eyes had picked out; she laughed at silly gulls battling one another for the scraps that fell from their gullets. Her heart went out to the sandpipers mincing so fiercely and delicately along the edge of the spent wave as they hunted sand fleas.

She came in the late afternoons when her work was done, just before evening, when the wind dropped down and the sun eased its intensity. The water was warmest at that hour, the sun sweetest, and the wind softest. And each evening at that hour, as she watched, her dead lover's body emerged from the foam to embrace her, cool as the waves and eternally alive, like a demigod. She never doubted him—he would be there, always, waiting. Vanessa was sick, ill with an elusive madness whose violence surfaced only in that frenzied moment when she ran to meet him in the waves.

With love hot in her veins, how could the chilly sea matter? Sun glittered off the ripples, lighting the cove, and lighting her mate's hair with coppery reflections that she alone knew. His eyes mirrored the green hue of the algae. His name was Victor, and he had triumphed over death. In life they could not break him; he had silenced himself to protect innocent lives. It was he who had mouthed to her, through misshapen lips and a face swollen from blows, the last time she saw him, "I will always love you."

That was the last time, and so her father held it arrogantly certain that he had won. Her father!...meting out life and death! From that moment on, Vanessa's madness progressed unspoken and unnoticed. Her grandmother alone came near the truth when Vanessa told her, "My father is dead, dead in life...." Thus she rationalized the existence of the two beings she loved most: her father and her lover. The one had died, the other still lived; he came out of the sea every evening to lie down with her in dunes warm from desert sun.

He sometimes accompanied her mutely as she rode the bus and cared for the ailing, winding a bandage, giving injections. Other times they would split up because he continued his hard
schedule of work and study, involved as ever in the lives of so many others. But he would meet her without fail in the beach twilight, to cuddle her if she needed it, or to drive her to an electrifying orgasm.

She had belonged to him since she was a child. She could never belong to anyone else, not even God as Padre Martin and Guillermo the fisherman thought. God demanded souls, but it was Vanessa's body that trembled with hunger—the insatiable, sexual hunger of youth which dogged her through the afternoon until, lying in nonexistent arms, she satisfied her obsession each evening.

At ten years old they saw one another for the first time. They were the same age, went to the same school, lived in the same neighborhood. They scarcely glanced at one another then, for neither had reached adolescence. Vanessa was a gangly blonde, with legs and arms too long for her body, and Victor was a coarse, brown, snubnosed kid whose eyes alone—huge and dark—attracted notice.

Later, bent on advancing his social standing, Vanessa's father moved the family to another town. Only when they were eighteen and convulsions racked the country, twisting people's faces, their souls and their ethics into grotesque mirrors of events, did the two meet again. Their parents were out of work, or in temporary jobs. The neighborhood was hushed, sunk in an unspoken terror. A curfew kept the nights short and dismal. Only those women Victor named "the headless ones" had reason to be glad, for their husbands came home early. They didn't bother to find out why—whether for love of their captivating charms, or simply because the bars and clubs had been shut down, and every other male in the country except those in power, in prison or in exile, was also held captive at home.

Those who didn't sympathize with the drastic measures strove to survive. People put on inscrutable expressions like masks, veils. While a carnival euphoria prevailed among the most powerful, to everyone else there remained only the stark second face used by the ancient Greek actors. The pressurized emotion in their eyes, during those bleak days of defeat, had shattered all interest, all joy, everything except the air itself. Some, suddenly recovering faith they had lost years ago, once again knew the true Christ who spoke to the suffering masses, not to the satisfied few. Vanessa's father took account of the situation, thought over his options, and became an informer for the forces of "order." Victor's father, laid off and drowning in bitterness, invented unknown forms of work for himself. A highly-trained workman, muscular and capable, he dragged a cart around selling bottles and newspapers, or dug through junk heaps after salable items, and in so fulfilling his basic necessities recovered a bit of human pride.

Victor and Vanessa met for the second time in the church square, and fell overwhelmingly in love in that instant. They never asked themselves why. Chemistry, Victor said. They went along at lightspeed, discovering their bodies and their souls together. Dispensing with the languid looks, the notes, and other silly trappings of young love, one afternoon in open country, beneath pine trees damp with dew, they simply became husband and wife. It happened without words as if their skin had conversed for centuries, through thousands of past lives. But love, oozing from their pores, glistening in their eyes, loosened their tongues as well. "Of the abundance of the heart the mouth speaketh," the Bible says, and a beloved one's name will turn up again and again in unrelated conversation, in pointless anecdotes without rhyme or reason. Such indiscretions, loudly announcing the love Vanessa tried to hush, did not go unnoticed by Juancho.

At first he didn't want to believe it. Startled, enraged, he found himself at a loss. Vanessa was eighteen, no longer his thin little girl but a silky-skinned woman with firm thighs and round breasts. There was a deer-like something in her thin waist—graceful without being crudely provocative—which made her body sway like a poplar in the wind.

Juancho could name the day and almost the hour when his daughter lost her virginity, for when a woman's body gives up its innocence her aspect mysteriously changes. Juancho's obsession with Vanessa worried her mother. In his unbounded affection for the girl she sensed something hidden, dangerous. She too understood instinctively that her daughter was no longer a virgin but a satisfied lover, and that her romps with the dog, the school books she tossed lightly onto the furniture, the songs she hummed in the shower, all sprang from a happiness she could not disguise.

Juancho held his peace and waited. He didn't tell anyone about his suspicions. He watched, snooped around, and within a month had discovered the man his daughter loved—his name, his family, his politics, and his clandestine activities. Victor assisted people on the run from political repression; he carried them in a buddy's pickup truck to more secure locations, then contacted a young priest who in turn would direct them further away. Arresting Victor was easy; making him talk, impossible. He sealed his lips with the full knowledge that martyrdom awaited him, knowing he would never marry Vanessa. He glimpsed her at the detention center door when he came out, herded with other prisoners toward a secret camp from which he would not return. For two seconds they stared at one another. In that stare and with those silent lips that barely moved, he communicated the message she understood unhesitatingly: "I will always love you."

She heard nothing more from him after that, neither him nor his buddies. Rumor had it they were dumped into an isolated cove of the sea, but even the sea kept its silence. The bodies never turned up. Right away neighbors pointed out Juancho as the informer, and one night, in the modest little house, father and daughter faced off with unwonted violence. Through the girl's pain and the man's anger the truth surfaced: she was his. She belonged to him by law because she had yet to attain her majority. Paternal power operated as it had in ancient Rome. No one was going to touch his little girl!

In his twisted mouth and wild eyes Marietta, his woman, and the three elder children deciphered Juancho's secret: He loved Vanessa with an incestuous love whereby, someday in the future, he would rape her. The next day they met to plan their escape. Juancho came home one evening to an empty house and a note on the table: "Don't try to find us—we're not coming back. And may God forgive you."

When Juancho got back from the bar he already knew exactly how he must proceed to catch his daughter. He talked to his mother while elaborately preparing for his departure.

"I'll be leaving tomorrow, mother. There's nothing to do here—no work, no fun, nothing. Just fish, sun, sand, and ocean. Thanks for letting me rest up a bit, but I'm going back to the capital."

"Very well, Juancho, I'd better iron your white shirt and make a sandwich or two." She had trouble hiding her pleasure. The next day he boarded the bus, but got off close to Los Pelícanos on the pretext of having forgotten something. As the bus diminished into the distance trailing a cloud of dust, Juancho started to walk. He was in no rush. The days were long, interminable, during November, and two hours of walking would put him at that enormous bay's corner, there where an arc of land enclosed the advancing ocean. Behind the beach, sustained by an estuary, bushes grew, briars and reeds where the pelicans roosted each night. On this beach set into the larger one, according to Martín the drunkard, his daughter bathed.

He knew that Martín had told the truth, he felt it with the instinctive surety of the frustrated male. With exact timing he would slip from behind a cactus to hunt the unsuspecting gazelle, the tarnished virgin, the female who had ceased to be his daughter.

As her grandmother had done, Vanessa saw him without seeing him, recognized him without recognizing him, when he emerged from the dunes. And it was not his walk or his stooped shoulders that started her heart racing, but the laughter rebounding from the rocks, audible even above the receding tide. Like a maniacal faun he laughed, like death, gurgling and shouting with each gust of wind: "Vanessa. Vanessa."

For her, likewise, he had become something other than a father. That apparently familiar form took on the shape of undisguised and pitiless agony. He came offering her life without life: shame and ruin.

Vanessa listened again, then stared at the sea. The monotonous waves rolled one on the next, sliding in without surging or breaking. Already brown and red from the setting sun, the ocean appeared to be trying to hush her to sleep. Gulls had begun to roost on the rocky point, and pelicans in bands flapped toward the estuary. Placidly, night approached.

She had arrived later than usual for their tryst, and Victor had not yet come to her out of the surf. But she sensed him in the transparent depths with a lullaby on his lips, singing to her:

> Look how they sleep, the fish in the sea.
> Look how they sleep, look again, and again.

She did not vacilate. Stripping off jacket, shoes, and skirt, dressed only in the red sunset light, she waded into the water without pausing, glad, sure of her escape because that death that stalked the beach, crying and calling to her, running along the waves' edge, laughing, was such a stupid death that it could not swim.

She waited for the first of the three strong waves that the open ocean infallibly sends against whatever or whomever seeks to enter it: those three waves that take or reject according to their whim. They carried Vanessa as they had Victor, forever.

Constables found Juancho the following day seated at the tideline, white face babbling, fists black and blue but still pummelling the sand. In his eyes lurked an insanity from which he would not return.

Months later the fishermen of Los Pelícanos invented a legend concerning an imaginary reef christened the Rock of the Virgin, after an imaginary virgin. Vanessa had been no virgin, just a girl in love, eighteen years old and driven to madness by the lunatics who, in that act like a thousand others, crushed her lover and extinguished the light of her generation...

Translated by Kent Dickson

# The Dress

## Marta Jara

"It's them." She knew immediately. She raised her head over the full-grown plants and watched. It's them!" The peddler and his wlfe. At that very moment they were heading over to sit on a rock shaded by a myrtle tree. "Yes it is..." she repeated, looking at them through the dark green tide of the potato patch.

She was crouched down, hilling up the potatoes and weeding along the rows on a low and not-too-distant rise.

She saw the man—he was not very tall—set his bag by the tree. He was wiping his face with a white rag. Perhaps a handkerchief. "He's wiping off sweat," she guessed. "It must be hot to walk the roads with such a heavy load."

His wife had just sat down in the myrtle's shade.

"They'll probably rest and then go down by the stream," she guessed. "If I take the road to the gate, I'll see them when they come by."

She knew she was deceiving herself. "That's not it. It's not just to see them." Turning her head, she cast a glance over her shoulder. Down below in the middle of the apple orchard the house seemed deserted except for the geese standing guard and solemnly walking in a row along the edge of the irrigation ditch. "Where can she be? She's probably inside. That's it. And she won't want...she's never wanted..." she grumbled as she bent down, her face tense and sad. Her lips trembled. "She'll die some day, but not soon enough for me to toast the occasion. I, too, will feel old—left with no company but the dog, the cat, the birds and the constant planting and hilling of potatoes. For what? For whom?" Suddenly she understood. "She's had everything she's denying me."

Before thinking it, almost as if anticipating it, she dropped her hilling tool and began to run through the potato patch, down the rise, and toward the house.

When she sped by, the startled geese cackled. She didn't stop but kept on running until she reached the barred gate. She straightened her dress and stepped into the ditch to wash off her feet. "They still haven't arrived. I have time to wash my face," she calculated. She smoothed back her hair. She wore it in a single braid that weighed against her back. She was a mature woman, strong, and robust like a man, with white skin and a sour, nervous face. She was barefoot. In the islands, the milky whiteness of her skin was rare.

"They have to come this way," she comforted herself. "There's no other road." She leaned against the fence post. A pleasant breeze blew and refreshed her hard, muscular legs, which were furrowed by swollen, blue veins.

"They have to come this way," she repeated, "and this time I will indeed buy a dress. Although she'll be opposed to the idea, I will buy it. to go to Chonchi to church on Sundays. I'll go after a good bath. with my hair combed and with my dress. They'll notice me. Somebody, somebody has to notice. I don't care if he is from Chiloe.. He'll be a man.... And although she'll he opposed..."

They were coming. She could hear their steps, their stumbling on the stones, the woman's chatter. She unconsciously smoothed her hair again. Her greeting surprised them. They approached. The man leaned his bag against the fence post before answering.

"Yes, yes. Good clothes. Would you like to look?" he offered. Then he looked at the woman accompanying him, seeming to indicate "You deal with this one."

"Where shall I show you the clothes?" It was the woman who spoke. "Surely you'll want to try something on. Isn't that right?"

"No, I won't. She probably won't let me buy anything." She threw an apprehensive glance over her shoulder and behind her in the doorway her mother was waiting. "I knew it," she said to herself. And making up her mind she suddenly lifted the bars to the gate.

"Come in."

She heard the man say to the woman, "You go. I'll wait down the road a little."

"What are you selling?" the cold, dry question stopped them at the door. She held her arms crossed over her chest, and like her voice her eyes glimmered with a slight irony.

"A little bit of everything. Used clothing, needles, thread, buttons, combs, soap, mirrors..." the itinerant trader recited her wares in a monotonous tone.

"We don't need anything," she interrupted. Without moving, she blocked any access to the house, her despotic tone of voice containing a quality stronger than her vary presence there before the closed door. Her look was mocking.

"Ah. Excuse me... I thought your daughter said...." she stammered, nodding toward the daughter.

"I knew it. I didn't need to hear her say it. She won't let me. She's always, her entire life, been this way: selfish."

The old woman smiled disdainfully. The result was a tension-filled silence.

"They hate each other," the peddler's wife guessed. She shrugged her shoulders. Ready to wait, she rested her bag on the ground.

"Mother, I wanted...They have dresses. I need one. I have the money. It's mine. I've earned it working. You know one never has a chance...."

She didn't finish the sentence and stared at the old woman,who understood her look: "You've been silent for so many years," it said, "and now finally you are letting go."

She confronted her. "It's an opportunity," she said. "You know full well that in town there are no..."

"Opportunity!" the old woman laughed and scathingly added, "Is that what you think?" But she moved away from the door, yielding but not backing down, as if to say, "Okay, see for yourself. Try it."

They entered the house. They walked along a dark hall, a closed door on each side, and there, beyond, at the end, a room equally dark but cool and spacious. On the wooden walls hanging from thick rusted nails were diverse farm implements. From the beams drooped nets and fishing gear, strings of mussels and dried, smoked meats. The woman examined it all with curiosity while feigning disinterest.

"You can put your things here," the old lady grunted, pointing to a round table with no cloth but dappled by the light filtering in the window. Through the foliage of an apple tree that nearly deprived the room of all light, you could see the garden.

She began to unpack her wares and scatter them haphazardly on top of the table. "What do these two women do here before the stove in winter, always face-to-face and dragging out their hatred?" she thought. "Just as there's a God in heaven, they probably fight the whole live-long day."

The spinster approached. She felt, although without seeing it, her mother's sardonic grimace. Not even the darkest shadows could hide it. "It doesn't matter. This time she won't be able to stop me. I'll wash real good and do my hair, and when I go to church, I'll put on my new dress. Somebody, yes, somebody, will have to notice me, if only because of the dress. 'Look!' they'll say, 'Isn't that Eloisa? She must have money!' I don't care what they say. I'm 46 years old and have some good land, a house, a boat, animals. My mother is old...it'll be enough for them to see me and they'll think....it doesn't matter to me you're here laughing. I have the right to have a man...just like you did. Be that as it may..." She picked out the dresses. Rather she rummaged through them haphazardly, almost without knowing what she was doing, confused by her own thoughts and her mother's inimical presence.

"The old woman's making her confused," the peddler thought, and she came to Eloisa's aid. "Let's see. This one should fit you just fine."

She held the dress up to Eloisa. She was amazed, for she herself was small and slight. "What a big woman! How can she be so big? If she tries them on, she's surely going to split the seams." With the patience necessary to her trade, she began to look for the ones she thought were of an adequate size.

"They aren't decent," the dry, clipped voice of the old woman lashed out systematically. "They aren't suitable," she smiled, savoring her triumph. "Have you no shame? How can you go exhibit yourself like that. It's not decent." she repeated.

They found one. Not very pretty, a solid color, pale green, faded from wear. She grew quiet. She couldn't say it was indecent. It was closed up to the neck, and its long, puckered sleeves hung down awkwardly. Leaving her corner, she came up to touch it and find fault. It would be too tight for her and the material, now worn thin, couldn't withstand the stress.

"It won't last you one wearing. You'll come back from Chonchi in tatters," she predicted.

Nevertheless, it was she who found the solution. Unintentionally, and unconsciously, her femininity, who knows for how long supressed and forgotten, surged: a blue cloth attracted her, the thick-linen of a skirt. She couldn't help but touch it.

"Ah!" the seller exclaimed. How stupid of me not to have remembered! This will fit you just fine. Try it on. The material is of a high quality."

She was indecisive. She wanted a dress not a skirt.

"Try it on!" her mother ordered. Her little eyes laughed sarcastically. "You don't like it, do you? It doesn't matter. It won't do for what you want it for, but it will be just fine for work." And directing herself to the other woman, she asked, "How much is it?"

"One thousand. One thousand pesos," she stated explicitly.

"Oh, no! That's high!" She didn't say any more, but that was enough to let them know she wouldn't give in.

"That's what it's worth," the woman responded without praising her merchandise. She presumed the sale would develop like a long, difficult sparring match.

"We can't pay that much. 500. Not a peso more."

"The old lady is stubborn, but she's not going to get the better of me. If I tell her 800, I'm lost. I will have to let her raise her offer." And to reinforce her position, she said, "No. One thousand. I asked a fair price. I can't sell it for less."

They contemplated each other: two cocks, ready for the fight, facing off, looking for trouble. The daughter entered. The mother made her turn around and again examined the cloth, touching it. Unexpectedly she offered, "Perhaps you would like a cup of tea?"

She caught the seller, and even her daughter, off guard .

"Yes, thank you. Why not." Her empty stomach was what ventured an answer. She hadn't had lunch, the morning was drawing on, and her man would probably be making a fire somewhere around there.

"She doesn't want...she won't let me pay so much. I know her..." the spinster informed her with a bitter expression, after her mother was gone. She touched the skirt as if caressing an already dissipated dream.

"I can let you have it for 800," she conceded. "Not a peso less. If you can't pay it, you'd better take it off."

"She won't want to. I know her," she said disheartened and added to herself, "She's as stubborn as a mule." Suddenly her face lit up. She spoke quickly and softly, whispering. "In front of her, let me have it for 500; later, outside on the road, I'll give you the difference." She didn't manage to explain any more; she barely had time to shut her mouth. Her mother entered bringing a steaming cup and in her eyes an inquisitive and malicious expression. She deposited the tea on the table.

"Sit down," she invited. "Help yourself." She put the sugar within reach and remained standing, observing them. She smelled something going on, but wily as a fox, she asked no questions.

The other woman began to sip her tea slowly. She praised it, wanting to flatter. After a while, as if the cup of tea had softened her, the tradeswoman pointed to the daughter. "I'll let you have it for 800."

Unflappable, the old woman replied, "No. 500. "

She kept drinking the tea slowly. Why hurry? She had her technique and now she would let the old lady witness it.

Unable to contain herself the spinster approached the table, still wearing the skirt. Mute and looking annoyed, she began to rifle through the dresses.

"It just may be that this fool will ruin everything." She hurried and drank the rest of the tea in a single gulp and stood up. The old woman was looking at her out of the corner of her eye when the peddler surprised her by saying, "Well, what do you think is a fair price?" As she asked her question, she proceeded to pack.

"500. Not a peso more."

"But mother! I..."

"Take it off!" she demanded, energetically interrupting.

"All right, I'll let you have it for 500," the woman acceded, "to repay your kindness. For no other reason."

"Go, bring the money!" she ordered, spitting out the words with a disdainful bitternes that seemed to imply, "This is what you get, and it's not the dress." She again sat down in her chair in the corner, from where she oversaw the payment. She smelled the trap but couldn't detect it. They said their good-byes. The seller gathered up her things and, unaccompanied, she headed toward the hall.

"I'll wait for her outside on the road. This one won't trick me. She's not capable" she deduced. She left. When she closed the door, she could hear the old woman say , "Go with her down to the road."

They walked together following the path alongside the irrigation ditch .

"There below, where she won't be able to see us, I'll give you what I owe you," the spinster whispered. "She must still be watching us." Then she surprised the woman by saying, "I've been thinking about your for days. I saw you in Chonchi. And from that day on I've been telling myself, 'This is my chance'. If I have a new dress, it's possible someone will notice me. Even though he's from Chiloe. We–and my mother notes the difference–are descended from Spaniards. Once I had a suitor. My mother was opposed: 'A Chilote,' she said. 'Never. I would rather see you dead!' That was many years ago. I never had another chance." She talked without stopping, telling all the essentials, exposing her life in short sentences. "I'm forty-six years old. I'm getting old. It has to be now. Although he may be from Chiloe, he's still a man. A man is a man, and my mother is now old. My father died, and one day I will inherit all this." She gestured, attempting to show the property with a sweep of her arm. "Anyone can understand that I will inherit all this. I just need someone to notice me, that's all. That's why I wanted the dress. To go to Chonchi."

The peddler, worn out by the weight of her bag, listened without looking at the speaker's face. Astounded, she heard her out. She saw only the bare feet, leaving in the dust wide footprints, the firm mannish step.

"That's why I wanted a dress. It's more noticeable than a skirt," she pointed out regretfully.

They arrived at the gate.

"Come on. Come with me a bit more," the peddler's wife insisted, pointing to a nearby spot. Surely around the bend her man would be waiting for her. She stopped. "He doesn't have to know," she told herself, taking the money for the skirt and keeping it. "He'll never notice." Then she opened her bag and began to take out clothes. She found it almost at once. She unfolded a red blouse and put in the spinster's hands.

"Here, this will fit you nicely and it looks good with the skirt. It will draw attention but it's decent," she said, employing for the first time the Chiloean expression. "Put it on when you go to Chonchi. It's a present." She warned her: "Don't show it to your mother, don't tell her a thing. She's capable of ripping it up. And when you find what you're looking for, whoever he may be, do what you have to do and don't be scared. You're too old to be afraid of your mother."

She didn't wait to be thanked. She left the spinster, stunned, in the middle of the road She walked off. Beyond, on the side toward the beach, was a column of smoke waiting for her like a signal. "There's my husband," she told herself. Before rounding the bend, she looked back. The woman was still standing there, embracing the blouse as if it were a man.

Translated by Martha J. Manier

# Elegance

## Ana Vásquez

The black crepe or the blue silk? The silk one because it goes well with the color of her eyes. But the cut of the skirt is no longer in style, and besides, she doesn't have blue shoes. Then the black. She puts it on decidedly and walks slowly to the mirror, smiling and greeting herself as if she were somebody else. But no, too long. She looks like a nun dressed for Sunday Mass. She hikes it above her knees and turns around to see the effect: a little shorter would be even better. She shortens it hurriedly. Daniel said around ten o'clock; it's already 10:15.and she still has to iron it! But black looks good on her, it gives her a dramatic look. And it hides the size of her hips, which are too wide. The fabric is soft; she likes the way it drapes on her. It makes her feel a little less anxious. Tonight it's absolutely necessary, indispensable, that she look elegant so no one will think, not even for a second, that she's just an office secretary.

They fired me, her father said, and at the time she really didn't comprehend the impact of those words that would change her life. Her teachers at school spoke of recessions and economic crises but suddenly unemployment ceased to be a mere statistic and instead became a grouchy, unbearable father who now spent the whole day at home. And at the end of the year she was told that instead of studying she would have to get a job.

She takes another look at herself in those new, open high heel shoes that make her appear taller. The woman who smiles back from the mirror seems to be somebody else, maybe an actress, or at least one of those women who struts haughtily in the pages of fashion magazines. The makeup case always terrifies her. She hears her mother's voice: "Don't paint yourself like a clown". Her mother always worried about good manners. Such a lady. It's getting late. What will Daniel's friends be like? What will they talk about? She dips a piece of cotton in the facial cream and removes the makeup from her eyes only to paint them once again, nervous, trying to make her hand stop shaking, so she doesn't have to start all over again: a thin line, a lot of mascara and that's it. Perfect!

Perfume and anxiousness. She sits on the edge of the bed, looking for her image reflected in the mirror. Where is that woman she sees every day, the one who runs around in blue jeans, laughing with Daniel, provoking him with her ironic barbs, that secretary who prefers to skip lunch to go see the latest exhibition. Here she is hidden beneath the mask of an elegant woman, looking the way her mother looked when things were going well for them, or like her aunts who, whenever they went out, wore leather gloves and very complicated hairdos that could only be controlled with a ton of hair spray. What a shame she'll have to put on that horrible rabbit's fur coat. She hesitates: always before going out she feels that stab of fear, as if she is about to abandon a shelter where she feels protected. Outside, she will no longer be able to undo what's been done, put on something else, excuse herself and not go. And if she doesn't fit in? Will it be awful? Of course not! To be dressed badly isn't such a big deal; there are things that are far more important in this world: misery, war. But that intellectual she so much wanted to be, a secretary, granted, but self-educated through her frequent visits to museums and exhibitions, that woman who says that what matters most are people and not what they're wearing, that same woman knows she is living a lie by spending an inordinate amount of time trying to look elegant, even though she doesn't have much money. But she's afraid to look bad. She couldn't face the embarrassment of knowing that she's somehow inadequate. And when she locked the door with its double lock she set in motion the irreversible. She takes another look at herself: you really look like a secretary. She decides to leave her overcoat. Rather catch pneumonia. She'll wear the black shawl.

Daniel hadn't given her a clue; a small get-together, a party. He'd shrugged his shoulders to give less importance to the word party. "Just a few friends. I'm sure you'll like them."

"A coming out party," she'd observed in her typically joking tone of voice, because that was the personality she'd invented for herself when she arrived in the city, and she enjoyed perfecting this personality for him. She realized that she fascinated him with her playful, challenging answers.

"A happening," replied Daniel, playing along with her.

She takes a final look at herself, like a general reviewing his troops before the attack. Now she really has to get going.

Those months during which she had to make her way through the indifference of the great unknown city and of the imposing company that she worked for. Eight floors, hundreds of employees, and she just another ant working hard at the ant factory. The architecture department, last floor. "An interesting form," she remarked as she faced the calendar. "Is it a Klee?"

He looked at her surprised, because architects move in other galaxies, and when she recognized a Klee it showed him she wasn't necessarily an idiot just because she was a secretary. She began to develop a real enthusiasm for those endless jousts of humor and culture in which she would always end up disconcerting him with one of those indifferent replies that only those who have seen and read everything would perhaps make. It wasn't true, of course, but she not only represented this type of character, she embodied the type so well that it seemed as if there weren't a single museum she hadn't visited and that her comments—although somewhat sarcastic—weren't completely original.

And that woman of the world she pretended to be, that new persona she invented and perfected every day, that image of the mocking intellectual served as a mask that disguised the little girl from the provinces who tried to get into the university, who cried with emotion the first time she saw a Rembrandt, and who sometimes became desperate at her typewriter, typing up one bureaucratic letter after another while the architects, inclined over their drafting boards, went on designing things completely unaware of the privileges they enjoyed. Now, finally, about to enter the world she longed for, just where she should have been from the very beginning, she gives the address to the taxi driver, wondering, nervously, if she looks good in her black dress. At the same time she hates herself because she knows that her feelings of insecurity are stupid, she shouldn't worry so much. What matters is what they do and say, not what she's wearing.

Laughing, a boy in faded blue jeans and red tennis shoes opens the door and stares at her with a questioning look on his face. Just by the expression in his eyes she realizes she isn't properly dressed Looking over his shoulder she sees a part of the room: soft and discreet, a beige wall-to-wall rug; a group chatting on the floor. Not one of the women that she could make out is dressed like she is. One has on a rose-colored velour warm-up suit with matching running shoes, another crosses and uncrosses legs wrapped in leather pants that must have cost more than a month's salary. She sees tanother one get up slowly and come to the door in frayed blue jeans and a silk smock. She realizes, as if in a sudden revelation, that her shoes are not only out of style but also something only someone from a small town would wear, and it's obvious that her black dress is a Burda design. In those few seconds during which the young woman walks toward her in that disinterested but distinguished way, she tries to overcome the waves of panic that are making her turn red and perspire at the same time. Panic...and rage, because they would never let her into a party in her town dressed in those torn blue jeans and people back home would have said that the woman dressed in the rose-colored warm-up suit was running around in her pajamas and that the other one looked like she just got off a horse.

There wasn't just one kind of elegance but many, and she was to blame for interpreting the word party in terms of dresses and jewelry when as far as Daniel was concerned only middle class people wore ties and high heels. Why hadn't she figured out that in the happenings he organized people showed off their casual simplicity and that for them this was elegance. Because good taste is a code that is understood by the in people, and it's always something different and unattainable for the uninitiated. In intense and continuous flashes of insight she clearly realizes that for them, the big city intellectuals, simplicity is the most sophisticated of styles and she hates herself, for, although she considers herself so intelligent and refined, it never occurred to her that her black dress would be ridiculous and gaudy as a neon sign.

Holding the door partly open, the young man, along with the woman dressed in jeans looks at her. "Who are you looking for," he asks without inviting her in. If he'd spoken to her in the familiar form of address it would have meant that he'd recognized her as belonging to the group, which, of course is not the case. No one recognizes her, she doesn't see Daniel; she can still say she got off at the wrong floor, take off, run down the stairs, take another taxi, return to her hide-out, lock herself in before he has a chance to see her, before the impact of her faux pas became irreversible. Tomorrow she could excuse herself with one of her brilliant phrases, she could come up with something: an unexpected visitor, a sick relative. "I didn't have a chance to let you know."

"What a shame; I would have liked you to meet my friends; I spoke so much to them about you."

"You don't know how sorry I am, but you'll invite me again to another happening, won't you?" And the next time she would go dressed in slacks, in boots even, like the women who stay late at the office doing exciting things and who like to be noticed.

"Daniel?" she asks timidly, as if her disguise as an idiot has taken control of her. She feels like fleeing when they have her go in; she imagines locking herself in a bathroom, leaping out the window or of covering her face with the black shawl to make sure no one recognizes her. No! I'm not this woman. She's only a poor naive thing who's disguised like me. Beneath the masks and the disguises, where is she? Is she by chance the reserved and distant secretary or the other one, the one who dreams of throwing her typewriter out the window, of pouring paint all over the top of her desk and of painting her passion and fury with her hands. Maybe she's still the girl who wanted to leave her small, stereotypical town, to make time hurry by so she could settle into her own present; the one who broke with the mommy-and-daddy protect me routine and dared to set out on her own. But where was the so-called break if, now that she imagined herself to be free, she kept dressing the way others wanted her to? She, who had always ridiculed the careful-how-you-look, the-make-sure-people-don't-take-you-for-what-you're-not approaches was now discovering that the contents of her suitcases bore the indelible mark of "what will people say."

In high school when one of those pretentious girls who tried to look elegant arrived, she and her friends would give her one of those amused looks, a look that slyly took in the poor social climber's outfit, scrutinizing each and every detail, the quality of the material, out-of-style fit, the shoes that didn't match the rest of her outfit, and they would immediately classify her: she's-not-one-of-us. Side glances assessed her lack of upbringing, because they already knew that upbringing was important. Accomplices, they winked at each other discreetly: Did you see? Did you notice that...? And with the gestures of great compassionate ladies, even though they were only eight years old, they said, "I'm sorry, but I don't think they'll let me go to your house." The cruelty was almost deliberate, because at that age you already know with whom to be seen and with whom to associate.

Why had she come dressed in that ridiculous dress, making herself the victim, the stupid social climber, humiliated as she made out just partial gestures, heads that furtively turned with just the requisite slowness so she would realize what was going on. She could almost hear them commenting on her open, high heel shoes and her golden earrings, cataloguing her not for what she was but for what she seemed to be. The arrogant frown of the one in leather pants, and the other in rose who imperceptibly shrugged her shoulders and turned toward the wall to hide her condescending smile. Alone, at the entrance to the room, humiliation invades her completely, deforming her body, which seems to shrink as if disdain can mold and diminish her.

A door opens and Daniel approaches. Tweed trousers, a worn cashmere pull-over and, a tray loaded with drinks. "Hi, Daniel" she smiles. His eyes express happiness and puzzlement.

"What did you dress up as?" Did she really hear him say that or did she imagine it? Perhaps it's what that surprised look on his face is asking. She feels like curling up in a corner and howling with rage and frustration.

But no. Not her. Heads or tails. Do it.

"I dressed up as my alter ego," she hears her own voice say decidedly. "I am Woman-object" He observes her, maintaining a certain distance, not showing a single friendly gesture, not saying a single word. "I am Woman-object," she repeated laughing. "Didn't you tell me it was a happening?"

At last Daniel understood the joke. Echoing her laughter, he carefully placed the tray on the carpet, took her hand and led her to the center of the room. "I am happy to introduce you to Woman-object", he announced, as if he were the owner of a circus hawking his own show. If looks could kill she would have died at that moment they observed her, undecided, still not sure whether to remove this tasteless little idiot from the pigeonhole in which they had placed her.

She can no longer retreat. On the contrary. Get on with it or you're dead. She opens her mouth slightly and flashes a toothpaste commercial smile then takes several steps forward, giving everyone a big wave as if she were a famous trapeze artist. "Ladies and gentlemen", she says in a loud voice, but in the falsetto tone of a clown, "as Woman-object I am happy to initiate for your pleasure tonight's happening".

But nothing happens, nobody laughs. She turns completely around. Nobody reacts. Indifferent eyes produce chills. She takes a deep breath; better eccentric than to have bad taste. She raises her arms and begins to swing her hips imitating Rita Hayworth, "Gilda" and intoning "Put the blame on Mame, boys," begins to remove one of her leather gloves.

She quickly wonders, "If my aunts, who epitomized the height of elegance in wearing gloves wherever they went, were to see me now, what would they think of this initial strip-tease." A part of her sins as she moves to the rhythm of the song, removing each finger slowly from the glove, taking note (in spite of the fact that her eyes are languidly open) of the interested and even appreciative looks she is getting, because it's true that if she dares to imitate the glamorous movie star it is because she's confident not only that she dances well, but that the famous black dress fits her like a glove. But another part of her is terrified by that mad woman now imitating a strip tease, wondering how she's going to get herself out of this mess. In that internal struggle, Gilda's imitator, daring and magnificent, prevails over the coward, and tossing the second glove with a theatrical gesture, takes a bow. They applaud her, but she knows it isn't enough; she has to do something else to convince them.

"Ladies and gentlemen," she announces again in the voice of a clown, "in the name of all artists I have the honor of bestowing on the owner of this circus the surrealistic earring." Removing one of her earrings she solemnly attaches it to Daniel's pull-over. Hurling the word surrealistic at them immediately after Gilda's dance was like winking at them: she isn't really a Woman-object, she's just acting. And from that moment on she succeeds in making them accomplices; they finally realize that she's one of them, a refined person. Better yet, an eccentric one. And then they applaud her enthusiastically.

But she's so excited she can no longer stop herself. She raises her hands to quiet them. "Ladies and gentlemen, I have a secret to confess." She pauses to intensify the suspense. She slowly removes the other earring and shows it to them as if it were a trophy. This poor little earring that she bought with such illusions; from the jewel that it had been it is now transformed into an extravagant object. "This precious gem of gold and rubies is the prize that the person who is most bored at the party will win. Any nominations?"

"Pedro!" shouts Daniel.

"No!" protests the woman dressed in the rose-colored warm-up suit, "Juan Pablo's the one. He's the best candidate," she shouts with that big smile that reminds you of a TV announcer. "Gentlemen, begin your nominations." And when everybody starts to take part in the game she suddenly recognizs Julio Lascasas, the younger generation's best poet (according to the critics) shouting nominations at her for the most bored, and then Toti Langer, the pianist, laughing uncontrollably at Daniel's side. She manages not to feel intimidated in the presence of all those people whose pictures frequently appear in the newspapers. She is too much into the whirlwind of her own game—until she has to stand on tiptoes to pin the earring on a huge man surprised at her kissing him on the cheek. The trump card, she says to herself, because now there no more looks of compassion. The distance between them and her has been erased, they speak to her, they even fight over getting to know her.

"What's your name, Woman-object," the huge man asks her.

"Cinderella," she replys without hesitating, as if she can think more quickly than they can. "Cinderella," she repeats, "the secretary who went to the ball." And removing one of those horrible shoes of hers, she raises it as high as she can. "I offer my glass slipper to one of the princesses here tonight. A young girl extends a careless finger and she hangs her shoe on it; she takes off other one and throws it, letting it bounce toward the door. "That's a signal for Prince Charming," she explains calmly.

Suddenly, without her earrings and shoes, she feels a lot better but she's tired and empty, the way she felt when she returned home after an especially difficult exam. Daniel approachs her with cashews to offer, but this is only a pretext. He really wants to whisper in her ear that his friends find her delightful, that thanks to her a real happening is now in full swing because now the Langer woman is playing jazz on a tiny white piano, a discreet little piece of furniture that she hadn't even noticed when she entered the room. Daniel's lips rub against her ear, she feels his warm breath on her neck and that voice she likes so much it sends chills up and down her spine is now asking her if she's having a good time. Between the emptiness and the euphoria that she's feeling she allows herself to bask in the pleasure of listening to him, and only then does she forget about the dress she's wearing; she forgets that during the entire day her only concern was with looking elegant, that she spent hours trying to decide whether or not the dress was out of style and whether it matched her colors. Sitting on the beige carpet she forgets everything so thoroughly and completely that she doesn't even give the slightest thought to that poor, insecure simpleton she had been.

The car's abrupt stop throws her against the back seat. "We're here, Miss, says the taxi driver. "Sorry for stopping like that. I wasn't paying attention. That's the building you want."

Translated by John J. Hassett

# The Department Store

## Flor María Aninat

Every day you see her seated in the middle of the department store in the women's section. She gives the impression of having slept in that same spot, because you never see her come or go. Some say she's the owner and likes to keep an eye on things. Others say she's only a mannequin.

But everybody talks just the same. She has the pose and bulk of Buddha, always wears black dresses, and, as her only adornment, a necklace which glistens around her throat, a different thick chain every day to show, perhaps, vanity, or that she has some place away from the store and jewelery to display. That she has a history.

There are those who say that her story is really quite different and that the chain covers a horrible scar from some other time, when they were going to hang her and the rope broke before asphyxiating her.

They say that from that time on her tongue has grown longer and if she's careless, she looks like a panting dog. Thus her silence. But those eyes—denuded of lashes and not without a certain mystery—speak to every person who passes in front of her, even to those fearful ones like the girl who at this moment is crushing a handkerchief between her fingers.

Elena knew the symptoms: the intense perspiration which, along with the agitation she felt, was separating her being from her actions. She had always been like that, since she was a child, since she was born, perhaps even inside her mother. Curiously, her mother never stopped reproaching her for it. Now those pink boots were hypnotizing her, making her a puppet. A profound anxiety directed her eyes to the boots and also to the sparkling necklace around the neck of the fat woman. From her platform, the figure seemed to introduce herself into Elena's consciousness, eyeing her, upsetting her.

The specter's teeth chattered and her eyelids fluttered. Elena thought that maybe these were signals to someone near her. When two women pushed her as they passed by, Elena's uneasiness increased, and she thought she had been found out. But both of them were engrossed in looking at fabric and in going through the bins with the daily specials. They didn't even notice. Nor did they notice when the man dressed in jeans and a light blue shirt fingered the bottom of one of their purses, taking a wallet from it. Not even the most discerning person would have noticed.

Arturo was happy. Now he could go have the much-desired coffee and avoid the crush of stupid, common people. In spite of his scorn, he felt good in a crowd; only a few times had he worked in parks or on lonely streets, and there he was afraid, a coward. He liked his work; it was emotional and intellectual. He did it not only with his hands but with his head. He had to study the people. Pure psychology, he called it. Even there, in that place, he was intrigued by the pale girl who looked from one side to the other, blinking, making faces as if she were about to burst into tears. She hadn't moved from the shoe section, but he hadn't seen her try on anything. She was the kind of person he wouldn't approach, the kind that was sensible, shouted violently and attracted a lot of attention. He was about to draw his gaze away when he noticed that some boots, one of the most outstanding items in the display, were disappearing into the depths of her enormous purse.

When he froze in his surprise, he caught sight of those motionless eyes which, for some time now, he had been trying to avoid. He didn't know if she were the store owner, a wax figure, or only a hallucination, so extreme was her immobility. Still, he felt that she had seen every action and that those dead eyes had alighted on the girl with the pink boots. He thought about warning the girl. Who knows, they might even come to be partners. In spite of her nervousness, she seemed competent. But when he looked her over again, he found he to be of a different class and felt a barrier between them. Her elegant dress and the way she carried herself made her actions incomprehensible: to his way of thinking, she should have been the victim, not the villain.

He wanted to continue studying her. She attracted him. But the fat woman seemed to absorb him, bewitch him, and spoil his plans. That scarecrow sat still as if glued to her stool, although there, amid the folds of her dress, he thought that one of her enormous hands was clutching something that moved softly, as if she were passing her fingers along the beads of a rosary.

Elena reflected on her now-carried-out intentions and wondered why she was dissatisfied. Other times, she had felt a happy release. The pink boots were in her purse. No one had seen her. She had no other reason to stay there. But today wasn't like always; something kept her there in that place. She'd been conscious of it since her image was reflected in that thick gold necklace. Only in the necklace, not in the eyes of its owner. Only in the metal was her figure reproduced.

The heavy woman wasn't a symbol, she wasn't an allegory, not even a guard. She didn't move, although she should have, being pushed constantly by that careening crowd which with each shove transmitted their failings to her. She no longer felt the anger she'd felt at first, or the exasperation she would feel later. It was a weariness that was eating up her insides, but not a weariness as severe as it would be when she was done. Her reasons...they didn't matter...to remember, to remove a past she would soon be able to avenge. Her hands passed lightly over the cord she held, tying knots and more knots—knots that did not come undone like that knot had before.

The man and the girl didn't run into each other when they left. Elena walked, clutching her purse, looking for the shadows of the wall, avoiding the golden brilliance. Arturo smiled there amid the crowd. The girl never saw him; he had forgotten her.

There is no joy in the store, only a thick air—like a winter fog. It's an emptiness, a feeling that what's real doesn't matter, and the knowledge that something is missing, something sensed and seen, but no longer remembered. Yet some people have good memories. They notice more and know that now the stool is empty and that the previous day a woman filled it, her eyes vacuous and fixed. Those who notice things with even greater care say that there between the folds of her dress, they thought they saw two doves emerge but on looking more closely, realized it was only her hands stealthily moving and that from them surged—to later hide—a very white cord in which she had finally tied the perfect slipknot.

Translated by Martha Manier

# Cleaning the Closet

## Margarita Aguirre

I discovered it on a Sunday afternoon. Autumn was just beginning and I was cold. I was alone in my room. I decided to straighten up the closet and there, toward the back, hidden by the faded flowers of some old wallpaper, I found it. I think it all happened when I tried to pull out a shoe box that had stuck to the wall. Actually, it wasn't a wall, but some sort of partition, I believe. When I tore the paper the wooden slats fell out by themselves. Then, (I should make it clear that I had removed my clothes from the pole that stretches across the closet), when the boards fell out it revealed a dark space, warm, clean and enticing. I didn't have time to think about anything once I was inside.

For many days I stayed there completely still with my knees against my chest, my head between my knees, and my arms wrapped around my body. I no longer felt the cold. I don't think I slept at all— I knew I had discovered happiness.

As soon as I entered, happiness began to overwhelm me like one of those fogs that descends in the afternoon, clouding over the street lights and shrouding the entire city in its warm, humid mystery.

I didn't talk to anyone about my discovery. I loved having something so absolutely mine. Finally, I had managed to be truly absent from what was going on in the house and everywhere else. And above all, I was finally protected, protected by something of my own, something I had discovered all by myself.

I locked myself in my room and took down the clothes one by one and left them spread out on the bed. Then I took out the shoes and the boxes of sweaters and underwear. Everything ended up on top of the furniture like mute witnesses to my departure. I looked at them before entering as if they would guard my absence, which, in fact, they did.

Around the house they got used to hearing me say, "I'm going to clean the closet."

"She's really in a cleaning mood," I heard one of my in-laws say, but I didn't pay any attention.

I don't know how long it was before I dared to move forward in there, but one day when I was inside an infantile curiosity made me unwind one of my arms—the right one—and with outstretched fingers, I groped toward the interior. The space extended infinitely. Then I thrust out my other hand and arm and stretched my legs. Slowly, I uncoiled myself to find what was in there—waiting for me. My movements were light and I felt like I was floating on cotton. In order to get out, I had to return to my original position.

When I came out I put away my clothes without bothering to organize them and I fell asleep on the bed still dressed. When I went back in the next morning I managed to stand up, but I felt dizzy. I was afraid, so I left quickly, hung up my clothes—this time very carefully—and went down to eat.

"We thought you weren't going to eat with us today either," they said.

I smiled. I have the habit of smiling because many years ago I discovered that a smile is the best defense. I sat down and ate hungrily. It seemed that everyone in the house was glad to see me so happy, "so alive," as my mother said. After eating I didn't feel like cleaning the closet again. I fell sound asleep and slept through the night.

I had to work the following day and so I couldn't announce that I was going to my room until the afternoon. By now I was saying very little about the closet, perhaps slightly afraid of being found out.

I let two days go by before daring to go for my walk again. As usual, it was very clean inside. If I had to define it, I would say that it is bright, although what is in there is not exactly a light.

I have always waited for happiness because I am one of those who believe in it. But I must confess that I never expected to find it in such a casual manner as cleaning the closet. Ever since I've been walking inside the closet, I have felt so absolutely happy that I spend entire days locked in there.

Around the house they're beginning to worry—I detect it in little ways.

"I'm straightening the closet, rearranging my things," I tell them, and notice that they look at me with pity.

I've heard it said that a person's happiness can make other people sad. It's a shame to see that happen, but there's nothing I can do about it.

Yesterday I stayed in there all through the night and I felt complete, full of happiness. It was dawn when I returned and hung up the clothes. Naturally, this morning I fell asleep and couldn't go to work, which is happening more and more frequently.

At lunchtime my mother pointed out that I had missed many days of work and that they had been calling to ask about me. She said it in the tone of, "I don't know what to tell them any more."

My mother is odd. I always hear her say that she would do anything to know I was happy. Now that she knows it—because my face is radiant and I shiver from happiness at the mere thought that I'm going to return as soon as I finish eating—I can see that she is worried. At times it seems that she wants to speak to me, but I don't give her the chance. If she can see that I'm happy, what could she want to tell me? Isn't this just what she has always wished for me?

And the rest of them? Why do they have to look at me with such pity? It's these incomprehensible attitudes that are tempting me to go inside and not return. I am sure that I can do it without great difficulty. It's possible that I'll do it this very night.

Winter has arrived. I can't stand the cold in my room and even less at the office, in spite of the electric heaters. In the dining room at home my brothers light the fireplace, but it's still cold and even the fire complains, crackling in vain. My grandmother comes down to dinner wearing mittens. The mittens are gloves... Well, I'm not going to waste time describing my grandmother's mittens.

It will be better if I go. Yesterday at the office I announced that I was quitting my job. The staff wants to give me a going-away party. They say that they've never had a better colleague. As a matter of fact,

I never fought with anyone and my bosses appreciate me.

"Is there any special reason for your resignation, Miss? Because we can talk about it and work it out."

I can't explain my discovery to them and even less to my friends in the office. No one would understand it. They don't even understand it at home where they claim they have always wanted to see me happy.

"When our last child marries (that's me)," my father tells his friends, "we'll be happy and relieved."

When he says it he always speaks of my timidity, and some neighbor or one of my mother's card partners always adds under her breath that it won't be an easy job because I'm such a "nobody."

That's how I've heard myself defined. Also as "the plain one," "the shy one," and even "the weird one" or else "the old maid" in spite of the fact that I'm not old enough to be called that.

None of that matters to me now.

Tonight I will remove the clothes, the shoes, everything, and I'll leave them on my bed.

Inside, the road is long. You float softly. You don't think about anything. You embrace yourself and roll along as if you were a shining star.


Translated by Margaret Stanton

# Maternity

## Marta Blanco

It's positive they told me and that's that, not a thing to be done about it, what happiness, can you imagine your whole life changing just like that, swelling up with maternal pride at this huge surprise, maybe it's even twins I thought, and what a beautiful day it was, blue and transparent—one of those days you got so used to up here at the house in the mountains, when the snow would seem about to slide right through the dining room window and the kids took early showers and drained the hot water heater with their sporadic bursts of hygienic zeal, and the coffee smells wonderful, fresh and rich, and it's barely seven o'clock in the morning and it's time to comb the youngest one's hair, she has hair like a porcupine poor thing, but she's so lovely; I hadn't the slightest doubt about it being good news, in addition to giving me back a sense of my own maternal identity that goes along with being a young woman, right, and no one likes to walk around feeling incomplete, it's a little like having just one eye, and you had always wanted a child, once you'd even wept, you were really good at weeping, because the two of us weren't able to have a child and all because it was my fault, sterile I assumed, stupid fool, and maybe that's why I looked after and cared so much about yours, who dated from before, from way back, from your previous life and that's not so unheard of, what with the problem of annulments this country gobbles up the poor women who are dragging babies around with them, there's not a thing to do about it if the other person won't sign the paper, so you end up living alone on pure love and who was going to doubt that, not me, I was all wrapped up in cotton candy, I was a candied chestnut, sweet as syrup and always being careful of your pride which is a bigger deal than protecting the Pope's pride, boy do I know your weak spots, that's why I never asked you for anything that was off limits, never talked about what's prohibited or impossible, marriage didn't enter into our secret language, we were together out of need for love, in daily busyness and friendliness, in a mysterious state of grace, a modern alliance, and I listened to Pedro Vargas every day because that was part of the repertory of your personal obsessions even though sometimes I'd have liked watusi or "When I left Cuba" and sometimes at sunset I yearned for Vivaldi, all that when I was tuned in to culture, but you always preferred Bach, and the sonatas made my heart ache, they were too violent, I wanted to regard them as incomprehensible, what else could you do with those sonatas that announce death I said and that's how it turned out, how could I have known I had an aptitude as a Cassandra, fortunetellers amused me, although sometimes I sought them out, like that time with the witch on Mariposa Hill, in Valparaiso, who smoked a cigar and read the cards and turned out to be a shitty witch because the truth was something altogether different, totally different, and now I'm caught up in this melancholy that makes me feel curiously languid, but it must be the sun, which makes me dizzy with its heat, and the house, which is still full of familiar sounds and furniture that is too solid, it should be ghostlike, vaporize at the slightest hint that the established order is perturbed, it's very hard to stay on in the same place, send down roots, love the places where one is most oneself in some way: I always envied you that, your great capacity for flight, for change, for sleep, that incredible ability to keep moving along without looking back was dangerous, no one is happy and the next minute miserable, no one should have that capacity for flight and be that close to people, love them furiously, chase after them, write them letters, become part of their lives and then like someone who isn't even doing it on purpose, just all of a sudden walk right out the door one day because that's it and how can we help it and you're reborn just like that, you submerge yourself in the baptismal font, and shazam you're a new man and you go right back to the game of adoring—and adorning—and the next poor girl falls for it because it's so hard to resist the words which transform the world into a game of mirrors, the stained glass is so gorgeous, we saw Saint Chapelle together, do you remember, and it was like being beyond this world, transported by all the light the glass transfigured and because the play of the sun through the blue and that deep red is truly disorienting, hallucinogenic, so that now I had the security and had passed the test and all that I said okay now, this puts me into a new position, into a pretty good position at the least and human beings should love each other, isn't that what the commandments say, what a bastardly thing to abandon a pregnant woman, the whole scene was just too romantic, I was eating myself up with love for you and it seemed as though you were about to love me a little, give me back just a little bit of what I'd given you in so many years of living together and supporting each other, and that even though one does these things without knowing why, there are moments in life when you just have to risk it all for someone, go for broke, especially since you were so alone and abandoned, so wretched and miserable when you fell into my arms, I'd have sworn that you loved me, it's revolting to feel that I was your feather pillow, with the soul of a feather comforter the poor dear, barely a rung on your career ladder of liberation and aspiration, but I'd have sworn that right now you were going to react decently, I'd have sworn it, couldn't you just die laughing, how could I possibly have guessed that you couldn't stand me, it was absurd, there was no clue, no hint of that at all, except that you raced out and said you had to think it over, whatever happened you had to think it over, an equation is something you believe is set in concrete, if you feed new data into your IBM you'll get different solutions and that's why I told you, what a really dumb idea of mine that was, to think of you as human after all, a person capable of weeping I used to say on those sleepless nights, that's a person I really have to love and respect and of course when you called me up on the phone sounding like a funeral home director I began to suspect it, that there was nothing to be done about it, and maybe you should have let me know about it some other way, let time heal it a little but you're made of other stuff, you wanted to smash the world, wipe out everything that had gone on before and the funniest thing is this idea of yours of putting castling into practice, even though you hate chess; anyway you made a queen's opening gambit here today, there tomorrow you'll have your arms wrapped around someone else and be loving someone else and you'll have moved right along, turned the page and have done with it as easily as saying abracadabra and who gives a damn about someone else's pride, but to call up on the phone and say it like that so coldly I don't love you any more dear and how can anything separate us since nothing unites us, it sounds pretty, doesn't it, but it wasn't like that, the only important thing was that you loved her, how great, pure Bogart and Clark Gable, love is repaid by love, and that is just trite, but you're fascinated by trite statements, you practice the liturgy of words and she's nothing to me any longer you said, and if I can't live with her otherwise and if she's going to be one of those who wants to get married first, I prefer to go to hell, and of course, one of those who wants to get married first, what kind of pride could distinguish me from her, from that Anastasia Filipovna, than that of a document signed by a justice of the peace or that of a priest's blessing, you had abandoned me in no man's land, with the child of nobody in my womb, for me there wasn't any wedding, you got married before, you said, and I'm still married to her and then to the priest for the blessing and the pledge and the holy water and I didn't have any pride at all left, five years together and all of a sudden I find out that you hate me, that you've hated me for years, poor little you, suffering away loving someone else and without saying a single damn word to me, not a single warning, happy at home with you and in half an hour you could die of a heart attack, of apoplexy, here today gone tomorrow, how am I supposed to understand this, you have to excuse me for not being too smart, for being so thickheaded, my trouble is that I practice loyalty, what a crazy idea, and besides, right in the midst of an entire life built up of small daily habits, always assuming I'd see your familiar expression, the brave look, some gesture of real affection, but now I understand that it doesn't matter to you at all, that this matter of a child isn't of the least importance to you, maybe the most astonishing thing is having lost all fear of death, me who went around always scared of life, almost not daring to enjoy it because I was so afraid of losing it, I felt so lucky to have one day after another, with you at my side, and that gave me enormous strength, even though I knew right along that it was all a big crapshoot that I could lose or win like the lottery, but I gave myself up to it far beyond anything reasonable, the only way to love you was with the total commitment you wanted, not holding anything back, and I'm made of flesh and blood after all, you'll see how true that is, five foot three and yearning to get married, I was walking around the world with a guilty conscience even though just being with you gave me the strength to cut loose from my bourgeois conventions and all of a sudden that phone call, and that impersonal voice, and the wedding, blue suit and grey necktie they said, how amazing, here I am in the middle of my life learning how to deal with being rejected with no clue as to why this had to happen to me, why to me of all people, and it really doesn't matter any more, even though this guy's got me sitting on a filthy old chair, like those out in the country, a chair where there isn't even a crossbar to rest your feet on, oh well, it doesn't really hurt, just the scare of having the anesthetic, but that's because my heart was beating so fast and since I don't have a heart anymore now anyway I can just calm down and then you wake up stretched out on a dirty cot, with a yellowed plastic sheet under you and a grey blanket over you and the world is all blurry and atta girl there you go, all done, just wait right here now until the bleeding stops, what a mess, my God, it's running down my legs all sticky and warm, viscous, the truth is that blood is really red, too red, and they make me walk up and down, that's really unpleasant, I can see the nurses grabbing me under the armpits and dragging me up to walk one two, one two, you have to keep walking, you can't drift off to sleep but it would be so nice just to go to sleep, how irritating that they're making me walk up and down this shifting floor, dragging my poor cramped up legs, and a shot in the butt and rest your head on your knees, I don't want to rest my head on my knees, my knees are too hard, like two old granite blocks, I probably should have gotten someone to come with me, it's so hard to drive along San Diego Street but they aren't letting me leave, that moustached guy in the white apron already told me that, who do you want me to call ma'am, as though there were anyone to call at times like this, the noonday sun is streaming through the window, it's a filthy window with the paint flaking off, I'd like to open it to see what's on the other side and it's impossible to let her fall asleep someone says, and they drag me around the room again they make me stumble back and forth over floorboards that creak and rock up and down, this room keeps growing and shrinking, sometimes I see it as big as a gym I'll never get to the other side, but coming back now one two one two and sitting down again with my head in the lap of an old toothless woman, no teeth, my God how weak I feel, what's happening to me, why, it was probably a little boy, a little girl, maybe it was such a special child this seed you planted in me as a last humiliation and I can't think about those things now, it doesn't make any sense while you're off on your honeymoon in the Caribbean, I *was only a speck in your eye, dear,* that's my song all right, *and you've wept me* out in a single tear, the old woman is rubbing my neck and I hear her say I'm through the worst of it now, that now I can leave and that I should drink a cup of strong black coffee and a glass of lemon juice, and they're cleaning off my legs with cotton balls, now I'm realizing that they never took off my shoes and I'm squishing along in blood, how disgusting, I'll have to throw them out before I get home and then I have to go out to the street and get into the car and I walk along the sidewalk as though I were floating, it's true, as though my hands were disconnected, as though my head were an immense globe but I'm not afraid, and on the corner I buy a bunch of violets from the florist who looks at me with concern, I'd swear he looks at me with concern and the sun is shining like it does every day and it's Thursday at two o'clock in the afternoon and I get into the car and close the door and I drive along Alameda at sixty and I'd swear that I'm not crying, I swear it, I don't have a single tear in my eyes, what's happening is that the sun is really bothering me, my eyes are stinging a little but that doesn't matter and I floor the gas pedal as though the red lights were all made of the blood of dead babies and I refuse to obey them.

Translated by Mary G. Berg

# Insignificance

## Luz Orfanoz

She wasn't born in the fall, even though her mother pushed and pushed because she didn't want a winter's child.

The girl arrived one night while the ocean was roaring and the woman had to walk against the wind, her nose searching for absent smells of roses and oranges and her heart resentful because of her poverty.

She first appeared omewhere between the door and the folding screen dividing the room, still attached to the umbilical cord and with the appearance of a drowned cat. There was no midwife or doctor. The fashioned hem of a skirt smelling of candle smoke covered her.

They bit off her only bond of union with that woman who still didn't know whether to form her belly button or leave her and flee to a world free from anger and passions:

She named her Narcisa, after the father. Whenever she looks at her, she's completely overcome by sadness. "What the hell else can happen to us!" she says to herself and squeezes the child as if to make her enter into her chest.

Both of them survive from one winter to the next. The flies of summer follow them as do the rats of the rainy season. Soups made from chicken bones warm their innards and hate gives them the strength to fight.

Narcisa grows. With monosyllables and lost looks she chases after trees and water while drawing herself out like a hungry worm. In the midst of slabs and phonolites she seems not to see or hear the drunks who enter to ride on her mother. Perhaps at that moment she is absorbed in a feather that flew down from the old grape arbor or is mentally sketching a fourth leaf onto the clover she has picked.

Never again does the woman give herself a child. "Enough!" she shouted and one abortion follows another until they form a scale of curses and sorrows.

The day Narcisa celebrates her twelfth birthday, and her belly begins to grow, her mother takes her amid the rain and the wind to look at the sea, once again beating up against the jetty. Without saying a word to her and with her face dried up from her own misfortunes, she pushes her in where the waves break.

Translated by Martha Manier

# Accelerated Cycle

## Luz Orfanoz

Crossing the street, a motorist shouted at her: "Hurry up, old lady" and she aged, and to make the aging process rapid, she changed the twenty-four hours of the day into twenty-four minutes and the sun couldn't manage to rise since the moon had already forced it to set, and in the rainy season only a sauce-pan of rain water fell, as spring filled the land with flowers and the air blew the clouds far away.

She didn't get to enjoy the mild temperature; the sun had grown in such a way that the winds feared it.

Between one birthday and another she could not manage to eat all the chocolates given to her, and the boxes started to accumulate behind the doors and closets, saturating her entire home with a sweet smell and naturally rats appeared and the need to acquire a cat. And so she asked one of her grandchildren to buy a hunting cat.

The cat didn't find the rats, but instead it devoured all the food stored in the kitchen. She then begged her family not to give her any more chocolates. Her mind was made up to abandon the house since only her bedroom remained secure. The rest of the house was the domain of rodents and the cat.

The children met in the sitting room and discussed the problem, resolving to look for a safe place for their grandmother.

But just as time advances, on the way to the nursing home, the grandmother turned into a great-grandmother, dying upon arrival at her new residence. So the relatives put her in a small black box and brought her to her final resting place in a horse-drawn carriage to comply with the wishes of the deceased. The coachman raced crazily through the paved street and, with so much jolting, ashes started to come out of the box to the point that at the gate of the cemetery the urn didn't weigh anything, in view of which they proceeded to open it, verifying that it was practically empty.

They then decided to transfer the remains to a snuff box kindly offered by one of the mourners, who had intended to pass by a pharmacy and have it filled on the way back from the graveyard.

Translated by Elizabeth D. Hodges and Doris Meyer

# Sailing Down the Rhine

## Sonia Guralnik

The air is warm, there is no breeze, the trees hold their breath, everything is immobile, waiting for the last passengers. At the end of the dock a bus comes into view, and slowly advances until it comes up next to the boat. A very tall woman is the first to step down. She is wearing thick-lensed glasses.

"Good afternoon, Frau Braun."

"Good afternoon, Captain."

"Allow me. I will count the tickets."

She observes his blue jacket, his white hat, from under which some gray hair protrudes. The captain has fine lips, which are drawn between two vertical folds. He is young and wears a gold-buttoned jacket. Just how old can he be? He has grown a small mustache, which he dyes black. That much is certain.

The old women appear at the bus door and begin their descent with great difficulty. Some lean on canes, others walk in pairs with slow, march-like steps. All wear lace-up shoes, all have twisted legs, but each one presents her deformities in different ways: At times the knees come together, or they are held incredibly separated. Those who have long legs wear short boots like a child's and those with legs like short parentheses wear tall boots like a hunter's.

"I'm not getting on board!" one of them says. "The Rhine's water isn't as clear as it used to be. It's dirty." And she crosses her arms.

Another whispers: "I don't want to go. I become so seasick on boats.."

An old woman shades her face with a parasol so as not to receive the sun's glare from the street, and she frowns unceasingly.

"Hurry up! Hurry up!" orders Frau Braun, beating her hands together in a steady rhythm. "The boat is waiting for us."

There's a yellowish old woman who wears a hat and gloves. Someone makes fun of her:

"I never go out if I'm not properly dressed," she says affirming her gloves. "People might confuse me with the servants."

They have placed four wheelchairs on the deck.

Madame Grete thinks herself nobility. She wears a crown and has put an ocher lace blouse on beneath her coat.

"Is everyone here?" the captain asks.

"Everyone!" shouts Frau Braun from below. And she pushes the old woman who gets seasick up the gangplank.

The ladies sit on the main deck in rows of twos. They have been promised hot chocolate if they behave. They hold hands and begin to sing with shrill little voices when the boat departs.

Their voices grow faint as the noise of the motor increases and suddenly they can no longer be heard. The boat pulls away, leaving behind the houses and the suburbs with their chimneys, parks, bridges, and sown fields.

A young woman on board sells postcards to the tourists. She, too, seems suddenly older as she approaches the old women. "They are post cards of the sites after the war. This is how Cologne looked after the bombing. Only the great cathedral was saved," she tells them, and she passes the cards close by their eyes so they can see but not touch.

At noon, Frau Braun lifts her chin and makes the old women march up to the top deck to enjoy the sun. They all hold hands: "Hanschen Klein, gin allein..." they sing. Madame Katz goes through her purse: her glasses must be there in the bottom. Madame Ursula hasn't been able to put in her teeth. Someone has taken them. How is she ever going to sip chocolate and nibble pastries...

They have stolen Madame Grete's watch.

"There's a thief among you," Frau Braun says, shaking her index finger. Then she turns to the captain and explains :"All of them get confused, they imagine days, things, dates; they forget..."

"I don't forget," thinks Madame Katz. She bows her head to rid herself of the formless memory that has haunted her ever since she entered the home. She has seen this women somewhere else. Where? How can she remember? Wasn't it in the spring of..." Suddenly her memory is invaded by the warmth of her daughter's body, and all becomes clouded in tears she is unable to stop. She sits very erect. She again goes through her purse. Who could possibly have taken her glasses? She is sure she had opened the drawer to take them out before she left... "I can live without my glasses. I no longer read," she thinks.

Frau Braun chats with the captain. She is 60, tall, strong, her short hair grows quickly. No one knows she was a torturer in the concentration camps. Nor does any one have any reason to know. The old women fear her. That helps her maintain discipline. She is capable of tiny tortures that leave no telltale marks: she hid Madame Ursula's dentures, she has just thrown Madame Katz's glasses into the river. She has Madame Grete's watch up her sleeve; soon she will drop it into the milk. She will add salt to the chocolate but no one will find out because the old women frequently imagine things and besides they never say anything during the commission's annual visit to the Paradise Home.

Madame Katz continues contemplating the captain. There is something about him that seems false, just like this boat, and this sunny, happy day. She looks at him more intently and suddenly a light illumines her old eyes: the mustache is a fake. Mustache. MUSTACHE. That's it! The jailer at Bergen-Belsen. They called her Mustache. My God! They say she shaved everyday, but even so a shadow appeared at noon. It's noon. Almost without daring, she looks at Frau Braun, who has the sun in her face...

"She took my Annie from me," Madame Katz thinks with great difficulty. She swallows the heavy tears that rise through her entire being, the sharp-edged tears that pierce with feelings of everything she has lived through.

"No, you just can't imagine how they are," Frau Braun is talking to the captain. "They forget their way; it's difficult to manage them; at times they are mischievous as mice....

The captain looks at her.

Madame Katz is determined. She shouts. "Frau Braun is the torturer at Bergen-Belsen! Frau Braun is Mustache!"

Like the rustle of dry straw, the old women's voices begin:

"Where were you during the war?"

"In many places. And you?"

"I was also in Bergen-Belsen."

"Auschwitz."

"Dachau."

The old women roll up their sleeves.

"In Ravensbruck."

"I was also in Auschwitz."

"My parents had no burial, no kaddish."

One of the women tries to stand up, the one with the bowed legs and short boots. She falls. Madame Ursula begins to cry and shout.

Madame Grete stammers trying to control the situation. She wants them to listen to her. She's the queen. She will speak.

All of them mill around Madame Katz. The groups of old women there in the back don't understand and ask over and over, "What's hapening?" Madame Katz drills on, her voice low and her punctuation perfect. She prounounces each syllable: "She is the one who mixes up our boots, she is the one who takes away our fresh bread and leaves us the scraps before we enter the dining room, she steals and destroys our glasses, she is the one who puts salt in our chocolate, she is the one who turns off the heat when we are shivering in the darkness. Ursula, she is the one who shouts behind our backs, the practical joker she calls them, she is the one who cuts the historical items from the paper, she is the one who pulled my Annie off the barbed wire, pulled her away from me in pieces!."

In the distance, Frau Braun claps her hands together, distractedly. There is no doubt, this captain is very nice.

"Go wash your hands," she orders half-heartedly. And she turns to the captain commenting: "Look how their hands are stained with age spots. Hands won't hide a woman's age ."

The captain has gone up to the bridge.

Madame Katz keeps talking in a hoarse whisper. The old women nod assent to each phrase. Finally she says: "It will be after lunch." The whisper travels throughout the boat, the slurred whisper that no one else hears.

They old women have taken each others' hands again. But this time a current of life runs through them. The old branches straighten in the storm. "Where were you?"

"Auschwitz."

"...my brother..."

"Bergen-Belsen."

"...my brother..."

"On the third day they broke our legs. The post war reports call it rheumatism. What a laugh! Rheumatism! My legs, the ones I used to show off and get what I wanted and now they are bowed."

Madame Ursula, terrified, mops the floor with her new skirt, repeating, "Quickly, quickly, she's coming." They pick her up and go to the dining room. They can no longer wait. All follow the movements of Madame Katz.

"Will you hurry up," Frau Braun howls, planting herself before them with her arms on her hips. Madame Katz approaches, coming so close that Frau Braun can see her sharp wrinkles, and says, "No. First we will sing a round. Ready! HANSCHEN KLEIN / GING ALLEIN / IN DIE WEITE / WELT HINEIN!"

The captain and two crewmen have looked for Frau Braun for a long time now and with no luck. He must now look after the old women. The boat has arrived in Koblenz.


Translated by Martha J. Manier

# The Englishwoman

## Marta Jara

I saw her arrive one night at nine o'clock, gaunt, pale and blonde, at that indefinite age of some Englishwomen somewhere between twenty-five and sixty years old. In her hand she carried an old suitcase and, resting on her recently permed curls, an unstylish hat, yellowed and faded.

"Miss Hutchinson...I'm Miss Emily Hutchinson...," she stammered in English with an awkward, pathetic voice, when, after the apprehensive sound of the bell, we rushed to the front door. She gave my parents a vigorous handshake and, looking at me kindly, asked me my name. I remained silent.

"Answer," ordered my father, severely. "It's the English governess who has come from Europe."

"I will never answer her," I responded timidly, "I don't like her..."

My parents looked at each other, horrified. Looking back, I think my father's eyes said, "I have made a great financial sacrifice. The governess has come on a freighter, cheap, to be sure, but still too expensive for my earnings. A great sacrifice. And this stubborn little girl..."

"She's very tired," explained my mother. "Tomorrow's another day."

Days, months, a year passed. And I continued to act haughty in my rebelliousness. "Doesn't she understand it's for her own good?" my father would exclaim. "Doesn't she see the benefits I'm trying to give her? Doesn't she feel it's necessary, indispensable, to know English? Having another language is like having another soul." And seeing my lowered head and sullen expression, he would grasp his head with both hands murmuring, "Some children are such donkeys! Donkeys!" Meanwhile, I envied the luck of my brother, who, after school and with our two cousins, took lessons with Mr. Bingle, an exuberant Englishman, light-hearted and eccentric, who quickly became my teacher too.

"Fine," warned my father one day, looking at me resolutely. "As long as you keep acting this way, you won't get any dessert."

"If you want, I'll answer 'yes,' but no more than 'yes,' " I agreed, letting out one of those deep breaths children take before crying.

That "yes" was the only connection between my small self and the Englishwoman who, each day in the house, felt more alone and more disoriented, enduring the tremendous loneliness of exile, to which was added the isolation of not being able to speak or understand. She knew no Spanish and no one in the family spoke English. A terrible form of prison. Until, one day, seeing the uselessness of her presence in our home, my father sent her back to her country.

Poor Emily Hutchinson. Today, when I think of you, something quivers and stirs in the bottom of my heart. One day, you embarked on a trip, very far away, prompted by the urgency of your unknown destiny, leaving behind the few belongings and humble memories that until then had made your life bearable. The embroidery in the pattern of a cross, and your needle, remained unfinished in the old drawer of the bureau. And the clumsy table clock, inherited from your grandmother, solitarily chimed the hours in the boarding house. You left for hostile climates and surroundings and your story became entwined with that of all the unfortunate and anonymous souls whose insignificance drags along, moribund and hidden. Souls who never realize their great ambition. And—as you know, Emily Hutchinson—between toiling and uprooting, life passes, slowly withering away like a tree that hasn't been watered.

Children cause suffering without knowing it. Later, through a magnifying glass, they look at the harm they caused in their unawareness. And they would give the world to change it. But they can't always touch the ashes of the past.

Today, I don't know why, from the depths of my childhood, I see the aimless Englishwoman arrive with her absurd hat and her gaunt figure. An immense pity, a longing to pronounce the word that my childish lips didn't know how to say, wells up with the quickening beats of my heart

Translated by Jennifer Bayon and Doris Meyer

# The White Bedspread

## Elena Castedo

Approaching the closet, Audolina meets María in the mirror. María is her name in the Anglo houses. They are all María s here, nobody can remember "Audolina," "Filomena," "Mirella," such simple names. Audolina places her ear against the door one more time, then takes the carefully folded Garfinkel's bag la Señora gave her from the closet. This is the most delicate operation of the whole week, the most dangerous and eventually the most satisfying. It requires speed and precision. Someone's coming up the stairs! María drops the bag and looks in the mirror to take a hairpin from her chignon, then puts the pin back. Even with her face all flushed from the scare, her image looks so dignified in front of the attic room, like the pictures of saints with landscapes behind them. *La Virgen Dolorosa* be praised; a bed white as a dove, with her own bedspread, in a room with a door that stays closed all night long.

The sound of steps is interrupted. Then they go down. Audolina takes a deep breath, opens the Garfinkel's bag and carefully places a pork chop, wrapped in double tin foil, to keep the cursed dog's nose out of it. Steps come up the stairs again. Audolina drops the bag nervously. She observes María in the mirror remove her apron. When the lines of the chest and the rump go flat, and hair shows gray, and the months are put to rest, it's the way the body shows what goes on in the soul. Then a woman can become pure again. The steps are almost at her door. She walks around the bed, caressing out every non-existent wrinkle. How beautiful. How lovely. Finally, her own bedspread, a dream for more than four times as many years as she has fingers. The girl opens the door without knocking and walks in, wearing a slip and teen bra. For the Sacred Virgin, still flat as a tortilla, wearing a bra... "María , hook this bra tighter for me, will you?" Audolina joins the two ends of the satin cloth; it feels dry compared to the live satin of the girl's back. Rougher patches announce her skin's imminent changes. "María , if you stay this Sunday, you could tell me stories. Like the one about that delivery man. Did he really leave you a red rose? Are you sure you didn't make it all up? You can tell it to me again." The girl's lips stretch an unsteady smile over braces.

"Why you ask me to stay, Missy Jenny. You know I got and see the friends in La Mamplesa."

"Give me a break, María ! It's not Mamplesa, how can you be so ignorant! It's Mount Pleasant."

"Is what I say, Missy Jenny, Mamplesa. I get ready now; in a minute la Señora, your mama, she take me to the bus stop. I got to fix my hair now, I got to change now." She lifts her arms to take the same hairpin and puts it back.

"You're so vain, María , always smoothing your hair to the back of your neck, and always putting cream in your hands. Don't tell me old women have boyfriends in Mt. Pleasant! Wouldn't that be a riot!"

"Vain no, Missy Jenny. A woman have to be neat and clean, and, when the woman is young, she...well, she got to have no choice, but all the bad time have the end, then a woman is not so young, then a woman can be neat, a woman can be...clean again. Missy Jenny, you eat more, you put some meat up front, not a good for nothing bra you have. Next week we are together, and I fix you the most best sopaipillas. Delicious, O.K child?"

"Child! Have you gone nuts? I'm not a child! You know very well I'm not! It's been five months now; I'm a woman! And I'm almost taller than you. Look, See? And what makes you think I need you around all the time? I have friends. I have a friend called Megan. If her parents hadn't forced her to go to the Greenbriar with them, she'd be right here with me, right here. And other friends too. And I'd rather not have you around at all. You can leave, just leave!"

The girl slams the door as she walks out. Audolina listens at the door. She must work fast. From the wastepaper basket she retrieves the small packages and tiny jars. Who'd look there, even if they should get suspicious? The rich have a fear of trash. She's so clever it makes her smile. She places the banana—also wrapped in tin foil, so the child won't pick the aroma. Then the scissors that appeared—a joyous miracle—inside the family room's old couch while she was vacuuming it. She'll admire them later. Maybe she'll trade them for Corina's canned artichokes, or a scarf, or a belt; Corina's very bold; she'll take anything from her Señora. Now some of the little jars; Audolina's very conscientious about collecting small containers ahead of time; never leave things for the last minute, her grandfather used to tell them. Actually, nowadays she could buy some of these things if she wanted to, but it's for prevention and, why not; she's very good at it. Empty prescription jars are the best; light, small, easy to pack and ideal for a Sunday's supply. Plus some left over, to go on filling the larger containers in the room she rents from her country woman, Doña Rosa.

*Ave María* ! Steps up the stairs again! Audolina dumps all the small jars with lilac bath salts, dish soap, cooking oil, vinegar, laundry soap, bicarbonate of soda and butter into the bag and drops it in the closet. There's no peace to be had. The steps go down the stairs. *Virgen Santa,* out with the bag again. The little jar with face cream fits snugly. Yes, she's still vain in some ways, Up Above forgive her. Last is the whiskey. She'll invite Doña Rosa and Corina, and they'll go to La Latina to buy the best empanaditas and croquetas and olives in all of La Mamplesa, and come back to listen to Celia Cruz sing those Ayayay! merengues in Radio Borinquen, and drink on the rocks, and laugh until their cheeks hurt. She brings no perfume; none of that rich woman's perfume; the smell still tugs at her stomach. In the houses of diplomats from her own country, every time she heard those faint male steps come into her room at night, instead of asking aloud, "Who is it?" or turning on the light, she would dab la señora's perfume—kept in a Kaopectate bottle—in the dark...

Steps run up the stairs and the girl bursts in with shiny eyes. "Look what I brought you, María ! The jewel box my father gave me; it's for you." The girl puts the box on the night table and opens it. "Isn't it beautiful music? It says here it's 'Rachmaninoff's prelude in C.' You're going to stay, aren't you, María . We can do fun things. If you want to, we can watch *telenovelas* on the Spanish channel; nobody'll be home but us."

"Gracias, gracias, Missy Jenny, but this is not for me, but it is for you. I come back Monday and now I get ready."

"Well, I don't care if you go away for all of Sunday, or the whole week-end for all I care! You think I'm going to be begging you to stay? No way! You really think you're the cat's meow, don't you? Well, there're lots of things you don't know. I bet you don't know I don't have a thing under my slip; no panties. Sexy, huh?" The girl lifts her slip playfully above her bony knees. "Ayyy! Shame, shame!"

"Missy Jenny, you go, pleese; and take the pretty box; your mama, la Señora; she very busy and she go to her office, and she call me in a minute..."

"C'mon María . Pretty soon you'll be telling me your sob stories about no father, and 'thees vallee of teears' and working in houses where your soul split and all that crap. I know it's nothing but lies, because you won't tell me why your soul 'split.' What nonsense. And you won't stay and tell me. And your stupid stories; a red rose, give me a break!... María , María ... I, didn't mean it, I like your stories; I want you to stay, and you can tell me whatever you want. O.K.?"

"Pleese, Missy, you go now, pleese, I get ready now..."

"Listen, why don't we pretend that my mom and step-dad are going on a trip today, instead of just going to their offices to work all week-end, that way we can walk to the bus, and we can go to the space museum and get ice cream, like we did when they went on trips. Hey! We can go to the river again, and walk there, and sit on the rocks under the bridge, and watch the water, and you can tell me things, all right?"

"Missy Jenny, now I pack to go; things I need for the Sunday. Your mama; ask la Señora... ask el Señor to take you..."

"C'mon, María , you know perfectly well that my mother can't; she has all that law work to do. And my father lives in Chicago, of course, he can't. And my step-dad; he always has work to do; always, always."

"Well, your señora mama she is a lawyer very important. You call some friend from school, Missy, you play."

"Play! listen, María , why don't you get it through your thick head; I'm not a little kid! I'm a woman! And kids from school, they are busy; they have to go shopping with their parents, and they have to go eat out, and all that. And... they'd come but they can't..."

The girl observes María . María 's standing firm. The girl goes to the bed; with a grand gesture that follows the music, she picks at the bedspread, leaving a big wrinkle. "Missy Jenny, pleese, the bedspread is very good, very good bedspread, you know I paid the money for a new, white bedspread, is not for play." Another big gesture, another tug, another big wrinkle on the bedspread. Audolina freezes.

"Do you want me to leave you a red rose on your bedspread María ?"

"Missy Jenny, the bedspread is very important...like the bra for you. Pleese, for Santa Catalina, *protectora* of young girls..."

"María aaaa! Why aren't you downstairs! I'm in a big rush!"

"Ay! *Virgen Santísima!* La Señora, see? I said to you...now you make me very mad."

Audolina attempts to bring the girl to the door. They push and pull. "Let me go! Let me go! You're scratching my arms! You horrible old woman! You're the worst maid I ever had!" The girl wiggles free and runs to the bed. She lifts her slip and sits in the middle of the bedspread. "Guess what, María , guess what time of the month it is for me-e." The braces shine as she forces a smile.

"Missy, please, Missy, I not can buy another bedspread, please...go, go now..."

"María aa! Are you coming or not! Jenny! Where's everybody!"

The girl gets up and leaves the room with dignity. In the middle of the white bedspread there is a red spot. Audolina forcefully pushes back a savage assault of unending trampled territories. Where, where is that territory that can't be trampled on. With a flushed face, she quickly rearranges the ham piece and the sandwich bag filled with oatmeal. She drops a sweater on top of the bag. This sloppy work is against her principles, but she has no choice. The music stops. María closes the door and rushes downstairs, taking care not to jiggle the bag, holding it so it appears very light, saying loudly, "Sí Señora! Sí Señora!"

# Down River

## Marta Brunet

First the house was made out of woven reeds plastered with mud. But with the passage of time, the man began to bring rocks up from the river, and around the existing walls he made additional ones of stone. It was like one house stuck inside another house. Or rather, like one room stuck inside another, because the house was nothing but that double-walled space with a door and two little windows, though it was surrounded by several sheds that served as kitchen, barn, and dismounting area. Next to the high wall of the mountain in a crevice in the rock, the house was sheltered from the wind. A gorge cut by a river separated it from the mountain on the other side.

In summer the river was a wretched trickle among the sands and the golden brown rocks. In fall it grew until it swallowed the stones, whirling precipitously, without even a patch of quiet water to give it the color of the sky, or a star to remain still in the deep night of its mirror. Winter came and the fine persistent streaks of rain blurred everything. But the noise of the water's furious surging still drowned out the falling of the rain and the beating of the wind, if not its long howl. Spring with its melting ice and snow provoked flash floods that carried away logs and jagged stones, often forming dams that the current pushed against until it surged forward again noisily. The thaw would come to an end, and the river would take on the appearance of a copper thread once again, imperceptible at times over the reddish hue of the sand, between the walls of the gorge, also red, like the barren mountalns that formed the horizon's boundary.

In the house, life was guided by the water. The dry weather of summer marked the time when the woman, singing sweetly the four notes of an Indian melody, performed her domestic chores beneath the sheds. The old woman would spin, half-blind, in her little chair facing the abyss, looking at the haze of her own eyes, her eyelids wide open, reddened by the sun, the wind, and the years. She was carved out by wrinkles, and her hands were strangely hurried as they moved the distaff back and forth. The girl helped her mother, she guided the old woman, and she went down to the river for water, sure of her fifteen years, holding her head high. Her skirt revealed the outline of her stomach. gently rising and falling, and her skin had the smooth texture of a piece of fruit that knew it was ripe and wanted to be eaten. The two children came and went, helping the mother, helping the old woman, helping the girl, frolicking around the mountains with the goats, looking after the donkey, helping most of all the man working down below in the dry river bed, splitting logs, turning them into firewood, wood tied in bundles that he would go to the distant town to deliver. A business enterprise to live from, a way of wrenching from the mountain a few crumbs that he exchanged for money. A business for the summer, because afterwards, in the fall, the rain destroyed the possibilities for this work, turning the roads into sticky clay, making them impassable.

Then the woman wove blankets on the primitive loom. The old woman continued spinning as always with her eyes fixed on her own haze, the girl came and went from shed to shed with a coat over her head to defend herself from the rain, along with the children similarly adorned. Meanwhile, the man, with the fine expertise of an artisan, fashioned the decorative border on the baskets, which, like the blankets, were work for bad weather. But the rain enclosed everything, absolutely, and the house, without a view, was left with its inhabitants inside by the hearth that burned in their midst, a slit open in the roof to let out the smoke, and a diffuse light coming in through the chinks in the windows. They seemed dazed by inaction, attentive only to a possible let-up in the rain that might allow them to rush outside for some quick chores.

There were just a few hours to work. The light was gone at mid-afternoon and a candle burned with its wavering flame, but only sometimes, because the woman was cutting back on that luxury. Generally the glow of the fire was sufficient to pass the mate around and afterwards the sleeping mats were brought up to the glowing embers, one for the man and the woman, another for the old woman and the girl, another for the children. They sought in the warmth of the coals a defense against the cold, which was becoming palpable, as if the night were pushing it through the seams of the door, through the chinks in the windows, through the slit in the roof, and inside the room as if it were attaching itself to the bodies there. The children fell asleep, quickly wrapped in their dreams. The old woman prayed long rosaries, drawing herself close to the warmth of the girl and wearing her superstition like a black cat around her neck between her braids and her shawl. The man and the woman exchanged ritual words, sentence fragments, listening to the breathing as it grew louder and louder.

"They're asleep..."

"Maclovia's not..."

"Everybody is."

"And the old lady?"

"Her? Forget her..."

The old woman knew that it didn't matter to them whether she was asleep or not, and when the first moan reached her, for an instant she interrupted her praying while a smile lifted her upper lip, exposing the gaping holes in her sparse teeth. But sometimes a more penetrating moan disturbed the girl's sleep and put her on the verge of waking, if it didn't wake her completely. The girl was left yearning, aware of what was going on there, seeing it without seeing it, sweating in torment, her breasts suddenly aching and her thighs trembling, one pressed against the other. But the silence returned, and she, slipping through a kind of beatitude, began to feel her muscles relax and that she was slowly entering the realm of sleep once more. When spring swept the horizon clean of clouds and a flock of tiny parrots went by screeching their delight at the sun, it was necessary to remake the path that led to the little town, to go sell the blankets and the baskets, to buy "the essentials."

"Where's your father?" asked the woman.

"Not my father; your husband. He's there, down below," the girl gestured.

"Won't you ever learn to call him 'Father'?"

"Never. My father died. This guy's your husband."

"Okay...." And the woman was left staring at her, stricken, without the strength to do battle with that stubbornness.

"You wanna go get him? The sun's already high and the kids are starving. That man always takes his own sweet time...."

"He's a hard worker...." broke in the old woman. "You hadn't ought to gripe about that. It's tempting Fate."

"Send one of the kids," the girl answered unenthusiastically.

The woman looked at her again, with that slowness that made her eyes look like a cow's, expressionless. But suddenly she reacted and shouted furiously: "You're gonna go get him... Get a move on... He's not some mangy dog that you can just ignore..."

The words seemed to slide over the girl, who was standing planted over her outspread legs, strong and naked legs, with her hands crossed behind her back. She looked at the woman from an angle, her thickly lashed eyes half closed. She raised her shoulders, and with her hands still behind her back, she started walking down the steps of the narrow terraced path that led to the river.

She was in no hurry. A little parrot that had discovered her glided curiously above her, attracted by the brightness of her blouse. A goat. which was perched on a large rock and supported as if by some miracle, stopped grazing and, with its foreshortened head, also looked at her curiously. The girl kept walking slowly, full of sunlight, her wide feet taking control of the earth at every step. She stopped a moment and, guided by the chipping, changed direction. She already knew where to find her mother's husband.

"They're calling you," she said, shouting from up above.

The man turned around to look at her. She stood above him, on an outcropping of stones and fallen logs, looking at him from between her eyelashes, serious and nevertheless with a kind of tenderness that fixed her mouth in a trace of a smile.

"I'm coming," he answered.

He had the hatchet in his hand. He swung it, sinking it with one sudden blow into the log that he was cutting. His entire self seemed to reach out at the effort, as if his muscles could beome part of the hatchet in order to penetrate the wood. He turned around, rubbing his hands together. And his eyes fastened on the figure up above him there, viewing her from below, with her bare legs and her gently rounded stomach and the tips of her upaised breasts, and above them her chin and her whole face thrown back, distorted and unfamiliar, with her hair dishevelled by the hand of the wind, a hand like a man's, desiring and caressing her.

It seemed as if he were taking root. He stood there staring and staring at ther. As if the roots were going into the earth, reaching that dark region of undergrund currents, cold and warm springs, both rising through his feet, up his legs and his trunk; flooding his chest, one against the other; reaching his arms, his hands, rising through his arms again, making that whole wave of confusion pound in his brain, throbbing there, pressing with its intense ebb and flow. Like streams of hot and cold water. And as if the sun had suddenly caused all the Spanish broom plants of his childhood home in the north to blossom, and as if the fragrance were a drunken festival that made the mountain tremble. The girl looked at him with half-closed eyes. The man ripped out the roots that held him, he cut them in one stroke, impelled by the same force with which he would chop down a tree, and he moved forward until he was almost pressing his face against the girl's feet. He raised his eyes. He saw her up above him still, firm and unflinching. Suddenly he pressed his forehead to her legs. He raised his hands and pressed them to her legs. And for a moment, they stayed that way, like part of the landscape, unthinking, feeling only the tremendous instinctive life that fused them together.

The girl stared at him, her eyes narrowing. When she took a step back, the man's face and hands stayed in the air, not attempting to keep her there. The girl turned around and began to walk. And the man, in one springing leap, hoisted himself up to the path and took off after her like a blind man to whom the unequivocal presence of the sun is miraculously revealed.


"You're being real fresh." the woman yelled.
"I can be if I want to." answered the girl, shouting just as loudly.
"Go wash the clothes."

"I don't feel like it."

"Go wash the clothes."

"I don't wanna wash the clothes. I don't feel like it. You hear? I don't wanna wash 'em. You wash 'em."

"You go wash 'em because I'm telling you to. I'm your mother."

"I don't feel like it."

"What you're gonna get is a good thrashing. "

"Ha!" laughed the girl. "Just try!"

Not with a stick, but she did try to get her with a good slap in the face. The girl dodged aside quickly, and the woman, from the force of her own movement, lost her balance and went crashing into the wash tub.

"You're gonna pay for this," she shouted, furious.

"Leave her alone," said the old woman. "Just leave her alone. You're not gonna get anywhere with her. She's worse than a mule."

"But she didn't used to be like this..."

"She's a teenager," the old woman went on. "Just leave her alone; she'll get over her pig-headedness."

"I'm gonna tell your father on you. Let's see if you mind him. "

"He's not my father," protested the girl from a distance, leaning against one of the dismounting shed supports and making S's in the dirt with her foot.

"Yeah, I already know. He's not your father; he's my husband,' the woman said bitterly.

"Your husband...," and she narrowed her eyes. Looking at her while an expression like the old woman's revealed in her mouth the teeth of a little carnivorous animal, strong and cruel.

"You'd better go up with the goats," interrupted the old woman. "They're the only ones that can put up with you."

"You, too, the way you spoil her, you'd think you didn't have any grandchildren besides her... " The woman delivered her reproach as the girl was leaving, her hands, as always, crossed behind her back.


Each woman seemed like a copy of the other: the old woman with her eyes wide open, expressionless, her whole self like a rust-colored stone, with the spindle for once lying motionless in her lap under her hands. The woman sat facing her, in another chair, her tear-washed eyes open, her features paralyzed by pain, her hands in the hollow of her skirt, like forgotten useless objects. Behind them the house was vanishing in the shadow that rose slowly from the ravine, preceded by a fresh breeze. In the sky there was only a speck of a star, and a bird stubbornly warbled its call. Suddenly dusk was gone, leaving behind the insistent croaking of the frogs, alive and scattered in the night .

"And the kids?"asked the woman in a thread of a voice.

"They already went to bed," the old woman said softly.

"They didn't wanna know how I was?"

"You know the way they are. All they can think about is old lady Barbona's two goats."

"And...what about her?"

"She's acting real relaxed..., as if nothing had happened."

"Did she fix dinner?"

"And who'd ya figure was gonna fix it for him?"

Not only did she take her man away from her. She took away her home, her responsibility for the life of the home, her right to be in charge. And she was her daughter... The muscles of her face went slack and the tears came gushing out through her eyes, silently flooding her cheeks, entering her lips, leaving a bitter taste in her throat. At times a sob was about to break loose, she felt it rising from the pit of her stomach, ripping her insides apart. But the woman pressed her apron convulsively to her mouth in order to make it die right there, without any noise. Because they had told her "that they didn't want to hear her" after the morning scene, when she found them locked in an embrace and exploded in anger, howling insults and threats that only served to make the girl, getting up calmly, look at her contemptuously, and to make the man, cold and brutal, put the new situation squarely before her. The woman could do whatever she felt like. If she wanted to stay at home, fine. If she wanted to leave, she could. But no sad looks or shouting. She could keep the old woman company, she could spin, weave, whatever she liked best. But the "head of the house" was now the girl.

"She's my woman. My woman," said the man, with a voice that shot out into the air like wheat into the furrow. "My woman."

When she wanted to strike out at the girl, the man raised his strong arm, preventing it. Let her get over her bad spell! Let her go off to the river or the woods, let her try to calm down! That's the way things were and that was it. That's the way life was..., as the old woman told her later, when she dragged her to the bottom of the gorge, both of them stumbling and clutching each other. At her age she could talk like that... But herself! With her adoration for the man, with her passion for him bonded to her skin, a wall that takes on new green life with the climbing vine that gives it its shape. The old woman! Just like the others. Like everybody else, hearing how she had been pushed aside. Trying to calm her down, to make it seem unimportant. The old woman, wanting to go back up to the house, denying her even that wretchedness which her company was to her, leaving her alone in her desperation, abandoned to her suffering, gnawing on her humiliation and her impotence.

She thought about leaving, walking along paths leading to anywhere. Throwing herself into the river, climbing the mountain and throwing herself off some cliff. She saw herself wasted away by hunger begging at farmhouses. Or cold in the water, bloated deformed, like a drowned animal that appeared from time to time out in the current. Or smashed among rocks and earth. She thought about her death like an event apart from herself, a spectator of other people's reactions in order to see them suffer. To see them torn apart by remorse. In order that they might never dare to look at each other, as if separating them in her soul. She cried, staring into the face of death. It was as if she were crying for some other dead person that was not herself. Little details of daily life in which she found some repose inserted themselves among those images. It would no longer be she who kneaded the dough, but the girl, exhausted over the board and afterwards her face inflamed by the oven's breath.

But when they were eating, maybe he wouldn't like bread made by other hands, complainer that he was, and he would miss her... By grasping this thread, she held on to hope. He would miss her... If not in the carnal embrace, in the routine of daily life. It was possible that the girl could end up content just to be "his woman" and she might leave room for her to be "the head of the house." But the idea that she should be "his woman" hurt her like a physical pain, like the suffering of having given birth to her, to her daughter, to the one who was now stealing everything from her. She wept again, alone in the bottom of the gorge, next to the impassive face of the jagged rocks.

The approach of nightfall with its ancient summons made her seek out furtively the protection of the house, and she found the old woman waiting for her, confident she would return.

New she had to keep them from hearing her. That's why she covered her mouth convulsively, her hands clenched over her apron, choking back the sobs. She couldn't let them hear her! She had to put up a good front. To disappear if she could. And to wait, wait... Dawn always comes eventually.

"I'm going to bed," the old woman said. "They've all been asleep for some time now."

She picked herself up, groped for her cane, grabbed hold of the chair, and got ready to set out for the house.

"Aren't you coming?" she asked in a tone of voice that cracked with unexpected tenderness.

"I'm coming, Mother," answered the other woman, picking herself up, too, with the sensation that she did not have a body, that her legs were not going to obey her, that she would not be able to remain standing, much less manage to move. But she picked herself up, she grabbed hold of the chair with the same gesture as the old woman and behind her, slowly, she started walking along the path to the house, terrified, as if edging her way through a bad dream, where despair sat crouching in the void, stalking her every step.

Translated by Elaine Dorough Johnson

# Encounters With the Skin

# The Pond

## María Flora Yáñez

*"There are more things in heaven and earth, Horatio,*
*Than are dreamt of in your philosophy."*
—Shakespeare.

A mere coincidence led me to that old country house situated in a
gorge far away from civilization. At dawn, on that day, I set out for a
drive with three friends. We spent hours on dusty, white highways,
stopping briefly at a hut close to the base of the mountain to eat a
quick lunch under the branches of a cattail plant. After lunch, we
continue hurriedly on our way, our eyes filled with visions of the
country, as the glow of the afternoon sun fills the sky. The car glides
forward rythmically, fast, scratching through the gauzy air, but suddenly, on the deserted road, the car breaks down making it impossible for us to continue our journey.

As there are no houses or people in sight, we decide to split up and
go in search of help. I walk to the east and, without knowing how,
captivated by the wild and desolate beauty of the countryside, I enter
into a labyrinth of small, winding paths until I become completely
lost. Disoriented, I stop for a second. Which way should I go to make
it back to the broken-down car? I find no clues to point me in the
right direction. At every turn thick vegetation obscures my vision and
blocks my way. Rosemary, cherimoya and hawthorn stretch across
the path making it narrower, almost impassable, and my feet can

153

barely move forward because they are embraced by thistles and unruly weeds. Finally I let out a quick cry of joy: in the distance, lost in the solitary exuberance, is a huge country house, looming and quiet. I pick up my pace because the sun is about to set and, ten minutes later, I enter the enclosure of a somewhat exotic looking park, at the end of which stands a clump of gigantic olive trees that envelop the lofty outline of the house in trembling shadow.

Two things surprise me as I cross the carved wood porch, in the eaves of which are perched several motionless doves that add a milky tameness to the picture. First: a profound silence all around, so profound it is as though existence has been suspended here in this threshold; and then, the endless red, colonial brick corridor that begins right at the entrance of the house. It is so long, so long, that it gives the impression of leading to the end of the earth, into the middle of space, to a place where human beings cannot go.

The heavy wood door squeaks as I push it open and I enter, surprised, into a big furnished room that is deserted. Then from one room to the next, all identical and impregnated with a faint odor that I remember having smelled before in places that have been inhabited by many people and things without ever being altered. All around lamps, mirrors and pendulum clocks, bathed in warm exhalations of human lives, watch me.

I call out. No one answers. My over-excited imagination incites me to continue through the dusty silence of the house, but at that moment I think I hear, close to me, a hasty murmur of voices. I anxiously follow the sound: in an enormous dining room, around a mahogany table replete with food and under the lights of a heavy and rich crystal chandelier, sit countless people, of all ages, talking. Some of them have such an ethereal, transparent appearance that they seem like ghosts.

I do not know anyone and no one pays any attention to me. My silent arrival does not interrupt the chatter. I situate myself in a corner, ready to observe. Very close by, an elderly man, with grey hair and strange, luminous eyes, speaks with authority, and a group of people listens to him religiously. Like the others, I, too, listen attentively. "...leaving the prison of our body" he says, "in order to follow the esoteric trail of the unknown. For example, nothingness is black, dense, impenetrable, but beyond nothingness..."

I sense that he is about to say extraordinary things and eagerly fix my eyes on his lips. But at that moment, the murmur of voices next to me prevents me from hearing the rest of his sentence. Who is this person? In spite of my interest in him, I feel uneasy in this setting, an outsider to the worries and joys of these people. I prepare myself to leave, when a man with bright eyes, a small and agile body, and an energetic and bitter mouth, advances hastily toward me from the far end of the room and whispers, looking me directly in the eyes: "Is it you?" I immediately understand that this young man is, like me, out of place in this old house. I have not seen him before and, yet, I feel that we have come a long way together. "Is it you?" he asks again impatiently. I nod yes. "I have looked for you through time," he adds. "Do you want to come with me? My name is Gerardo." His tone of voice is both authoritative and imploring. Without waiting for my answer, he breaks through the noisy crowd and leaves. I follow him in amazement. Any thoughts of the broken-down car and my anxious friends on the deserted road left my mind some time ago. What does all that matter now anyway? The most important thing is this new world I have unexpectedly entered, a world that is magical and fascinating like an illuminating flame.

I follow his silhouette with ease. Outside the night begins to lower its black curtain over the countryside. All is quiet and the park's vegetation fades to hues of death. The olive trees appear more open, clearer, and the shadow of their foliage traces trembling reflections on the ground. Beyond the park, in front of us, the steep heights of the gorge come together to form what seems like a deep, aromatic bed. What does it smell of? Of broom bushes, or rather, lilies, trampled lilies, and yet it is strange, because winter is upon us. "You are like a part of the landscape," Gerardo says to me.

"Where are we going?" I ask.

"What does it matter'" he answers fervently. "We are not following a trail. On a night as bright and beautiful as this one, it is impossible to stay indoors."

His words please and surprise me, but I remain silent. We cross endless paths and immense clearings swaddled in grey twilight. The landscape is so varied that I feel like I am leafing through a great book of pictures in which with each turning page the subject becomes more colorful and intense.

How far away the old house is. How far away is everything that is not the present minute. My worries of yesterday are no longer worries; my happiness of yesterday, is no longer my happiness. Only one thing matters: continuing, continuing forward. Because while I walk along side of him, of Gerardo, a strange, gentle breeze transforms me. I discover in myself the strength of a swallow, I who was always weak; I find in myself the strength of an explorer; I who was always timid. I continue, continue happier with each step, without my curiosity needing to break the spell by asking pointless questions. What for? I am already tied to Gerardo's destiny. Where are we going? It does not really matter. We are going...that is what is essential.

At the foot of a mountain inhabited by animals, he stops suddenly and smiles at me. "Would it be too difficult for you to climb?" he asks.

I answer him with another question. "Have you noticed that in this region the insects are an intense and violet color even at night? And there are millions of them. I've never seen so many wings together..."

"Indeed, it is curious and very beautiful," he observes. "Let's climb, if you want to..."

The impression that, with him, I am penetrating a marvelous and new world, is now clear. We pass through the universe of wings that form a transparent curtain. Up above, the night is as clear as day. Tired from the steep ascent, we let ourselves fall onto the slope of the mountain under some old pepper plants. Oh, how I love pepper plants with their slightly spicy fragrance and their little branches that look like blushing pearls.

We still have quite a way to go before reaching the top. And what does it matter if we do not arrive? We continue lying on the hard, crisp-leaved ground of the incline. The winged insects have now disappeared from our view, but in their place a legion of red ants invades everything. They crawl up my dress, caress my bare arms, my back, and so many of them weigh down the hem of my shawl in a thick red line that it gradually slips from around my shoulders. In the distance a continuous and harmonious noise, like that of the running waters of a great river, can vaguely be heard.

"You are even prettier without your shawl," murmurs Gerardo, looking at me. "Do you know that when I found you, I found myself? I long for your skin, I long for your eyes... I bury myself in the pleats of your wool dress and it seems as though I am entering a new country, only recently discovered, inhabited by only two people. Who are they? Where did they come from? What are their names? It does not matter. All of a sudden they are other, distinct beings, without origin or name. They simply found themselves."

"Yes, they found themselves," I murmur like an echo.

"I could spend hours looking at your long fingers. They remind me so much of the delicate roots of a lily," he continues. "And the strands of your hair that blow in the wind and that shimmer like lights. I don't know your name, but I carry you within myself, like a caress, next to my heart. Come, next to my heart..."

I feel his longing breath on my face. "Triguita..." he stammers. Why is he calling me Triguita? Perhaps because he does not know that my name is Alina, Perhaps because my skin smells of wheat fields and shows the golden signs of the sun...

"Triguita," he continues, "you know and see that you are the truth for me." I do not answer, but rest my head on his shoulder, then I lie down on the grass of the mountain and his arms embrace me and I hear the pounding of his heart in my ears. Our two beings become as one and the force that binds us is so superhuman that it seems that our souls have escaped their physical casing and blended together.

But suddenly our energy is interrupted by a fleeting premonition. I abruptly release myself from his embrace and look around me in the nocturnal clarity. A tall shadow materializes next to us: a grey outline traced on the rugged undergrowth of the ground. What intrusive specter is this that comes to disturb our marvelous fusion, our encounter that takes place beyond the abstract depth of time and space?

"Let's continue on our way," I beg Gerardo in a low and quivering voice. "Something inexplicable has come to break the spell that was enchanting us."

We try to continue walking, but, at that moment we are cut off by the same man of uncertain age, grey hair and luminous eyes who we left pontificating back in the old house on the plain. How did he get here? How did he get ahead of us when we practically ran here and have only recently fallen to the ground to rest? When we left the strange house he was still in the dining room leisurely sipping a cup of tea and showed no sign of wanting to leave. Now he is here on the slope and seems to be coming down from the top of the mountain. How did he do it? It is impossible to get here by carriage because of the steep roads and dense vegetation. He must have come on foot, like us. But what mysterious shortcut did he take? It is all a mystery that I cannot solve. The only thing that I know for sure is that now, standing in the middle of the path, he is blocking our way.

"Why are you interrupting our solitude? Why are you holding up our walk?" Gerardo rebukes violently.

"It is pointless to continue," answers the old man.

"Why?" Gerardo asks.

"There s a dreadful epidemic. If you insist on continuing you will go completely blind because that is the effect of the epidemic in this region."

"But...we can't stay here all night out in the open. And we can't turn back because we can't find the trail. Besides, once we mix with people again, we won't be ourselves anymore and everything will change."

"Do as you please, but I warn you: further on, total blindness awaits you."

"You don't convince me," Gerardo exclaims. "We will keep walking."

And with a harsh movement he pushes the grey-haired man to one side. But the old man places his transparent and aged hand on my shoulder saying calmly, "She will not proceed."

"Gerardo!" I scream. "This seems like a dream."

"It is a dream," murmurs my friend solemnly.

At that moment, an enormous bird flies between the two of us and its soft, dark wings almost brush against my forehead. Is it an owl? I manage to perceive the ironic look in its round bird-of-prey eyes before it disappears into the red-streaked sky. I feel an empty sensation inside of me and reach out my arms. But, horrified and desperate, I see that Gerardo is no longer by my side.

All of the blood in my veins rushes to my temples in dizzying pulsations.

"Gerardo!" The scream that comes from the very center of my being hurls itself down the mountain only to crash and dissolve in the immutable nature that surrounds me. How can I explain Gerardo's abrupt and unexpected disappearance? What has happened to him? Where is he?

The man with the luminous gaze, the same man who had no pity or understanding for us and no faith in us, looks at me sadly, as though he wants to help me. But his presence now seems terrible to me, like fate or a hurricane that in its blind passage hits and destroys everything.

Meanwhile, the sky becomes livid. Rolling scraps of clouds aggressively link together and drag themselves over our heads. And the night is a living thing that oppresses me. The animals that live on the mountain seem to have suddenly awakened because all around a sound like the rising tide can be heard. Loud, clear calls, wide-spread commotion, a strange symphony that defines itself in an interminable, impassioned chorus. The entire mountain speaks. The trees also seem to come to life, they sway, they approach, they recede, in continuous vibration.

I am paralyzed with fear. I cannot get used to the rough swaying, which casts me, without reason, from a world of light into a world of awful darkness. Gerardo violently erased from my life, just because, and I am left in the middle of a hostile and upsetting nature! Without him I am like a plant whose roots have been ripped from the earth. And my laxity, which is even greater than my fear, makes me incapable, like in dreams, of moving any of my limbs. I do not want life to go on! I do not want the sun to shine anymore now that I have lost Gerardo! I do not care if I remain in the desolation of this mountain forever. All I want to do is to collapse exhausted in the profound darkness.

But suddenly, from my very weakness I draw strength and without thinking about the vigilant man whose penetrating eyes always cut through me, I flee like a wounded animal downhill.

Here there is a blank in my memory. I must have slept out in the open air for a few hours, I must have walked a long way, because, suddenly, in the middle of my emotional upheaval, I notice that the morning light is timidly breaking through the blue membrane of the sky. A few minutes later I find myself on the outskirts of a city, in front of a big white building.

My dress is torn and covered with thorns. My wool shawl remains caught in a thistle bush, the prisoner of the army of red ants. Dizzy from lack of sleep and from the unforeseen magic of that peculiar day, I enter the white building without knowing why, maybe because, like a goal, it stands there before me. But I am astonished to see that beyond the threshold, blocking my way, stands the elderly man with the luminous eyes who, consciously or unconsciously, destroyed my fusion with Gerardo. He approaches me with ease.

"Do you want to see him?" he asks calmly.

A single word leaves my lips: "Gerardo!"

"Come..." he says leading me down a narrow, white corridor. I realize that we are in a hospital. Doctors, teachers and nurses bow obsequiously before my companion. We enter a big, empty room and there, lying on an operating table, with his forehead hidden under one arm, I see Gerardo. I recognize with painful yearning his small, agile body, his brown hair.

"Gerardo," I stammer. "what have they done to you?" When he hears the whisper of my voice, he turns his head toward me and his blue eyes, as bright as lights, look at me. I realize almost instantly that they look at me without seeing me. Then his hands touch me, they feel up and down the pleats of my wool dress.

"Don't worry about me," he whispers. "Being physically apart is bearable, but being spiritually disunited is intolerable. And that is not going to happen."

The voice of the doctor in charge sounds out authoritatively. "It s a strange illness," he says. "It isn't ordinary blindness."

Meanwhile the nurses in their white caps flutter around the room like innocent doves. But suddenly, the doctor frowns and exclaims gravely, "It's useless to try anything now: he has passed away."

I do not know why I cannot properly comprehend the terrible catastrophe that this death represents for me. The doctor's words slide over my somewhat unconscious stupor and again I feel as though I am dreaming. Everything has happened at an uncontrollable and fantastic pace as though one step removed from reality and time. I am unaware of all that surrounds me, and I feel lost in an incoherent night, beneath whose darkness the events take on a tortuous, pendular motion: yes.. no...yes...no...

I cry softly. I am shaken by the harshness of a stocky blond nurse with accentuated features, who coldly says to me as she covers Gerardo's body with a sheet, "Crying is not allowed in this room." Other nurses, many others, enter the room bringing with them sprigs of long, pale, unidentifiable flowers. They begin to throw them on him, but then something extraordinary occurs: when the petals touch him, his livid skin takes on color, his stiff body begins to tremble. A wave of fear passes through the room; the nurses stop the kind gesture of their hands, while the doctor, feverishly, takes the pulse of the dead man.

"This man is still alive," he exclaims. "His heart has started to beat again."

I feel a surge of blood rush to my chest and my cheeks. What does all this mean? I know I am not dreaming. And yet...I hurry over to the operating table and again sigh: "Gerardo." As he does not answer me, I lightly touch his brown hair with my fingers. Then, like the first time, he lifts his head and looks at me. But I let out a horrified scream because it is not him, it is not Gerardo. Instead of the unrealistic, passionate features of my friend, I find before me, another. An Other.

It seems that my destiny now is to live in this exasperating, pendular motion: yes...no...yes...no...

"Gerardo has disappeared!" I scream. "This is not him, they have replaced Gerardo's body with another."

I have not finished my sentence when again the grey-haired man, who has played such a strange role in these happenings, appears next to me. His bright eyes, more ghostly each time, now resemble the empty gaze of a statue. He fixes his veiled, mysterious eyes on me and slowly proclaims, "This man is like Gerardo; he will play an identical role in your life. What does it matter if they have changed his body?" The patient, as if to support the old man's sentence, smiles up at me from the operating table. Doctors and nurses nod in agreement.

But I am still petrified. Oh, I had found perfection, but perfection only exists in dreams and it is logical, now, that it should disappear. What have they done with the blind Gerardo? At what moment did they manage to switch his body with another without my noticing?

Stop the hours, stop the day, stop life... I make useless attempts to understand what is happening. With pupils dilated from anxiety, I go through the rooms searching for eyes, mouths that I can read like the living book that Gerardo's eyes and mouth were for me. But I find nothing. Bodies, indifferent bodies. Eyes, indifferent eyes.

I leave the strange place and cross the white city that has neither history nor name. Outside there is an afternoon glow in the sky. I follow the pale face of the sun and head back into the countryside. Always searching for Gerardo. Finding him is like regaining my own breath again. I feel that in order to find him I must go back to where I started, to the big, looming, silent house. But how? Which way should I go?

Guided by my instincts, I walk with feverish haste. Flocks of birds pass by in a black line over my head. Cormorants. Could the sea perhaps be close by? A straw-colored reflection covers the land. "I mustn't be frightened by this yellowish tint that hangs over the countryside," I tell myself. "I mustn t be frightened..."

Here, again, there is another abysmal hole in my memory. The complicated tapestry of my memories seems like a huge piece of torn gauze. I do not know why the threads that weave together the plot of that day are continually being cut. I must have walked a long way, like before. What worries me now, all of a sudden, is not finding the mountain inhabited by the animals. Could it be that I have gone the wrong way? And what if I never manage to find my way back again? I sigh nervously. I am exhausted, I am thirsty and hungry. But... Oh, what a relief! A happy cry comes from my chest because, all of a sudden, I recognize the grove of olive trees that preceded the house. The curious thing is that I cannot see the mountain... It does not matter anymore. A few more steps, a crossroads, and beyond that, the day before, the big, warm friendly house in the gorge appeared in front of me like a magical vision. Now I stop perplexed.

"Either things lack common sense or I am dreaming," I say to myself., because I have crossed the little forest, the park, the crossroads that I know so well and... Nothing! No signs of the gorge or the house. Nevertheless, like the day before, I begin to smell broom bushes and trampled lilies. If I am living in the unreal, how kind these ghosts must be, who, in winter, make everything smell like the breath of spring.

I continue walking and further on, there where the house should have been, the smell that delighted me in the melancholy setting of the deserted rooms comes up to greet me. That evaporating, undefinable smell that is emitted by old things that have-been trampled down over time. I do not know what to think. Maybe emotion and fatigue are preventing me from perceiving the objects around me and are making me the victim of hallucinatory spells.

It must be late because now there are stars in the sky. But neither the house nor the gorge, nor the long, colonial brick corridor are anywhere to be seen. "There were lamps, mirrors and pendulum clocks here," I say to myself thoughtfully. "Mirrors more than anything, innumerable mirrors clouded from the passage of time."

"There is still one left!" I exclaim out loud in a surprised voice. "There is one!" Because at my feet appears a huge mirror in which I see the reflection of my image, stretched out and unreal. I lean forward as if to merge myself with this image of mine that looks up at me from below. But I step back quickly; the mirror in which I see myself is a pond, a huge pond, still and green, whose waters emit a strange, subtle, depressing odor like ether when it floats sickeningly in the atmosphere.

Now I am absolutely certain that, on the other side of this motionless body of water, I will find Gerardo.

"Triguita!" His voice vibrates urgently, calling me through space.

"Gerardo!" I answer joyously. And I think to myself, "I could go right up to the pond or run on it as though it were really a mirror.

But I cannot do either because, at that moment, something incomprehensible and unusual happens: to this day I cannot explain how, a shooting star suddenly falls from the sky into the cloudy waters of the pond. In the complete silence is heard the crack of the star as it breaks through the thin, flat surface, leaving innumerable circles in its wake.

The pond, like a monster being violently roused from a dream, becomes choppy, swells, bellows and rolls itself into a stormy and rising surf. Now, in place of the sleeping mirror is an angry force that devours paths and trails.

Then I understand that my determination to unite with Gerardo anew is in vain. I will never see him again. That marvelous fusion of ours was a miracle and, like all miracles, it will not be repeated.

I do not even hear his voice anymore, as it has been suffocated by the monstrous surf. In a spark of supernatural clarity of my senses, I manage to make out a vague silhouette far away, very far away, on the other bank of the pond. But I am not suffering anymore. The awareness that fighting back is useless envelops me in a sort of sweet resignation. So much effort, I tell myself, so much fighting, to reach this resigned state, this meekness when faced with the inevitable!

I understand, without pain, that we will always remain on opposite shores, separated by something uncontrollable and relentless. I understand that his shadow will fade away in the distance. And that I, for as long as I live, will have to remain on this side of the water. Alone.

Translated by Alison Ridley

# Scents Of Wood and Silence
## Pía Barros

*To Cecé*

"You seem different this morning."

"It's just that I dreamt about sea gulls," she said, jumping out of bed to toast and eggs, steaming coffee and the daily ritual of shared breakfasts.

She didn't hear him when he said, "That's strange, you've got green grass between your fingers."

It had been a game so doing the laundry wouldn't be so dull. She began dreaming about hands that reached out of the sheets searching for her breasts, they should be large, coarse hands, bony and neglected, with long fingers, that would touch her painlessly, vigorous hands, rising and falling over her nipples, tracing her bristling skin, roaming all over her.

She smiled when she saw that the washer has quit running long ago and shook off her lethargy, plunging into the sheets and pillowcases that she would hang up, still perturbed by that caress.

For a time, she closed her eyes and in the shadows, while Ismael slept, she let herself be carried away by those hands, she took them, in turn, to show them the secret trace of her pores and her trembling pleasure.

Ismael was eating his breakfast as always, immersed in the news, and he found her beautiful and transparent. Life was secure and he felt fulfilled.

One afternoon when the heat flushed her and made her dream of lakes in winter, she wanted him to have narrow hips, small tight buttocks to dig her fingernails into, dark down outlining his genitals.

He found her asleep on the rug, with rumpled clothes and slightly open, moist lips. He put down his briefcase on the table and wanted to make love to her right there, but he controlled himself, because the image seemed virginal to him, and she was so delicate that he didn't want to attack her, and he sat down for a long while smiling, watching her sleep, so abandoned, sweet, with a face made childlike by her dreams.

But she was licking hips, kissing buttocks, clawing.

He didn't worry about her paleness until much later, when he noticed how obsessively she was sleeping. She seemed to seek out every possible moment to close her eyes, and when the house began to show neglect, he asked her to see a doctor, because he had heard that excessive drowsiness was a symptom of anemia. The tests came back normal and he didn't mention it again.

Autumn arrived when she wanted him tall, though not too tall, just enough so that embracing him would bury her face in a chest that made her feel vulnerable. She spent long hours roaming over him with her naked body, her nipples rising and falling as if sketching out his flat stomach. She adored the extreme thinness with which she had dreamt him and she liked imagining how her bones left traces on his stomach. Sleeping was gradually transformed into an art of not being caught, and she liked using differently colored sheets to cover herself up and go away, far away, where intimacy offered a refuge where she could give voice to her fantasies.

Once, the vertical rain over the darkening city seduced her, and the window widened for her until she could imagine the countryside and wet horses in the distance. Winter kept her drowsy and rain splintered the landscapes. It was then that she gave him a face, and she thought with a shudder that from that moment on, she was being unfaithful. She brushed aside that idea because he didn't exist, he was only multiple pieces of many somebodies, fragments of attraction that made her guilty of nothing but her dreams. She smiled, relieved and anxious, and she desired him with a green horizontal gaze, thick dark eyebrows, and she felt safe, because she understood that he was far away, on the other side of the threshold, where it was possible to invent his salty skin to lick bit by bit., unhurriedly, until taking it, making it hers, reshaping it.

Ismael began to monitor her sleep, to see the thin dark-haired man smiling in her slightly open eyes. He knew she was going toward him, that he was waiting for her...but then she closed the tunnel of her eyelids all the way and left him on the other side, defenseless, aching, and laughing at himself, while she, far-away and other, tossed in the sheets and smiled.

"Why did you take so long?" he said, tall and enigmatic, just as she dreamt him.

"It was hard to fall asleep," she responded, hugging the body that smelled of wood and silence.

She knew that on his side everything was her own, that he would love her, aching and torn, his soul full of horses. On the other side remained pressing tasks, guilt, schedules.

Morning surprised them as she wanted it to, their skin intertwined, and he said, "Don't go yet," and he began kissing her, looking for answers in her nipples, questions in her buttocks, and she was dressing and walking toward the door of the cabin and he was following her, all grinning and boyish, and he was throwing her on the grass and he was loving her with a delightful penetration, where the sea gulls of time exploded in their fingers, and orgasm came with all the sky in her eyes and she grabbed onto a blade of grass so that she wouldn't feel as if she were dying, in the midst of the commotion of a bird flying overhead and the hoarse, deep laugh that flowed free, full, vibrant.

Ismael's hand had broken through the threshold and he was saying, "You seem different this morning."

"It's just that I dreamt about sea gulls."

Ismael watched her. He waited until she fell asleep and then tried to see through the intermingled space and her drowsy eyes to where they were making love, toward where she was looking. The cabin, the lake, and the sea, those were her refuges, the islands anchoring the dreams that left him injured, defenseless. Ismael discovered small objects that she brought back from the threshold and left around, forgotten: some grains of sand, weeds, a small paper boat, the remains of winter in the middle of summer, or the blades of turf tangled through her hair when she awoke. He had grown accustomed to inspecting the sheets, painfully searching for the traces, humiliated by the mist he didn't know how to fight, hiding the proof of her faraway dreams.

She slept, reared up or transparent, spending almost all of her time on the other side of the threshold. In the house, dust accumulated under the furniture and dirty plates spilled their contents around different spots in the kitchen.

The rain made her close her eyes again. "Come here," she had heard in the distance. He began nipping her, licking her, bending her, making her submit. She wanted to dream about sea gulls again, but each bite hurled her toward strange images, a mouth crying out in the darkness, a half-smile slightly parted by a cigarette, a man's shoes on the grass...his tongue and teeth clawing her nipples launched her directly toward an angry sea and the urgency of her desiring skin, toward a flaming inferno that dried out her mouth and blurred her own voyeur's silhouette spying on the game...the hand and the green gaze crawled over her skin and she opened her thighs calling him, with an ancestral scent that she didn't even recognize in herself, and the cabin became a fissure in the rock that was scraping her shoulder and the sea was there, bellowing, licking the calves that she raised to keep astride the vertical man who seemed to be trying to topple with its waves, and the foam roaring over her buttocks and her legs crossed over the back into which she dug her nails trying to mark, to leave a trace, and the man attacked her until her eyes clouded, leaving a small thread in the juncture of her lips...

This time, she wouldn't be able to hide her scarred back, the teethmarks on her hips. Ismael stopped smiling, but he didn't ask questions. He was afraid he wouldn't be able to stand the answers. There was no one to blame.

Bit by bit, she became thinner, and by then she didn't even attempt the parody of getting out if bed. It was useless for Ismael to raise her head to make her open her eyes and swallow a couple of spoonfuls of soup. She was over there, in delirium, offering fingers and possessions, "because I exist in you, it's my flesh that's heating you up, come on, lick me, let your green eyes glide over the water...." Fever arrived slowly one day, when the sheet became damp, leaving the trace of two sweats. Her bony, translucent fingers barely rose to gesture for a little water. The fever gradually impregnated her hands, her forehead, and began taking her dreams far away.

"Ismael," she called out in the darkness, "I can't dream, help me."

Ismael feared the anguish that hoarsened her voice. But later, a long while afterwards, he smiled and quit giving her the medicine.

In her delirium, she was asking him to help her remember, to reconstruct the lake and his eyes, and how I made his chest, Ismael, the size of his hands grasping my hips to push inside of me, help me Ismael, this afternoon there would be kites and laughter and our skins would call each other by name up there, Ismael, up there, where guilt has no place and no bird will ever go astray...

But Ismael only put water to her lips and smiled.

"Everything will be alright, I promise you, everything will be fine again."

She struggled desperately, trying to grasp his hands, his hair, something that would take her back over the threshold, while fever was erasing the contours of the cabin, the man's smile, the coarse hands that scratched as they caressed, the scents of woods and silence.

Help me Ismael.

Everything will be fine.

She was crying, while in the distance, the anguished voice faded as it called, "Sleep, dream me again," but it was no longer a voice, it was the memory of having heard some voice and the horror and emptiness and hips and shoulders and the green gaze diluting until it disappeared.

Afterwards, there was only a long silence and the end of winter, while her fever dropped and a taciturn paleness began to take hold of her body.

Sleep found her empty and too weak to dream him again.

Ismael opened the window to change the thin air of those months, and she felt that air take away with it the last vestiges of memory.

The window was only a wide frame, displaying buildings and streets and pavement.

She gave up the fight, it was no use. In her forlornness, the sheets became dull stains once again. It would be impossible for her to restore in them the scents of wood and silence.

Translated by Alice A. Nelson

# Subway

## Ana María del Río

"Good-bye," I say, not even bothered. She doesn't say anything. She opens and closes her mouth behind a car window framed in sky-blue. Her words are probably enclosed forever behind the glass, sketched like soap bubbles. Their expressions, more elegant, the ones in blue and gray, persist, full of courtesy nonetheless.

When a subway car stops it's like a moment of life is detained and everybody gets themselves ready, polishes themselves up and hides their small sins, rolling them inside their coats like teeny apples. But what sins could those of us who take the seven o'clock subway of fatigue have submerged in stupor and snarls?

"Well, good-bye," I tell her, and I don't move toward the stopped car. This time I'm not going to allow her to probe me, to push her head of brown hair—which wouldn't hurt a fly (who knows, now)—in between my eyes, gauging my well-being in the objects that I need, as if I didn't exist, smoker's toothpaste, that tobacco, so expensive, that...

All the conversations we've had over these twenty years (and I've realized it, furious, in a second) have revolved around me, as if around a white flag, a nameless island, where have you been, how'd it go, simple cover-ups for your secret eyes.

I know nothing about you. Suddenly, it strikes me that I've seen your vague round form, in your shell of a sweater and a Scottish kilt, on the street, on the subway, as if they were all women who were more or less comfortable or not, smiling-tired who go floating around the boulevards, letting themselves be carried along by the group, the sales, the remnants.

And I, all those years, speaking pompously about myself, and even giving details: I have an aching back, right over the third vertebra, mine is not a normal lumbago And I, like an idiot, believing that we were a couple, that you came undone when I went out (or better, that you were afraid), that you could never read my books; it was magazines for you and, like an idiot, believing that your children were dammed up inside you, little balls of wool, first teeth; like an imbecile I have believed, my high collar high for so many years, that I was your solution, especially when you were much younger, with your waistline and your minuscule yes-es, your pained looks, and I mounted my steed and right away defeated that doctor who tried to seduce you between operations in your aunt's clinic. At least she appreciated what I was worth and always looked at me like your savior (and at times like your father, I believe). She used to throw me huge smiles for not letting the scandal spread around that teeny town and for taking you without asking so many questions and more than anything else for being interested in the clinic (she left me her living room set exclusively for that reason, I think). More than anything, that time when your cousin, the blonde one, let everybody know about her secret fears that a pregnancy would result from the surprised kiss between you and that doctor, the married one (it seems that the state of matrimony granted him an extraordinary state of fertility). It was all a scandal that threw itself against cotton armor, and I, who didn't understand much about Latino dramas, saw clearly that your aunt's clinic was the most famous in town and you, the most enchanting of the nurses. I got you out of there, legally of course, and once you married me, you didn't go back to work, you had children.

If anyone ever made you sigh, it must have been that doctor, the married one, because with me, no sighs, nor did you complain. You never said no, really. Your wide consenting mouth with its upturned corners, your eventually round body agreed to everything.

If I had only known... A violet shame warms me.

Quiet on the orange bench in the subway station, with its cold walls spilled into millions of brilliant chips, I keep myself from moving.

Actually, I was at one time, perhaps the fifteen days before our wedding, your true salvation, goodness personified. At least that's what your aunt's smiles, in the midst of reverential teas, made clear.

And it was really a surprise that the metallic blue one followed by the grey one should approach us, like any couple among those that nod off on the subway trip home on a weekday with our arms behind one another, that they should approach, should signal with their chins to the ones at the other end, should grab you not at all softly by the shoulders, appropriate your arm, open your wallet and showing up in it the bill, the hundred denomination bill, those of the last regime, the prohibited ones, the unlucky ones, one of those, the rebels' password. The uniform took the bill with a handkerchief and then took out a piece of paper and confronted you with the composite drawing and it was you, eye for eye, tooth for tooth. The blue arm still had the remnants of high school about him and said, ma'am, I have a duty. I, outside the car, with all the others, looking through the window, neither defender nor macho, nothing like what's the meaning of all this, simply looking like a fish through the glass with my mouth open and closing, because all beginnings are unknowns, there won't be enough air, and you aren't part of my rib or my lumbago but somebody as distant as an assassin in the newspaper. I stand there looking at the composite drawing.

And why did you have the hundred denomination bill, you who clean out your wallet every two weeks, just like your aunt taught you and you who don't even listen to the news.

I droop on the bench holding my chin between my rage and my hands, diving among all the memories for who could have been the coward who put that in your purse and then the ire that he would have put it there, what was the coward doing in your purse, with what right, that was really unbearable, so I was happy to see you, to just imagine you, hidden behind the door at home, hiding the surreptitious bill in your heart, like a treasure, secretly making phone calls, living with a mask of fear and inexorable movement, walking tiptoe through the house and a whole series of unimaginable acts for you, ample and serene.

You stood there, looking at me through the glass. You helped take all the infinite things out of your purse: blusher that had never been used (never been used?), multicolored kerchiefs, nail polish remover, napkins, but I was watching you carefully and when they got to the envelope with the eclair-colored fastener you blushed. They opened it and they looked at you, you blushed and I felt like I was alone on the subway and that everybody was my enemy and your friend. The whispers wound between heads. Now not even your sweet smell will enter my eyes, no one will hear your little words.

You open and close your mouth. Pink palms with threads of sweat in the lifelines that trace your pink life, your silenced words saying how could I know, making memory out of the forgotten frown, your hand, your oh-so-small hand, loaded with ten short fingers without seductive fingernails, which take my wrinkled fingers like a little girl, that beckon to me through the glass door, as if to say come save you. On some afternoons, you seemed infinite to me like the earth, bowed like the earth, soft like the dust, predictable like the dawn... You were the perfect mixture, I used to say. Just one winter with me was enough to make you suddenly grow up and devote yourself to putting cutlery and sheets in order and providing tea-time with the inexorable cookies.

I'm not going to go. At the end of the station's frozen grave looms an orange bench. I will sit on it and I won't move until everything has passed. The one and only reason why we separated were the glass doors: in one blow, the knives of air separated us.

I sit down. I have already been completely investigated and it was like the examination of a sock, inside and out. In fifteen minutes they read me all of her and she dragged herself, colorless, through the yellow pages of the report...

"A peaceful man, eh?" the one in grey said.

"How did you find out about the bill," they say.

"I didn't know about it," I respond. Her file is under mine and it's much thicker.

"You're going to have to wait," says the secretary, looking at his machine and writing without turning around.

"I'm not in any hurry," I say, and then I get scared because it's true.

"I'm sorry to have to tell you," the grey one says, looking toward the window from which the stopped car can be seen.

Then I get up. I go up to the desk and I look at the grey one and I try to find his eyes.

"Is it true?," I ask him.

"When did you find out about the bill?," he returns the question.

And since I don't answer, he goes on. "This is serious. She meets the description," he says at me looking above something. "Under arrest, for now. You will be able to be in touch with her."

"I don't want to," I say and I light a cigarette.

The secretary stops his machine.

"What did you say?" with his finger in the air.

"That I don't want to see her again," the old man says and his wooden shoulders droop and creak.

"But you can see her, if you want," the grey one says.

"We don't object to the presence of the spouse, on the contrary..."
Then the old man looks at his shoes and says, "She's not my spouse."

"Companion?" the secretary's thin voice waits, finger in the air.

The old man nods and stoops a little more.

"If she's guilty, take her," he says.

All of him creaks as he gets up and, with his face of a spouse who can't take it, he makes it to the doorway.

The gray one lets him go. In the doorway, the old man stops and turns halfway around. He straightens himself up like a soldier and for a moment his somewhat damp coat seems to float above the office.

"Do your duty," he says and leaves slowly, dragging his feet and the knots of his hands that can no longer hold the cigarette. The secretary shrugs his shoulders and rips the page out of the typewritter.

Translated by Elizabeth L. Rhodes

# The Fish Tank
## Alejandra Farias

The bathroom is a lousy place to spend the night, but it's the only place I can go to escape the sound of Elena's moaning. The floor is freezing, and the tiles feel as cold as death against my back. The toilet bowl is convenient, though, somewhere to flick the ashes of my non-stop cigarettes. Elena continues to shriek, headed for her fifth orgasm of the night. And tomorrow morning, as she puts the kettle on for breakfast, she'll casually say, "What a night. I barely slept a wink."

I'll smile, as if congratulating her, still able to feel the frozen tiles against my back. The dawn that appeared from behind the water tank, then crashed into the mirror. The sickening fact that I pay half the rent for this place.

And that stupid song they play as background music. I've lost track of how many times they've flipped the cassette—"close your eyes"—and rocked the damn mattress with the force of the earthquake she is, and he's dressing her ceremoniously, getting ready to summon the police. Maybe my final revenge will be to put on her tombstone a delicate marble plaque etched with her last words: "Go deeper, my love." Someone's snoring. It's him. How could I not recognize his snore, its used to be the only thing that could put me to sleep. Even now I try to recreate it with the static of a badly-tuned radio or the snowy buzz of the television test pattern late at night.

"Well, honey, what's wrong with the boy? Either you care about him, or mommy takes over, because her maternal instinct is so strong, she can't stand to see men unhappy." Like an idiot, I thought she was joking. I thought she talked to him so much because she wanted us to be happy together. It's not the first time this has happened to me. Back in school a girlfriend of mine used to answer the love letters that I'd write to the best looking boy in our grade, while she'd make out with him on the park bench every afternoon after class.

I keep losing out because I have this stupid illusion of being understood without having to explain or reach out. I want to simply meet someone on the street, in an elevator, or in this stinking, narrow bathroom that she never cleans when it's her turn because she doesn't want to ruin her fingernails. The nails that I suppose are at this very moment softly buried in his warm skin. The skin that entertained me every night as I smelled it inch by inch in an effort to memorize its odor. Nights of smoke, love, and terrible fights about why Cortazar put Moreira in the second half, or about real time in "La noche boca arriba." I bet they haven't spoken more than twenty words to each other. She's incapable of reading anything other than the weekly ladies' section of the newspaper. Part of her game plan was to borrow a few of my books to leave on her night table when she knew I'd be getting home late.

Only now do I realize the source of the drip that creates a huge puddle every morning. It would make sense to call the plumber, or better yet, to wait until the hole is so large that it will spew enough water to drown them both. I'd be the lucky one to make the big discovery. Both bodies nude and swollen, almost purple, floating among the furniture and the books, covering their bulging and about-to-burst eyes. Maybe I could turn on the shower, get under the water and rinse off the stinking lechery that fouls the air. I'd get dressed and take a walk through the streets where only the pigeons are up. By then they'd be aware of my presence. They'd go back to their moans, and the mattress would once again go on the attack, deafening me until I fell, insane, to the ground, vomiting all the cockroaches of the world in one uncontainable and humiliating retch. It's better this way. That they not be aware of my presence, although I feel my every movement is coldly calculated, thought out, and graceful. The infallible predictions of that witch who gives me sappy greeting cards on my birthday—For a very special person who makes the world a warmer and friendlier place—and at Easter—May the peace, love and joy of the holiday remain in your heart, bringing you a year of happiness, fulfillment, and success, Elena.

The first minibus stops at the corner and then continues down the road with the same kind of effort. It probably has its lights on, and a student is perhaps getting ready to climb aboard at the next stop. He'll have to hide his college I.D. in his pocket, hail the bus at the last minute, get on, then remove the covering from the card right under the driver's nose. With this slightest of gestures he becomes cromagnon man, and throws the measly change into the box protected by the Virgin of Carmen encased in a small glass tube. Then the ticket dances toward the floor. It will have to be retrieved from between the driver's deformed and split shoes so that he won't be able to resell it, torn into little pieces, then thrown at him as if he were a Homecoming Queen. Finally one gets off the bus some twenty blocks beyond the school, having fought the most ridiculous battle of the day.

The minibus added a new movement to this macabre symphony. If I stay still I can perceive every movement that occurs in this space; the water that drips at intervals from the shower, the sink faucet, the movement of my diaphragm, rising and falling as I breathe in and out, the rhythmic contraction of my heart, the pilot light of the water heater, the movement of their bodies which from my hiding place I intuit to be rocking slowly, liltingly, my eyelashes that move and therefore allow me to perceive the light that is streaming, more strongly now, through the window, the footsteps of the man who lives above us, a cashier in a bakery, the raspy breathing of the small, dying fish that someone has taken out of the water.

She came to wake me at about noon. She had put on her white terry cloth robe. The one she always wears when she has an overnight guest. Several times I surprised her in front of the hallway mirror trying out different neckline possibilities. I watched her from my bedroom, and tried to figure out what she was thinking each time she spun around on tiptoe. She took my face in her small hands and kissed my forehead, and said, "Baby had another depressing night." I tried to smile, but sleeping in such cramped quarters had given me a stiff neck, which combined with the night chill, kept me in bed all day.

More lovingly than ever she took me to my bed, and when we passed her room I stopped to see if he was still there. She laughed and said that he had left at the crack of dawn, and that he had asked her to say hi to me. While Elena whistled, and clattered the few pieces of crockery we had left in the kitchen, I tried to figure out why he had sent his regards. Maybe it was another way of laughing at me, or some kind of coded message, like the ones we used to send each other whenever we simply couldn't stand being apart any longer.

Elena arrived an hour later with something that looked like breakfast. Except that the eggs were raw, the milk full of curds, and the toast utterly burnt. She sat on the floor and wolfed it down, then took off her robe, laid down next to me and slept for the rest of the afternoon, as was her habit following an exhausting night of lovemaking.

I felt sleepy again, and laid down. Elena's hair was tickling my nose. I was bothered by her sweaty, hot skin each time it rubbed against me. He had been there, and traces of his smell were still in her hair. How would his hands cup those rounded shoulders? Surely he would have run his wet tongue along her white and well-shaped back.

I dreamed that Elena had become a fat old slug that was trying to swallow me. I escaped among the dense green hills of the fish tank, but it became harder and harder to breathe, until at last I woke up full of anxiety because my gills were drying up outside the water. I got up. It was dark outside, and pouring rain. Stupidly, I sat by the phone hoping someone would call me.

I'm here, alone, in the dark apartment. She's asleep in my bed now, and he's gone who knows where to forget who he is, to forget that last night he was repeatedly raped by an insatiable woman who wasn't even thinking of him. She was thinking of me, the way my eyes get sad whenever she mentions his name, or the thousands of poems she finds scattered throughout the living room, on the table, in the kitchen or on my bed. They all start with the same Chinese proverb: Suan-chu dreamed he was a butterfly, and when he awoke he didn't know whether he was a butterfly that had dreamed of being Suan-chu, or Suan-chu who had dreamed of being a butterfly.

It is cold, and a wet, injured pigeon takes shelter on the window sill. I watch her from the other side of the pane without having enough pity to let her in. She closes her eyes and lowers her head onto her wounded wing. Years ago I used to see them land on the ledges outside the classroom, and while the teacher insisted that we draw little lines straight down the page, I would watch them mate after flirting with each other for a long time.

The wind picks up and the rain smashes against the window. Thousands of rivers explode in my head, and become confused with the spurts of liquid that run down the gutter. It's my blood that flows from my veins in a crazy and unstoppable gush. Someone comes up the stairs singing, I feel uneasy, but I lie down on the rug again when the steps continue on to the next floor. Apparently, nobody's going to take Elena from me tonight.

The pump in the fish tank seems like a monster that breathes every once in a while.

On winter nights, when the rain danced on the roof, my mother would sit on my bed. On her lap she would hold an enormous story-book from which she would read if I would agree to go to sleep. There was a drawing, made up of many lines, all on top of each other, that depicted a young prince who had been transformed into a knight, and had to confront a terrible beast at dawn. In a very dark grotto, under a waterfall, he kept watch all night long over his weapons. I light a cigarette, and the smoke rises slowly, messily, reaching the lamp that hangs from the molding illuminated by the streetlight. The beast waited for the prince outside the cave, roaring every now and then. The water running through the gutter sounds like a bubbling brook. Elena moves in my bed, breathing quickly, almost a cry. The serpent must be moving, marking my territory. Her hands will hide under the pillow, and her hair will fall upon her chest.

Now I shouldn't sleep.

On the nights he stayed with me, Elena would pace back and forth until I'd get up. It was almost dawn, and I'd leave the room to have a cigarette or, for no reason at all, to simply chat with her in the hall-way. I fear her sadness. It's as if an enormous building could be knocked over by a slight breeze. Then I have to touch her, put her head on my belly, and stroke her hair until she falls asleep crying, sobbing. It's cold and there's a real threat that I could run out of cigarettes. Someone's singing in the apartment above us.

He often used to make up songs with the last words of my sentences. He'd sit at my window and compose lyrics that he could never finish. He had begun to spin in that apathy of smoke and silence.

She's in my bed and I can't sleep.

Maybe the sun will come up tomorrow and erase all the puddles from the sidewalks, and with them, the pending battle, and these still hands will no longer be knives.

I could call him on the phone and wait several fear-stained seconds for his voice to come through the receiver in the usual cheery way he answers all my calls.

One must be alone to watch over the weapons.

Elena continues to turn in my bed. I suppose she's dreaming of the snake. It follows her up the stairs, and just outside our door it wraps her in its cold, hard skin. It squeezes her until she howls desperately, profoundly. I get up, and with unusual speed, I'm at the foot of the bed. Ready to jump on her and free her from all her monsters which are mine as well. I pause at the edge of the bed, as if it were a giant, inevitable cliff. I become paralyzed on the edge, repressing the impulse that could save us, or make us fall into an illusion even more macabre than the one that has us spinning in circles. Always one inside the other. Her outline and mine are so blurred that the pain hangs between our breaths. The moment has not yet arrived. I retreat slowly towards the window. The city is traced beyond the window pane, and the light that keeps watch on the hill continues to blink despite the torrential rain. It threatens to either sleep like Elena, or to stay awake forever, like me.

Elena is naked on the bed. I pick up the quilt and cover her cold body. Suddenly I remember when we used to sit on the steps and laugh after insulting each other like crazy because once again she had left the keys on top of the refrigerator. We'd flip a coin, and the loser would have to plead with the woman next door, then climb over her balcony to ours, a dangerous and regular adventure. Elena always forgets everything, especially to pay the water bill, and when we least expect it, the apartment turns into the Sahara Desert. She very solicitously takes the big tin cans to get water from the tap at the front door of the building. I do my best to wipe the soap from my body with a towel, but the shampoo remains hard and sticky on my head.

When he was around things were different because he'd go down to the concierge to get the key needed to restore the water. Without any problem we'd be back to our comfortable routine of turning on the faucets and seeing the rush of transparent liquid. But she, with the same attitude, would lug the heavy cans upstairs, then empty them into the dishwasher without saying a word. That was my cue to leave as quickly as possible. I'd make up any excuse to escape the temper tantrum that would inevitably take place, the kicking of the furniture and whatever else got in her way. I'd grab my survey file and go do the blocks I'd been assigned. I'd ask housewives still in their robes what brand of toothpaste they used. What differences did they notice between brands. The taste, for example, was relevant, a clean feeling, or as they say, the taste of freshness. Though the color, consistency, and smell would also figure in the coveted selection. All morning long I'd stand in the beating sun with my pencil poised to check off a) Very good b) Satisfactory or c) Bad.

Whenever I had a good day, that is, whenever I came up with more than twenty women willing to answer the survey, I bought cakes at the corner store. As soon as Elena opened the door, even though she hadn't undone the chain, I'd thrust the package under her nose, and that was enough to make her jump with joy around the apartment. She'd make an effort to set the table properly, even going as far as to roll the napkins into little tubes and cinch them with the silver rings she inherited from her filthy rich grandmother. She would appear in her best dress, her hair pulled back and tied at the nape of her neck, while the tea and bread turned cold.

As we eat, she doesn't gesture wildly with her hands and never sits with her legs apart as she usually does. She passes the bread in its basket, and doesn't make me negotiate for the butter. She goes out of her way to chat about her work and to express interest in mine.

But it's not always so. Sometimes she is completely warped. Once in a while I'll get home and she won't open the door even though I can hear her cassette in the player, and I am careful to knock only every ten minutes so as not to upset her. When she lets me in, the place is a mess, as if there has been a battle, and the casualties are the smallest fish whose bodies are strewn all over the floor. Refusing to speak to me, as well as to anyone who might happen to phone, she lifts the receiver then lets it fall instantly back into place. She puts on enough water for only one cup of tea, and toasts a single slice of bread. She sits down to eat silently at the kitchen table. I know that on days like these I'll have to lock myself in my bedroom, emerging only when she starts sobbing for the usual at my door.

Again she removes the blanket from her shoulders, the shoulders I've always considered perfect. But I came to hate them each time I'd see them peeking at the edge of my bedroom door while he was there. They'd tell me that her entire body, in the nude, would be entering momentarily in search of the ash tray, the robe, the newspaper or the nail polish remover that never was in my room to begin with. Once Elena would leave, he and I would be very quiet, trying to understand her frame of mind, each in our own way. He interpreted her behavior as an invitation to stroke her soft skin. For me, it was just another clumsy attempt to paw me with affection. Nevertheless, after each of her nude entrances, we ended up making love in a strange and desperate way.

Elena is now sleeping peacefully. I can't help watching her. Her eyes have stopped moving back and forth under the lids that she has always covered with black shadow, ever since we went to see a ridiculously romantic movie about gypsies and bullfighters. The gypsy wore all kinds of tulle skirts that flew up around her neck whenever she twirled. Half the audience couldn't take their eyes off her tiny red panties. Except Elena, who studied the woman's make-up in order to replicate it later. Elena wouldn't stop dancing. We listened to Paco de Lucia for weeks on end, and I had to rearrange the furniture so that she would quit dancing on the table or any other platform available to be punished by her tap shoes. But I never did get her to stop putting roses between her teeth and then placing them at my feet. She'd do it even when we had company.

Things became a bit more normal in the apartment when Andres began to drop by. At least the dancing stopped, and the furniture was put back in place. Much of Elena's happiness faded with the Spanish music and the setting of the autumn sun. Instead she acquired a weird sort of maturity that staggered into the walls and corners of the apartment.

He would bring me baskets full of treats that she was unable to enjoy. She was like a child whose aunts had stopped watching just as she had begun to perform. Every now and then I'd catch her scrubbing the toilet bowl, mascara running down her face.

She had a complete fit when I asked to borrow her keys in order to have a copy made. That night she brought home two friends who, within no time at all, were running around naked trying to catch her. I put on my coat and went to sleep at Andres' place, and as punishment for my desertion, had to put up with the two little friends for the rest of the week.

The nights Andres worked the late shift he'd get up at one in the morning and leave after wolfing down a couple of sandwiches. I'd wait to hear Elena's footsteps in the hallway. Sometimes she'd take forever, and I'd see her hat pass slowly by, headed for the kitchen, then the bathroom. The signal had been given, and the game could begin.

She enjoyed slipping by my dark doorway wearing the hat which had belonged to my grandfather, brandishing the kitchen knife, and walking like Jack the Ripper. She was perfectly silent. She'd disappear for minutes that seemed like hours, then suddenly appear, her hair teased into a lion's mane, her hands transformed into claws, and circle my bed in the darkness. Her eyes had an unfamiliar gleam, her breathing was heavy. I pretended to be asleep. When she used the sheer curtains as a bridal veil, she seemed to me a self-absorbed widow in search of revenge. The return of a missing lover who had perished in a long ago and far away duel. After several hours of her strange and macabre games, she'd stand in the doorway and ask if I, too, had insomnia. Indifferent to my response, she'd lie down on the bed and begin to tell me stories about her childhood. She didn't even realize that she had been wearing costumes and stalking me in the dark.

It has stopped raining. I'm stuck to the armchair that faces the bed where Elena is still dreaming. If I could annihilate distances, or penetrate them in order to meet her, free of all these memories. They only serve to keep me from her true self. Perhaps if I could forget last night. I'd also have to forget all the other nights, an endless, painful series of nights. How could I forget her warm hug as we left the clinic, and her voice trying to take me beyond the pain that wracked my stomach and my consciousness as the blood gushed out in torrents. We got to the apartment, and with great tenderness she sat me down facing her fish tank in the living room. Quickly she put everything back in place, straightened the beds and whacked the dust with a broom. She put me to bed. She found a shrill station on the radio, then left, closing the door behind her. She returned with a bouquet of flowers which she put in a vase. Or that sunny day in spring when, after running crazily, wildly, I found her and some other friends in a basement. They had come from the plaza at the School of Engineering, which was teeming with bullets and beatings. Elena took my hand and told me not to be afraid, that it would soon be over, they would clearly have to let us go that night, it was all in a day's work, we'd get used to it. Once again she was right.

She can slip right through my defenses and sit in an unfamiliar place inside me, from where she either grants me the pleasure of her company or sabotages my peace of mind. I don't want to sleep.

I want to extract from her, by means of a complex exorcism, the answers I need in order to keep on living in this apartment, tonight, in this body.

Elena, if we started over and didn't allow this sinister grief, which we seem compelled to tear from one another, to overwhelm us. If we could forget the hidden labyrinths that lead to our minotaurs. If we followed the rules, and kept our distance, like normal people. Perhaps we could avoid the battle that will either destroy us tonight or give us new lives, restoring the solitude that was ours at birth, the solitude that we've managed to deceive all this time.

But at this point we've run out of excuses.

You and I are in this enormous fish tank that spins like a fiendish carousel. Both frightened fish staggering into the glass walls of the tank.

Are you dreaming right now about what I am plotting? So many times before you've prevented my escape because you were able to intuit it, then stop me with a perfect move. You, the eternal keeper of my children. The puppeteer.

The moment has arrived, this complicity is killing me, and the moss has become so thick that your old-friend smell is destroying me.

# Alejandra Farias

There isn't a single place in this humid apartment where I can hide to escape your thousands of tentacles. To come to terms with my own limitations without being under your thumb.

I walk toward the bed where you groan. Toss and turn. Call out.

My knife-hands cross through the only distance that we sacredly respect. They run down your stomach, they become tangled in your pubic hair, they pause on your breasts. I slowly put my naked weight on top of yours. Our breaths become one. Finally I am on top of you.

The first shafts of light enter through the window and get tangled in your hair and mine. Outside, on the streets, the bustle begins.

A memory pops into my head—it is of the first sunbeams illuminating the tips of the waves. We are not one of them, Elena, we are two. Despite the fact that I can understand all your winks, and you can always guess my next move.

I'm sorry, but I must destroy the fish tank that you wanted us to share. Not even all the humidity we are expelling could prevent it.

Your shoulders try to escape from my hands, you struggle, but even as you do, I sense that your shoulders are seeking my mouth. You move your neck from side to side, shivering, breathing heavily, as if to increase the speed of the waterfall into which this wave must crash. It has to break.

I capture the contours of your lips, I memorize the bridge of your nose, and I kiss your eyes. Perhaps someday I'll be able to walk alone through the puddles left by the rain, which now resumes.

This huge wave does a final summersault and falls with a crash on the becalmed sea. Silence takes hold of everything. Only a drop that falls intermittently to the floor and is drowned out by the sound of the air pump in the fish tank.

I could never by satisfied with just a memory of you.

Translated by Nancy Abraham Hall

# Not Without Her Glasses
## Carmen Basanez

The meddlesome old man threw the envelope on the desk. It was exactly when I was thinking about Nancy, the night we had just spent together, and the surprising thing I discovered. She couldn't make love without her glasses. That's what she told me.

That first time she climbed into bed naked and wearing her glasses struck me as very strange. I realize that it inhibited me, and to top it all off, after so many beers I was a failure, a complete failure.

The second time she was more considerate and I was more virile. Smothering her in kisses, I threw her glasses to the floor. It was she who couldn't function. I remember it well, for later we both laughed about our mutual mishaps and became close fricnds.

On that same day Gacitua decided to send to a certain Federico Palacios the envelope that he had been holding on to for a long time. It wasn't just to find out about his arrangements with Nancy; it was a matter of serious problems between subordinate and boss—arriving late to work, telling lies and making excuses and the ironic tone he used to greet him—"Good morning Mr. Gacitua, pretty day, isn't it?" or "Hello there, Mr. Gacitua, how is your mother this morning?" And then with innocence dancing on his face, he would put on this pretense of being a man devoted to his job, typing out bills and looking out of the corner of his eye at the lovely curve of Miss Nancy's fanny when the boss had her take down some files so that he, too, could enioy that very same fanny. Being the owner of the firm and all, he had more right than the illustrious Palacios.

On the other hand, Gacitua was sixty years old, a bachelor, the only son of a nearly blind mother who waited for him at home. Working full time, he had no time for love, and suddenly he was sixty and had no one to share his life with. Until now—when Nancy makes his lower belly grow taut and he pretends he has a stomach ache and keeps his legs together while the others wink at each other behind his back and Federico, the cynic, begins the gossip. He noticed it on the occasion of the department's anniversary. A few too many drinks made him look at Nancy too much, and from that point on everyone openly joked about it. That's how the persecution began. Gacitua personally revised Federico Palacios' time card and kept an eye on his movements more than on his own, to the point that he forgot several times to zip up his fly when he had gone into the restroom to spy on him. Nancy was the first to notice it; he had called her in to dictate a letter.

She arrived towering above him in her high heels and sat down with her note pad; he came out from behind his desk because it made him very nervous having her so near. He walked about dictating. His long strides gave him a better perspective af her plump neck bent over her paper and allowed him to take in everything including the overpowering perfume she used behind her ears; it made him a little dizzy. He finished the first paragraph in no time, and it was at that moment that he saw that her face was red with embarrassment, as though she wanted to say something. "Miss Nancy, you want to interrupt me and you're succeeding; please continue the letter."

But she kept looking at his fly until he did too. Sticking out of the opening was a small white, unpretentious lump. He closed it with an unfortunately quick movement, so unfortunate that the zipper got stuck, pinching the cloth and something else, too. He doubled up in pain, crying aloud; she was doubled up too, but from laughing so hard; fortunately she had the wisdom to get out of his office as quick- she could. At that moment he decided that Federico Palacios to blame for this humiliation and he would get what was coming im.

he old man likes Nancy. I put myself in his place and considering at had been caught in the zipper, I was sure it hurt to go to the bathroom; I was sure you slept with your legs open just as virgins do while hoping for their dreams to come true. Old man, I want to tell you about Nancy, how she likes to make love with her glasses on, the same ones she uses to enter records and write your letters; she even spoke to me about the letter you have for me, the one you've left on my desk. I know what it's about; I'm ahead of you even in that. I can manage because if I talk to you about her and I tell you that you can have all the Nancys in the office, you'll reconsider; better still if I invite you for a drink after work, you'll have more time to think about what it costs to provide for a family. Certainly, your heart will soften and you'll reconsider my firing. The next day, old man, I'll hand Nancy over to you on a silver platter so you can again pretend that she doesn't interest you and you can begin the little game that fills your life just as the noodles that she prepares twice a week with white sauce and grated cheese fills mine.

That Federio Palacios doesn't make such a bad impression on me. I've had a couple of weeks to reconsider things; he's not late any more, and Miss Nancy is safe when she works in the files. Best of all, she has really changed; now she has the courage to tell me when I forget to close my fly; there's a new form of communication between us; everything is more intimate and pleasant for me, I can even calmly zip up my fly in front of her and not pinch anything.

Federico Palacios is a good man after all; he's been in the section for several years and besides...

I can see it in your face, Gacitúa! You're going to forget about firing me and start all over. I confess that I'm really relieved; after all it's not easy out there.

The three of us again begin our game, Gacitúa, you dreaming about Nancy, Nancy remembering your forgetfulness and I asking about your dear mother. Amusing, isn't it. Satisfied, you will answer, leaning back in your chair so you can scratch your stomach and thinking how well you did leaving me there and changing the office files; while I, dear Gacitúa, think that in reality you've done well, because now I don't see Nancy over and over again in the department. Thus I enjoy her more when she waits for me, but not without her glasses—the same ones (how I'd like to tell you, old man) she wears when she writes your letters.

Translated by Janet Spinas Cunningham

# A Requiem for Hands
## Alejandra Basoalto

He was large, pale and had warm hands. And she loved him. She loved him for nearly a decade of floods in streets and highways, an earthquake in the metropolitan area, and several sweltering summers during which she rarely ventured from her home before seven in the evening, that is, if she didn't have a meeting with him. (Here the narrator reserves the right to omit details about the origin and type of relationship which united them in order not to hurt the feelings of his wife and her husband.)

During the '86 flood while they were wrapped up and carried away in their bubble of sentiments and silences, the phone rang incessantly but he did not answer, finally the noise stopped. Nevertheless, when the ringing violently began again in the midst of thunderclaps, he had no choice but to answer it It was his wife alarmed by the television news reports showing blocks of inundated streets, downed trees, and cars stalled in the rising water.

His answer, rather brusque, indicated to her that he was transgressing norms and found himself in the midst of a strictly family situation. But he wasn't a man of submission and with no great explanations at all he immersed himself again into the bubble, iridescent in the soft lamplight.

His hands were warm. Delicate. She liked to hold them in the midst of the desolation, when all outside was precarious, when the world's voices could no longer shelter her. Then she would hold onto those hands as if to an anchor, not noticing the perspiration that was spreading over them in proportion to the intensifying throbs of their hearts. She was sure he had entered into the game in spite of his silence.

And she loved him with the obstinacy of an unsatisfied woman. For years she had hoped he would take her in his arms and kiss her. For years she had dreamed of his golden member in her mouth, on her legs, in the feverish scorpion of her belly. But he kept his distance. Only his eyes passed over her in a burning flame that left her trembling.

She was a good letter writer. On wide, white paper she would write long missives, always typed and with no signature. He would read them attentively and try to hide any indication of his reaction; but she would spy on him, interpreting any flutter of his eyelashes, any brief movement of his hand, or any increased rate in his respiration.

The tenor of the letters was, with some variation, basically the same (but the narrator cannot reveal it). Then they held long conversations with regard to the matter, and she felt he would slide away from her territory as from the recently fallen snow.

And so it went. Someone whispered to her that that he didn't like women and perhaps had unrealized homosexual tendencies. That idea had also crossed her mind each time she heard his quiet, soft voice and observed his gentle gestures, with no brusqueness to them at all. Later, she rejected the thought with the certainty that there are men like that, delicate in their tendernesss, men of air, transparent in their vital steadfastness.

She was fire, however. Violent and direct like Sagittarius' arrow and she decided one day she would go away forever. Forever lasted a month in which she found herself immersed in feminist organizations, never ending meetings, and structuralist discussions that bored into her brain but left her heart intact in its longing. And she went back to him. He welcomed her with the same old smile, as if that absurd interval had never occurred.

And so the months passed, months in which she suffered periods of infinite thinness, and periods in which, if it hadn't been for his very words, his precise silences, and his lighthouse hands which reached out to her, she would have succumbed. Both of them dove into the perfect circle of emotions without slipping, as if knowing the contact of their hands gave them the roundness necessary to keep on living.

Suddenly, one afternoon, her hands grew cold. The doctors said it was a hormonal disorder, her circulation, a weight loss... (here the narrator does not have access to the private medical files and I cannot give the exact details of the origins of her illness nor its later progression or treatment).

The fact is that she began to change. She told him she needed time to be alone, that other activities required her attention for several months, and she began to extend the time between their meetings. Apparently he wasn't offended by this, but with the passage of weeks he could no longer stand it. One afternoon in April 1989 and contrary to his established patterns, he called her to a non-agreed upon meeting. She almost couldn't go, but the force of the custom of complying with one's obligations (*nota bene:* she took it as an obligation) made her delay another meeting almost as inevitable as it was mysterious (the narrator doesn't consider it necessary to provide details of these new activites) and she arrived punctually at seven.

He summoned her to this most unusual encounter by giving some quick as well as absurd reasons: He said he had become confused, that he wasn't sure of the agreed upon date, that..., but she didn't believe him for a second; he never left things to chance. He was a living, breathing watch with his timing perfectly controlled.

The words slipped by with strange shades of meaning. He watched her, hoping for some special gleam in her eyes. A tear perhaps. But nothing. She had dry eyes and a smile with which she controlled the situation. Then came the ritual of the hands. His hands could not warm the skin grown thin over the frozen bones of her fingers. She felt that her hands would never again be corrupted by any heat whatsoever. They were condemned to eternal ice.

And almost sadly, but with a daring voice, which surprised even her, she let the definitive words escape. She decided she would not come back.

Translated by Martha Manier

# Encounter on the Margins
## Lucía Guerra

(A conversation with Juana Manuela Gorriti,
Argentinian writer born in 1818.)

By sheer chance I came upon your name in a lengthy and tedious
history of Argentinian literature. I began looking for your work only
because you are a woman—a prejudice of mine, I admit. Hidden away
among hundreds of volumes published by the intellectual men of
your country, I discover your books: a few short stories, a succinct
memoir, and two novels which scarcely fit into the genre: they number ninety-six and one-hundred-and-four pages, respectively. In keeping with our encounter in the territory of the unpredictable, I find (in
a book on Peruvian literature!) the only portrait of you in print. Your
face resembles that of a thin and morally-outraged old aunt, the kind
who lowers her eyes before uttering a reprimand. And although I love
the tango about blonde Mireya, I dislike your blue eyes and fair complexion—those Anglo-Saxon features which so remind me of the old
aristocracy and its contempt for common people. Then suddenly,
three provocative new pieces emerge from the puzzle of your life:
your scandalous cigarettes, your lovers, and your illegitimate children.
Thus you lead me across the threshold of questions not yet asked in
the critical disquisitions men have composed about literary creation.
Were your cigarettes and your illicit love affairs part of the same
audacity that led you to become a writer? Other women authors

(Gertrudis, Mercedes, and María Luisa) nod affirmatively from their tangle of lovers and letters inscribed in the web of their writing, lasting testimony to their passion and frustration in love. Is, in fact, writing a subversive impulse for women, as opposed to what men rather vaingloriously define as craftsmanship?

But this fertile flow of information takes an abrupt new turn, a darker journey, the course unclear, obscure, the images dim as fog in a forest. An American critic, adopting the tone of a righteous preacher before the pulpit of absolute truth, defines your texts as failed attempts to mirror reality. Another, from your homeland, comments scathingly that you used to wear trousers and dedicated much of your time to practicing an oriental religion. Juana Manuela, you have been assigned a short paragraph in the prolific, Amazonian realm of critical discourses written by men. Indeed, you are Juana María for the absent-minded scholar who copied your name from an old book in a probably dark and possibly cold library. Like a handful of worn-out chords, the same data about your life rings wearily throughout the books I consult: the date of your birth, the complete names of your parents, you trip to Bolivia to escape the persecution of Facundo Quiroga and his barbaric henchmen, the assassination of your husband, the president of Bolivia, who was shot in the doorway of his palace by a general making a prearranged social call, and always, for some inexplicable reason, your embrace of Juana Manso on her deathbed.

On the rebound from this wall of repetitive information, this echoing chain of masculine mimicry, I stumble across a fictionalized biography of your life. Like a captive staked to the sand in the Sahara, I am forced to ingest the dry and unpotable contents of four-hundred-and-eight pages of pure unadulterated drivel.

Left with no other alternatives for my preliminary research, I decide to cross the bridge that you built with black ink and your goosefeather pen. So I begin reading you, using a letter opener to separate the still-uncut pages of one of your novels. Published in 1885, it had sailed along the entire coast of South America to the United States, and in more than a century, no one had read it. I confess to disappointment with your plots, which are typical of those cheap, sentimental novels from the nineteenth century: tears from a broken heart, women who faint in the throes of love, etc. I turn my back on you with contempt and stomp across the planking on your bridge, deciding that you are, unfortunately, a waste of time.

But in this I am mistaken.

Weeks later, while driving on a highway in California, my radio picks up a primitive rhythm and I listen to a teenage singer inflamed by eroticism who sings to a girl with wounded thighs. He wants to lick her blood-stained skin, tongue her bruises. Oddly, she reminds me of one of your characters: that anguished bride, still wearing a bloody white veil, who searches among the battlefield dead for her betrothed. I slow down; cars continually pass me, honking. I look at license plates and see instead a choir of women singing a *De Profundis,* their moans deafening the ears of Juan Manuel de Rosas, the dictator who devastated your country. I also see a pilgrimage of shawled women collecting lillies-of-the-valley for the graves of husbands and sons killed in the civil war. Brides dressed in black appear before my eyes, their breasts torn by terrible knife wounds. And suddenly it comes to me that in your work, behind the mask and subterfuge of love stories which were not offensive to your countrymen with their long beards and curly mustaches, you firmly denounced the sinister tide of historical events created by masculine voiolence.

So once more I traverse the bridge you built so long ago, laboring under the flickering light of a candle. And now I explore the foliage of your love stories and discover the you concealed in the deceptive net of feminine sentimentalism. Your true self lies at the bottom of a well of blood, surrounded by damned archangels with the faces of killers and souls hard as rock. I encounter not only you but myself as well, because we share the horrendous experience of dictatorship—that monstrous beast forever stalking our continent. In your time, Rosas hired retarded dwarfs to perform somersaults for his amusement, while Pinochet arrested clowns for transgressive behavior. You saw your people surrounded by the *mazorquero gauchos,* who spied in every corner with their eyes of steel; over one hundred years later, I saw soldiers in brown berets torturing the people of my country, transporting them along the streets in open trucks, their hands tied behind them, their heads covered by burlap sacks. *Mazorca* from *más horca,* meaning more hanging, more rifles, more victims, more... An evil *coyuyo* rises Phoenix-like from the ashes of disaster for each generation, announcing its willingness to serve in a strident call that arises from hell and echoes across the Andes.

I return to the present, leaving behind the well of blood where I encountered you. In a here which is also a there—past and present braided together by injustice—it is my duty to revive your memory, to rescue you from the blank pages of forgetfulness. I shall exhume the virtues of your writing by weaving a new design into the canonized tapestry of literature—Sarmiento, Alberdi, Echeverría, Mármol—moving these hallowed legends to the fringes of fame and making space for you to occupy your rightful place. Your sad *pacui* melody, a sparrow's lament so often silenced by the masculine cries of eagles, now soars in a song that speaks for all the women in our continent, always in the margins of all battles. Sitting on your patio, which is also my patio, you knew that men are the only ones who rattle their sabers, mouthing words to fit their ideas in an incessant and never-changing, one-note samba called Man. You knew that they would transform you into a mute, a marionette in the Argentinian style, at your hearth in Salta, the city of your birth, or in any marriage bed in any bedroom in the world. Amidst cigarettes and lovers, I embroider you in black, red, and white. I do not accept your God and His imminent compassion. I love your bride who reappears as a ghost and takes vengeance on the evil colonel by throwing him off a precipice. I'd have tossed him off myself. I bow to you, my sister, in homage.

Translated by Richard Cunningham and Lucía Guerra

# Up to the Clouds

# The Boy Who Took Off in a Tree
## Jacqueline Balcells

Mrs. Pérez was watering the orchard when someone knocked at the door of her house. At that same moment, she noticed that a new orange tree had appeared among the other trees. The Pérez's orchard was very small, and she was sure the tree hadn't been there before. At a glance it appeared to be like all the other orange trees, *but*...there was something strange about it: her farmer's eye, familiar with every type of plant, told her that something was wrong. Wouldn't she have seen it before? Why did the tree's scant leaves have a rare, metallic sheen?

Her children interrupted her thoughts. The three came running from the house, shouting with excitement.

"Mama! Mama! Someone left a package at the door!" panted Manuel, the oldest, out of breath.

"No...stupid. It isn't a package. It is a bundle wrapped in a sheet," remarked Melisa.

"Mama...Mama...come see it! It's like a big bug; it moves and makes a strange sound," said José, the youngest.

Mrs. Pérez, drying her hands on her apron with a sigh, walked slowly toward the house.

She entered the kitchen, crossed through the old dining room, and reached the front door, which was partly open. She pushed it open a little more and...there on the ground was the thing that had caused the children so much dismay: it was a piece of cloth, so white that it reflected the sun's rays as if it were snow.

Something moved beneath it, with a noise like paper wrinkling.

Mrs. Pérez stood there, not daring to touch it.

"Children, didn't you see who left this here?" she asked them.

"No, Mama. There was a knock at the door, and when I opened it, no one was there," replied Melisa.

"I even looked up the road," added Manuel, "but all I saw were rocks and trees."

"Aren't you going to look at it, Mama? What are you waiting for?" shouted José, pulling at her skirt.

Mrs. Pérez replied, "Stand back, in case it is something that jumps!"

And cautiously bending over, she grabbed the white cloth by the corner and pulled it back. The cloth flew through the air and immediately disintegrated like a spider web blown by a fierce hurricane. And what remained on the ground between Mrs. Pérez and her three children was so unexpected that the four of them stared at it with their mouths open.

On its back and completely naked, a fat, rosy baby looked at them with two enormous black eyes. He kicked his feet, waved his hands, and made a curious sound that wasn't a cry but more like the shrieking of a bird. His little face was bathed with tears.

Without a moment's hesitation, Mrs. Pérez leaned over and took the baby in her arms. The baby immediately stopped crying.

"Poor little thing! Poor little thing!" said the good woman, while she rocked him. At the moment, she couldn't think of anything else to say.

The children, in turn, were full of questions.

"Mama, who does he belong to?"

"Who could have left him here?"

"What are we going to do with him?"

Leading them inside, the mother answered, "For now, I am going to dress him and give him something to eat. Then, we will see..."

In the evening, when the sun had set and work in the fields ended for the day, Mr. Pérez returned home. As soon as he opened the door, the children threw themselves at him to tell him the news.

"Papa, we have a baby!" said Manuel.

"Papa, we found a package on the doorstep!" shouted Melisa with excitement.

"Papa, I don't like how he cries...he sounds like a horrible bird!" added José.

"What are these silly things you are telling me? Where is your mother?" asked Mr. Pérez.

"She is with the baby!" the three answered in chorus.

"If this is a joke...," threatened the father, a little angry, "you will see what will happen!"

And in two steps he crossed the living room and entered the kitchen. There, Mrs. Pérez was seated on a bench, giving a bottle of milk to a robust baby dressed in clothes that were too big for him.

"Who left this child here?" he asked his wife.

"We don't know," she answered with regret.

"What do you mean 'we don't know'!" shouted Mr. Pérez.

"Someone left him on the doorstep!" said Melisa, who was standing next to him.

Mr. Pérez clenched his fists and began to speak in an overly calm tone: "Wou-ld yo-u li-ke to expla-in to me what this is abo-ut, be-fore I be-come ve-ry an-gry?" And he pointed a finger at the baby, who looked at him placidly from Mrs. Pérez's arms.

Mrs. Pérez then recounted, calmly and in detail, how they found the baby. When she finished, her husband turned and stormed out of the house, saying, "This cannot be! I will find out who left him here..."

He went to the nearest neighbor's house and then continued into town. He spoke with everyone he knew; he even went to the church and the police station. But no one could tell him anything.

He returned home worried, his head hanging low. The children were already sleeping, and the new baby was next to his wife's bed in an old crib that she had rescued from the basement. Mrs. Pérez asked her husband what he had discovered. After hearing what he had to say, she remained silent for a long while. Then, when Mr. Pérez was already half asleep, she said to him: "Did you know that a new tree also appeared in the orchard today? It is an orange tree, but it doesn't look like an orange tree...Very strange, very strange..."

"Stop your foolishness," he answered grouchily. "We don't know what to do with this baby and you are worried about a tree...."

The next day, the baby's cry—like the squawking of a bird—woke them. Mr. Pérez sat up in bed at once and said to his wife: "This isn't going to work! This very moment you must take the child somewhere that will take him in!"

"But...where?" asked his wife with anguish.

"To an orphanage in the city...I don't know, we will find a place..."

Mrs. Pérez looked at the child and her eyes filled with tears. "Poor little thing! It's going to be hard to give him up... And if we were to keep him?"

"Keep him? Are you crazy? Just when we are in a terrible drought and the harvest will be poor? Also, I don't like his eyes: they are too big and dark; they don't seem human."

"You are crazy! He has beautiful eyes!" she said, furious. And, getting up, she took the child in her arms and left the room.

Mr. Pérez, who loved his wife very much and knew she had a good heart, followed her and spoke to her gently, "Well...you are the one who will have to take care of him. In the long run, one more mouth..."

He hadn't finished the sentence before his wife hugged him.

"Thank you! Thank you! You will come to love him! Also, he has brought us good luck: on the day he arrived I discovered a new tree! Now we have four children and four orange trees!"

"A good-luck baby? Come on, woman. With this drought, luck and children aren't worth much."

The days and months passed. The interminable drought dried out the land and the fields. Nothing sprouted. But in the Pérez house, two things grew at an incredible rate: the abandoned child and the strange tree.

Everyone had agreed to call the child Galo, short for Regalo, gift. He already wandered through the entire house. He was truly enormous for his age, but still didn't utter a single word.

"I think Galo is a little stupid, Mama," said Manuel.

"And he is so clumsy! He trips over the smallest thing! He breaks everything he touches!" added Melisa.

"And I can't stand the awful way he cries!" continued José.

In reality, the three children were enormously jealous of Galo. They didn't like it that their mother worried about him so much. And their father agreed with them.

"Woman, don't you think you are spoiling this child? Our children are right: Galo is strange, clumsy, and mute. Who knows what his parents were like!"

So, to change topics, Mrs. Pérez spoke to her husband about the tree. "Have you seen how much the strange orange tree has grown? In only a few months it has grown taller than all the other trees. It is as tall as a poplar."

"Yes," answered Mr. Pérez, "I have seen it, and I intend to cut it down. I don't know if you have noticed, but it has not one bud and only a few leaves! It will never produce fruit. We have to conserve the little water that remains for the other poor trees. If I cut it down, at least we will have firewood!"

One day very early he went to the orchard with an ax and prepared to cut down the tree. Galo had followed him in silence, as usual, but upon seeing his adopted father take the first hack with his ax, he began to scream as if he were crazy, as if the ax were cutting him into pieces. Stumbling forward, he grabbed Mr. Pérez's arm.

Wrenching his arm away, Mr. Pérez called his wife to take the child back to the house. "This tree is harder than a rock, and in addition I have to listen to this stupid child and his squawking."

"It's his favorite tree," Melisa told him. "Maybe he thinks the ax will hurt him as well."

"Whenever he breaks a toy and we scold him, he hides behind this tree," added Manuel.

"I found him hugging the trunk one day, like the idiot that he is," concluded José, the youngest and meanest.

But although Mrs. Pérez took Galo where they couldn't hear his cries and Mr. Pérez chopped at the tree all he could, he couldn't remove more than a splinter.

"Damned tree!" shouted Mr. Pérez, exhausted and furious. "Tomorrow I will pull up its roots!"

That night Galo didn't eat even a crumb of bread, and Mrs. Pérez thought he was sick. The good woman got up to check on him several times; each time, she found him awake in his bed, his large black eyes wide open, staring at her in anguish.

The next day Mr. Pérez took his pickax and went right to the tree. Again, the child tried to follow him, but Mrs. Pérez locked him in the house and gave him an aspirin, because she thought he had a fever. Galo cried and cried and tried in vain to open the door to the orchard. The other children laughed at him, telling him that his tree was already on the ground.

Meanwhile Mr. Pérez desperately tried to yank the roots out of the ground with the pickax. The roots were bigger, tougher, and deeper than he had ever seen before. They seemed to have grown as far down as the branches at the top had grown toward the sky.

"Devil tree!" exclaimed Mr. Pérez, exhausted after three hours of effort. "I would need to destroy half the orchard to pull out these roots!" And he went inside, furious and defeated. Fortunately, learning that his tree was still standing, Galo had calmed down.

The days and months passed without a single drop of water falling from the sky. But the strange, bare tree continued to grow, even though Mr. Pérez didn't water it anymore. In turn, the other three orange trees barely survived with the little water they got. Galo, for his part, had grown so much that he was already taller than the oldest child. But he continued to be clumsy, and he still didn't say a single word. He made noise only when he cried, and then the only way to quiet him was to let him hug his tree, even if it was cold or dark.

Summer arrived, the fields burned, and the oranges in the orchard were practically the only food left. Mr. Pérez felt helpless, and Mrs. Pérez prayed the rosary. Manuel, Melisa, and José climbed the three sad orange trees searching for fruit. Galo also tried to climb, but although he was big, he wasn't very coordinated, and he always ended up falling to the ground. The children laughed at him and ate all the oranges. Galo huddled by his tree and watched them with sadness.

"Eat the oranges from your tree!" teased Manuel, Melisa, and José.

One afternoon, Mr. and Mrs. Pérez went to church to pray for rain. The children were alone in the orchard, searching for any remaining oranges hidden by leaves. Suddenly, José, the youngest, shouted, "Look! Look! Up in Galo's tree, at the top! An enormous orange, enormous!"

And it was true. On top of the giant tree, ten times higher than the highest branch on the other three orange trees, a unique, golden orange swung gently in the breeze.

"Why didn't we see it before? I'm going to pick it!" said Manuel, the oldest. And he immediately began to climb the tree. But he had only climbed a short way when–kerplunk!–he fell to the ground.

"Oh!" he shouted. "The trunk seems to be covered with oil; it's slippery."

"Slippery?" responded Melisa. "Watch how fast I can climb it!"

She reached the first branch, then the second, and then–boom!– she also fell to the ground.

"It isn't slippery. Its branches shook me loose!" she exclaimed angrily, while she brushed the dirt from her bottom.

"You two are afraid of heights and don't know anything!" said José. "Watch me!"

He began to climb the tree like a monkey. But when he reached the third branch he began to yell: "Ouch! Ouch! This tree is pricking me. I can't stand it any longer!"

And he dropped to the ground.

Galo stood in a stupor, watching the enormous orange that hung from the top of the tree. He didn't appear to have noticed what was happening with his brothers and sister.

At that moment, Mr. and Mrs. Pérez returned home. In pain, the children showed them the orange and told them of their efforts to reach it. Their father proclaimed loudly, "Horrible tree! I will get that orange, children . . . ."

But Mr. Pérez didn't even reach the second branch: he had barely gotten off the ground when he fell like a sack of potatoes. His wife and children, frightened, ran to him and helped him to his feet.

Limping, Mr. Pérez raised his fist and shouted at the tree, as if it could hear him, "You will see, hateful tree! I will throw acid on your roots; I will bomb you; I will call in the army to destroy you . . . !"

The orange at the top of the tree seemed to laugh at the Pérez's efforts to reach it.

Father and children stood nursing their wounds when they heard a rustle that came from above, like the sound of the wind through leaves. They looked up and saw Galo struggling up the tree trunk. Although there was no wind at all, the entire tree shook.

"He is going to kill himself!" cried Melisa.

"He will fall on us!" shouted Manuel.

"And he will start to cry again!" exclaimed José.

Frightened, Mr. Pérez, shouted, "Galo, come down immediately!"

And Mrs. Pérez, desperate, begged him, "Galo, my son, that tree will kill you. Don't go any higher! You are going to fall! Come down, please, come down!"

But Galo didn't appear to hear them, and he had already reached the first branch. The tree moved now as if a hurricane were thrashing it, and the sharp whistle of the wind drowned out Mrs. Pérez's pleas.

"How terrible! He will fall! I don't want to watch!" she cried with her face in her hands, while her husband and the three children stared, immobile and open-mouthed, as Galo continued to climb, undaunted by the commotion on the ground.

"He reached it! He reached the second branch! The branch is bending...! He's going to fall!" screamed the children.

But Galo, despite his clumsiness and the shaking of the tree, didn't fall or become frightened. And when he reached the third branch and continued to climb higher, the Pérez's realized that they were witnessing a miracle: the tree was actually helping the child to climb. All the tree's movements were to support Galo's hands and feet every time he hesitated. The thickest branches bent like human arms to support and push him higher. Galo never once looked toward the ground where his adoptive family stood.

"My God! My God!" the mother cried silently, seeing him grow smaller and become lost in the immense height of the trembling orange tree.

Pale, Mr. Pérez didn't move a muscle.

"He's going to reach the orange!" shouted Melisa, clapping her hands.

And finally, at the top of the tree, supported by the weakest branches, which encircled him like fingers, Galo reached up and grabbed the enormous orange. And suddenly, the tree stood still and the deafening whistling stopped. Mrs. Pérez, without knowing why, let out a horrible cry. As Galo touched the orange, it glowed like a lantern and began to swell bigger than a melon, bigger than a pumpkin. And from the top to the roots, the tree lit up as if it were made of glass. As it grew, the orange lost color, until it was a white, radiant globe that dwarfed Galo. Mr. and Mrs. Pérez weren't able to move or cry out, and the children opened and closed their eyes, deathly afraid of the tower of light that the tree had become. At that moment, from the peak, Galo turned toward them, shook his hand, and opening his mouth, shouted with a supernatural voice, "KIKLI KILI NITI LISI NIFLI TIKLI MILI."

A hatchway opened in the side of the globe, and Galo entered without hesitation. The hatchway closed, and despite the blinding light, the Pérez family could see the small shadow of the boy who had been their brother and son moving inside the sphere.

A tremor shook the earth. Lightning and thunder joined together, and Galo's tree became a silver rocket that slowly lifted from the ground.

The five members of the Pérez family were speechless. The three children, clinging to their parents and very frightened, didn't dare open their eyes for a long time. A dull, distant sound arose from the bottom of the deep hole in the ground where the tree had been. Blup! Bluuup! Bluuuuuuup! Stronger every moment, as if a giant corkscrew were uncorking a bottle the size of a house, the sound rose and rose. The Pérez family, paralyzed with fear, had their eyes fixed on the hole in the ground.

Bluuuuuup! Bluuuuuuup! BLUUUUUUUUUUUUUUUUP! The sound got louder and louder until it ended in a pop like a cork popping out of a colossal bottle of champagne. And from the hole left by Galo's tree, a great stream of pure water spouted high into the air. In an instant, the Pérez family had in front of them what they had been missing so desperately for so many months: a wide and deep well full of water.

"Water! Water!" repeated Mr. Pérez, as if in a trance. "Water for my crops. We are saved!"

The children approached the edge of the well and touched the water with their hands.

"KIKLI KILI NITI LISI NIFLI TIKLI MILI...," they shouted in chorus, without knowing whether to laugh at the strange words or to cry at Galo's disappearance.

Mrs. Pérez laughed and cried.

Suddenly, José said, "Look there! Something shiny is floating in the water!."

Melisa ran to find a branch. With the branch in his hand and stretching his arm as far as he could, Manuel brought the large golden orange to the edge of the well.

"Galo's orange!" shouted the children.

"Or a similar one," Mr. Pérez corrected.

"I will peel it," said Manuel, who tried to dig his nails into the peel But he couldn't even scratch the surface.

"Let me try!" shouted José. But he was unsuccessful as well.

"I will try!" exclaimed Melisa. But the orange's skin was as hard as a rock.

"Give it to me" ordered Mr. Pérez. But he couldn't even cut it with his penknife. Tired, he passed it to his wife for her to keep as a remembrance of Galo. As Mrs. Pérez took it in her hands, the peel began to fall off by itself. Segments as red as a ruby appeared beneath the skin, and Mrs. Pérez ate one without a moment's hesitation. Mr. Pérez and the children stood watching her to learn from her expression what flavor the strange fruit had.

"Oh, my poor Galo, my dear son, now I understand!" exclaimed Mrs. Pérez. With her eyes full of tears, she gave her husband and children the remaining sections.

And when they ate them, they also began to cry, looking toward the sky that, in the meantime, had filled with stars.

Thanks to that orange, the only, last, and strange words that Galo had spoken resonated now with clarity:

KIKLI KILI NITI LISI NIFLI TIKLI MILI.

"Earth mother, thank you for raising me. I leave to search for my own. I will always be your son in the stars."

Translated by Janice Molloy

# A Dog, a Boy, and the Night
## Amalia Rendic

The sun was fading softly into small golden rays. The weak light from the streetlamps was not enough to fight the darkness and the fog that threatened to invade the mining camp. A small crowd of pile drivers, machinists, ore crushers, and miners, was returning home. Because of the breathing difficulty caused by the high altitude, they walked slowly and silently. The Chuquicamata mine is 2,800 meters above sea level.

When they came to the Brinkeroft quarters, they began to scatter toward different sections of the camp. Through half-open windows and doors it was possible to get a glimpse of home lights. Juan Labra, a hard-working machinist and a loyal friend, was walking along one of the many lanes of the town; and he could still hear the painful noise made by whistles and sirens from the factory. He had a face with deep wrinkles resembling veins of ore. All of a sudden he didn't feel worried anymore; waves of tenderness could be seen in his eyes. He accepted his family's love as a natural present. There Juanucho was, as usual, every evening, waiting for him at the door of their house. He was a nine-year old boy, with lively and inquisitive eyes. He was pretty strong for his age, and very fond of walking around. He knew the mine like the palm of his hand, inch by inch. He was very talkative too and only his smile could make him stop chattering. He pressed his face against the iron gate of the small garden and looked with curiosity at a very tall American who was walking behind his father.

"Dad, a gringo is following you; he is coming to our house!" he hurriedly whispered as he greeted his father. The street was deserted. Juanucho was obssessed by Black, a big German shepherd standing by his master, Mr. Davies. Black was for Mr. Davies one of the few beings that he had accepted in his affections. For him he was like a companion in his lonely life abroad.

"Come on in, Mr. Davies. What can we do for you?" said Juan Labra, taking off his hard hat while he opened the fence door. He hardly could conceal his astonishment at seeing one of the company's executives at his place.

"I'll be brief, Mr. Labra. I need a favor from you. I'll soon be going to Antofagasta, and I'd like to leave Black with you. You are kind, you are a member of a society for the protection of animals in Calama, as everyone knows," said Mr. Davies while looking at his dog.

"Very well, Mr. Davies, thanks for your trust. Your dog will like it here. We'll make sure he doesn't miss you too much. My own son Juanucho will take care of Black while you are gone," Juan Labra answered, adjusting his jacket and feeling a strange sensation of self-satisfaction.

"I leave him in your hands and thank you very much. So long, Mr. Labra. I'll see you soon, Black...Ah, I was forgetting his canned meat. It's his favorite food."

Both the owner and the dog looked sad. Black pulled at his master's pants and Mr. Davies stooped to pat that head with a pointed snout. Then he left. The dog wanted to follow him but Juanucho's arms retained him as if by a chain. Black barked falteringly, scenting something in the air. His red wet tongue was hanging out. The boy closed the fence. Black stood erect and didn't look very friendly. His shining fur, his slenderness, his bearing, everything in him pointed to his expensive origins. He was worth his weight in gold and had been the winner of many dog shows.

Juanucho began to talk to him as if the dog were his little brother. They looked at each other for a long while without even blinking. The dog's eyes were motionless and the image of the boy was reflected on them like small dots of light. The boy timidly patted Black's back; the dog sniffed and then answered with a gentle wag of his tail.

Juanucho persisted in his strange monologue with Black. Both of them began to take a liking to each other. After the dark hours of the night, dawn came wrapped in mist, and later on the day broke as usual between the two huge masses of St. Peter's and St. Paul's volcanos. Everything looked like a wet blue color.

Black awakened up in the yard of the working family's house and when he heard the first sirens blow and saw the miners' procession, it was as if something very big had awakened in his chest. He greeted these new impressions with barks that sounded like explosions. First thing in the morning, Juanucho, in his fantasy world, went out to see his new friend and for days and days they went together everywhere.

Challenging the wind, they used to run on that great winding ribbon that is the road to Calama. Without feeling any fatigue they entered the vast spaces of the desert. They played diving into the grey copper residue of the mine pit, that shapeless and majestic mass of dirt. They would try to collect the green-blue and yellow reflections that produce entrancing colors in the sunlight.

Thus many hours went on and nightfalls came and the friendship ties between them became warmer and warmer. However, a growing anxiety clouded the short-lived happiness of the boy. He thought the dead-line would be here soon. Without a doubt, Mr. Davies would return.

"Dad, couldn't you ask the Mister to give us Black? Why don't you buy Black from him?"

"No, Juanucho, he'll never be ours. He's too fine, he's worth his weight in gold. They are dogs for the rich. The gringos like to walk them and take them to shows," the worker answered with a bitter smile.

"When I grow up I'll buy him!" Juanucho answered with decisively. "I don't want them to take him away, he's my friend!" the boy almost shouted at his father.

One day, when they were coming back from the banks of the Loa River, a nasty mountain wind began to blow. They were wet with the silk-like mist. When they arrived at their door they stopped as if they were facing something they feared and anticipated.

Mr. Davies! He was back. The boy tried to explain what the dog meant to him but the words that had welled up from his heart got stuck in his throat. It was a sad moment.

"Good-bye, little friend, good luck!" he stammered. His eyes were wet and he was wringing his hands.

Mr. Davies thanked him warmly. Like a young honest man, the boy didn't accept any payment at all.

Black reluctantly followed his former master and after examining eagerly every corner, he said good-bye to the workers' quarters on his way to the American camp. Juanucho, after his first attack of despair, tried to understand what was going on; he knew—an expensive dog was not for him. Black kept walking. Harmony had been restored on both sides.

But night and its solitude came, that hour when the minds ponder on each and every fragment of their lives, and everything was useless for the boy. Juanucho's defenses collapsed and he began sobbing. A communicating flow started between the feelings of the boy and the animal and at that very moment, in the American camp, the dog began howling. Images of Black were parading by the boy's mind and, as if a secret influence were operating, the dog barked furiously, asking the wind to transmit his message. At the beginning it was a plaintive message; but then it became deafening.

Juanucho cried all night long. His moaning also turned into a strange concert whipped through the quiet streets of the mining town.

Mr. Davies was perplexed with Black. What can a man do with a crying dog? A new truth took hold in the gringo's mind. Black no longer belonged to him. The dog didn't love him any more .

Labra didn't know how to comfort his tearful and feverish little man. After all, what can a man do with a crying boy? Labra wanted his son to laugh again with that nice and free laughter he had. He felt obliged to win back Juanucho's smile. Poverty had stung him many times, but this he was unable to bear. Something unexpected would have to happen during this exciting night in the mining town.

As if the hour of universal brotherhood had already come, he threw a poncho over his shoulders, took a flashlight and began walking toward the American camp to check if a miracle could be true. He had to give himself courage and be daring. He, a modest worker, always shy and asking no questions, would go and ask one of the company's executives that Black, that fine, beautiful, prize-winning dog, be given to him. He breathed deeply and he shuddered when he realized his own boldness. He was ascending the road to the American camp.

Unexpectedly, some brown phosphorescent eyes shone under his flashlight. Labra was startled. A smell of pipe and fine tobacco and the sound of a familiar barking made him stop.

Mr. Davies himself was coming to receive him and was walking toward the workers' quarters!

Both men felt as if something were pressing their hearts. Words were not necessary anymore.

"He's not mine anymore," the American whispered while he put in Labra's hands the heavy leash he used for Black.

Labra took the animal in his trembling hands and a sad happiness warmed his smile. There were no effusive thanks but a mute and reciprocal understanding. Black, who was tugging his leash, forced him to follow the tracks toward Juanucho's neigborhood.

At the very moment of the miracle, there was a new warmth over the night of Chuquicamata.

Translated by Joy Renjilian-Burgy

# Butterfly Man

## Elena Aldunate

The child is bored. With her nose and sticky little hands pressed against the glass, she gazes out the window at the afternoon activity. Inside, the din grows louder. Children, lost in their own world of make-believe, run around, shouting, wrestling, or sit silently playing strange games with pebbles, rags, papers, or forks.

The afternoon is bursting with activity, but the little girl, who has just celebrated her fifth birthday, stands on her knees on the big chair, rubbing her patent leather shoes against her light blue stockings. She watches the activity outside, that street outside where the grown-ups don't permit her to play.

She is not a pretty child—the mouth, round eyes, straight black hair, pale complexion, and broad nose all give her the appearance of a little Indian girl. Nevertheless, she has a beautiful look of sadness, of tender resignation in her eyes.

No, she doesn't want any more cake. She doesn't want her little jeweled birthday crown. She hates the colored balloons. She hates her cousins. She wants to get out of this house which is full of noise, restrictions, and new things.

So, here, pressed against the panes, she gazes hungrily, until, deep within her agile little mind, the idea begins to take form. Outside, outside. That big "no-no"—that's what she wants.

In the midst of the hubbub and sounds of party horns, children running races, and crying, she crosses the dining room, the living room; she slips down the hall, approaches the forbidden door, and, tiptoeing in her new shoes, she reaches out with both hands and turns the big brass knob. It opens with a click! And there right before her is the outside, that same street in which a few moments before she had buried the loneliness of an only child.

Suddenly, without looking outside, someone closes the door after her so the children won't go out.

The slamming of the door brings to life the unknown surroundings, makes the walls grow higher, heightens her awareness of being alone, and turns the sky black and angry, revealing on every corner the scary shadow of the boogieman. Cars turn into dragons with glowing eyes, roaring and making the ground tremble as they gallop past. A world of fantasy, fear, and emptiness closes in upon the child.

Behind her the house is safe and warm; before her, fearsome, magical, uncontrollable images take shape and then vanish as they whirl about her in a mysterious dance of fantasy.

Wide-eyed, the child steps into the great world where the grown-ups have forbidden her to go. She ventures forth like a small ray of pink light, moves along the walls, to the street corner which looms before her like a monstrous mouth, while evil, bejeweled beasts with hot breath stalk her.

With a child's natural fear of unfamiliar surroundings, she arrives at the Plaza with anxiety...and, little child that she is, after all, she soon stops sobbing and begins to smile. Her pounding little heart slows to its normal beat as she strolls aimlessly down the sidewalk, full of curiosity and expectation. Now, she is as calm as if she were in her own yard. No longer afraid of anything, she sits right down on the curb, elbows on her knees, resting her head in her sticky little hands. She stares intently into space. She sits there, staring, staring so intensely that she penetrates the hidden dimension reserved for children. And suddenly something wonderful appears right before her.

Is it a firefly? The midnight sun? A small lost planet? No, it's a house, a house of light, a house of butterflies. Butterflies, blue, yellow, red, white, green, lilac...butterflies of all colors.

They are beautiful, more so than balloons. Balloons burst. Better than candy, prettier than the five little candles on her cake, finer than Mama's gold bracelets.

Standing, eyes sparkling and arms outstretched, the little girl laughingly defends herself as they flutter about her, between her hands, under her short dress, between the blue bows on her sleeves; they brush against her face and legs, softly, gently. They are wonderful. Confident now, they alight in her hair, on the palm of her hand.

Suddenly, she jumps up and down, clapping her hands.

The butterflies take flight, and she laughs with glee.

Little by little the butterflies return, and they play the same game again and again, two times, ten times, three, just as the magic ritual of children prescribes.

Only this time the grownups won't stop her from arriving at the magic number. And so, there they are, in the house of light, the little girl and the butterflies, the butterflies and the little girl, playing on and on, until, in the midst of everything, a man appears. The little girl and the butterflies flee. The man speaks softly and smiles; his eyes are blue, his hands big and soft, but now our little girl is running back down the sidewalk as fast as she can, screaming at the top of her lungs, until she reaches the great door, open again now, through which she entered this forbidden place.

Back inside, nothing exciting is happening. Lights, balloons, party horns, things are winding down. Children are crying, some because they have to leave, others because they don't want to go. And later, she's in bed, much later than usual just because it's her birthday. All alone in her own room, her cheeks stained with tears, she sleeps without dreaming.

There will be many more afternoons like this one, day after day, inside the little house of light. The little girl and the Butterfly Man, she shouting with joy, her eyes sparkling and her hands filled with candy and covered with butterflies. He tells her stories, laughs with her, plays games with her, and treats her with infinite patience, great tenderness, and much love. Never does he show the slightest boredom with her, nor does he treat her as grown-ups usually treat children. And so they become friends. It is their secret, a secret so great it cannot be told to anyone.

Curled up, with her dark head resting on his knees, her eyes lost in the flight of the butterflies, the little girl listens to the same stories over and over again, stories about magical roads where the sun always shines, and where there is sweet fruit, and flowers and birds, soft furry animals, and princes and princesses who fall in love. Sailing the seas, she sees whole cities submerged in the depths. She travels to enchanted galaxies where happiness reigns. She hears songs and lullabies which lull her to sleep. During this same time she is learning to count, to read. She is taught that the world is round, and that there are many countries, many things with strange names; that she is loved, that she has a soul, a heart, and a home of her own; she also discovers that she is not awkward or ugly, that she can go to sleep without being afraid and wake up without crying; she realizes that it doesn't matter if her hands are dirty, or if her stockings get wrinkled because she can take them off and throw them away and run about the house barefooted and get wet and make little animals out of mud. And, you know what? When she takes them to the Butterfly Man, those little animals fly and talk and walk about. She can come and go as she pleases. She can touch whatever she wants. Or eat whatever she wants. But there is one thing she cannot do: she cannot tell a lie. When she lies, her friend becomes sad and the colors of the butterflies fade.

It's always that way; she must not tell a lie.

And sometimes, when she eats too many rolls and ice cream cones or fruit, she feels sick and has to go home and at night she wakes up crying and Mama gets mad and gives her that awful medicine.

Weeks go by, and each Saturday afternoon the little girl is in her own private world with the birds and her friend whose gentle hands caress her tenderly. How full and warm is her heart! How she looks forward to her future, as she grows day by day!

So time passes, until one Saturday summer comes, and it is time to go to the beach. The little girl is frantic because she realizes that she wil not be able to get away that afternoon and the Butterfly Man will be waiting for her. She has to tell him. But how? They are leaving at three o'clock, at three, three! In the midst of the packing and the arguing, the hustle and bustle of putting things away and closing up the house, all you can hear are the maids who say, "Yes, Ma'am!" And Daddy who says "This doesn't fit!" And Mama who says, "Where can that child have gone?" The little girl slips out to the street and runs faster than she has ever run. All out of breath, she sits on the curb and looks and looks, until her eyes hurt from looking.

Nothing happens. Maybe this isn't the place; it must be farther ahead, or perhaps not this far. She goes back and forth looking, searching but finding nothing. Only the street in the afternoon sun, and walls and houses, just like any place else.

Her friend doesn't appear.

How many hours does she spend searching for him?

Suddenly she realizes that the sun is no longer bright, that she is hungry, that it is getting dark, and that the Butterfly Man has abandoned her...

Sadly she walks up and down, tears streaming down her face, sobbing louder with each step. She feels the deep pain of being all alone, as only a child can. She huddles on a park bench, and cries and cries, until she feels hands on her shoulders and a man's arms which pick her up and shake her.

"Child, child, what a scare you have given us! It is not nice to run off like that. You have been a bad girl...but, what's the matter? Why are you crying? Are you hurt?"

The child opens her swollen little eyes, expecting to see her friend at last, and then she is afraid, when she sees the stern look of her father.

"Daddy, please don't get angry, but I had to say goodbye. Mama says that's the polite thing to do."

"Say goodbye? Who have you been with? Who spoke to you? How many times have I told you not to talk to strangers? What am I going to do with you? Now answer me?"

"Daddy, it's just that the Butterfly Man...it's all his fault....he's gone! He's gone, and he will never come back, and I love him so, I just love him so much."

"The *what* Man?"

The child's voice is filled with such anguish, her crying so heart-rending, that her father feels that something is seriously wrong and that she can't tell him.

Confused and worried, her father holds her head to his chest and caresses her tear-stained cheeks as he wonders what he should do; and as he looks up at the late afternoon sky, already getting dark, he notices that as the streetlights come on thousands and thousands of butterflies are attracted and flutter around them.

"Silly little girl! Do you know what happened? It was your imagination. Look at the streetlights. Look how the butterflies want to get into them to find out what's inside, to possess what they can't understand. I'm going to tell you a story, a story that will help you see why the butterflies love the light so much...Your Mama and I work hard to make a nice home where you can be happy, but sometimes we work too hard and don't have time to..."

"A story? You're going to tell me a story, Daddy?"

"Yes, I am. Once upon a time..."


Translated by Kenneth M. Taggart

# Up to the Clouds
## Ana María Guiraldes

Soledad makes sure she is alone in the house. She goes in to the large bedroom. For a while she observes the threads of light that filter through the closed Venetian blinds and fill the room with brilliant dots. Abruptly she opens the blinds: the restrained sun spills out in a wave over the interior.

She walks directly to the dresser. She opens the small box. Searches. Chooses among some accessories a smal embellished shell comb, covered withtiny stones. She secures it to one side of her black hair and steps back to see the effect. She moves her head to set off little sparks of light from each bead. Absorbed, she looks over the perfume bottles.

Suddenly, she remains still. Decided, she runs to the closet. She has to hurry.

She searches among the light and colorful confusion of clothes. On other occasions she doesn't vacillate, and now, when there is no time to lose, she is totally confused. A hanger slips from the rod: the dress falls softly at her feet. She takes that as an omen and begins to undress.

Nervous, she tugs, she pulls off her blouse without worrying about the button which flies off; with a toe she kicks the green skirt high in the air, and it falls on the bed. She picks up the dress from the floor; she feels the freshness of the cloth on her slender shoulders. She runs to the mirror. She has to put on makeup, if only lipstick, at least! If she controls her pulse, there is no problem. She smiles: her eyes shine like two honey cakes as she wipes with a finger a red streak that smears across one of her teeth.

She almost forgets her shoes. And her purse? She fidgets. The bags fall on the floor. Impatient, she picks them all up and with both hands pushes them, as well as she can, back into their places.

She's ready.

She walks through the house satisfied with the quietness that surrounds it.

She goes out to the street.

Her high heels hit on the cement with an ever-increasing sureness. She feels the dress flutter, pleasing, with each step.

Two men look at her. She senses they follow her with their eyes. She tries to walk straight, without looking back, especially when she hears them laugh.

She stops before crossing the street. A car slows down. The whistles sound sharp, persistent. She manages to maintain her seriousness for a moment, but laughter escapes and a dimple sinks into her smooth cheek.

From the car they make exaggerated motions for her to pass. Prideful, she crosses without looking at the excited waving hands.

She spots the park full of children. Shall she cross it or go around? The shade of the trees is tempting. She walks on, slowly, because her heels sink into the gravel. The nannies look at her; they tug at the little ones without ceasing to observe her; they whisper. She thinks they're jealous of her, and she touches the shell comb which is still in place. She shakes her hair so the sun will shine through its looseness; she sits down, legs crossed, on a bench, next to a large urn of flowers.

She waits.

She smiles at a child who totters and falls down then sits next to her. Some girls are swinging; each time the swing takes them higher, they shriek. She opens her purse. She looks at herself in the tiny mirror, and she presses her lips hard so the red lipstick will stay on. The sunlight is reflected in the glass, and it sends a silver spot to the grass.

She's tempted: she focuses the brightness on the face of a little girl who is resting in a swing. She sees how she rubs her eyes, confused.

Soledad laughs. She gets up, walks over to the swing.

"Want a push?" she asks.

The child, with her eyes very open, shakes her head yes.

"Hold tight, because I'm going to send you up to the clouds," she advises.

She begins to push. She tries not to dirty her shoes. The arc of movement is more pronounced each time. The child in the swing gives out little cries. Her skirt goes up and down, up and down, up to show her thin legs. Her braids swing, too, next to her red cheeks.

"Up to the clouds!" shouts Soledad, and she increases the heave of each push. The child bounces each time she reaches the top of the arc, and looks with terrified glee at the tree branches. "O.K., stop me!" she yells.

The nannies, absorbed in the contemplation of Soledad, maintain control over the children only by tugging at their clothes.

They nudge each other when the wind raises her pleated skirt. Soledad stops the swing. "Did you like that? she asks.

The child shakes her head yes. "Now it's your turn," she offers.

Soledad laughs. With a jump, she lands on the swing seat. The pebbles scatter under her shoes when she backs up on her toes to get the maximum push. The swing begins its slow movement, back and forth, Soledad's legs go up, then they double back, skillfully, to launch herself strongly forward.

Her purse flies off her arm, the shell comb slips down to her ear.

"Up to the clouds!" Soledad cries out in a high-pitched voice.

The too large shoes fly off. The long dress flies about. And her mouth, which begins to blur with lipstick, smiles and her smooth ten-year-old cheeks fill with dimples.

Translated by Russell O. Salmon

# The Family Album
## Ana María Guireldes

When Don Elias sighed his last breath, the newly widowed Mrs. Adela Lopez realized that she did not have time to cry. But her eldest daughter did cry, the three younger children cried and baby Thomas cried because it was his feeding time. In the midst of the sobs and whimpers, the doctor handed the widow the death certificate which stated that Elias Jaramillo Valdebenito had departed this world at 10:40 a.m., victim of a cardiac arrest.

With handkerchief in hand just in case, the widow directed the preparations for the wake. And thus, Don Elias, in his new three-piece suit with a pine-scented handkerchief in the breast pocket, was placed in the casket half an hour later. The four children obediently changed their clothes and washed their face and hands before taking their places in the living room, a properly grieving but dignified family. The nanny held little Thomas who had awakened in a bad temper that morning and was still crying.

Doña Adela, in her black suit and suede dress shoes, stood next to the casket looking at her dead husband and thinking that luckily there was enough coffee for the guests. The deceased, unaware of the commotion his death had caused, remained flat on his back prepared for a long day of being contemplated.

The first visitors to arrive were three teachers—two women and a man. Neither they nor those who arrived later noticed the cleanliness of the house or the perfection of the children who were all lined up, secretly poking and pinching each other at the sight of Miss Zoila's beard and Miss Silvia's teeth. Nor did anyone admire the swiftness with which the housewife had prepared everything. They all knew that Doña Adela had managed to organize a Christmas party in a half hour and had collected shoes for poor children in a single morning, distributing them herself because she didn't trust anyone else. Even more reason, then, to expect her own husband's wake to be perfect. She was one of those women who never made a mistake or were caught off-guard. Until that day.

The two maids perspired as they hurried around the house under the commanding eyes of their boss. The cook opened the door for the guests, wiped the floor to erase the marks left by the professor's rubber soles and removed the empty coffee cups. The other maid, who was rather slow and easily frightened, walked Tommy around shaking him whenever he kicked her, and fretted because the child wanted to look at his father sleeping in the big box and she didn't dare let him. The deceased man might wink at her like he used to when he was alive and then appear to her later in a cloud of smoke, wearing wings. The lady of the house herself went off to the kitchen several times to keep an eye on the preparations for lunch: the children weren't about to starve just because Elias had died. She even had enough presence of mind to give Samuel the gardener, who was charged with receiving the wreaths, a black tie and told him not to smoke because it was disrespectful.

All of this considering that Elias had died suddenly. If he had been ill a long time, she at least would have had time to mend the sofa so that the oldest daughter wouldn't have had to sit on the tear all morning to cover it up.

But no one is perfect. And so it happened that the music teacher Miss Silvia, a piano and harp specialist, asked to see the family album. "I would so much like to see a picture of Don Elias surrounded by his family. He was such a solitary, hard-working man that I never had the pleasure of seeing him as the father of his family," she said in her sharp voice, her chest quivering.

Doña Adela, who was glowering at the little ones as they giggled at the drop of saliva that fell on Miss Silvia's lap when she pronounced the word "pleasure," stood there dumbfounded. And since Miss Silvia spoke in the high-pitched voice she used in class, everyone heard her:

"Yes, the family album, Doña Adela...Don Elias and all of his off-spring, Doña Adela..."

And so Doña Adela, who never missed a detail, realized in the middle of her husband's wake that she didn't have a picture of the family. And for good reason: Elias was a Rotarian, he ate out every week, he was president of whatever they asked him to be, a fireman, a friend to his friends...In short, a thousand excuses tumbled out of the mouth of the distressed widow who had the habit of examining what was done, not that which was not done.

But, while out of the corner of her eye she watched her eldest daughter wriggle around on the sofa thus revealing the rip, she searched for a solution: a way of adorning the wall with a photo of poor Elias with the family he had managed to create with some effort and good humor, next to his wife who had accompanied him through good times and bad, and perhaps next to the maids who had served him during the last ten years (Doña Adela's maids stayed with her a long time). To show that hers was a family that understood the value of tradition and most of all, so that no one could say that she, the widow of Jaramillo, had overlooked such an important detail, she decided to take her husband out of the casket. Without any crying or hysteria, as natural as could be. Besides, she would have done the same thing if she had discovered a scratch or some other defect in the casket. As she was giving Samuel, (who had been smoking behind the rose bushes), clear instructions about getting the photographer, she noticed that Elias' face was beginning to look strange.

The teachers rose to the occasion. They immediately joined forces to help with the tasks at hand. Besides convincing the widow that it would not be necessary to open the drapes because the photographer always used a flash, they also informed her that luckily he was just returning from a neighboring farm where he had taken pictures of a newly arrived family that wanted to be immortalized under the region's apple blossoms and blue skies. The photographer, Jose Sotomayor, had been with the family for two days and had not heard about the recent death. Samuel, the odor of flowers and cigarettes still on his hands, had to do some talking to persuade him that Doña Adela needed a family picture because Elias was about to embark on a long journey, (Samuel smiled a little as he said this), and that it would be good business because they would pay him double for the hurry. Jose was finally convinced.

When he arrived at the traveler's house, everything was ready. The entire family was waiting for him. In the place of honor, very rigid, shoulder to shoulder with his wife and the cook, stood Don Elias, impeccable in his blue suit. To either side were his children, wide-eyed and silent. The nanny, with Tommy asleep in her arms, wore the expression of having seen a ghost.

Doña Adela brusquely cut off the photographer's repeated pleas for Don Elias to smile or raise his half-closed eyelids. And finally, clearly indignant, she told him to take the picture once and for all and that she did not want to hear any more jokes about Elias looking exhausted from having been out all night. Reprimanded, the photographer said, "There, there, that's it, smile, sir," because Elias' jaw had fallen slightly. He had the wife step back a little to be in line with her husband who had no intention of assuming a more elegant pose. The camera clicked and Jose excused himself to go to work in his studio.

And so, after some hustle and bustle in which everyone participated—retrieving the casket from the dining room and the wreaths from the pantry, returning to the foot of the casket the red carnations that Doña Adela had placed in a vase on the table to liven up the picture, giving the nanny a tranquilizer because she was sure the master had been staring at her, serving the children lunch and, of course, installing Don Elias in the same comfortable position he was in at 11:10 that morning—Doña Adela took her daughter's place on the sofa to receive the remaining guests who came to pay their respects. And finally, a couple of days later, with the first and last family picture hung on the wall, she went into her room to cry in peace and remember Elias who smiled softly at her from the photograph.

Translated by Margaret Stanton

# Endless Flight

## María Cristina da Fonseca

I was thirsty, and flew quietly and near the ground to the water hole. She surprised me there. Somehow, I always knew she'd find me, even though each and every one of my actions was fashioned to avoid her.

My chest hardened, my nerves tightened, and my neck turned to stone.

I could see that the ocelot was beautiful as she came toward me, death perched on her golden haunches.

I wanted to take flight, but my wings were caught. I tried to send forth a song that would tear open the skies, but I could 't give it voice!

In a matter of seconds I was just a pile of bloody feathers caught between the mighty teeth of her feline jaw and the steel of her claws.

Before starting out on this last flight and closing the circle of life that held me, no thoughts gave me anguish, nor did my soul lament. She ate, licking my stiff body. And there I remained, scattered into pieces, until a thousand secret lives silently came to inhabit me...

At first I was just a poor dead bird, the remains of the ocelot's feast, slowly and sickeningly rotting in sun and wind.

But one afternoon, rain came to wash the scrub oak and the huge green leaves of the plantain trees. It came to knock down the enormous red hibiscus petals with its drops, and to take me away...

First it took me in its arms of water and wind. Then I traveled and traveled, a thousand times removed from myself, and divided into millions of scattered particles until I came to dwell at the foot of a great hill.

Then I became a mountain...

And from the mist, a man came with a hoe and a shovel. He cut me in two, made me into furrows, and filled me with seeds. I nourished these plentiful seeds with my old crumbled bones and my ancient blood, which had turned to ash. And with my own entrails I fed and watered them a thousand times.

And so it was that later I became sap and passed through the fragant green labyrinthine innards of the plants and gave them my liquid.

Yet something of myself stayed within the earth...until one bright morning when other men dug into the heart of the mountain and built their homes with straw and the clay of my soul.

And I became a cave.

Later, an old Indian woman came looking for me. Part of me went with her to the shadowy interior of her hut. There, with her wrinkled hands and the wisdom of centuries, she tirelessly kneaded and molded me. I became a vessel with a rounded body and polished face. When I was finished, the woman—I could have called her "mother"—took a long look at me from beneath hooded eyelids. And before casting me to the flames, on my face she drew with her fingernails two slanting eyes, whispering in a low voice, "Every crock needs eyes to see when the yucca is cooked." And I learned how to open my insides and give food to ease the hunger of every day.

Then Alfredo, the potter, came to the hut. "Give me some of your famous clay," he bid the old woman. And he carried me to his wheel and table where he spread me, turned me inside out, and pounded me a thousand and one times to make me supple and compliant.

"It's the best clay I ever held in my hands," he told anyone who could hear him. "You could even say that it talks, you could even say that it sings every time I put a fold in its skin. I can feel how life still trembles within it. And sometimes I think I hold in the palm of my hands the throbbing breast of a bird ready to fly away."

The potter worked hours and hours until he had made my clay body into a beautiful pitcher decorated with a splendid long-tailed alligator.

And I became a vessel to keep water that calms thirst.

Nevertheless, while forming me, the pot maker lost an important part of his soul, and it remained forever joined to the reptile that embellished my pitcher-shaped body. "It seems to move and breathe. One of these days it will get out through one of the cracks!" was the comment of all who looked at it.

I believe that's how it will happen one of these afternoons when the sun caresses, and the wind blows tirelessly, because sometimes I feel the sand I am made from trembling with the soft tickle of nameless cells that endlessly come together and then divide. It beats beneath a fleeting ray of light that is only barely lit. And it seems that I can sense once more within me the old undulating of blood that proclaims life's magnificent kiss.

I feel that at any moment, since the wind blows so much, the body that was dust and clay, dwelling, food, and water shall rise from the wasteland. I will be an alligator, painfully loosened from a vase, or perhaps a fish with gleaming scales, or a crane flying once again in a sea of ivory clouds.

Translated by Diane Russell-Pineda

# The Secret
## María Luisa Bombal

I know many things no one else knows.

I could tell a million wonderful stories about the earth, and the sea, and the heavens.

This story, however, is only about the sea.

Way down in the depths of the sea, deeper than the deepest and blackest level of absolute darkness, the light returns to illuminate the waters. Its golden rays shine on giant sponges, making them sparkle yellow as the sun.

There are all kinds of plants and living things in this undersea world of icy summer light which shines eternally....

There are broad meadows thick with green and red sea anemones to which transparent jellyfish cling tightly before continuing their wandering through the waters.

There are dense hard white coral reefs, opening and closing slowly like flowers, where fish with dark velvety skin dart about.

Now I see sea horses. Really, they are tiny little warhorses of the sea, their algae manes flying, casting a soft luminous glow about them as they gallop silently by.

And, if you would just pick up a certain ordinary looking gray seashell, I'm sure you would see a little mermaid weeping inside.

And, now I remember. We used to play among the rocks by the sea when we were children. Often when we were jumping from one rock to another, we would stop short when we suddenly came to a narrow gorge. After the waves crashed through, they left a thick rich blanket of sparkling foam and made a moaning sound, like someone in the throes of a slow death, as if they were whispering some final words.

Did you understand, then, what they were trying to say?

I don't know whether you did or not.

As for me, I must say that I did.

I understood that the dying foamy waves were trying to whisper the very secret of their noble origin into our ears.

"Way way down in the very depths of the sea," they whispered, "there is an underwater volcano in a state of constant eruption. Night and day without ceasing, it spews silvery molten lava from its crater to the surface of the waters...

But what I really want to tell you is a strange story, now long-forgotten, which took place in these depths.

It's the story of a pirate ship which, centuries ago, was caught in a giant whirlpool and pulled down into the depths, passing through unknown currents and past submerged reefs.

A giant octupus clung docilely to each mast, as if they were sitting in the crows-nest as ship lookouts, while shy starfish were calmly making their nest in the hold.

When he finally regained consciousness, the pirate captain woke his crew with a harsh command and gave the order to weigh anchor.

And as soon as they came out of their stupor, the crew stepped lively to obey. But no sooner had the captain taken a second glance at their surroundings from his turret than he began to curse.

The ship had run aground on the sands of an endless beach clearly visible in the soft green light of the moon.

But there was something even worse—he aimed his spyglass in every direction, and there was no sign of the sea.

"Damned Sea!" he roared. "Damn the tides, ruled by the very Devil himself! Be damned, I say! Leaving us stranded inland like this...who knows how long it will be before the accursed hour when the tide turns and refloats our ship..."

Full of anger and frustration he looked up, searching for some open sky and stars, and the point from which that moon was casting its eerie light.

But he found no sky, no stars, no moon.

He swore by the very Devil that all he could see above seemed black, and quiet, and still...as if it were the mirrored image of the same diabolical desert sands where he had run aground...

And now, as if all that were not enough, there was something else even more strange. The full black mainsails—pride of his ship when they billowed full—were slack and still. There was not a breath of wind.

"All hands ashore!" "All hands ashore!" The command was echoed throughout the ship. "Take daggers, and packs. Reconnoiter the coast."

The gangplank dropped straightaway, the crew, still in kind of a daze, disembarked meekly, their captain the last in line, pistol in hand.

They sand they tread, sinking almost to their ankles, was fine as powder...and very cold.

Splitting them into two bands, the Captain orders one to head East, the other West, to find the sea. But then...

"Avast!" he shouts, stopping the headlong rush of his crew. "Cabin Boy, stay here and stand watch. The rest, carry out your orders. step lively!"

The cabin boy, son of humble fishermen, had longed for adventure and booty and had run away from home to go to sea with "the Terror" (which was the name of the ship as well as the Captain). Obeying his orders, he turns and retraces his steps, head down as if he were studying the tracks he had just made.

"Dullard...clumsy oaf...step lively!" the Pirate Captain swore, once the boy stood before him. Though only fifteen years old, the boy was so short he barely came up to the massive gold buckle of the Captain's bloodstained belt.

"Boys on board my ship!" he thought, suddenly aware of an uneasy feeling he couldn't describe.

"Captain, Sir", says the cabin boy in a soft voice, interrupting his thoughts, "have you noticed that our feet leave no tracks on the sand?"

"And also that my ship's mainsails cast no shadow?" snapped the Captain harshly.

Then, his rage cooled slowly before the innocent questioning look of the cabin boy.

"There, there, son," he muttered, placing his rough hand on the boy's shoulder, "we'll find the sea before long."

"Aye, Aye, Sir," the boy murmured, as if to say thank you. Thank you. Prohibited words on a Pirate ship. His lips could burn before he would say them.

Did I actually say thank you, the boy wonders, alarmed by the very thought.

I called him son, the Captain thinks, struck that he might say such a thing.

"Captain, Sir," says the Cabin Boy, "at the time of the shipwreck..."

The Pirate Captain bristled and regained his brusque manner on hearing these words.

"...I mean, when that happened, I was below. When I came to, what do you think I saw? The hold was filled with the slimiest creatures I have ever seen..."

"What kind of creatures?"

"Well, starfish, but...they were alive. They make me sick. They throbbed like the innards of a man just slit open. And they moved about, looking for each other, massing together, and even trying to grab me and pull me in..."

"Hah! And you were scared stiff, right?"

"Well, then quick as an eel, I opened all the doors and hatches to get them out of there, kicking and sweeping to clear the decks. And then how they moved out over the sand! But, Captain, Sir, I have to tell you something...I noticed that they did not leave tracks behind them..."

Captain Terror didn't reply.

Side by side they stood stiffly in that dim eerie light; the silence was absolute, not even an echo. It was so quiet that after a while they began to hear something.

They heard the rising of an unseen tide within their very beings. It was the rising of a strange feeling they couldn't describe...a feeling a hundred times more powerful than rage, or hate, or fear. A feeling which gnawed at their very consciousness like a persistent nightmare. And their will, unable to resist, meekly crumbled before its onslaught.

"Sadness," murmured the Cabin Boy finally, without realizing why he had chosen that word. It had just come to him.

And then the Captain made a supreme effort to shake off the nightmarish reality around them by reverting to his harsh, blustery manner.

"Belay that, Boy! You are a pirate now! We've taught you to plunder, to use your sword, to take booty, and to burn..., and yet, I never ever heard you curse."

After a few moments, the Pirate Captain lowered his voice and asked softly, "Boy, you must know, tell me, where do you think we are?"

"Captain, Sir, I believe we are right where you think we are," the boy answered timidly.

"Well, damn me then!" the old Pirate guffawed. "We're hundreds of leagues down into the depths, at the very bottom of the sea!" But just as he burst out with the hearty laughter he was known for, he cut himself off, the sound still in his throat.

Because what he intended to be a hearty laugh came out as a tremendous groan, the anguished cry of someone else speaking from deep within his heart who had taken over his voice and his feelings; it was the voice of someone desperately trying to regain what he knew was forever lost...

Translated by Kenneth M. Taggart

# Hualpín

## Sonia Montecinos

A gentleman from Hualpín once described a tremendously wide island by the edge of a river. The residents of this island raise animals, in particular cows and sheep. The island is covered with sand. He said that from time to time tiny people appear on the island; they are born small and stay small.

One May day, the gentleman's neighbor went to round up his animals. He thought: "It looks like it's going to rain tonight, and the water could rise. I'm going to get the animals."

It was late. The fog had fallen, and it was very dark. The man got lost. Every time he tried to find the road, he ended up in the same spot. It was already midnight. He didn't know what else to do, so he said to himself, "I am going to have to stay here all night, sitting on the ground." All of a sudden, he encountered a little, old, white-haired woman wearing a shawl.

"What's wrong, young man?"

"Do you live here?" he asked.

"Yes, I live here. What are you doing out here in the cold? I will give you a place to stay. Follow me!"

He said that the tiny woman opened a door in the earth. Going down a stairway, they entered a huge house below. There was a lion on either side of the door, protecting it.

"Grr Grr!" growled the lions.

"Don't do that," the little old woman told them. "He's a guest."

The man passed through the door. Inside another little old woman

237

was cooking pheasant's feet in an big pot over the fire and was toasting flour like crazy! Every so often she would dip the pheasant's feet in the toasted flour. The little old woman who had found him had a rock and started to make flour furiously. They did this all night long. They sat him at the edge of the fire. He said the lantern's light was so bright that it seemed like daytime.

"Do you want flour? Do you want a little to eat?" the old woman asked him.

He asked himself, "What kind of flour could it be?" but responded, "Yes!" because he didn't want to refuse.

They served him water and flour on a clay plate with a wooden spoon. He ate it, but it was a bit sour so he left a little. He said that he looked up and noticed it was light outside. It was dawn, and the two little old women were still making flour and cooking over the fire.

One of them said, "Don't tell anyone that we live here or that you stayed here. Tell your daughter or son, but no one else. Don't bring anyone to look for us, because if you do, you will die. It is light out now; you should go home."

When the man left, it was foggy but light. One of the little old women pointed and said, "Follow that path." He followed it to the road, reaching his house around ten in the morning. The young man was with the Wün Kuzé, which is what the little people who live in the earth are called. When you see smoke rise from the earth in the morning, it is the women of dawn who are still stoking their fire and making flour.


Translated by Janice Molloy

# The Body That Talks

# Bicycles

## Agata Gligo

*Para mi hijo, Luis Cristobal*

It isn't easy to read the numbers on the buildings when the sidewalk is narrow. You end up walking along the curb to gain some distance at the risk of falling into the street. It has always been this way on Cathedral Street, even in the aftermath of the earthquake. Destruction lurks invisibly in the hopeless decrepitude of these houses. I think about this as I ascend the stairs feeling the wood creak beneath my feet. The other people on the stairway with me must be thinking about it too. On the landing, an arrow pointing upward tells me I'm going in the right direction. I read, "Criminal Court No.123," suddenly realizing that the number reveals the existence of one hundred and twenty-three criminal courts. Before, there were fifteen, twenty, twenty-four at most. One-hundred-and-twenty-three is an incredible number! But it is not surprising that they have steadily increased.

The waiting room is filled with the odor of stale tobacco from the cigarette butts that have been ground into the unwaxed floor. Tweed jackets and ragged sweaters divide the lawyers and the suspects into two distinct groups, while I sit at the end of a bench, the tiny flowers on my corduroy skirt trembling as I cross and uncross my legs. A tall, young man calls out my name in a loud voice. His strength gives me confidence. I follow him. He settles into the chair behind his desk. I wait for him to offer me a seat, but he doesn't. Putting a sheet of paper in the typewriter, he types for a long time, offering me a view of his right cheek, right ear and sideburn, the corner of his eye, his entire profile, implacable, unmoving, never looking at me.

"Age?" he asks.

"Thirty-eight."

"Place of birth?"

"Santiago, Chile." I separate the syllables, enunciating Chi-le, compelled by a sudden thirst for solemnity.

I decide to sit down while the questioning continues. The harsh voice reverberates off the high walls of the room. Whatever made me think he radiated masculine energy? He's nothing but a bully in a shirt and tie.

"So much for first impressions," I sigh to myself.

The important thing now is for him to change his profile and look me in the face. From the hexagonal skylight, a ray of light seems to validate his obstinance. As long as he doesn't look at me, I don't exist for him. My complaint will disappear, become nothing, just as I am about to become nothing. Why does he despise me? Because I have had only two bicycles stolen? I've come all the way across town to report my story, a drama completely different, I know, from the bloody, unsolvable ones for which more than one-hundred-twenty-three courts now exist. If the judicial system is tangled in knots, with new judges exhausted from the start by inconclusive findings, it isn't going to unravel like magic just to solve my domestic tragedy.

"Value?" he asks

"What?"

"What were they worth?"

"I don't know, I just want them back. The children get tired when they have to walk to school."

"How much?"

"About one-hundred dollars each," I answer reluctantly.

"And why did you say in your first statement that the thief is someone who is familiar with the house?"

The length of the question gives me hope. "Because they climbed the wall and they saw that the door didn't have a lock, so there wasn't any danger of getting locked in. And because this isn't the first time that they've robbed us."

"What did they take before?" he asks indifferently.

"Seven bicycles."

His profile turns, it dissolves. A wide ray of light falls through the broken glass of the skylight, erasing his features and giving his new face the round, smooth rigidity of a statue.

He repeats, "Seven bicycles?"

"Yes."

"It says here, 'Residence inhabited by its owner, his wife and two young children.' How many children do you really have?"

"Two.

"And you have seven bicycles for two children?"

"I did have," I lamented

"Are you sure they were only bicycles?" he asks deliberately.

"There may have been a tricyle..."

"Where did you file the report?"

"I don't remember."

"Or didn't you file one? And why not? This is an unusual case. Don't you think that's excessive?"

"Yes, but it's only seven bicycles in an entire lifetime."

Challenged by his silence, I continue. "I mean, no, not in a lifetime. Since we got married. Well, that's not right either. Actually, since the children became old enough to ride bicycles. Yes, that's it."

The sensation of terror is reserved for catastrophes and deaths that occur everyday. I feel a modest fear, a second-class fear that doesn't succeed—as terror does—in completely subordinating the soul to the body, or the body to the soul. It's more like a suspicion. I'm afraid I have said too much. Bicycles. It sounds too much like motorcycles, a word with connotations of violence and all kinds of shady characters. This guy in front of me could complicate the whole thing, I'm sure. I raise my eyes to look for a cheerful poster to prove my innocence: a boy pedalling in a green park full of flowers, preferably with a butterfly net in his hand. I see only a plaster garland on the wall, the tips broken, the paint peeling off.

"How were they stolen?"

"By two's. First two, then we bought more; a few years later, two more were taken, and..."

"And the rest?"

"The last ones disappeared five days ago," I explained.

"And?"

"You're going to tell me that one is unaccounted for. Well, they stole one separately."

"Really?"

"But I'm reporting only the two that were stolen recently. I told you about the others to help solve the case."

"Did you or did you not report the previous ones?"

"No."

"No?"

"I mean, yes, I think so. It's so long ago, I don't remember."

When I walked down Cathedral Street this noon with the summons in my hand, the layout of this part of the city seemed orderly, rectilinear, as in my student days. You no longer saw the old, handwritten signs in curtainless windows offering to take in roomers or mend stockings. The ailing, depressed neighborhood was coming to life with the privilege of housing so many tribunals whose bronze signs lit up the gray layer of smoke, dirt and, most recently, smog, that coats the facades.

In the interrogation room, the lines of a fake column branch off at the top to get lost in a web of intertwining curves. It bothers me to look at them. How is a labyrinth born? Somewhere I read that it is futile to look for the causes of momentous events. And what about the common, everyday events, this particular event: my possible or imminent transformation into the subject—or object—of an unpredictable legal case which this man, again ignoring me with his right profile, is documenting in a file which will surely grow larger?

Like everyone who navigates through anguish, I futilely turn back in desperation to the road that was offered to me and that I did not take. I should not have hesitated and stammered. Stammering always implies guilt. I could have defended my rights, become proud, aggressive, derogatory, defiant, responding that the possession of seven bicycles proved that I was a powerful person, a model citizen, a staunch defender of the private ownership of the means of transportation, that pillar of family unity, especially that of my own family. And, although his posture allowed him only a sideways view of life, I could have suggested that biking together has an invisible, educational advantage, similar to singing hymns in chorus: it strengthens the bonds between people. But, just as I couldn't find the beginning of the design on the pillar, I found it impossible to retrace my steps and guess where this episode would lead me.

The stench of old cigarette butts from the dry wood floor seeps through the half-opened door. It bothered me at first, I admit, but now I am used to it. If this case gets serious, they could send me to another court. I wouldn't like that. I already know this old, rickety mansion with its shaky walls, where the light no longer enters, blocked from its new angle by the dust on the skylight. Suddenly, the face that is questioning me gets lost in the shadows, as my own face does; it can't see me, I don't see it, the typewriter has become silent. I remain rigid, immobile, scarcely breathing. Am I still a person or have I turned into a ghost? Little by little, I can feel my silhouette being erased, vanishing, but instead of anxiety, I feel relief; I don't want to exist for his eerie, judgmental eye. That is why I remain so quiet in the completely dark room. Later, invisible, cautious, I will try to retrieve the report. The children can walk to school. We can walk through our sad, dejected city and we won't even try to get the bicycles back. Seven bicycles in a lifetime are enough.


Translated by Margaret Stanton

# Because We're Poor

## Elizabeth Subercaseax

It's cold now. This year's flood was a major one and since the adobe never had a chance to dry the house is still damp. My grandmother is the one who says that such things don't matter. She says that the cold kills when it reaches the heart but that it's not so bad if you use Alamiro's blanket. She also says there are two kinds of silence, the night's and the living dead's. Alamiro always argues with her. According to him, the only silence that exists is that of the dead. But I like what Chepe said before he left, that there are two kinds of people in this world, those who give orders and all the rest. The president, the bishop and the mayor belong to the first group. And Chepe also said that if you write them a letter you have to put Excellency, Eminence and Sir. If you don't write it that way it won't get delivered.

My grandmother woke up with her vision blurred. Every year during the month of October a certain sadness overtakes her. Her face becomes silent, the spark in her eyes goes out, she hardly speaks and walks around the patio as if the earth didn't exist. She stares at the air as if Chepe were there. Because what she wants is to find him there.

Alamiro is the one who told me that when Chepe was born my grandmother had two pigs killed and he went and bought wine at the cooperative. On the day Chepe was baptized they opened the doors of their home and people from the pueblo say that it was the best fiesta they had ever seen. They danced the "calladito" and Alamiro got crazy drunk. He kept jumping around the patio, pointing at the stars and yelling at them. You're Josefina, and you, Carmela, and that one hidden over there is Adela and the pale one's Francisco! And that's how he kept naming them. When Padre Hilario arrived Alamiro had to dunk his head in the pool of water because his speech was muddled and his eyes cloudy. I agree with my grandmother that being tipsy in the presence of a priest shows a lack of respect for the Virgin. Maybe it was for just this reason that God, in the middle of the baptism ceremony, took Padre Hilario away with Him. My grandmother was holding Chepe in her arms, Alamiro and the rest of the guests stood around her and when Padre Hilario said in the name of the Father, the Father took him. My grandmother put Chepe back on the bed and began to rock the Padre in her arms. As if he had an attack, but he didn't. Alamiro says they buried him in the cemetery that's located on a hillside overlooking El Trauco, on the side where the wind blows and the volcano smokes. He told me that that day El Trauco was smoking more than ever and you couldn't even see your own hands in the cemetery. On account of that big, black cloud of smoke. It's a good thing that Baudilio knew where the grave was.

That's why Padre Orlando baptized my Uncle Chepe and why the Padre stayed in this area. Until the day he died. It was really because my grandmother, almost desperate at the thought that Chepe would come into the world without a name, forced Alamiro to go look for another priest. In these campos you don't find very many. Because there's no church. Alamiro, given the fact that he was worried and believing that Padre Hilario's death was punishment for his getting drunk, set out in a hurry to look for another priest. In fact, he left at dawn on the day following the burial.

I really like to listen to Alamiro when he talks to me about that day. I don't know why I do but I do. He said he set out when it was still dark. Somebody had spoken to him about Padre Orlando, who lived on the hill where the fireflies gathered, way over there, beyond La Toribia stream, closer to Rinconada than to where we are. The road seemed so long, lonely and dusty to him, that he started to imagine that that's what the path of death must be like. Alamiro isn't afraid, but he doesn't like to talk about death. Everything was submerged in the silence of another world and the only noise was that of his own footsteps on the dirt road. I wonder if they gave me the wrong address?, he says he asked himself, thinking that he would never get there, but he did. They hadn't told him that Padre Orlando's house was so poor. When he saw a house that was barely standing, needing paint, crooked and propped up by supports, he thought for sure that he had made the trip in vain. The Padre couldn't possibly live there. But he did.

At the end of the room, on a bed, plunged in a world of darkness, lay Padre Orlando. Alamiro says that his face was full of fear as if he had seen something terrible, and his throat was so thin and his hands so stiff holding onto a wooden cross that Alamiro got scared and instead of asking him if he could baptize his son, he asked him if he was in this life or the other.

In this one, still—said the priest smiling a bit.

That's the part I like best: "in this one, still".

That same afternoon they set out for here. And since the Padre had a hard time walking, Alamiro got Baudilio to lend him a wagon. They arrived on the following morning. My grandmother was peeling *mote* in the patio when Alamiro called her.

"I found a priest who does baptisms His name is Padre Orlando and he uses two scapulars. When he speaks about Jesus he raises his arms like a bird," he said to her.

"He's not sick from anything, is he?" my grandmother asked.

"No, not at all," Alamiro said as he blessed himself.

"Then, go get him," said my grandmother.

My grandmother went running out of the house and when she reached the wagon she stood on her tiptoes. She had never before seen such a foresaken and exhausted soul. With his gaze toward heaven, his eyes half closed and his arms crossed, he looked as if he had seen the evil eye. Resting on his chest were a rosary and missal.

"You brought us a dead priest!" my grandmother shouted.

"He's feeling a little faint," replied Alamiro as he looked at his feet.

"Stop looking at your feet and help me get him down."

Now my grandmother says that it was a real miracle that Father Orlando was able to baptize Chepe. But in these parts miracles tend to be bigger ones than in other areas, because Father Orlando died a week after Chepe left.

The fact that Chepe has left home I just can't understand. Maybe the death of the oxen had something to do with it. When he turned fifteen Alamiro told him that Fulgencio and Primitivo were his to keep. It's true that Fulgencio and Primitivo were old but not that old that they should die like that. It happened in the middle of that winter, on the way to Pilar's field. Chepe had taken them out in the early morining and on the way back he said he hardly made it to the high ground of Las Máquinas when Fulgencio and Primitivo sunk in the mud, raised their heads as if saying goodbye to the world, and then turned over and remained there, with their feet holding up the sky and the look of death in their eyes. Maybe that's what influenced Chepe. But my grandmother says that that same night they heard a helicopter, that the oxen's death doesn't have anything to do with Chepe's departure, but that the helicopter does.

Now my grandmother is sorry they went to such pains to give Chepe an excellent education.

"I tell you, Alamiro, if Chepe had studied in the school at Tapihue none of this would have ever happened."

Why did they sign him up for school in Lontué? My grandmother was always asking that question. The school in Tapihue had few facilities, just a one room school house, that's all, and only one teacher, Miss Lidia, but Chepe would have learned just the same, my grandmother was sure of that. Alamiro was the one who insisted. They had to give their son the best education possible and he was told that even a minister of the government had graduated from the school in Lontué.

By the time he turned fourteen Chepe was already saying weird things, reading political pamphlets and speaking to Salustio Moena. Everyone said that Salustio Moena's past was unknown, that he had come to these parts to preach strange truths and that he was stirring up the campesinos against the patrón. When he turned fifteen Alamiro decided to give Chepe the pair of oxen to see if he could get him enthused about farm work.

Alamiro says that the land ennobles the life of the poor. It doesn't matter that you have to use candlelight in the rural areas, but in the city it would be impossible because there there are no campos. Pure cement and nothing else.

Why didn't you say that to him before sending him off to the school in Lontué? My grandmother blames Alamiro. But Alamiro is not to blame for the things that started happening. He says that the country has fallen into terrible times. That was why there were helicopters hovering over El Trauco. That was why people were now afraid. I still hadn't been born but fear was even stuck like glue to the stones of the road and, understandably, even today you can feel it all around you. Especially when you go to the grotto and pray at Gilberto's animita.

Gilberto and Chepe were the only ones who studied in Lontué. Maybe that's why people respected them. They knew how to read and had begun to speak like gentlemen. Alamiro is the one who's always telling me about the day they threw Gilberto into El Trauco. It must have been a terrible day for everyone, but Alamiro says that in those days everything was terrible. That morning they were celebrating the feastday of the Virgin when that captain arrived in a truck. He was looking for Gilberto and here is where he found him. Alamiro tells me that Gilberto was sitting in this chair where I'm sitting now when the captain entered the house saying that Gilberto had to go with him. Chepe wanted to go too.

"Not you," the captain said, but as soon as the captain and Gilberto left in the truck, Chepe jumped on Nieblina and galloped after them. Chepe was the one who told Alamiro what he saw in Pilar's field. He told him that he remained hidden among the willows. In the middle of the field there was a helicopter and next to the glass bird was another man. Chepe had never seen him before. He must have been the pilot because he was the one who got on board first and took hold of the control stick which Chepe could see from where he was. Chepe said that Gilberto was pale and trembling, that a certain anguish arose in his eyes and that he didn't say a word. They put him on the helicopter, in fact they pushed him on according to Chepe. The captain got on board too and shut the bird's only door and then it began to turn a huge propeller located in its head and to roar and then climb. With the captain, the pilot and Gilberto all inside it. From his hiding place, Chepe saw how they soared and headed towards El Trauco, which was a little farther away.

At first Chepe thought about returning home, but he stayed. They might come back at any moment. But they didn't. The bird flew over the top of the volcano, over its smoke hole when Chepe saw the door open and Gilberto fly through the air and then fall into the mouth of El Trauco, just the way the queltehues do, like a bird cut down by a gunshot.

Afterwards the helicopter headed in the other direction, kept climbing until it was just a dot and gone from sight. Chepe told Alamiro that his vision blurred and that on the way back he couldn't see the road. Because his eyes were filled with tears and his heart was heavy.

Just remembering all this makes me shiver. It was on the following day that Chepe left. He only said that he had things to do in Lontué and that he'd be back as soon as he finished his errands. Chepe was like that, reserved, he didn't like to give explanations. He left with the clothes he had on. Alamiro says he didn't even take a coat. It was the month of October and in October it always rains here. Time went by. First weeks, then two months. And Chepe, as if the earth had swallowed him up. Not a letter, not a single sign of him. My grandmother became more and more desperate and Alamiro more and more quiet.

"Go look for him in the barracks," people told my grandmother.

"What would Chepe be doing in the barracks? Chepe didn't have anything to do with the military. On the contrary, he couldn't stand them."

"Exactly for that reason look for him in the barracks," the people kept telling my grandmother.

Alamiro began living as if he were paralyzed. That's why it was my grandmother who set out to look for him. Wherever she went it was the same old story. Your son's not here, they'd tell her. One colonel even said that her son didn't exist. How could Chepe not exist? And those golden-colored eyes, and that way of laughing that he had, and those hands that squeezed the clamp on his guitar to tune it up when he played the calladito, and the birthmark on his neck, and the sketch he drew right after he entered the school in Lontué which my grandmother still keeps at the head of her bed? How is it possible that Chepe didn't exist? But that's what the colonel said.

The house started to fill up with shadows. It was a good thing they brought me to live with my grandparents, because before I arrived this house was immersed in semi-darkness. My grandmother stopped combing her hair and Alamiro spoke to himself. Always about Chepe, the things he would say, his way of looking at life, even the jokes he would tell and sometimes he sang like Chepe, but little by little his voice became silent.

It was about two years ago that the lists appeared. Chepe's name was on one of them and when my grandmother went to speak with the mayor of Lontué they told her that Chepe had died in a confrontation. During the time of the military, they said. And soon they would hand over the first bodies. From that time on my grandmother and Alamiro have been going every other week to Lontué. But I don't think they're going to give us his bones. Because we're poor. That's why.


Translated by John J. Hassett

# The Bone Spoon

## Luz Larrain

*To Gabriel*

He looked for it several times, feeling a frenzy of uneasiness each time the cupboard drawers revealed only its absence. His chore of gathering the family together was coming to an end and the ritual was about to begin.

One by one the compulsory guests occupied their places at the dining room table. Aurelio was aware of the role that the utensil would play, now that all of them were together; the piano music and the melodies of the 40s almost seemed to enliven an atmosphere laden with tensions. "Brazil," "Muñequita linda," "Besamé mucho." The ladies picked up their napkins and casting charming glances at each other, they decided to settle themselves quite comfortably in their chairs.

"Where is it? Who took it?"

The master of the house perused the faces of his guests; he decided to give it up for a moment, considering the expectancy of those waiting for the roast beef to be carved.

"Could you have taken it hunting? Maybe last Sunday, Aurelio. Besides it's only a spoon." Berta whispered the last words rather impatiently, certain they would be a source of indignation in the key of F sharp major.

"You're always picking on me. Nothing's sacred." Aurelio countered with a rabid hoarseness in his voice that also eased the saliva caught in his throat.

"Ssh...speak softer. Think of grandmother." Rita took out her compact and opening it applied lipstick to her parched lips.

"The children...that's it. The children did it."

"What's it all about?" Everyone tried to help.

"It's not important. Why go on so about it?" Doña Berta preferred to leave things as they were As the lady of the house she felt duty bound to change the subject, especially in light of the emergency, almost obligatory, situation that had brought them together.

"I read in the paper today that by the year 2000 people won't have any hair."

Loud laughter overshadowed these prophetic words; she continued filling the intervals of silence with diverse anecdotes, all in a twelve-by-eighteen foot room that little by little was becoming an enclosure filled with murmurs and laughter.

In the adjoining room, Doña Adelaida, her eighty-some-year-old mother-in-law, was coughing, almost choking. Carola, her granddaughter, offered her a glass of water to ease the attacks. Six days and six nights of vigil had forced each of the relatives to take a turn.

"I love Carola," the old woman repeated monotonously.

Without a doubt the on-going gathering was comforting to the heads of the household, their weariness reflected in the dark cirdes under their eyes.

Aurelio again appeared. He was coming from the kitchen, exhibiting the object in question as though it were a trophy from some competition. It was the bone spoon.

"You can begin," he said, heaving a sigh of satisfaction. All looked at him, thinking their friend was crazy. Why was that object that distracted everyone so important?

"They say that Tamara dances Bolero as naked as the day she was born."

"That's awful!"

"What goes on in a person's bedroom is nobody's business. Don't you think?"

"It's in very bad taste."

"Maybe it makes her feel better. Psychologists make everything complicated now."

The tinkling of the glasses blended with the voices; in the adjoining room the old woman's cough rattling the window panes became more evident. Therefore, at this point, Berta thought it would be better to turn down the volume of the radio. A small earthquake hit the table when Aurelio sat down. The battle was lost; they were putting mustard on the meat using the traditional table spoon. His work of art postponed, iniquitously forgotten through the fault of someone who had hidden it in the farthest corner of the kitchen. Nevertheless, he slipped the bone spoon into the gravy boat with an air of dignity and slowly spread the gravy over his slice of meat.

"You're so artistic about everything, Aurelio." Agata took off her glasses and looked over her shoulder; meanwhile she moved the toe of her foot until it touched Aurelio's calf, hidden beneath the intimacy of the tablecloth.

"The greatest delay was the time it took to boil the bone; it was truly a time consuming job." Aurelio seemed really engrossed in his topic.

"Well then...tell us about it, brother. Are you saying that that little spoon you looked for so hard was a bone?" Rita laughed for no good reason.

While Aurelio related in detail the long process involved in producing the spoon, there was total silence. First, there was astonishment on discovering that the bone's anatomical form was perfect for conversion into an object for serving gravy.

"You can begin. "

"It's excellent, Aurelio. This time the meat came out just right."

"I like it cooked more."

"You're an outstanding cook. It takes a load off of Berta's shoulders." Their voices mingled tumultously.

The repeated coughing of the grandmother began to make the throats of the group hurt; all listened to the choking fit that now shook the glass in the entry door. Doña Berta raised the tone of her voice such that the noise produced in the adjoining room was immediately silenced.

"I propose a toast to the head of the house." Having said this, she took the spoon and put it in the gravy boat insinuating that it would remain there forever. Now Rita took over.

"We can no longer eat calmly. I remember when we used to go to Calera de Tango on Sundays." She tried to lighten the atmosphere darkened by that cough that was becoming more and more intense.

"You almost risk your life at midnight, don't you think," she repeated in a sharper voice.

"I worry when the motor overheats." Aurelio was chewing on the sinewy bits of meat, pretending not to worry about his mother's illness, while the nudges from Agata's shoe made it difficult for him to remain calm.

The door of the room opened and the slender figure of Carola stood there in the midst of all the rowdiness.

"Mama...it's grandmother. She wants to tell you something."

Doña Berta gestured for the others to continue as they were.

"I'm coming, Carolita. Take care of the dessert."

The immense room once again caught her unawares. The feather pillows were now strewn on the floor at the foot of the bed, the armchair and the washstand with the pitcher on the bureau, the smell of rice powder and sandalwood that covered the dressing table. She arranged the handkerchief that hid part of her mothers' white hair that had come loose from her bun.

"What's wrong? What's the matter now?" The grandmother moved restlessly. The cough turned into rhythmic, heavy breathing then worsened until it became a suffocating whistle. Then she unbuttoned her nightshirt and the poultice slid down to her yellow and wrinkled abdomen. The result of ten pregnancies, thought Berta.

"You'll see. This is going to help. "

She replaced the dry plaster with one recently wrung out in the pot that slowly boiled on the hot plate. Carola had entered very quietly, and taking her mother's hand, began to squeeze it affectionately. More than once she had thought her parents' friends were frivolous; she might say they were a group of opportunistic people—the relatives included—unaware of the course of their lives. Everything was reduced to eating drinking and above all laughing at nothing. Her father wasn't bad and she suspected that little or nothing was left of her grandfather's fortune for him to squander.

"Do you want a cup of coffee, Mama?" She looked at Berta's face, tired after so many nights watching the old woman die.

"I want them to leave, that's the only thing I want. Under the pretext of keeping us company, they're converting this house into a place of noisy uproar and confusion."

Around the bed were flying two moths attracted by the orange colored light of the faintly glowing lamp. As if this were not disassociated from the activities in the other room, you could clearly hear the sound of glasses raised in a late night toast and a few conversations fading out as the night fell over them. Little effort was made to put coherent phrases together.

"Mother...grandmother's eyes aren't moving."

Carola let go of her mother's hand and approached on tip toe, the floor creaking, afraid of the figure that had grown silent in the bed.

"Tell them to be quiet...those people out there and especially tell Rita; she has no compassion for her mother." Berta, also watchful, did not move.

The door opened as though by the wind and a profile appeared in the doorway.

"The wine is all gone. Aurelio says he can't find the keys, Berta."

Rita's aquiline nose stood out in the shadows. The hairpins had slipped out of her hair as though catapulted by the electricity in the air.

"Good Lord! None of you is worth a damn. Carola, tell them."

Rita, stumbling, took three steps into the room and looked toward the three figures grouped in an almost perfect geometric triangle. Carola had begun to bend over the pillows and her long hair was a curtain covering her face

"Has something happened?" Rita's hiccup cut through the question.

"Yes, grandmother died."

Translated by Janet Spinas Cunningham

# The House
## Margarita Niemeyer

On the outside it was nothing special, just some walls made out of bricks and mortar, a flat slate-colored roof and a few dusty geraniums trying to bloom. She had almost turned the job down, because she felt it was beneath her dignity to make money keeping a house like that clean. Even her own place looked better, with its bright pots of flowers that she watered every day, and the little painted bench Lucho had made her when he worked at the machine shop down in the harbor.

But to open the door was to plunge into the sunlight that danced on the multicolored throws covering the living room furniture, to hammer at the age-old copper and iron of the pots and pans and see her face reflected in them; to help tighten the leather thongs on the old fishing baskets and wrap in golden rays, piece by piece, all the ancient pottery of painted clay. For the master of the house was an archeologist, or something like that, and those were the things that kept him busy when he came on vacation, valuable objects, one of a kind, and she had to take very good care of them, being careful not to break them as she cleaned because they were part of our national heritage, or so the lady of the house had told her. And then the master told her how some Indians had once lived here and the most beautiful pot might have belonged to his great-great-grandparents, and as she listened she decided not to tell him he was wrong, because she had known his great-great-grandma, who she knew had never owned anything as pretty as that and who wasn't an Indian either, because she didn't look anything like the Indians on TV who were always fighting the white man, or those others called *mapuches* he says live down south. But she kept all that to herself, because the master was such a cheerful guy and such a gentleman, so interested in everyone, and he had always helped her, right from the time her old man got lost at sea and she was left all alone with her Lucho just a baby.

At first, and for a long time after, it was the sheer pleasure of coming down the hill each Thursday, as soon as her favorite TV serial was over, keys in hand, eager to get there and take a good look around before she started cleaning. She was sure she could list each object in order with her eyes closed—even the smallest, like that shiny needle which, the master told her, a very old Indian lady had worn in her hair. Even everyday things looked different there, like the dried-up old starfish on the ledge under the lightest-colored bookcase, which she would have kicked aside on the beach but would never have kept in her house, and there it was looking just right, as if it belonged.

Every Thursday she would carefully pick out the key to the door and go inside, throwing back curtains to let in the hot sun and opening the windows wide, so the fresh sea air could drive out the barely perceptible odor of dampness clinging to the hidden surfaces of the house. Then grabbing the broom and mop, she would proceed to clean much more thoroughly than she had been asked to, because she liked feeling the warmth of the pots against the roughness of her hands, those clay surfaces so satiny smooth that they broke through years of oblivion, taking her back to a prehistoric time of her own when she dared caress her breasts grown hard with fear and pleasure, over beyond the hill, among the secluded rocks.

This time, however, she wasn't looking for *huacos* or ancient pots to rearrange when she decided to skip her program. What she wanted was to sit quietly for a while in the doorway, and air her aching bones along with the stuffiness inside the house. The aching in her bones had started right about when Lucho disappeared and no one knew anything and her daughter-in-law just cried and cried and then got it into her head to go back to her own family and leave her kid with grandma. For a month now she had awakened with that same old aching sensation, starting in her knuckles, and right off she remembered her cousin Isabel, so young and with her hands all bent like claws; of course, Isabel would always have the kettle on before the frost was off the kneading trough, even in the dead of winter, no matter how often she had told her to wait until sunrise. But with so many kids, what else was a woman to do; she had always considered herself lucky to have only one, although now, well, at least Mercedes hadn't taken José Luis with her.

It wasn't arthritis, the doctor said, when the pain burrowed into her thighs and calves, it's nerves, try walking and drink warm milk, he told her, not telling her how to buy the milk she needed for José, and now that even the money the archeologist sends her is past due, the mail from Santiago is hit-or-miss, just wait they tell her, the only news that reaches here from outside is on TV, there may as well have been an earthquake. And it's incredible how things happen in pairs, like going to clean the house and smelling piss in a corner of the living room, strong, sharp, and sickening, pure ammonia.

At first she thought it was some freesias she had left in a vase the last time she'd been there. But no; the freesias were beginning to wilt in their own pungent but fragrant perfume, and the water smelled as fresh and clean as if it had just been poured. That other smell was old, like when someone piddles then takes off for good, like the smell of those dark wooden poles that drunks pee on as a way of saying they've been there.

She went back over the whole living room floor with steel wool, then waxed it again, even though she had done so the previous Thursday; and she wiped every surface she could get at with bleach and water. She used half a bottle of furniture polish on the hard-to-reach legs of desks and chairs, wondering if maybe a mouse had gotten in, but there were no signs of mice, or holes for them to crawl through, or anything like that. She washed the curtains and stayed later than usual, waiting for them to dry so she could iron them and hang them back up, so they wouldn't fade out there in the sun.

When she closed the windows before leaving, she noted to her satisfaction that the sickening odor was gone; then she walked briskly back up the hill to her house to see what kind of a mess José had made while she was out and to light the fire, these days kids are no help, now my Lucho, he was something else, and to fix dinner, because I won't have him playing with matches, something might happen to him too, God forbid.

The next morning the smell was back, stronger than ever. Now it permeated not just a corner but the whole living room, and it threatened to invade the dining room as well. Desperate, she opened all the windows, what will the master and his wife say when they come back, they'll think I don't clean; and she didn't even answer the phone, three times she waited on line to make that long distance call and now it's ringing and ringing and she doesn't answer, maybe it's the wax, but it's the same brand I've always used, sure that it wasn't the wax and that anyway, she had no money to buy another can unless the money order arrived, over three weeks late just when you're out of cash, it seemed everything was happening at once.

She cleaned, swept, checked corners, removed ancient cobwebs from ceilings she hadn't been hired to clean. She spent hours disinfecting the bathroom, kneeling on the floor in front of the toilet, and the sink, so often on her knees of late that she had lost count of the times, with that snapshot of Lucho dressed for his first communion, there were no others she had to explain, and they had laughed at the armband with his name in gold letters, at the candle in his hand, we don't know they'd say, come back tomorrow, sign here, they'd say; the Virgin of Andacollo, I must go see her with Mercedes, that silly girl, she refused to show them the wedding picture, maybe they'd recognize him, but maybe they'll take it away too she says. And I must go with José to visit Our Lord of Miracles, and pray to please let my Lucho be all right, the way I see it you have to try everything, cleaning the bidet inside and out, scrubbing at every sign of a crack on the impervious porcelain. That day she had no time for TV, the sun was long gone by the time she closed the curtains again, and it was dark when she got back home.

She spent all week waiting for the money order. She cared more about buying the wax than getting paid, there was no way she would let a bad smell take over her house and have it end up like the big old place those glue-sniffing hoodlums burned down last year, after turning it into a public bathroom and who knows what else. But that other house had no owners, because the owners were all dead and their heirs—just distant cousins and in-laws who cared more about the land than the house, anyway—were too busy fighting over their money.

Every day she called the number the lady of the house had left her, but with no luck. The phone just rang and rang, deaf to her silent prayers. No one ever answered. On Wednesday, after they paid her for a load of wash, she decided to act on her own and buy the wax, they'd just try and make do, she and José, until the money order arrived, after all, now they'll have to send two months worth at the same time and that way you come out ahead.

On Thursday morning she thought she would have much more to do than other days, and it occurred to her to take the kid along to help with the windows.

That afternoon, however, she caught herself dragging her feet and making idle woman-talk with that do-nothing neighbor of hers; and she even thought about stopping by to collect what Señora Susie over on the next block owed her for some ironing.

Buying the can of wax was a drawn-out affair as well, complete with discussions about brands and different types and lots of haggling that ended with it's a real giveaway, I'm only selling it that cheap 'cause it's homemade, and an embarrassed Jose tugging on the sleeve of her jacket.

She clutched harder and harder at the keys in her right hand as she approached the house. She decided to check thoroughly before opening the door, in order to avoid surprises. Outside there were no cat or mouse turds to be found. Everything seemed in good order. She gave the geraniums a good soaking, washing off the dust from the street and finally, holding tight to her can of wax, how silly, an old lady like me, she took hold of the key and opened the door, as simple as that.

But the stench was still there, hideous, all over everything, suffocating her, sneering at her, everything had hit her all at once, her Lucho in big trouble and now she's alone with José Luis, Mercedes leaving, saying she's afraid, saying she'd better go home to her mom, if Lucho shows up he can come after her she says, sure, that'll be real easy, anyhow, where can Lucho be, hidden away somewhere, he must have been arrested, why doesn't anyone say anything, and now what to do about this nauseating smell of piss here in the house, and the money they used to send me for cleaning and buying the wax and the furniture polish and all that, how do they expect you to clean, they stop sending money and they don't answer the phone anymore, just when Lucho disappears, just when Mercedes ups and decides to leave and with no one saying a word, and it's like the only thing that's for sure is the TV series that goes on and on and never ends and the president who shows up smiling on the news, with his uniform all neatly pressed and his officials, cutting ribbons and kissing babies, he's looking out for them, he says—José, be careful—then, finally, in tears, because if I had known what to do about this smell of piss or how to get rid of it I would have done something, but I told you to be careful you lousy shit, and now you show up here to break the prettiest pot in the master's collection.

Translated by Louise B. Popkin

# The Journey
## Ana Pizarro

The passenger opens the window and the rhythm of the wheels of the train on the tracks enters with a few puffs of smoke that fill the entire car. He suddenly wanted to perceive it directly, without letting the glass of the window intervene as it turned yellow toward the edges until it penetrated the wood. The region is unpleasant and mountainous, almost deserted. A few hours ago the pine vegetation began, leaving behind the poplar cove. The landscape continued darkening until the intense green of the moment, favored by the afternoon light that filtered through the layer of clouds. The trip has been long; when he took the train yesterday and the ticket agent behind the window reminded him that it was a sixteen-hour trip, he appeared surprised as if he had forgotten the distance in these past ten years. Only from above, while he watched the steward prepare his bed, did he feel that there was something familiar in all that. Never had he seen a similar rail car in all his time travelling around the world. They no longer existed. They belonged to an older time—almost a century ago—when economic prosperity had touched the region because of the introduction of a salt peter refinery in the north. That caused the English to invade the country with trains made according to their specifications and convenience. The native inhabitants—workers, artisans, merchants—travelled in third class cars at the end, in wagons with wooden seats that creaked the entire journey and smelled of sweat. They travelled content, believing that progress had arrived.

When the conductor looked strangely at his ticket, he told him that although it designated the next station, he would get off at Trafquen. The conductor in turn, replied ill-humoredly that he knew what he was doing, but that they would have to make a special stop because there hadn't been a station there in many years. He barely slept during the night and told himself that it was probably because what separated him from the corridor and the other passengers was that heavy velvet curtain that maintained some of its old elegance in spite of its frayed edges. At daybreak he had finally allowed himself to be carried off by the sleep that usually follows nights of insomnia, when a hand touched his shoulder and rocked him. He then opened the curtain on one side and the steward asked him if he desired breakfast in bed. He decided to get dressed in order to view the landscape. He had carried this landscape within him for so many years, always fearing that he would forget some detail, miss the shade of green or the dark hue of the clouds. Only once, a short time ago, he was surprised by someone who talked about the moss on the rocks. This made him tremble. It was true: living there meant always being confronted by the moss on the rocks. Then he told himself that he had to return, even if it were only to see where he had come from. He was glad about his sudden decision and felt that his life almost suffered from a serene happiness because of it. He thought about the all-red face of the butcher and his surprise to see him again. He wondered if they had paved the streets and he felt nostalgic about his childhood.

Topahue had once been an important lumber center. For an instant he thought that he was breathing the smell of the sawmills, seeing the wooden huts where working class families improvised their housing and where barefoot, red-cheeked children played. When it drizzled, one could hear the clear and distant train whistle. There was no definite transportation from Trafquen and the only motor vehicle was the tractor of the lumberyard that took turns transporting the patrimony of the sawmills. People arrived by horse. However, it was always possible to find good-willed drivers who would transport neighbors who preferred the oxen's route to completing the journey on foot and dodging the puddles.

It had only taken him one week to prepare for the trip, and before boarding the plane that would bring him to his country, his children and his wife barely recognized him and were surprised to see him arrive with his grey hair dyed a dark shade of brown. He didn't have to give them a major explanation; they had learned to know when they ought not to question, so that he packed a light suitcase, said I'll return soon and left. In three minutes, the conductor tells him, you get off at the station and the train will continue. We are doing you a favor. When the train departs, he remains a few minutes in the middle of a deserted station, with his valise still in his hand, because his chest is pounding and he feels an infinite sadness that descends to his knees. A while ago, when the immensity of the river appeared in his window—tranquil, blue and enormous between the pines—he was sure.

I am from here, he said to himself, and the view innundated him for a moment. They still haven't paved the streets, and while he looks for a place to have some coffee it seems to him as if time has come to a standstill in the linden trees of the plaza, where he sees himself as a child arriving on horseback. Topahue? The woman prepares instant coffee. She is old and unkempt, and seems to be among the few living inhabitants that he has seen wandering aimlessly through the streets of the village. "Don't go over there, friend, it isn't worth it. It isn't worth it. Stay here. Here you can drink some coffee, or beer if you like. Over there you won't find anyone. There is no longer any business there, there is no commerce or activity. One can scarcely talk with anyone other than the dead, who don't leave you alone. It is a cold place. Before the military arrived, there certainly was a lot going on. They came in search of flour, sugar and coffee when they brought the wood to sell. You have probably heard talk about the corn festival, or about when they installed light. But then the lumber industry arrived with the military and the sawmills began to disappear. The slaughter of the people also came. They brought them through the poplar cove on top of the trucks, with their hands tied. People stopped coming from other villages as well, and then the blacksmith went away, they say, to the north. The bakery closed because they sold a black bread that no one ate. The masons had no more work. In the beginning one left and was followed by all of the remaining young men. It must have been when you left. The other lasted a little longer, but he said that the dead men would not let him sleep, that they followed him into the houses asking him about those who had not returned to the village. About those who had been carried off never to be heard from again. He said that that was their obsession because they feel lonely. He said that they go about taking possession of you until you end up with them. He was one of the last ones to go away. The lumber industry had already left everything bare. 'We will return in twenty years,' they said, when there are new pine groves. Later they didn't come back to look for anyone else because there was no one left to take away. Even the dead calmed down and returned to their homes without ever again thinking about the others. In Topahue and later in Trafquén everything began to dry up: the land, the animals and the people drying up like the trees, and they ended up like them, with their arms in the air, against the wind. Finish your coffee friend, there is no hurry. You say you want to return now; don't be silly. Don't go. You can't just leave here, you can no longer leave. The conductor won't even see you when he passes by. He doesn't make the train stop, because he knows that in this village, for a long time now, we are all beneath the earth. Sit down my friend, sit down. Drink your coffee, there is no hurry. And tell me: the ones they took away, those who never returned, where are they?"

Translated by Celeste Kostopulos-Cooperman

# Journey of the Watermelon

## Virginia Vidal

*It is the fruit of the tree of thirst*
*It is the green whale of summer...*
—Pablo Neruda

Today, Monday, the telegram arrived. My heart's pounding in my throat. I have to get out of the store, catch my breath, get some air and calm these palpitations. Just now a boat is crossing the river. Counting today, there's only three days left before I too cross it, take two airplanes and arrive at where he is. God. To cross more than two thousand miles. I'm going to pieces. I begin to pack the suitcase. What should I bring him? What does he most need? Everything! To think I thought he was dead. And now I'm going to see him. Already it's Thursday...and nothing's ready. I fold a stack of clothes. I put in his finest shirt and best outfit. I count my money. I calculate how much I'll have to spend on bus fare... I inspect the pantry shelves. Chocolates? Some preserves? How I'd love to put everything he likes into a huge shopping bag. And what about fruit? Where should I buy some? I'll go into the city tonight. The plane flight leaves early tomorrow morning. In the capital I'll have to take care of so many things. What if I don't have time to buy him something there? In the corner, over there, are some lovely watermelons. They say they're worth their weight in gold there. My neighbor told me that they sell them in slices which they call "monitos."

Yes, that's it. Though it may seem crazy I'll bring him a watermelon all the way from here... I leave my daughter in charge of everything. She understands: I'm going to see him, to smell that tart odor of his. How I desire to touch his beard, to have it prick me... The boat is moving so slowly. God. I'm so anxious. Slowly the islands pass by. The blue hydrangea stares out in a daze over the water. At last, there is the pier. I rush to the train station. All night on the train. No rest, no sleep. Everything welling up in my memory. Everything being brought back to life At first I thought he uas dead. Then lost... I leave the train station carrying my bags and suitcase. I try to orient myself. To the airlines. But there are no taxis available! And it's almost day-break.

I could just cry. I've reserved a flight for this morning, Thursday, which is the only visiting day. I should have left yesterday morning, early, on a bus and I'd be there by now, and I could have gotten a room somewhere and rested up a bit. I don't want to be wearing this distraught face. I'm so thin. Oh I know, I'll go to the hairdresser. I'll have them dye my gray hairs, give me a good cut. A beautiful hairdo. I'll look real pretty. Airborne at last. Now we're flying over the desert. It looks like an animal hide parched to the bone. Not one patch of green anywhere... God willing, I'll be with him at noontime. From the airport to the city. Then from there to the interior. It's funny: I've planned everything as though I were an expert, someone who's trav-eled here often, I who have always been so reluctant to travel. Truth is, I don't know anything about this region, but I ll ask...

Damn. I just missed the bus that goes directly there by only a cou-ple of minutes. I have to make a diversion on another bus that goes further to the north. On the crowded bus I adjust my luggage as well as I can, and cradle the watermelon in my lap with loving care. It weighs like the devil... Such a dreary landscape. We leave behind the hills that surround the city. Everything is an ochre color. A few barren ridges. Not even a blade of grass grows here. And this heat. I feel so drowsy. I'm sinking into the dry heat, into the whine of the motor... In the distance I hear the bus driver s voice: "Señora, do you see those chimneys way over there? That's it. You're going to have to walk quite a ways." The other passengers feel sorry for me. It's already past noon...

I start walking. And walking. The chimneys also seem to be moving. As though separating themselves from me. As though poking fun at me... Yes, I am going to see him... But it's difficult walking with the suitcase and bags. And this sun is piercing, scorching, pounding on my head. I cover myself with my jumper. Strange. It seems the wool actually offers some cool relief. My feet keep getting swallowed up in the sand. Ah! I can make out a stream bed up ahead. I pick up my pace. Ah, to relieve my feet in its cool water... I keep walking. And walking. I keep shifting the suitcase and bags from one hand to the other. I mustn't stop to rest. I must see him before visiting time is over... I almost feel like crying. It's not a stream bed at all; only where some greenish metal has run off. A mean trick. Off in the distance, I can make out what looks like a little field of watercress. This has to be what they call a mirage... I'm totally covered in dust. My shoes are cutting into me. The sweat is pouring off me. The chimneys seem to be getting taller. A blinding reflection is hurting my eyes. It looks like a steamy, shimmering pool of water... God, I'm so exhausted. I've no more strength left. But if I want to get there, I must quit this complaining and push on. I throw myself on the ground, rip off my blouse and clean off my face, neck and arms with it. Worse than black soot. I take a clean blouse out of the suitcase. It didn't occur to me to bring a little bottle of cologne... I take out my papers and money. I wrap them in a handkerchief and place it in my bosom. It's difficult abandoning everything. What's hardest is leaving behind the little gifts I'm taking to him. But I refuse to leave the watermelon behind, even if it kills me. Oh, what strength I'll have to muster so as not to abandon it... I drink what tea is still left in the thermos. Regrettably I open the package of sweets that I was bringing for him. With its little silvery wrapper I put one in my mouth. They're melted. I hug my watermelon and continue walking. And walking. My legs feel heavy and rough as wool. Sweat's dripping down my temples and it's driving me crazy. My lips are parched and cracking. My tongue's like leather. I'm so exhausted that my arms could just drop off, as if they just wanted to be rid of the bag. I toss it over my back, hook each strap on my shoulder. I keep on walking.

Oh beautiful. A lake of soapy water. No. It resembles snow. Like a frozen lake you can skate on. But if I approach it , I'll be going away from the chimneys. They're very close now. With all my soul I pray for the strength. God, remember how I cried over his death. It's a miracle knowing he's alive. God, please perform another miracle. Oh, let me see him again. I've waited so long and hard for this day... I continue walking on as much as I am able. The chimneys can't escape from me now. I know I'll get there. I know he needs me now. But this terrain is so strange. It's as if they had swept it totally clean. They probably had wanted to fence it in... Now I can make out the buildings. I hang the bag from one arm and then pass my other arm through the straps, so that it's easier to hold. I can barely walk. I'm dragging my feet. My knees are buckling, they're so weak... But I'll make it... The sound of a motor! They're shouting at me. Calling out to me. They're military. I turn around. They're shouting at me like I'm a criminal. Why don't they show some compassion and approach me? They're such jerks. They order me to walk slowly, even though I'm only dragging my feet along. One of them is screaming himself hoarse: don't put down the bag. They're crazy. If only they knew how far I've brought this watermelon... Finally, I start walking toward them. What do they want? Are they going to take me prisoner? Won't they let me see him? Well then. They can just take this bag to him... They keep on shouting at me. They order me to walk carefully, tracing the letter "S" in the sand. They shout at me some more. I'm only a few meters away from them and still they make no sign of approaching me. One of them starts to kick and raise clouds of sand... I feel like I'm about to faint. One of them finally comes over and offers me some water. A soldier comes forward and holds me up by my arm. The other one grabs the bag. They ask me if I'm out of my mind. That no one is permitted to pass through here. I don't understand. There's no warning signs, no scarecrows. I laugh out loud. What birds? Am I going mad? One of them shoves me around and stares at me with his strange eyes, I don't know what they're up to. Another one offers me some water. They carry me over to their Jeep. I ask them if it's still visiting hour. I tell them that I had to leave my heavy suitcase behind in the sand. They distance themselves from me. I begin to feel like it's totally hopeless. I beg them to let me go see him. I notice how strange they are. One of them says that we're already there, but that no one is allowed in without good reason... Then they inspect my things and finally decide to take me with them... My joy leaves me speechless. I don't even have voice enough to thank them. The jolting Jeep suddenly makes me conscious of my body, as though it were being revived. I watch them: the profile of the soldier at my side, the necks of the ones sitting up front. In their uniforms they all seem alike, but one notices their adolescent features under their burnt black skin... I think this is how my son must look... Such an unrelenting sun. Such an inhospitable climate... At my feet is the bag that I've kept dearly close to me. I stretch my hand and gently massage its smooth roundness... We arrive at a barbed-wire fence. A wide gate opens up. We enter into a kind of huge corral bordered by long, low shacks. Groups of men. A few women. Some children clinging to their skirts. And armed guards everywhere. Desperately I look around trying to find him. They help me get out of the Jeep. They take my things. But I refuse to let go of the bag. A soldier gives an order... Finally I spot him. Oh, my son! He's all bones. His skin is black. He starts running toward me... I'm frozen to the ground. He comes over and embraces me. I bury my head in his chest. I hug him. Kiss him. I touch his face, his hair. I start kissing him again and again...

"What's in the bag that you won't part with?"

How stupid. I follow him with the bag on my arm. Half-embarrassed I say, "Oh it's just a little something: a watermelon for you."

Why is it that his face seems to relax, as though relieved? He smiles. A soldier starts shouting, furious. "This woman is out of her mind. She just walked through the minefield."

Another launches into a tirade. "These women are going to be the death of us. It's a miracle she wasn't blown to bits."

I notice that my boy is trembling. Then, in a barely audible voice, he says to me, "Is that true, Mama?"


Translated by Richard Schaaf

# Mitrani

## Bárbara Mujica

My friend Isaac Goldemberg introduced me to León Mitrani several years ago. According to Isaac, Mitrani was born in Staraya Ushitza, and in the great swarm of migrant Jews that trekked across the continents early in the century, León made his way to the unlikely town of Chepén, in northern Peru, not far from the Ecuadorean border. As Isaac tells it, Mitrani's feelings of cultural isolation in those hinterlands populated mostly by Indians and mixed-bloods eventually drove him from paranoia to madness. It was during the War, when tales of Nazi depravities began to penetrate even remote Andean towns, that León's mental health first began to show signs of faltering. When Peruvian troops marched through Chepén on their way back from raids across the Ecuadorean border, Mitrani was convinced that they were Nazi soldiers coming to get him. In the end Mitrani died loony as a goon. Because of his religion, not because of his insanity, he was refused burial in the local cemetery, so poor León was left to rot somewhere in the desert, as isolated in death as he had been in life. Finally he became a *dybbuk* in search of a body, and still haunts the environs of Chepén. That's the way Isaac tells it, anyway. And I believe it. But there's more.

The truth is that I knew León Mitrani even before Isaac introduced me to him. In fact, I knew him better than Isaac did. I never said anything to Isaac about it, though, in order to avoid one of those embarrassing situations in which somebody tells you a long story, and then you deflate his balloon by saying that you've already heard it. Or maybe that's not the real reason I didn't tell him. Anyway, the part about the *dybbuk,* that part I didn't know.

What happened is that right after the War, in 1946 or '47—Isaac wouldn't know about this because he was just a baby then—Mitrani left Chepén and went to Chile on business. He had a small store, and at that time it was easier to get certain merchandise in Santiago than in Lima. It was a long trip from Chepén to Santiago, and León planned to spend several months in the Chilean capital. He came to like Chile a lot, and if things had gone differently, perhaps he would have stayed.

During those years my aunt and I kept a small rooming house off Calle San Antonio, in one of those tiny streets behind where the Hotel Tupahue is. Back then it wasn't such a bad area.

It didn't start off to be a rooming house. What happened is that in 1945, when I finally got out of Germany—with little else but a concentration camp number burned into my arm and a box of surgical equipment I had stolen from a doctor I had been forced to assist—I wound up in Santiago, where I had a relative named Raquel Berkowitz. Aunt Raquel had been in Chile for years. She was a widow and she lived alone in a large although unpretentious house. Stories of holocaust terror reached her every day through newspapers and the radio, and Aunt Raquel, severed from her relatives in Germany and Poland by the miles and by the decades, was convinced that she had no one left in the world. Day after day she sat, engulfed in solitude, mourning for kin she felt she had somehow unwittingly abandoned. And then I appeared.

Aunt Raquel was overjoyed. She took me in without hesitation, and during the months that followed, we built up a relationship cemented by reticence and grief and a shared need to rest a throbbing head on a hospitable shoulder. For my sake Aunt Raquel, who had long ago abandoned Jewish usages, began to light sabbath candles and separate *milkh* from *fleysh.* For my sake she softly chanted *baruch atohs* on Friday night and baked challah on Friday morning. For my sake, because she knew how I needed to grasp at those threads of custom in order to keep my anima intact.

In time we were joined by others. Others who were not relations, but whom Aunt Raquel had heard about here and there. Men and women who were floundering in a city in which they had no roots and no kin. Jews from Czechoslovakia, Hungary, Germany, Poland, with scruffy shoes and shattered psyches. Aunt Raquel would find them and take them in, and when they could, they would slip her a couple of *escudos* to help her meet expenses. That's how Aunt Raquel's house came to be a *pensión*.

The edifice, like the souls of those who inhabited it, was in grave disrepair. Peeling paint hung from the front door in thin silverish strips. The stucco of the walls was cracked and, in places, crumbling. The deteriorating French-style shutters were all but falling off, their bluish veneer only faintly reminiscent of the ultramarine they had been. The third floor front window had a crack, caused when a Nazi zealot had thrown rocks at the Berkowitz dwelling in the winter of 1939. Aunt Raquel felt that she didn't deserve to have it fixed and so left it, an external sign of the guilt she suffered for being physically comfortable in her spacious home off San Antonio in Santiago, while her relatives were being gassed at Auschwitz. What had once been a garden was now overrun with weeds, for in the long years during which radio news broadcasts told of ovens and venoms, Aunt Raquel had neither the heart nor the stomach to tend her roses. Inside the house, the once-burgundy sofas had faded to a dirty-looking pink, and the mahogany cabinets were in want of waxing. The walls, formerly radiant with yellows, blues, corals, and ivories, were now uniformly drab. Aunt Raquel kept no servants. She distrusted gentiles, and would not let a mestizo woman into the house, even to scrub the floors.

As the house began to fill with people, improvements came gradually to be made. An old Czech named Franz took an interest in the garden and pesky honeysuckles finally gave way to a new crop of silky pink roses whose fragrance filled Aunt Raquel's living room in the late spring. Celia and Frieda Cohen, sisters—and enemies, in the way that only sisters can be—saw eye-to-eye only with regard to the need to refurbish the window dressings. Hour after hour they sat at the dining room table hand-stitching curtains—yellow for the living room, pink for the kitchen, white for the dining room, blue for Aunt Raquel's bedroom, mint and white for mine, and so on down the spectrum until all of Aunt Raquel's eight guest bedrooms had new window furnishings. While they sewed, Frieda jabbed at Celia as steadily and ardently as the steel needle in her hand jabbed at the pliant pink chiffon. Celia was way too heavy, Frieda said. Celia was young yet, but she would never get a new husband if she didn't stop stuffing Raquel's buttery challah into her cheeks. Celia winced at every jab, but she knew that her sister gutted the air with words for the same reason that she herself gutted her stomach with food: in order to forget, in order to drown the searing pain of memory. They had been seven sisters in all: Bessie, Else, Anna, Molly, Celia, Frieda, and Channah. They had all been married and among them there had been thirty-three children. Of those forty-seven people, only two had survived: Celia and Frieda. Remembrance was close and suffocating. Boxcars filled with agonizing humans, but also infants delicate and rosy and humid, eyes filled with wonderment, lips touched with a first ingenuous smile, oblivious to the soldiers who would toss them in the air and impale them with bayonets before their mothers' eyes, to the experimenters who would flay them to ascertain how much pain they could endure, to the sportsmen who would set dogs upon them, then sit back to enjoy the spectacle as the beasts ripped apart the live tender baby flesh...

Other members of the burgeoning household accepted other chores as a matter of course, without being asked. Rebecca Weinberg, a spindly Austrian cellist with ravishing red tresses, had bought her life by serenading her captors night after night. She took care of the dusting and waxing and sometimes helped Franz in the garden. Johanna Goodman, a motherly German Jewess who had lost her only son, the apple of her eye, took over the kitchen. Taciturn and morbid, Johanna communicated only with the batters she converted into aromatic *Streuselkuchen*, *Pfeffernussen*, and *Obsttorten*. But the challah she left to Aunt Raquel, who took a special pride in her breads.

There was Abel Gottlieb, once a master carpenter, now mender of Aunt Raquel's fences and French shutters. There was David Baumgold, a wisp of an old man who years before had been one of Germany's most noted accountants and who now earned a few *escudos* keeping the books for a café owner named Schwartz who went by the pseudonym of Suárez Valdivieso. David Baumgold, who considered his position as Schwartz's bookkeeper profoundly degrading, did odd jobs around Aunt Raquel's, sputtering curses at everyone and everything. And then, of course, there was León Mitrani.

León didn't contribute any work. He was a businessman, and Aunt Raquel's first regular paying guest. Aunt Raquel didn't find him; he found her. During his first hours in Santiago, a Hasidic Jew with greying side curls had told him in Yiddish that there was a Jewish *pensión* in a little street off San Antonio, and Mitrani had made it his business to seek it out.

It was the first time in years León Mitrani had found himself completely surrounded by his own kind. He listened while Frieda and Celia told of their lost children: little Hilda with the soft brown curls, a budding pianist, she would be seventeen now; little Max with his sickly constitution, would he have survived until manhood? And on and on. They spoke with bitterness, sometimes choking back tears. But they needed to talk and Mitrani needed to listen. Like Aunt Raquel, he was overwhelmed by a sense of culpability.

It seemed to Abel Gottlieb that Celia was falling in love with Mitrani. I heard him mention it to Franz, who said that it was true, that he had once seen her sobbing into León's ample chest while the gentle Peruvian stroked her honey blond curls. But León was married. He told us all about it. His wife was a Christian woman, as crazy when she married him as Mitrani himself later became. She was blind, he said, and involved in all kinds of secret mystical rites. He suspected that she was a witch.

I suppose that he told us about her in order to clarify things so that Celia wouldn't get her hopes up. He was an honest man, León Mitrani. And a kind man. Isaac always spoke well of him. I mean, years later, when he told me about how Mitrani had befriended him in Chepén.

Celia wasn't the only one who found solace in Mitrani. Baumgold was another. Often I would see the two of them—Mitrani and Baumgold—walking down San Antonio. Or sometimes I would catch sight of them seated at a small table in Schwartz's cafe, smoking and chatting softly. Baumgold's smooth head would inevitably be bent, his eyes half-closed, as if he were ashamed to face the world in his downgraded position as Schwartz's bookkeeper. At five in the afternoon, when most Chileans take *once*—tea and assorted rolls or pastries—Aunt Raquel would serve verbena and some of Johanna's magnificent *Kuchen*. But Mitrani and Baumgold would nearly always abandon the group for Schwartz's, where they would lose themselves in interminable conversations. Baumgold did most of the talking, I imagine, telling Mitrani of the economic turmoil that plagued Germany before the War and how he, Baumgold, could have singlehandedly saved the country with his own particular formula of financial sorcery if only he hadn't been hauled off and flung into a pit behind barbed wire. Mitrani, I imagine, would take Baumgold's arm or place his own massive arm around the old man's shoulders and calm him with just a few syllables, not particularly eloquent or erudite, but heartfelt. Mitrani understood pain. That's probably why he went crazy in the end.

All of us confided in Mitrani. Johanna, so reserved with the rest of us while at the same time lavishing her love in the form of *Apfeltorten*, would sit next to León on the faded pink sofa in Aunt Raquel's parlor and once in a while a laconic remark would pass between them. But after those long silent sessions, Johanna's face would soften, the taut jowl and the inimical gaze would relax, and if you examined that physiognomy you could catch a glimmer of the mirthful young mother she once had been.

Frieda, Abel, Franz, Rebecca, everyone poured his heart out to Mitrani. He was an outsider, in a sense, one who hadn't been through the horror, but who could empathize and who listened insatiably, avid to absorb it all. Mitrani seemed to consider it his calling to help us survive the aftermath, the psychological devastation, as we had survived the camps. It was a mission he shared with Aunt Raquel.

Probably the one who looked most to León for consolation was I. It took a while. Sometimes he would ask me questions about what my life had been. He knew I had been a nurse, and that I was trying to learn enough Spanish to take a course and get a license to practice nursing in Santiago. He knew that because Aunt Raquel had told him. As for me, for a long time I told him nothing. It wasn't that I didn't trust León Mitrani. It was just that in those days I kept it all inside, like a rotting carcass too bulky and too tightly lodged to heave up. Sometimes Mitrani would put his arms around me or place his hand on my wrist and say simply, "Lenore..." I knew it was an invitation to talk, nothing more, but I'd pull away as though he had made an indecent advance.

One day when I was dusting my room, Mitrani came ambling through the hall. I had laid my box of surgical equipment on the bed, open. Mitrani caught sight of it as he was about to pass my room and stopped short in the doorway. I could feel him looking at the instruments, even though I was turned away from him. I could feel him sizing them up, evaluating what each piece was capable of doing, conjecturing what I had done or helped do with it. I didn't know how much Aunt Raquel had told him about my nursing, but it was common knowledge what Jewish doctor's assistants were forced to do during the War. I shifted positions and turned toward him, but neither of us spoke. It was as though Mitrani's eyes were piercing my memory, delving into the images that were embedded there, into the scenes I had witnessed. His eyes went from the scalpel to my face to the miniature steel scissors to my face again, to the clamps, to the pincers and then back to me. I sensed that Mitrani knew, knew in ghastly detail, the kinds of operations I had assisted at... I had been forced to assist at... Forced, in order to save my own life... I felt myself release a wail from some deep recess of my gut, although I didn't hear a sound. My back and shoulders were so tense that the tightly contracted muscles sent excruciating pulsations from my cranium through my spine to my knees. Mitrani remained silent. And then the aching began to subside and I was aware that my lips were trembling and I was biting, biting hard in order not to sob or to shriek again. I felt overwhelmed by vertigo and nausea, and my eyes were filling with tears in spite of my squeezing the lids shut. My lips were beginning to part and to quiver and the inside of my mouth was chafed from the rubbing of my teeth. My inner cheeks tasted faintly of blood. I couldn't hold my lips still. I grimaced. Scorching tears seared my temples, and there was a glutinous mass in my throat that was unable to buffer the sharp, even pain. It was as though the very scalpel that lay in the black velvet-lined box on the bed were stuck in my throat and there were no way to dislodge it.

I heard another moan, an ululation that seemed to emanate from some gravely wounded animal, and I made myself realize that it had torn itself out of me. Mitrani was pressing me close to him, caressing the back of my neck, picking each sticky brown hair off a cheek, viscid with tears, and placing it back among the rest of my hair. All the time he said nothing, but his muteness enveloped and calmed me magically. Words would have been superfluous.

Who knows how long we stood there, my lacerated soul in silent communication with him. But I understood at that moment that between Mitrani and me there existed a secret bond, and that he would do anything to help me ease the anguish, that he would make any sacrifice.

I told him, then. I told him about the instruments, what they had done, what I had done. I'm not going to repeat it all now. I can't... I don't want to talk about it... I stole the instruments and kept them with me because I didn't want to forget—as if I could ever forget—what one human being is capable of doing to another.

Things ran smoothly at the *pensión* for several months after that incident. Little by little we all learned Spanish. Gradually each of us found a job—Johanna at a bakery, Celia in a dress shop, Frieda as an assistant to a seamstress. Rebecca at first worked as a waitress at Schwartz's cafe, which the owner had recently renamed Las Delicias. When she had saved up enough money, she bought a cello and began giving lessons. Abel Gottlieb did odd carpentry for the neighbors, and I found work as an assistant at a public hospital. Only Franz stayed on at the *pensión* during the day, not only tending the garden now, but also sweeping and vacuuming and performing other chores for which Aunt Raquel no longer had the energy.

In the early afternoon we would gather back at the *pensión* for *almuerzo*, the large midday meal. After prayers over *fleysh* and wine, we would eat and talk in hushed German and Yiddish syllables, somehow still mortified by the possibility of being overheard and dragged off.

On Fridays at sundown Aunt Raquel lit the Sabbath candles, and we'd huddle around her like small children witnessing an act of great wonderment. In April, for Pessach, there was a Seder and for want of a male child, old, bald Baumgold asked the four questions.

With time we learned to live again. In time the individual bridges each of us had built to Mitrani extended and touched the others, until we had created a network that cemented us together into a family.

Mitrani was the keystone. When we unburdened ourselves to him, we felt cleansed, revitalized, able to reach out beyond ourselves.

Our collective recuperation was halting, but we emerged with that resilience intact that had been nearly wasted away by the War. In September of 1947, when Aunt Raquel died, there was only a brief period of mayhem. The *pensión* continued to exist. I quit my job at the hospital and took over Aunt Raquel's duties.

Mitrani had been saying for months that the time was coming when he would be leaving Santiago. His business needed him, even if his sorceress wife did not. And yet he stayed on, lulled by his routine of daily promenades down Calle San Antonio with Baumgold, culminating regularly now with a stop at Schwartz's café, where the ex-accountant and he formed part of a *tertulia*, or conversation group, that met to discuss such topics as the deadly shenanigans of Stalin and the imminent formation of the State of Israel, the latest soccer scores, Gene Kelly's movies, the purchase of the dry cleaning establishment on Calle Centurión by a ragged Arab, and the marriage of a grey-eyed society girl named Lucinda Santa María to an American with mining interests in Antofagasta. Lulled, too, by the lilting sound of Friday-night chants presided over now by me or sometimes by Frieda; and by the perfume of Celia's voluminous frothy curls on his shoulder as he read the *Mercurio*, Santiago's leading newspaper, and listened to the others chat softly in Yiddish or in German.

Mitrani would have stayed forever, perhaps, if it hadn't been for Levine.

I don't know who told Levine about the *pensión*, but he arrived on the doorstep, suitcase in hand, one day in November.

It had never been Aunt Raquel's custom to turn away anyone, and so I welcomed still another errant Jew into our midst, although I told him that he would have to share a room. He said he didn't mind. He said that he needed somewhere to stay and that he was happy to have found a place among his own. He didn't speak a word of Spanish.

The only room large enough to accommodate another person was Mitrani's.

León was not happy about having a roommate.

Levine was an imposing fellow. Corpulent and flaxen-haired, he charmed the women with his textured baritone voice. He seemed to be a jolly sort, and on those increasingly infrequent occasions when devastating memories invaded the spirit of one or another of the members of the household, Levine would try gently to coax the sufferer out of depression with stories of village life in the remote corner of Bavaria where he had spent his early childhood. What Mitrani had accomplished with patience and tenderness, Levine often managed to accomplish with humor, and it was clear by the time a month had gone by that Rebecca and Johanna, at least, preferred Levine's techniques.

Yet, like the rest of us, Levine had his restive moments. More than once I saw him standing alone in the garden, lost in some private void, lips pursed.

After Levine came to live with us, life in the pension underwent some subtle changes. Johanna's desserts became more lavish. For her *Honigkuchen* she chose only the finest of honeys purchased at an exclusive *salón de té*. Almonds, which in the years immediately following the War she had often had to do without, she now located in food shops in neighborhoods into which she had never before ventured. And spices—cardamon, cinnamon, cloves—Johanna found them all, employing a resourcefulness of which most of us had not believed her capable.

In the evenings, when we gathered to read or to converse in the parlor, Rebecca serenaded us on her newly purchased cello, accompanied by Frieda on the piano. Frieda was not her friend's equal as a musician, but she practiced with diligence in preparation for the nightly concerts. While they played, Levine, a music lover, hummed softly to himself in obvious enjoyment, and the women, encouraged by his appreciation, often played late into the night.

Life at the *pensión* was tranquil and harmonious. Only Mitrani seemed ill at ease, alienated.

One morning, as I was straightening out the silverware, Mitrani came and stood next to me. After a short silence he said evenly, "Have you noticed, Lenore, how Levine always remains quiet during the Kaddish?"

I didn't respond right away. Mitrani's question struck me as petty. "So?" I answered finally. "Some people don't like to pray out loud." I thought León was peeved at all the attention Levine had been getting.

León looked pensive. He sat down at the dining room table and lit a cigarette. "You don't think," he said solemnly, "that it could be that Levine doesn't know the prayer?"

Later, at lunch, I saw Mitrani eyeing Levine surreptitiously, as though he thought that there was something about the man that didn't quite ring true.

The rest of us were delighted to have Levine in our midst. His good nature and effervescent cobalt eyes had a regenerative effect on the group, drawing out a levity that had been repressed much too long. Johanna, especially, was more cheerful than any of us had ever seen her, and Celia and Frieda and I wondered if we might have a wedding at the *pensión* before the following year was over. They were about the same age, Johanna and Levine. They were both in their mid-forties, with plenty of years ahead of them to rebuild their lives.

Mitrani, in the meantime, grew more and more taciturn. He began to plan in earnest his return to Chepén. One by one, he sold those belongings that he did not intend to take back to Peru. Sometime in mid-January he wrote to his friend Jacobo, Isaac's father, that he would be in Lima within the month.

León Mitrani didn't say anything more about Levine until one Sunday afternoon, when the two of us were sitting alone in the dining room. In Santiago the summer months—December, January, and February—can be mild or they can be oppressive, asphyxiating. But even on the worst days the residents of the *pensión* almost always wore long sleeves to cover up the numbers branded on their arms. The day in question was a scorcher, and Baumgold and Gottlieb had worn short sleeves in the house in the morning, even though they would never have worn them in the street.

"Levine," Mitrani told me, "never bares his arms. Not even when he goes to bed."

I was vexed. I thought Mitrani was nitpicking again. I got up and started to set the table without commenting.

"Lenore," Mitrani said, grasping my wrist between his thumb and index finger, "I wouldn't exaggerate. I sleep in the same room with the man. I am telling you that I have never seen Morris Levine's arms. He puts on his pajamas in the bathroom. Doesn't this seem strange to you, Lenore?"

I wasn't sure what it was that Mitrani was getting at. "All of us are self-conscious about the numbers," I said.

"Or what about the lack of a number?" Mitrani's voice fell at the end of the sentence, as if he had articulated a statement instead of a question.

At dinner that evening I kept an eye on Levine. I watched him devour Johanna's superb *Kuchen* and I listened to him discuss starting a bakery next to Schwartz's Las Delicias with Baumgold.

As Rebecca and Celia played Bach in the parlor, I pretended to concentrate on the blue and white vest I was knitting, but in reality I was spying on Levine.

Nothing he did seemed out of the ordinary. I did notice that he always spoke German, never Yiddish, but that in itself was nothing. Most of us felt more comfortable in German than in Yiddish. German had been our primary language, spoken at school, at work, and in the street, while Yiddish had been reserved for the home.

The next time Mitrani and I spoke of Levine, it was I who brought up the subject.

I had done an extremely unethical thing.

Mitrani's apprehensions about the newcomer had kindled in me certain qualms. One day when I was sweeping Levine's room, I got it into my head to go through his belongings. There was a miniature suitcase that he kept under the bed. I pulled it out and tried to open it, but it was locked. I knew that Levine had gone with Baumgold to see the premises of the projected bakery, and supposed that the two men would be gone all morning. I attempted to pry the clasps of the suitcase open with a nail file, but they remained steadfast. I went to my room and took out the black box with surgical equipment. From it I removed a hooked device. I went back to Levine's room and began to work on the suitcase. I had to jiggle the pins for a long time, but finally I manipulated the clasps open.

There wasn't too much in the small valise: a passport with the name Morris Levine on the first page. It might have been fraudulent, but then, many of those who escaped Germany before the end of the War traveled with false papers. There were several documents written in German. One was a birth certificate, badly damaged and nearly illegible. I could barely make out the name: Kurt Georg Stahl.

I articulated the name silently, cringing. A shiver progressed up my spine to the base of my neck, then entwined my neck and formed an icy spike in my throat. I felt the same nausea I had experienced the day Mitrani had walked in on me while the box of surgical instruments lay open on my bed. I reread the name, scrutinizing each letter individually. Then, gagging, I groped my way down the hall to the bathroom. The release of vomit provided no relief. I tried to steady myself against the cool green-white wall of the bathroom. After a few minutes, I began to regain my equilibrium.

Dr. Kurt Georg Stahl. I had never met him. He had been the director of medical experiments at the clinic I had been assigned to years before in Germany. I had heard his name an infinite number of times. It was wedged in my mind like a mangled nail in a complex piece of machinery that is prevented from functioning properly by the obstruction.

When I thought I had regained my composure enough to express myself coherently, I went to look for Mitrani. He was in the garden. We went into the parlor to talk. We talked a long, long time. It was nightfall before we finished.

The next morning it was Johanna who rushed down the stairs with the dreadful news. Alarmed because neither Mitrani nor Levine had come down for breakfast, she had gone upstairs to see if they had overslept. She had knocked gently at the door, she said. There had been no answer, so she had called softly, "Morris, Morris, León." Johanna was perturbed by the lack of a response. She knew León to be an early riser.

She had tried the door, expecting to find it locked, but the knob turned and she pushed and called again. Then she opened the door and milliseconds afterward let out a shriek, turned and rushed down the stairs, stumbling in her urgency.

Johanna whispered a few inaudible words before succumbing to hysteria. It was impossible to grasp the gist of her ranting, but it was evident that something horrendous had occurred. Baumgold and Gottlieb bounded up the stairs. Johanna wailed uncontrollably and Rebecca, pallid, was biting her lips and trembling. Frieda and Celia were clutching one another's hands, their eyes dull and unfocusing.

From the top of the stairs Baumgold communicated the message that Johanna had been too distraught to articulate: Morris Levine was dead.

Franz, the old Czech with a love for roses and peonies, made his way up the stairs and moments later confirmed that Levine was lying in sheets saturated with blood, this throat slit from ear to ear, his wrists slashed, his genitals mutilated. Baumgold, who had followed Franz back into Levine's room, had pulled open the bedclothes and discovered that excrement covered the lower part of the bottom sheet. Morris Levine had undoubtedly released it in the trauma of death. The stench was unbearable.

León Mitrani was nowhere to be found. Celia was the first to bring up the fact.

It was at least an hour or an hour and a half before we had recovered the degree of serenity necessary to function once again as a group, at least on a rudimentary level. By that time Johanna had dissolved into silent weeping and Celia and Frieda had gone into the kitchen to fetch glasses of cold water to calm everyone's nerves.

There was no phone in the *pensión*. Abel Gottlieb, the gentle carpenter who had mended Aunt Raquel's shutters two years before, offered to go for the police, but I felt that before we notified the authorities we should knit together our statement. Mitrani had obviously incriminated himself by his disappearance, but there was no sense in adding fuel to the fire. We decided to remain tight-lipped about León's dislike of Levine. We were, after all, a family, and even though one of us had met with hideous misfortune, survival of the clan dictated that Mitrani be protected as much as possible. We also determined that Abel would not go for the police for several hours. That would give León more time to make his way toward the border. We would tell the officers that we had assumed Levine and Mitrani had slept late, and had not investigated their absence until it was nearly lunchtime.

Finally, about 3:30 in the afternoon, Gottlieb set out to inform the authorities.

It took an absurdly long time for the two *carabineros*—one swarthy and obsequious, one fair-complected and indifferent, both coarse—to get to the *pensión* with Gottlieb. They interrogated us first as a group and then individually. Later they were joined by several heavyweights with guns in conspicuous places and a detective who examined with diligence the room that had been Mitrani's and Levine's. León had left most of his belongings, taking with him only his documents and a few essentials for the trip back to Peru.

The police surmised that the murder must have taken place about 11:00 the preceding night. Levine's corpse was starting to appear grotesquely deformed.

Reproducing in my mind Mitrani's journey from Santiago to Lima, I calculated that León might well be close to the border or even have crossed it. Soon he would be hiding out in some godforsaken Andean village where no authorities of any national government had ventured—a village where he would be in all probability the only white, and in all certainty the only Jew, but in which he would carve a niche for himself in order to survive. I wondered if he would ever make his way back to Chepén.

The Chilean police had no jurisdiction in Peru. Relations between the two countries hadn't been amicable since the War of the Pacific, and the officer who questioned me remarked that no cooperation could be expected from the Peruvian authorities. Extradition was a pipedream. The murder of an errant foreigner named Levine... it was hardly worth making into an international issue.

It wasn't until much later that I found out that Mitrani did in fact wind up back in Chepén. I never found out the details of his passage, but about Mitrani's eventual demise, it was Isaac who filled me in. By the early fifties, León's mental health had severely deteriorated, and he had lost touch with reality. According to Isaac, on Sunday mornings he would stand in the plaza in front of the church and scream epithets at the populace.

The investigation of Levine's death really didn't amount to much. The police concluded that the guilty party was unretrievable, and the whole thing fizzled out with only a brief mention on the fifth page of the *Mercurio*: "Nazi Camp Survivor Murdered by Fellow Jew."

Several months later, on a languid fall afternoon, when everyone else was out of the house, I went up to my room and took out the box of surgical instruments that had been opened only once since that day months before when I had jimmied the locks on Morris

Levine's valise. The police, knowing that I had been a practicing nurse in Germany and a medical assistant in Chile, had paid it no heed. I opened the box and examined each instrument.

Each was spotless. Not a trace of blood. Then I closed the box and wrapped it in several pieces of old newspaper. Finally, I dropped the package into a basket and slipped the handle over my arm. Then I went out.

I crossed San Antonio and walked toward the Cathedral. It was a Sunday and Mass had let out a few minutes before. Families walked in the streets, four or five abreast. Men and women, many of them of English, Italian or Slavic stock, chattered animatedly and waved to friends. The soft musical sounds of the particular brand of Spanish that is Chilean floated into the crisp air as one friend called to another, "*¡Cómo estai, gordo! ¿Qué e' de tu vida?*", or as a man addressed his neighbor, "*¿Cómo le va, don Fernando? ¿Cómo está su señora?*" Chilean women, some blond and fair-skinned, others dark, of Spanish or mixed Spanish and Indian background, wore chic sheaths, mid-calf length. Their jackets were smart and padded at the shoulders; some of them had fur collars. Their shoes were high-heeled and of the best Chilean leather. The men wore dark suits and white shirts. At strategic points on the street were vendors selling *empanadas*, spicy meat pies with raisins, sliced eggs and olives. The fragrances were inebriating.

I yearned to savor the morning. I felt euphoric, as though I had finally reached a goal long striven for. The trauma of Mitrani's escape was over. I had received word via a Hungarian Jew who had recently arrived from Lima that he was safe. If it had gone otherwise for him, I might have gone mad with guilt.

A small mestizo girl, ragged and barefoot, peered out from behind a park bench. She thrust an outdated magazine at me. I smiled and gave her a coin for it. In appearance and demeanor she contrasted dramatically with the cosmopolitan churchgoers who were gathering in small bunches near the Cathedral to fill each other in on the week's gossip.

The River Mapocho is polluted and malodorous. It runs through Santiago between the Hill of Santa Lucía, now converted into one of the world's most attractive urban parks, and the Hill of San Cristóbal, upon which there stands a large statue of the Virgin Mary, a gift to Chile from the people of France. Occasionally the Mapocho threatens to inundate the city, although this menace has been reduced in recent years by numerous flood control projects. Even so, the river is an unfriendly element in an otherwise hospitable city. To the southwest of the center of Santiago the Mapocho flows into the Maipo, a mother of ill-repute, long accused of being a source of typhoid fever in Santiago Province.

On the southern outskirts of the city, the Mapocho is surrounded by *callampas*, conglomerations of makeshift shacks of tin and plywood, where the poor camp. By the time it reaches these *villas miseria*, it has become a cesspool, a health hazard against which both municipal and federal authorities have long battled.

I took a roundabout route, crossing the Plaza de Armas and wandering through *galerías comerciales*—passageways lined by shops of every type. I didn't get to the slum section until mid-afternoon. By then the basket was weighing heavily on my arm. Children reminiscent of the little girl who had sold me the magazine that morning were playing along the river's edge.

It was time to get rid of the basket. I walked along the river until I came to a deserted area. There I opened the receptacle and took out the box of surgical instruments, still wrapped in newspapers. I did not unwrap it. Instead, I hurled it as far as I could into the infested waters.

I was done with it. The instruments had finally served their purpose. I had performed my last and only worthwhile operation. It was the only operation I had ever performed voluntarily and entirely alone.

I watched the package plunge. Within seconds it was gone. I closed my eyes and said a silent prayer for Mitrani. Then I put the empty basket down on the river bank. Some needy person would surely find it and make use of it.

# A Matter of Distance

## Sonia González Valdenegro

I can just see you sitting there in the dining room with the rest of the women in town. And hear you discussing what was in the news back when I came here—one after another, mouthing the same clichés. And my image of you and the others is faded, frozen in time. Reminiscing aloud, you ask old Eulalia, the best reader among you, to go back over the last paragraph in my letter, starting a few lines before that "I'll be there soon" which you dwell on with obvious pleasure. And I can see the old lady grabbing the paper from on top of the sideboard, putting on her pince-nez, clearing her throat and beginning to read, while the others yawn and tug on their knitting wool. Meanwhile, the third candy from the package sticks to my palate and I push it around my mouth with the tip of my tongue. At the end of the street the sunset is yellow, and after two days of heavy rain the puddles at the curb are full of debris. When she's through reading my letter for what must be the fourth or fifth time, you wonder what I'm doing just now. And that's when I'd like to tell you it's Friday, that here in the city on Friday, people get together after work in different places, reclaim personal attachments and animosities dulled by their weekly routines, go to the movies, to cafés where they linger over cups of coffee and cigarettes, and the sound of their voices —energetic, if not festive—floats from table to table. The shops are all lit up and in the windows the chocolates, the candies wrapped in brightly colored paper, are so beautiful they could spend the whole night looking at them. There's also the option of going home early

and watching something on TV; there are so many ways to avoid
being caught up by loneliness and thrust into the tunnel of broken
dreams, but they're all the same, because loneliness lurks just as read-
ily in front of a TV screen as at the entrance to the movies. The lady
in charge of the boarding house, who—like all city-dwellers—prefers
human voices to silence, invites me into the kitchen to watch the
movie with the others. But I refuse. I refuse because that's not what
I've come for; I didn't leave the backwardness of a small town to end
up in an ice-cold kitchen, hearing old men and women tell the same
stories over and over, just like at home. The same old ways of killing
time, *viejita*, and if only you could see—see and remember—the way
I'm seeing and remembering as I move a few steps further in the line
(though maybe I'm not really moving at all, just shifting my weight
from one foot to the other), those times when your friends would
bring over their knitting and sit there with you saying I shouldn't
leave; they'd say that looking at each other out of the corners of their
eyes, because they weren't sure whether certain rumors about me
were true. But I would escape out the back door whenever I saw them
coming, because staying at home would have been a lifetime proposi-
tion. I preferred to walk out to the edge of town and dream the vague
dreams we cherish when we've never lived. Whenever the sameness
of streets and faces narrowed my vistas, a soaking rain would fill me
with what must be hope—the idea that things have got to change, that
it's possible to change them. I would wait for all the women to leave
before heading home; and when I got there I'd open all the windows,
to rid the house of the musty odor of lamb and old age left there by
them and their wool. Sometimes you'd come into my room, sit down
next to the bed where I pretended to be asleep and stroke my hair.
And then I'd remember—as I remember you now—what I had
promised myself that afternoon out in the rain, and one by one, I'd go
back over every face in town, and I'd hold my breath until I heard
you leave, turning out the hallway lights as you went. Now as I pull
out a bill for my ticket and hand it to the lady at the box office, I can
just see you coming out of the house for a chat with those farmers
who must still go by our door, driving their oxen that could scarcely
move under the weight of the yoke; you would exchange a few
words—no opinions—simply acknowledging the existence of a cloud,

a bird, or confirming a rumor circulating at the time from one old lady's mouth to another. And now the look in the eyes of the man standing three people behind me in line suggests a different conversation—also about everyday trivia, but different. I begin anticipating what will happen next: like, maybe going back to the boarding house to daydream (would it really be that awful?); then I'm still at the movies and the next show is about to start (anything but that huge, silent house, damp through and through, where each night at ten the boarders shuffle back and forth in their slippers between their rooms and the bathroom with their pitchers, cotton swabs and chamberpots). But I also think about things like still working at the parcel service across from our house, and you're happy to have me near by, where you can just pull back the curtain and watch me arranging things behind the counter. I think about those things now and at other times when I remember you, because loneliness brings with it the illusion that anyone who's not around can fill the void. And right now anyone who's not around means you, who couldn't understand why I came here all by myself, because you didn't know what the whole town was saying about me, about me and Segundo, or about me and José, and on and on—about me and every man in town because in those dull afternoon conversations, who cared about one, but two were as good as an army. And I can just see José knocking on the door and asking you when I'll be back. But me, go back there...no way. No way, I think, sitting in the theater now, and the guy who was waiting on line before comes over, saying excuse me because he knows I'm one of those, that I'm like him, that we're both the type who recognize each other at first glance by the boredom and anxiety written all over our faces. Then the roaring lion appears and now—finally—it's here: the start of this Friday whose images may bring the sign I'm looking for—the sign that has to come, even if it takes forever. This time the movie's about a girl watching a movie, and suddenly she's recognized by one of the actors who steps off the screen to follow her. I offer the man sitting next to me a candy, which he takes and pops into his mouth. In the movies people are born, fall in love, quarrel and die so fast that they never have time to be bored. I think that and the thought brings back feelings like sitting by the oven waiting for the bread to bake; off in the distance a radio reports the news that's always forthcoming here in the city, this city that, nevertheless, hasn't come forth with anything else since that day, several months back, when I got on the train and you told me not to forget to stay warm, eat properly and write to you—because in small towns what matters is wearing the right clothes and eating the right food—and of course, you couldn't even imagine how pretty the shoes are in the shop windows, or the price of that gorgeous two-piece suit I want to buy so I can be like the other girls who work at the office, the ones who wait on people instead of pushing papers in that cramped and dingy backroom. Yes, I'm telling you these things just because, because I want you to know them too, like I'd tell you that while I'm chewing on this candy which by now, is eating away at my tongue, the girl in the film shows up again all alone and tears start rolling down my cheeks. And of course, the guy next to me must think I'm crying like all women do, because I'm so sensitive to the suffering of movie heroines. But the truth is, I'm not crying for her or for you surrounded by all those old gossip-mongers but for myself, because now the guy takes my hand and I feel so tired, so at the end of a pointless struggle, and I know I won't say no this time either, this time or ever again, even if I sometimes would like to. And yes, we'll leave here and in the street, maybe he'll take my arm and anyone who sees us will think we're a real couple, like the ones who sometimes argue (without ever really knowing why, maybe it's to rid their faces of signs of annoyance, so each one's smile will look broader and better to the other). Yes, as we walk by the people waiting in line for the last show, anyone would say this man and I...but no, *viejita*. There are big bags of garbage in the street and we avoid them just as we do the puddles; leaning on each other we take a walk around this city that will never belong to us or anyone like us, this city you'd look down on if you could see it because of all the things that are foreign to you, that you detest and that add up to the difference between us, *viejita*. Now it's completely dark out. I could go into detail about how we deceive each other, but no, we both lie just like every Friday because the faces are different, but we've both been at it for weeks now—exchanging false names and addresses, making up different phone numbers and claiming to lead the lives of people we would have liked to be, ideal, perfect creatures calmly enjoying a Friday night on the town. Anyway,

# Sonia González Valdenegro

I'm telling you all this while we look for a hotel one of us has been to before, and as we walk down the dark, silent hallway that could be part of a hospital or an insane asylum because to tell the truth, *viejita,* this is sheer madness. It's madness to rush around getting dressed later on, for fear of being seen in broad daylight—because if we get a good look, we're liable to recognize each other on the street with this desperate Friday night neediness. So, separately, as fast as possible, it's back to the same clothes, the same dreams each of us took into the movies. Those are the things I'd like to tell you, *viejita,* instead of repeating, as I will first thing tomorrow morning (I get up every Saturday and write): Dear Mom, I hope this letter finds you well. Yesterday was Friday, so my friends and I went out to an evening movie.... All the things I can't tell you because you never learned to read, so my words have to be deciphered by Doña Eulalia and the others, who are right when they say that heaven only knows what I came here for, when they tell each other—while you go to get the teapot—that the things I write you are lies.

Translated by Louise B. Popkin

# The Authors

MARGARITA AGUIRRE (1925) is a distinguished writer of short stories and novels. She worked as Pablo Neruda's secretary in the 1950s. Among her works are "La oveja roja" (1974) and *El huésped*.

ELENA ALDUNATE (1925) is one of the most well-known science fiction writers in Chile. She has also written children's literature. Among her works are *Angélica y el delfín* (1977) and the novel *Candia* (1980).

FLOR MARIA ANINAT has taught English and worked as a journalist. Her novel, *Coroney,* appeared in 1984 and a collection of stories, *Andares desordenados* in 1987. She is a member of Soffia, a writing workshop, along with other Chilian writers such as Carmen Basánez, Digna Tapia, Sonia Guralnik, Luz Larraín, Margarita Prado, and the Peruvian Elena O'Brien.

JACQUELINE BALCELLS (1944) was born in Valparaíso and published her first book of stories, *Le raisin enchanté,* in Paris. This book later appeared in Chile in a collection titled *El niño que se fue en un árbol,* published in 1986. She has continued to publish, and her most recent work is *El polizón de la Santa María* (1992).

PIA BARROS (1955) has distinguished herself with her fervent literary activities and by organizing writing workshops. She has two short story collections, *Miedos transitorios* and *A horcajadas*. She has also written a novel, *El tono menor del deseo*.

CARMEN BASAÑEZ (1943) believes the most important event in her life was discovering herself as a womn. Besides having stories appear in anthologies, she has published *Tiempo de ventnas* (1990) and is working on a novel.

ALEJANDRA BASOALTO (1950) published a collection of stories, *Territorio exclusivo*, in 1992.

MARTA BLANCO (1938) was a prominent and distinguished Chilean journalist in the 1960s. She later retired to a very secluded life. Among her works are *La generación de las hojas* and *Todo es mentira*.

MARIA LUISA BOMBAL (1910-1980) is considered one of the most innovative writers of Chilean literature. Among her works are *The Final Mist* (1933) and *La amortajada* (1938).

MARTA BRUNET (1897-1967) was considered, along with Bombal, to be one of the most distinguished writers of her generation. Her works include *Bestia Dañina* (1953), *Aguas abajo* (1943), and *Cuentos para Marisol* (1966).

ELENA CASTEDO won the American Book Award for *Paraiso* in 1990. She is now working on a collection of short stories.

MARIA CRISTINA DA FONSECA is a human rights activist, lawyer, and short story writer. She writes mainly children's fiction.

MARIA ASUNCION DE FOKES was born in Barcelona and moved to Chile in the late 1930s when she was in her teens. She participated in literary workshops during the 70s. This is her first published work.

ANA MARIA DEL RIO (1948) is one of the most popular Chilean writers of her generation. Together with Pía Barros, she directed a writing workshop called Soffia. She won the María Luisa Bombal literary prize in 1991 with her novel *Oxido de Carmen*.

CLAUDIA ESCOBAR (1962) began her career in the workshops of Antonio Skármita. Her stories have been published in various anthologies, among them *Santiago: pena capital* (1991).

# The Authors

ALEJANDRA FARIAS (1962) earned her degree in literature and began her work in the workshops of Skármita and Marco Antonio de la Parra.

AGATA GLIGO (1940) is a well-known lawyer. She began her literary careeer witha biography of María Luisa Bombal. To date, she has published stories and a novel.

SONIA GONZALEZ VALDENEGRO (1958) rose to prominence with the publication of her collection of short stories, *Tejer historia*.

LUCIA GUERRA is a writer and a critic. She is the author of *Más allá de las máscaras* (1983), *Frutos extraños* (Letras de Oro award, 1991), *Premio Municipal de Literatura,* and *Muñeca brava*. Her short stories won the Plural Award in 1987 and the Bienal Cuento in 1994. Her book, *La mumer fragmentada: Historias de un signo* was awarded the Casa de las Américas Prize in 1994.

ANA MARIA GUIRALDES (1945) is one of the most popular writers of children's stories. Her most important work is *Cuentos de soledad y asombro* (1991).

ANA MARIA GURALNIK (1911, Ukraine) migrated to Santiago early in her life but did not begin writing until 1980. She has published two short story collections, *El Samovar* and *Retratos en sepia,* and a novel, *La mujer gusano*.

MARTA JARA (1922-1972) distinguished herself as a *costumbrista* and published three short story collections, the most noted of which is *Surazo* (1960).

LUZ LARRAIN (1930) began her literary career in the '80s with a collection of short stories entitled *La cuchara de hueso*. She has also written historical novels.

SONIA MONTECINOS (1954) is an anthropologist, novelist, and storyteller. Inspired by the Mapuche traditions, among her most memorable stories is "El zorro que cayó del cielo" (1987).

# The Authors

Barbara Mujica (1942) is a professor of literature at Georgetown University. Winner of the E. L. Doctorow International Fiction award, she is the author of *The Deaths of Don Bernardo.*

Margarita Niemeyer is a literary critic and a member of José Donoso's workshop. She published *Mujer frente al espejo,* her first collection of stories, in 1992.

Luz Orfanoz (1932) began to write fiction after raising a family and retiring from her job as a secretary. "The stories are in my head," she says, and "I just have to write them down." Her first collection, *No son todos los que están,* was published in 1991. A second collection is in preparation.

Ana Pizarro (1940) is an essayist and literary critic. During the military coup, she was exiled to Paris. Currently, she lives in Geneva. She has written literary criticism and literary historiography. Her stories have been published in numerous anthologies.

Violeta Quevedo (1892-1962) offered Chile a new way of making litererature: with ingenuity and travel journals. Her first collection was published in 1962.

Amalia Rendic (1928-1988) is considered to be one of the most outstanding authors of children's literature. She also wrote one novel, *Pasos Sonambulos* (1969).

Elizabeth Subercaseaux (1944) is a journalist and writer. She distinguished herself with her work during the military regime with a book of interviews with General Pinochet. Among her most important works are *Silendra* and *Canto de la raíz lejana.*

Ana Vasquez (1945) is a Chilean sociologist and a distinguished writer. She has lived in Paris since 1973. She wrote *Abel Aánchez y sus hermanos* and her most recent novel is titled *Mi amiga Chantal.*

# The Authors

VIRGINIA VIDAL (1920) is a writer and journalist. Among her books are *La emancipación de la mujer* (1972). During her exile in Venezuela, she received various awards for her stories.

MARIA FLORA YAÑEZ (1893-1962) was the author of numerous novels and stories including *Juan Estrella* and *La Piedra*.

# The Translators

JENNIFER BAYON, ELIZABETH D. HODGES, and MELANIE HUGHES, are 1993 graduates of Connecticut College. Majors in Hispanic Studies, they have collaborated with Doris Meyer on their first published translations for this collection.

MARY G. BERG is a writer and translator who lives in Cambridge, MA. She has taught Latin American literature at Harvard, Caltech, and UCLA, and has written critical biographies of several Latin American women writers. She is currently writing books about Clorinda Matto de Turner and Juana Manuela Gorriti.

RICHARD CUNNINGHAM is a writer and translator. His books are *The Place Where the World Ends* and *A Ceremony in the Lincoln Tunnel*. In 1980, along with Lucía Guerra, he translated a collection of María Luisa Bombal's work entitled *New Islands*. He is currently working on a novel about Columbia and continues to translate with Señora Guerra.

KENT DICKSON moved to Buenos Aires, Argentina after studying English in college. He is currently pursuing graduate studies in the Department of Spanish and Portuguese at UCLA. He lives in Los Angeles with his wife, Nicole Pinsky.

NANCY ABRAHAM HALL, raised in a bilingual household in México, lives outside Boston with her husband and children. She holds a Ph.D. in Romance Languges and Literatures from Harvard University, and is a specialist in Hispanic-Americanliterature. She teaches Spanish language classes at Wellesley College in Massachusetts.

# The Translators

John J. Hassett is professor of Spanish at Swarthmore College in Pennsylvania. Former editor of CHASQUI, he co-edited *Chile: Dictatorship and the Struggle for Democracy* and *Towards a Society that Serves Its People: The Intellectual Contribution of El Salvador's Murdered Jesuits.*

Elaine Dorough Johnson holds a Ph.D. in Spanish and has translated works by Luisa Mercedes Levinson, Emilia Pardo Bazán, and María Cristina de Fonseca, as well as additional stories by Marta Brunet. She is currently conducting research on Brazilian women wriers.

Celeste Kostopulos-Cooperman is professor of Humanities and Modern Langues at Suffolk University, Boston, MA. She won the ALTA Prize in 1993 for her translation of Marjorie Agosín's *Circles of Madness.*

Martha J. Manier is professor of Spanish and women's Studies at Humboldt State University. Recent publications include an article on Fernan Caballero and the translation of Pía Barros' *Miedos transitorios/Transitory Fears* in collaboration with Diane Russell-Pineda.

Doris Meyer is professor of Hispanic Studies at Connecticut College. She has published a biography of Victoria Ocampo and other books and articles related to contemporary Latin American literature.

Janice Molloy is a Boston-area editor and translator. Her translations have appeared in numerous anthologies and publications. She translated two books by Marjorie Agosín: *Women of Smoke* and *Mothers of the Plaza de Mayo.*

Alice A. Nelson teaches Latin American literature and culture at The Evergreen State College in Olympia, Washington. She is currently completing a book kon gender, hostory, and resistence in Chilean literature of thePinochet period.

# The Translators

LOUISE POPKIN is translator and co-editor of the volume *Repression, Exile and Democracy: Uruguayan Culture* (Duke University Press, 1993). Specializing in Latin American poetry and fiction, she is a frequent contributor to literary journals and anthologies.

ELIZABETH RHODES is an Associate Professor in the Department of Romance Languages and Literatures at Boston College, where she teaches Early Modern Spanish Literature and Women's Studies courses. Her primary field of research is feminine spirituality.

JOY RENJILIAN-BURGY is a faculty member at Wellesley College and a visiting lecturer at Harvard University. Co-editor of *Album: Cuentos del mundo hispánico,* her translations have appeared in various literary anthologies,

ALISON RIDLEY is a p;rofessor of Latin American literature at Hollins College and author of essays on Golden Age literature.

DIANE RUSSELL-PINEDA lived for many years in México City, where she worked as a translator and teacher. She is currently pursuing a doctorate in Latin American Literature at the University of Maryland, College Park, where she teaches translation.

RUSSELL O. SALMON, a professor a Indiana University, is the director of the Center for Latin American and Caribbean Studies. His most recent book is a translation of Ernesto Cardenal's *ONVIS de ORO/Golden UFO, The Indian Poems.*

RICHARD SCHAAF is editor of Azul Editions. He lives in Washington, D.C. with his wife, Lise.

JANET SPINAS-CUNNINGHAM is Professor Emeritus of Spanish at Humboldt State University, Arcata, California, where she was Chair of the Foreign Languages Department. She received her doctorate in Romance Languages and Literatures.

MARGARET STANTON is assistant professor of Spanish at Sweet Briar

College, where she teaches Latin American literature and directs the Latin American Studies Program.

KENNETH M. TAGGART is an Associate Professor of Spanish at Trinity University in San Antonio, Texas. He has written on Rulfo, Fuentes, Garcia Marquez, Vargas llosa, and currently specializes in the works of Isabel Allende and women writers of the Post-Boom.